ACCLAIM FOR THE
EXPERIMENT IN TERROR SERIES

"Seductively entertaining…I'm convinced that it has some secret ingredient (like the sauce on a Big Mac or the coffee beans at Starbucks) that makes it immediately addictive."

–Bitsy Bling Books

"I don't think, short of being completely ridiculous, I can encourage you more strongly to read this series. It has quickly moved to the top of my favorites list."

–The Bookish Babes

"A ghost hunting adventure with original characters guaranteed to please!"

–Romancing the Darkside

"Loved it, loved it, loved it. I can't say it enough. I've never related to a character as much as I did to Perry Palomino."

–Pretty Opinionated

"Halle's first-person narrative is written in a breezy fashion that instantly made me feel like I could hang out with her protagonist."

—Forever Young Adult

"Perry and Dex are two charismatic and slightly crazy characters that carry you in kicking and screaming along for the ride."

–Naughty Between the Stacks

Also by Karina Halle

THE DEVIL'S METAL

Karina Halle

DIVERSIONBOOKS

Diversion Books
A Division of Diversion Publishing Corp.
443 Park Avenue South, Suite 1004
New York, NY 10016
www.DiversionBooks.com

Publisher's Note: This a work of fiction. Names, characters, places, and incidents are the product of the author's imagination or are used fictitiously. Any resemblance to actual events, locales, or persons, living or dead, is entirely coincidental.

For more information, email info@diversionbooks.com or visit Karina Halle's website at www.khale.wordpress.com

First Diversion Books edition February 2012

eBook ISBN: 978-1-938120-96-1
Paperback ISBN: 978-1-62681-008-2

To the musicians who've inspired this crazy, beautiful journey: This one's for you. Thanks for helping me escape hell.

CHAPTER ONE

"Are you ready to rock and roll!?"

Melanie's voice boomed through the barn causing a group of pigeons to take flight from the dusty rafters. Moonglow raised her head back in annoyance and gave me the eye. As a flighty Arabian horse, she was never too impressed with Mel's approach.

"I'm ready!" I hollered back and quickly finished brushing down Moonglow as she stood uneasily in the crossties, her weight shifting from one leg to the other.

In seconds, a boisterous Mel appeared beside me, a thin sheen of sweat on her dark brown forehead.

"How the hell could you even be riding in this weather?" she asked, words popping with energy. She was returning Moonglow's wild-eyed look and I couldn't help but snicker at their exchange. It was Mel versus horse and Mel usually won.

"I have to practice," I reminded her, wiping the sweat from my face. I probably deposited a million white horse hairs in its place. Even though Mel was obviously bothered by the oppressive heat that swamped the Kittitas Valley in late July, she still looked insanely hip and bitchin' (as she liked to say). Me, on the other hand, well let's just say I looked like I belonged in a stable.

"I know you have to practice," she said, tearing her eyes off my horse and ducking under the crossties, "but the concert starts in an hour and...you're..."

She trailed off and gave me an unimpressed squint as she looked me up and down, deciding to finish her sentence by plucking a few strands of hay out of my unruly hair.

I snatched them out of her hand and flung them onto the concrete floor.

"I'm fine," I told her quickly and gave Moonglow a few more quick brushes down her legs. I was going to put her away slightly sweaty which was never good, but Mel was right. I was a mess and I had a concert to cover. I'd always made a point of looking as natural and professional as possible at shows just so people wouldn't think I was some groupie. Still, being covered in sweat and horse hair wasn't a good look either, even for rock and roll.

"If you say so," she said and crossed her arms. The movement pushed up her breasts in her low-cut scarf top. Mel was totally tight with the whole groupie term. Then again, she wasn't the one trying to make a career for herself in the music industry. She just loved rock—and its men—as much as I did and made one hell of a fine partner in crime for live shows.

I gave her a dismissive look and took Moonglow to her stall, locking her in just as a rumble of thunder shook the ground.

"It's a bit early in the season for thunderstorms," I noted as we made our way out of my father's small barn. The air was ripe with electricity, and a mess of dark gray clouds loomed on the rolling horizon, spilling down the brown hills like dust bunnies.

She patted at her small afro. "As long as it doesn't mess up my hair. Now aren't you glad I got the car for tonight?"

I lived a bit outside of Ellensburg on a small cattle ranch, turned hay farm, turned waste of space, and a symbol of lost money. I never had a car and my dad crashed his truck into our neighbor's fence earlier in the year, so it was either my three-speed bike, Moonglow, or my own two feet for getting around. Or Mel, when she managed to snatch her older brother's car keys.

We called it the Dumpster. It was an ugly Gremlin, patched and peeling paint, and it constantly smelled like garbage. Its newest nickname was the Shaggin' Wagon, based on the rotation of chicks her brother picked up in Seattle when he was there for school. Something about city chicks being easy. With Ryan, my ex, going there for college in the fall, the idea made me feel sick to my stomach.

Mel must have caught the look on my face as we crossed the narrow road of crumbling asphalt to the Gremlin, because her brows furrowed.

"Is Eric home?" she asked. Her voice always sounded small when she said his name.

I shook my head and looked back at the aging farmhouse, empty and terribly dark despite the evening light. It was Friday and my brother was finishing up summer school. He should have been home an hour ago, so I hoped he found some friends and was hanging out with them after class. As for my dad, he was out at the bar. At least I knew where he was.

Mel stopped and put her hands on my shoulders, peering up at me. I was tall for a girl, 5'9", and she was a tiny little thing. I tried not to let many people boss me around, but she had a way about her. She leaned in close and peered into my eyes.

"Dawn, tell it to me straight. Are you okay? You don't look okay."

I gave her a quick smile. My lips tasted like sweat.

"I guess I'm just feeling overwhelmed," I admitted.

She gave me a nod, reached into the open window of the Gremlin's back seat, and pulled out a flask. She tossed it to me and I caught it with ease.

"Drink that," she said. "Shut off your brain."

I opened my mouth to protest but knew it would be useless. I tipped the flask back into my mouth and got a burst of warm whiskey as it poured into my throat. I swallowed it quickly and wiped my lips, trying not to cough.

"How about tonight you stop worrying about everything…

and I do mean everything," she said, emphasizing the last word, "and just enjoy the music for music. Don't even take notes. Just be. I love you girl, but you're trying too hard. It's the fucking summer. You're not even writing this piece for a paper, right? So take the time to live a little, you dig?"

I wanted to argue with Mel about needing to keep going, about buckling down and trying harder. Being a music journalist in Ellensburg, Washington, home of a big rodeo and miles of Timothy hay, was difficult. Being a *female* music journalist was almost impossible. But I knew complaining to Mel would do me no good. She was black and she had her own share of prejudices and obstacles to deal with, even in a field like nursing. Even in everyday life.

I smiled just as another roll of thunder crashed across the waving fields. Goosebumps prickled up my arms, despite the sweat and waning sunshine.

"I'll *try* to have fun," I joked. "So are we ready to go?"

She took a small sip of the flask then handed it back to me, nodding at it. "Almost."

I sighed and took one more chug of the burning liquid. The baloney sandwich I made myself for dinner hadn't protected me in the slightest and I was already feeling buzzed. I tossed the flask back into the car and gave Mel an expectant look.

"Happy now?"

She took a pair of Jackie-O sunglasses out of her snug denim shorts and placed them on her face. She grinned, her white teeth flashing like lightning against a cocoa sky.

"Getting there," she said and opened the driver's door. That smell of garbage wafted out and we both tried not to gag.

"Seriously," I said as I eased myself onto the passenger's seat. "Does he haul trash around in here or what? You know, maybe he's living out of his car in Seattle, ever think of that?"

"Oh, I've thought of that." She started the car and it chugged to life. Within seconds we were roaring down the country road, windows open, Alice Cooper's "Hello Hooray" blaring from the radio. The breeze wasn't doing anything to get out the smell or cool down the car. My jeans stuck to the seat. Dust and heat blasted my face.

"Are you worried Ryan's going to start picking up trash once he goes?" she asked as she whipped the car violently onto the main road.

I would have laughed at that but it hit a little close to home. "A little."

She looked at me beneath her shades. "You know you have to give up on him, girl."

I shrugged and started paying attention to the way the wind was tangling my long, curly hair. I was going to end up at the show with a rust-colored rat's nest.

"We could make it work," I said with quiet determination.

"You mad? I mean, I love the dude like I love my brothers, but you know this fairytale ain't having a happy ending here. He was good for sloppy kisses and cherry popping and looking slammin' at our prom, but you guys have been dullsville ever since...well, ever since you started school."

This was all true, so I couldn't argue. Ryan was my first steady boyfriend in high school and we were the envy of everyone there. At least, I told myself that. We looked good, both of us tall and very athletic, both of us competed in the rodeo every year (me in barrel racing, him in calf roping), and we were one of those tongue wrestling in public, sickening couples. Since I grew up towering over most of the girls and was predisposed to muscles and a small chest (and therefore a plethora of teasing), I always felt that Ryan's love for me was like an award for staying alive or something. It definitely helped the high school years go down a lot easier. But after we graduated, everything changed—as it should, I guess.

"I don't know, Mel," I said, wanting to change the subject. It was making me feel hotter, dizzier. "We broke up but it doesn't mean the end. You never know where the future will lead us."

She snorted then shot me an apologetic look. "Hey, I just

don't want to see you spend the rest of the summer pining over him when you'll probably get hurt in the end. Dude was a creep for dumping your white ass anyway."

I leaned over and slapped my thigh. "And it's a good ass too."

"You can bet on it."

I grinned at her and looked to the dry, quaint streets of downtown Ellensburg as they came into view. I had to get Ryan out of my head. There were more important things to worry about, like the shitty run I had with Moonglow that afternoon, or the rock concert we were about to infiltrate.

The venue was this small club near the university called The Ripper. It was one of the few places in town that played all ages shows, which was awesome when I was underage, but now that I had turned twenty-one and was a lot more serious about music, competing with teenyboppers for the best spot in the house was always a full contact sport. Tonight's band, PASTE, featured Terry Black, the extremely foxy lead singer who screamed better than he sung—and that wasn't saying much. I had reviewed the band's debut album earlier this year for the college paper and called it "mediocre and malicious," but still secretly hoped I could score an interview with him before or after the show. The band was popular-city.

Yup, part of me dreamed that an interview with Terry Black could be my big break. I had been writing articles, interviews, and show reviews all summer long and sending them to Seattle and Spokane papers hoping to be picked up. Last year I wrote for a few community newspapers, highlighting up-and-coming bands such as Boys N Snakes, and my current obsession, Hybrid. This June I got my biggest break when the Seattle Times published a review I did of a Bad Company show. No one had really heard of the band, despite having the all-mighty Paul Rodgers from Free in it, so somehow my review got attention. It also got me a big fat check—which I promptly spent on groceries for the house and a bottle of Wild Turkey for my dad. Ever since then though, I'd had no bites. I was hoping Black would fix the slump and maybe get me enough cash to buy a new saddle for Moonglow. Continuing on with my wishful thinking, I was hoping Big Ears, the music section of CWU's paper, would make me editor and I could finally write about the bands I wanted to without hearing "but you're a woman, let the men handle the noise."

As Mel pulled the Dumpster into a packed parking lot full of blaring 8-tracks and Pabst Blue Ribbon, my hopes sank. Because I was writing on spec, I didn't have a press pass so I looked just like every other concert goer.

Except not.

The girls were young and beautiful, wearing short shorts and skinny strapped tops. Some had on bikinis, other see-through shirts made of crochet and netting. They were all tanned with ironed hair and large platforms. There were even a few wearing PASTE t-shirts that were clearly meant for children considering the way they showed off their abs. Their lips were frosted pink, their smiles drunk and seductive.

I was wearing a thin red t-shirt that stuck to my skin from sweat. From a quick glance into the rearview mirror, I could see my hair really was a rust-colored rat's nest, my dark brown eyes didn't have a lick of makeup on them, and somehow my freckles had multiplied in the last hour. My jeans were bell-bottoms, my shoes were Frye boots—with horse shit on them. I was going to have to compete against these girls for Terry's attention, and I had a feeling he wouldn't give a fuck that I was a so-called journalist.

Especially one that compared his voice to a cheese grater.

I sighed, suddenly not wanting to get out of the car.

"Dawn, you're doing it again," Mel warned.

"Doing what?"

"Turn off your brain." She began to reach behind her for the flask.

My hands flew up to my mouth in protest. "No, I'm fine. I need to think clearly tonight."

She gave me a wry look. "What is with you lately?"

"What do you mean?"

She nodded at the girls in the parking lot who were laughing, drinking, and oblivious to the thunderstorm that was hiding around the corner. "Where's your confidence, girl? You're gorgeous and you know it. Not only that, but you're one fine writer. A double threat."

"I'm just not slutty enough," I mumbled.

Mel ripped off her sunglasses and gave me the stare down. She had won in the staring contest against my horse earlier—I was powerless. I looked down at my hands and dirty fingernails.

"Are you calling them girls sluts because of the way they're dressed, cuz damn child you must think I'm a downright ho in my little booty boobie get-up here," she said with full-on attitude.

"You're not a groupie," I protested.

"Who cares? I could be. What's wrong with trying to get some rock and roll tail? Sex is sex, Dawn, even for the wrong reasons. I thought you were all for this women's liberation shit and bra burning."

I looked down at my chest. "I didn't need those bras anyway."

She put her hand on my shoulder. She wasn't gentle. Mel could fly off the handle and you never wanted her on your bad side.

"It doesn't mean you have to spread your legs if you don't want to," she told me in her I'm-a-year-older-let-me-lecture-you voice. "But let those girls be those girls. You be yourself, loosen up, and maybe, just maybe, if you try the groupie angle, you'll end up getting the real story."

I gave her fingers a quick kiss before shrugging them off. "You are a terrible influence Miss Melanie Jones."

She laughed, throwing her head back. "And you need a good shag, Miss Dawn Emerson. You can't have the rock and roll without the sex. And drugs. Speaking of..."

She brought out her saddlebag purse and brought out a joint from her slim cigarette case.

"What did I say about thinking clearly?" I reminded her. But I ended up taking a quick puff anyway. Pot was good for the musical experience and clearly I needed to loosen up a little. I felt as tense as the coming storm.

We got out of the car sufficiently high. I gathered my confidence, threw back my shoulders, and the two of us strode proudly toward the entrance to The Ripper. We were getting second glances from a lot of the guys. Naturally the sight of a short, curvy black girl and a tall redhead garnered a lot of attention in itself, plus there were Mel's boobs swinging around in her top and that flirtatious smile of hers. If they could get past the mess of hair and the horse-shit boots, I knew deep down I wasn't anything to sneeze at either. But was I "beat out the groupies and score an interview with a rock star" hot? That remained to be seen.

We showed our tickets at the door to a tricked-out bouncer, and after flashing him our IDs, he slapped a yellow band on our wrists, proclaiming to the world that we were of legal drinking age. I grinned despite myself. After years of watching the "cool" older kids have their drinks in the club, it was a relief to be able to do the same.

The club was packed even though half the audience still appeared to be tailgating outside. It was dark and blurry and reeked of cigarette smoke and cheap cologne. I felt like I was floating through the crowd, feeding off the energy of music lovers, intoxicated by the anticipation of a live show. I was in my element and the grass was working fast to mellow me out.

Mel did her usual thing which was to ditch me as soon as we got inside. She spotted a former flame of hers, this real creep from New York who thought he was a ghetto superstar, and took off to him like a moth to a flame. I didn't mind. I liked to be alone during a concert, the better to feel the music and really immerse myself. Plus observing the crowd was a major tool to creating atmosphere in music reviews, and that was hard to do when you had Mel squealing in your ear, dissecting the size of the lead singer's dick by the tightness of his pants.

I found a spot against the sweating wall to the left of the

stage, conveniently close to the backstage entrance. I kept a deceptively casual watch on it to see if I recognized any of the roadies or managers who were going in and out. So far, none of them looked familiar and after ten minutes the area around the door became crowded with the frosted-lip chicks. I felt my chest tighten. Mel was right, something really was wrong with me. With family issues, my worries about Moonglow's performance, and Ryan leaving me, it seemed like everything was stressing me out. Music was always the one thing in my life I could count on, the drug that took me away from reality and made me feel whole. Now, it just seemed like too much pressure to make something of myself.

I took in a deep breath of secondhand smoke and closed my eyes. I repeated a Zen mantra I had heard on a.m. television until I started to feel in control again. When I opened my eyes, Todd McFadden was standing in front of me. He worked with me on Big Ears and since he was into the same rock and metal as I was, I was always battling him for music reviews and shows. We were on friendly terms, but I really couldn't stand his chauvinistic opinions, nor the fact that he always had one long nose hair sticking out of his right nostril.

"Hey Red," he cooed. He placed his hand against the wall and leaned on it, thinking it probably made him look cool. It just made him look like he couldn't stand up straight, and after getting a quick glimpse of his red-rimmed eyes, it wasn't far from the truth.

"Hey Caveman," I replied. So I may have lied when I said we were on friendly terms.

"Oh, you like the chest-beating type, admit it." His smile was more reptilian when high.

"The only thing that should be beat is *it*," I retorted and turned my attention back to the stage. "So, beat it, I'm trying to watch a show."

"No show yet, babe," he said, stepping in closer. "Are you here to write or just listen?"

"Both," I said, crossing my arms.

He nodded but stood there, not really getting the hint. After a few awkward seconds he said, "Did you hear I'm interviewing Terry after the show?"

I tried really hard to not let that bother me. I failed. My eyes bugged out.

"What? How? For who?"

Todd shrugged. "Spokane. I got a job there for the summer. Beats the hell out of Big Ears."

I knew it did. Man, that pissed me right off. Of course someone like Todd would be able to land a job like that—he stole half my potential stories anyway.

He glanced over at the scantily-clad girls at the groupie door. "You know you might have a chance if you…"

He trailed off and looked down at my top with disdain. "Never mind. You got shafted, babe."

That did it.

I pressed both my hands into his scrawny chest and shoved him. Hard. He went stumbling off balance and landed on his ass on the greasy floor. People in the crowd cried out as their drinks spilled, then laughed at him and went about their business.

Todd glared up at me, his face growing visibly red in the darkness. Trying to stifle his embarrassment, he got to his feet and pointed a finger at me.

"Real professional, Red. No wonder you're not going anywhere."

And with that he adjusted the collar on his leather jacket and stormed off into the crowd, shoving a few drunks out of his way.

So much for de-stressing. Two seconds talking with Todd and my heart rate was all over the place. I hated, *hated* knowing he was doing better than I was and hated even more that he thought I was going nowhere. Well, I'd show him.

I tugged my shirt down and began to make my way toward the side door. I didn't get very far.

The lights in the house went down and the band—minus

Terry—took to the stage among cheers and hollers from the crowd. They were all young, fashionably skinny, and trying way too hard to imitate Alice Cooper with their weird boots, tights, and bleeding eye makeup. They looked like ghoulish long-haired clones of each other.

A single spotlight lit up the middle of the small stage, and as the drummer began his roll, Terry Black stepped out in all his glory. He was tall and thin like the rest of the band with hair carefully disheveled in long black waves. He was wearing a cape made out of sewn-on bats and snakeskin platform boots. He looked like an idiot and it was only because he had a handsome, albeit babyish, face that the women were going nuts for him. He raised his arms in the air like he was going to fly away and already a pair of white lace panties were tossed on the stage.

"Minions!" he addressed the crowd in a booming voice. "Calm down before your master."

Oh dear lord. I shook my head, wondering why I even wanted to interview this loser to begin with.

But the chicks went nuts and even the guys seemed to fall for his faux-metal bullshit. And that was why I wanted to interview him. Because he was popular.

Ugh, I was so close to being a sell-out.

I looked at the stage and saw Todd standing on the side of it, watching the band, taking notes and chatting with one of the roadies.

That's what I wanted to be? Double ugh.

After about twenty minutes, I had enough of listening to Terry scream and Todd shooting me smug looks from the side stage. I made my way through the sweaty crowd of overheated leather and underage girls until I was at the bar. The line-up was wild, with people shoving and yelling, and after a few minutes there I realized I wouldn't be getting a drink either. I started to look around for Mel and finally found her in the corner, sucking face with ghetto creep. She wasn't even watching the damn show.

I thought about approaching her and dragging her away, but

I knew better than to get between Mel and her man, whichever man that was. Frankly, I was a little jealous, too. She had no problems finding a guy to shag, where I was too hung up on Ryan to even consider anybody in the venue. Sure, I liked the looks I had gotten earlier but looks never went very far with me. If Ryan and I were actually really, truly dunzo, I was going to have a hell of a time trying to get over him.

I glanced at my watch. It was only nine and probably still light outside. It was going to be a long walk without the Gremlin but everyone was walking these days because of the gas prices and I was more than used to it. I shot one more glance at Mel, hoping she wasn't occupied but she still hadn't come up for air. And with the way ghetto creep's hand was manhandling her boob, I didn't think she'd be breathing anytime soon.

I decided to call her house and leave a message with her mother when I got home, just so she wouldn't worry about me, then pushed my way through the remainder of the concert goers and past the bouncers until I was outside. The sun had set but the air was still bathed in a sticky golden glow. The thunderstorm had passed though rumbles still emanated in the distance.

I only made it one block before a tan VW beetle puttered up to me. I was immediately met with chills, even though the air was heavy with warmth.

"Excuse me," a male voice called out from the car. I stopped and gave it a wary look as it came to a stop and the engine turned off. If he was wondering if he could give me a ride, he was shit out of luck. Ever since a few girls had been murdered and beaten on campus (including one from my English Lit class) earlier in the spring, no one wanted to take chances with strangers.

I straightened my shoulders and made sure my arms were flexed slightly. A weakling I wasn't and I wanted this man to know I could take care of myself.

He got out of the car, dressed in a white tennis outfit and thankfully stood on the other side of the vehicle. He gave me a short wave. He wasn't a bad looking guy at all, tall and dark-haired, and he seemed harmless, especially when I noticed his left arm was in a sling. But he gave me the heebie-jeebies like nothing else. His eyes didn't look…normal. They looked predatory.

"My name's Ted," he said, giving me an open smile.

I didn't say anything. I wasn't about to tell him my name. Normally I would have asked if he needed help, but I wasn't taking any chances.

I stared back at him. I wanted to look away but that would have been a sign of weakness and he looked like one of those animals who'd pounce when your guard was down.

He frowned a bit, perhaps confused by my stand-offishness, then put another smile on. It was about as fake as Santa Claus. "I was wondering if you could help me, I think my friend and I are lost."

I looked back at the car. I could see the outline of someone else in the backseat, a thin woman it looked like, but that didn't make me feel any better.

"Sorry, I have to go," I told him feebly. I turned to keep walking, though I was entertaining the idea of turning around and heading back to the venue for safety.

"But you're on the cusp of all your dreams," he called after me.

I stopped in mid-stride and shot him a curious look. If this was his equivalent of offering me candy, it was working.

"Excuse me?" I couldn't help it.

He smiled again and leaned a bit against the car. He was looking less handsome now. His eyes were devious and disturbing, his lips too small and twisted.

"Could you tell me how to get to the University?" he asked.

I could. But I wanted to hear more about the dreams.

"Turn around, head down Ruby and turn right on East University Way," I quickly told him. "What did you say about my dreams?"

He stepped back and gestured at the VW. "Come along for a ride and I'll tell you all about the journey you're about to embark upon."

Goosebumps prickled down my arms. "What journey?"

Walking home? *That* journey?

He shook his head as if he heard my thoughts. "Step inside. I'll tell you about how it all ends. In fire. With a man you'll never be able to save."

Okay, this was beyond creepy. This was run away, now and fast.

"Or find out for yourself," he added. He started to get back in the car, much to my relief and bewilderment. "It's your choice."

The door slammed and the car started up with a roar. The ending notes of a Hybrid song, "Sky Valley" wafted out from the windows. The VW quickly pulled out onto the road and did a U-turn, puttering away in the direction of the university.

As it went past me again, Ted kept his eyes on the road. But in the backseat I got a glimpse of the woman. She was staring straight at me, a blur of pale skin and long white hair obscured by the dirtiness of the rear windshield.

I held my breath, my heart racing strangely as they drove down the street. I waited until they were out of sight before I booked it home. Running in boots was noisy and hard on my ankles, but I went for a run several times a week to keep the weight off and I had enough stamina to push through it for forty-five sweaty minutes.

By the time I arrived home, it was completely dark out and I was soaked in sweat. I had never been so happy to see the farmhouse before. Even in its scrawny, faded condition it felt like a safety net after the night I just had. Just what the hell had happened with that Ted guy? Was he just someone sinister or had I just smoked too much pot? I made a mental note to take it easier next time, especially as my lungs were extra wheezy.

I opened the screen door slowly, knowing it squeaked extra loud at night, and listened for signs of life. It was quiet and almost dark except for a faint light coming from the living room. I crept toward it and spied my father passed out on the couch, two empty cans of cheap beer beside him. I sighed, though I should have been happy he had just been drinking beer and none of the hard stuff. I took the blanket off of the armchair and put it over him.

I loved my dad to pieces, except when he was drunk, which was often. It was a strained relationship at best, especially since I had been such a daddy's girl growing up. I was really everything he had until Eric came along six years later. But then Mom died and shit just went downhill. Still, I didn't blame my dad. Well, I tried not to. It was something I worked on every day. He still managed to keep his job at the repair shop, I just wished he'd pull himself together for Eric's sake. He needed extra care, more than the average sixteen-year-old, and I was tired of taking care of both of them. I knew that was selfish of me, but...

I tucked the quilt underneath his heavy arms and brushed the hair off of his forehead. It was dirty and graying and made me sad. I sighed again, my heart still thumping from the run, and went into the kitchen for a glass of water before bed. I remembered I had to phone Mel's mom and leave a message for her. It was getting late but she was used to the two of us calling each other all hours of the night.

I went for the phone and saw there was something addressed to me on the message pad. It was my dad's writing. For a second I hoped that Ryan had called while I was out and the skin prickled deliciously at the back of my neck.

Dawn! Call Maureen at Cream Magazine. 313-587-2837.

Huh. I brought the pad up to my face, as if that would help me understand it better. What area code was 313? And what was Cream? Did he mean *Creem* Magazine?

My heart pounded loudly.

I looked over at my dad who was now snoring loudly. I didn't want to wake him up, knowing he'd probably be drunk and disorderly if I did. I'd have to catch him in the morning.

Unless Eric knew something. I quickly filled up a glass with water and downed it before I scuttled up the stairs to our bedrooms. Eric's door was closed and I leaned against it, listening.

When I couldn't tell if he was asleep or not, I opened it quietly and peeked in. He was sprawled under his sheets, twitching slightly, the moonlight shining in through the dusty window. God damn it, why was everyone asleep in this house?

I carefully shut the door behind me and once inside my room, I flicked on my lights and collapsed on the bed. I rolled over on my back and looked up at my heaven—the ceiling. My bedroom was my prized sanctuary, always had been. Through my mom's depression, my father's collapse, Eric's affliction, this was the one place I felt…home. Even when a quick ride on Moonglow didn't wash away the blues, my room did, so as long as I put a record on my beloved orange player and slipped on a pair of earphones. I had a massive record collection that took up one wall of my room, competing for space with riding ribbons and trophies. I kept the walls more or less bare to showcase the concert photos I had taken and deemed good enough to frame. The ceiling was where my posters were, held to it with sticky blue gum. Lying on my back, it was easy to get lost in Pink Floyd's rainbow or Elton John's yellow brick road. Jimmy Page stared down at me with a sleepy look in his eyes, while Ozzy made goofy faces. Jeff Beck, The Guess Who, Dust, Wings, The Doors, and Wishbone Ash, jockeyed for position with Jimi Hendrix, The Rolling Stones, Alice Cooper, The Beatles, Ziggy Stardust, Queen, The Stooges, and The Allman Brothers Band.

Before I had time to wonder what Ryan was doing, if Todd was going to get his interview, who the hell that Ted guy was, and what Cream was all about, I swept away to sleep by the music in my head.

I dreamed of fire.

CHAPTER TWO

I was slowly woken up by sunshine streaming in through my window and the phone ringing from downstairs. Before I had time to fathom that I had fallen asleep in my disgusting clothes on top of the covers, my brother was yelling at me through the house.

"Dawn! Phone's for you!" I heard him at the bottom of the stairs, a small hoot and bark following the sentence.

I sat up and groaned, feeling it was far too early for anything, then remembered the message from the night before. I sprang to my feet and scampered down the stairs, my boots clunking loudly.

My brother was standing in the kitchen in his pajamas and eating from a bowl of cereal. He gave me a disgusted look as I came near, his head twitching.

"Ew, did you sleep in those?" he asked, placing the phone in my hand. His left shoulder shrugged up in a tic.

"I had a weird night," I told him. I quickly placed my hand over the mouth piece and whispered to him. "Who is it?"

"Who do you think?"

I put the phone to my ear. "Hello, Dawn speaking."

"Bitch!" Mel hissed from the other line.

Ah, crap I had totally forgotten about calling her mom.

"Hey, sorry about last night," I said, rubbing my forehead, trying to get the sleep out.

"Sorry?! You know I spent half my night looking for you? Tiny and I nearly turned the place upside down when I couldn't find you!"

Tiny was ghetto creep's real name. Figured.

"I'm sorry. I had to get out of there and I didn't want to interrupt you and ghet—er Tiny. You looked busy."

"I *was* busy, but damn girl you know you come first."

"Sorry again," I said. Eric was watching me, amused yet melancholic, cornflakes being shoved in his mouth. The milk spilled a bit from his shoulder tic.

"Well, what happened?" she prodded, sounding calmer.

I told her about Todd and Terry's supposed interview and how I had a minor panic attack of sorts. I didn't want to add in the part about Ted though, that would have only made her madder.

"Did I ruin your night?" I asked.

"No, you didn't," she said with a sigh. "I assumed you left, and I asked the doorman and he said you did and that you looked fine. I know you can take care of yourself. Still, Dawn, you have to be careful, you dig? You know, 1974 is starting to be a scary year with all them chicks going missing and stuff."

A shiver ran down my spine. I thought back to Ted's strange, otherworldly eyes and the way the girl in the backseat stared at me like she knew me somehow. I could barely see her but I had *felt* it.

"I know," I told her, wiping the image out of my head. "I was being paranoid, don't worry."

"*Make a joke and I will sigh and you will laugh and I will cry.*" She sang Ozzy on the spot.

"Don't insult my Sabbath love," I warned her. "Anyway, I'm home. I passed out in my clothes though so I've got to take a shower. I think Eric is about to lose his breakfast here."

I winked at him, and after promising to hang out with Mel tomorrow, I hung up the phone in its cradle.

I turned to Eric and ruffled the top of his head, something he hated but I would never stop doing. I got the tall genes in the family, along with the red hair and tanned, freckly skin. Eric was small, short, skinny and pale with a shock of dark hair. Our eyes were the same though, brown as coffee, and we shared our mother's slim nose and high cheekbones.

"What were you doing after school? You didn't come home," I asked him, pulling out a chair at the dining table. There was one brown banana in the fruit bowl and I decided to make it my breakfast. I wasn't a picky eater. I couldn't afford to be.

"I...I asked out Sheena Warner," he said, clearing his throat in another one of his tics. I could tell he was trying to suppress them around me when he shouldn't. See, my brother has Tourette's Syndrome. It's nothing like the stereotype. I mean, I guess there are a lot of similarities but my brother doesn't go around making obscene comments or swearing at people. I think the doctor told us that was in a different category. Even so, my brother makes these little hoots and barks, sometimes randomly, sometimes during a sentence. He has three tics that appear all the time: his left shoulder shrug, his facial twitch, and his throat-clearing. The shoulder one can be really violent at times and the more he tries to suppress it, the more stress he causes on his body. Emotions make the tics wilder, too.

He had a crush on this girl in his class, Sheena, for the longest time. She was pretty but not too popular and kind of bookish, and they were friends as far as I knew. But growing up in a small town and having a noticeable affliction made Eric a target for mean girls and bullies alike. At least once a month he was coming home with a black eye, or he'd lock himself in his room close to tears. I personally wanted to go down to the high school and beat up every punk that looked at him funny, but I would only make things worse. Having my brother in my life was a constant heartbreaker.

"Oh?" I said. I knew from the way he kept clearing his throat and the way his eyes were focused on the banana and not me that this wasn't going to have a happy ending.

"She said no," he said softly.

I gave him a pained smile. "Maybe she just wants to be friends."

His eyes flew to mine. They were watering from frustration. "She doesn't want to be friends. She said I attract too much bad attention and I'll distract her from her scholarship."

"What a fucking nerd," I spat out then put my hand to my mouth. "Sorry Eric, I didn't mean it. I just mean…you don't need someone like that in your life. Friends are your friends no matter what attention you get."

"But I need someone in my life!" he wailed. "I don't care who."

His shoulder jerked up and he screamed at it in agony, as if it were another being.

I got to my feet and tried to embrace him to let him know things were okay, but he pushed his way out of my grasp. Sometimes I forgot that even though I was more like a mother to him than a sister, sometimes boys didn't want their mothers either.

"Eric, I'm sorry," I called after him.

"Leave me alone," he mumbled and ran upstairs to his room. I heard the door slam, which made the spoon in the cereal bowl clatter.

When Eric was younger, we were told that he'd most likely grow out of the syndrome by the time he was eighteen. I know we were all holding our breath for that, but it seemed that he was getting worse over the years, not better.

Life, I thought. *You can be a real bitch.*

I threw the banana peel in the garbage and looked back at the message that was scrawled on the pad. It had somehow lost all the excitement I felt earlier, and I doubted it was actually Creem Magazine, the best rock and roll publication out there with all my favorite writers, because that was the stuff made of dreams, not the cards I'd normally been dealt. Still, I had to wonder. My dad was out at work, so I couldn't ask him about it and I wasn't about to bug Eric. It didn't matter anyway, all I had to do was call and I'd find out. I just hoped it wasn't a crank call or someone selling something because we couldn't afford to call long distance very often.

I took a deep breath and dialed the number. After a few clicks and crackles in the silence, the other end started ringing.

"Hello, Creem Magazine, Maureen speaking," a woman's crisp voice answered.

Holy Toledo.

I swallowed hard.

The woman repeated herself. "Hello? Is anyone there?"

I heard some clattering in the background and a few people laughing. If I didn't say something soon, she was going to hang up.

"Yes," I said quickly. "Um, yes, hi. Hi…Maureen? This is Dawn Emerson. I got a message from you last night, I think?"

There was a pause then she laughed. "Oh, sorry could you repeat yourself again? Dawn, you said?"

"Yes, Dawn Emerson."

"Of course! Dawn. Sorry, I'm dealing with a few hacks here blowing smoke in my face." She gave a little cough. I had to wonder what the hell was going on at Creem Magazine. Maybe they really were a bunch of hooligans like they painted themselves.

A bunch of hooligans who called *me*.

"Anyhow, Dawn do you mind holding? I'm just going to patch you through to Barry, mmkay?"

Before I could say otherwise, the line went silent. *Barry.* Barry Kramer, the pusher of rock and roll on America's impressionable minds. The founder of hooligan central. The man I'd always hoped would be my future boss, who'd have me sharing a house with the likes of Lester Bangs and Lisa Robinson. See, that's why I dug Barry. He put women like Lisa, Jann U, and Patti Smith to work for him. He didn't subscribe to the Big Ears bullshit that women didn't know rock from Adam.

The wait was agonizing. I started to fear it was a prank after all. Maybe Todd or some jerk got Creem to call me for kicks.

Maybe Maureen had actually hung up on me. Maybe they were all laughing at me while I waited, sweating in the kitchen, reeking like stale cigarettes and yesterday's ride.

Before I chewed off all of my split ends, there was a crackle on the other line and I straightened up, heart thumping.

"Hello, is this Dawn Emerson?"

"Yes," I said pathetically, in a voice barely above a whisper. "This is she."

"Dawn, this is Barry Kramer. I'm the editor at Creem Magazine."

"I know."

"Good," he said. His voice was smooth and youthful, not as intimidating as I had imagined. "I figured you would. Listen, Dawn, we've had something rather unusual fall into our lap and it involves you personally."

"I'm listening," I told him, wondering what the hell he was talking about. How could anything involve me? The mystery was warping my brain.

He cleared his throat. "First of all, I wanted to say I've read your work and I really dig it. You show great potential and all that kind of stuff. Your live review of Bad Company was engaging to say the least. I got some copies of your school's paper and the interviews are far-out. How did you manage to get Moe from Khaki Toast?"

"I ambushed him after a show," I told him. I didn't add the part where I bribed a roadie with ten bucks to let me backstage. I may not flash my boobs at rock stars, but I'm not above a little bribery. I had always thought it was too bad that the interview was wasted on such a small paper, but if Barry had seen it…well, this changed everything. My heart swirled at the thought of my idols actually reading my writing all this time.

"Well done," he said. "I like a woman with balls. And I hope you have big enough ones for what I'm about to ask of you."

He paused. My mind reeled.

"The reason I've read your pieces is because you were brought to my attention by Jacob Edwards. Have you heard of him?"

The name was familiar but I couldn't place it.

"It doesn't matter. He's the manager of Hybrid and I know you've heard of *them*. I read your glowing review of Molten Universe and your little ditty on the evolution of their sound. Pretty insightful stuff, especially for a band that's just coming into their own. We think they're ahead of their time and so do you. And so does Edwards. He wants you to write for us, joining Hybrid on the road for a few weeks next month."

"Come again?" He didn't, *couldn't*, have just said what I thought he said.

He laughed appreciatively. "Hey, it was a surprise to us too. From what I understand, Edwards caught wind of your work, loved what you said about the band, and he thinks a female voice would help win over the female fans. Hybrid is too aggressive for a lot of rock chicks, even though they have Noelle in the band, and that whole Graham and devil worshiping rumor definitely hasn't helped. I mean, it works for Led Zeppelin, but as hard as these guys try, they aren't Led Zeppelin."

That was actually a line from my review:

> *People keep trying to make comparisons between Hybrid and Led Zeppelin. I say, let the comparisons stop with their third album, Molten Universe. They aren't Led Zeppelin. This album showcases a unique brand of metal, more grinding, thunderous and—gasp—sexual than the English rockers. In this case, Hybrid is heavier than lead.*

It wasn't groundbreaking writing but it obviously struck a chord with someone. I just didn't think it would be with the actual band themselves.

And suddenly this was all too good to be true.

"Dawn? Are you there?"

"Yeah," I said warily. "I'm here. I'm just…are you sure you have the right Dawn?"

"Do *you* think I have the right Dawn?"

Good question. If I could eventually get over what was actually being asked of me, if I could pretend this was all real, I had to wonder if I was strong enough—good enough—to actually take this on. Writing for Creem Magazine? Going on the road with an actual fucking rock band? And a band I actually loved, a band who was slowly joining the ranks of Black Sabbath, Led Zeppelin, and Hendrix in the shrine of my heart?

I couldn't afford to doubt myself.

I had to be made for this.

I pushed uptight, worrywart Dawn somewhere in the back of my mind and said to Barry, "Yes. You definitely have the right Dawn."

"That's what I thought." He didn't sound as relieved as I would have thought. I guess this was a story he could either take or leave. "Obviously, we'll be paying you too for the story, if that helps. But the expenses for the hotels on the road and your food and all that stuff, that will be taken care of by Elektra, their record label. We'd probably want to run this story in the October issue, you know to take on a spooky slant or something like that, which means you'll have to turn over your copy at the end of August, beginning of September at the latest. You're green, so I expect we're going to have a lot of editing and fact-checking to do over here. Also, this is just a one-off thing. We don't know if you're the next Cameron Crowe or not, and we're not about to make any commitments beyond this story."

He yammered on about this and that for the next bit but I struggled to pay attention. Suddenly I was no longer in my kitchen, I was somewhere else. It was taking all of my brain power to get me focused on the fact that this was reality.

Oh lord, please don't let this be a dream. This was everything I had ever wished and asked for, and I had made that plea many a time while growing up. I always thought it went unheard.

"All right, Dawn. I've got to go handle something. Are you going to need a few days to think about this? I can give you one. They want you on their bus by August 2nd in Colorado, start of the tour."

"Can I let you know tomorrow?" I asked. As much as I wanted to do this, needed to do this, I did have my family to think about. And even though Barry said Creem would pay me, I'd be up and leaving my brother and father, and I'd be cutting into some crucial practice time with Moonglow. If I had to be there on August 2nd, that left me five days.

"Absolutely," he said. "Talk to you then."

The line went dead. I stared at the phone in my hand, unable to process what had just happened. I slowly hung it up on the receiver and was met with the biggest urge to break down and cry.

CHAPTER THREE

"So what rock star are you going to sleep with first?" Mel asked. "Robbie? Sage? Or Mr. Black Magic?"

I rolled over on my side and gave her the dirtiest look I could muster. It was the next day and we were lying side by side up in the hayloft, the only cool place around when the temperatures were climbing. The hay made a comfortable place to chill and sip cold beers, and today we had out every magazine I had that featured Hybrid in some way, including Creem.

"None of them. And I haven't decided if I'm going to or not," I pointed out.

She snorted and took a chug of her beer, finishing it off before tossing it over the side of the loft. It landed on the ground below with a clank and I could hear Moonglow startle in her stall. I shot her another dirty look, which she ignored.

"You totally know you're going, Dawn. Eric knows you're going. Your pa knows you're going. Your horse knows you're going. I know you're going. The only one who doesn't know is this Kramer dude, and you're going to have to call him pretty soon before he decides to give your assignment to someone else."

"Except there isn't anyone else," I reminded her. "Edwards

asked for me specifically."

"I know," she said thoughtfully. She pulled a beer out of the cooler beside us and took a sip. "Don't you think that's a little odd though? I mean, it's totally bitchin', don't get me wrong, but it's kind of weird that this guy wants you, right?"

I nodded and blew a piece of hair away from my sweaty face.

"It *is* weird," I admitted. "I've been thinking about it over and over. It's just too good to be true. The only thing that makes any sense is the fact that they need to win over a female audience, and maybe they didn't like the other female writers' voice as much as mine. Or maybe they asked, like, Patti Smith first and she said no. I don't know. It's far-out but it's happening. I think."

"Stop pretending you have to think about it," she said. She smacked me lightly on my arm. "I'll come by and make sure little Eric is doing all right. He can even come over for dinner when Mom makes her famous wings. And you know I'll have a few drinks with your dad."

"Don't you dare!"

"Whatever, your dad's cool. We ain't any better than he is." She took a sip to emphasize her point. "So what else is stopping you?"

I looked down at the dirt floor way below us. "Moonglow. She's not turning as fast as she used to be. I don't think I'll be able to just show up at the rodeo and win anything. I have to practice."

"Oh shut up about practicing. Give the damn horse a break! You've been doing the rodeo for long enough."

"I know. That's why this was supposed to be our last year."

"Well, maybe next year will be your last year. You're good at the horsey stuff but you're better at the writing. You're twenty-one, not twelve. I know your goal in life isn't to marry a horse anymore, thank god, cuz that was getting weird."

I sighed, wishing this whole thing could have happened at a better time. Preferably not one that made my head swell with the heat.

"So, then what else?" She handed me the beer, which was already growing warm. Beads of moisture ran down the can and made my hands slick.

I pursed my lips, pretending I was thinking when I wasn't.

"Oh, seriously?" Mel caught on. "Ryan?"

I shrugged. "I'd be on the road for who knows how long. They say a couple of weeks but if I don't get the story, that might turn into three or four. I might be there for the whole tour, I don't know. So what if I come back here and Ryan has already left for Seattle?"

She palmed her face and shook her head. "You're crazy, woman. Crazy fucking city, that's what you *are*, that's where you *live*."

It *was* crazy city. But it was the truth. The sad, pathetic truth.

She sighed and snatched the beer back from me. "So, you're considering not going on tour with one of your favorite bands. With one of your favorite musicians, the man you call the musical genius of our time, Mr. Sage Knightly, who happens to be one fine piece of ass. Because you're afraid that your loser creep ex-boyfriend might be gone?"

I cringed and opened my mouth to defend Ryan. Sure, he didn't break up with me in the nicest way, and I had caught him cheating on me (though it was only a kiss, he swears), but Ryan had my heart for the better part of my life and—

"Turn off your brain!" Mel yelled, interrupting my deluded thoughts. "I know what you're thinking! And guess what, he is already gone. I'm sorry girl, I hate to sound mean but you really ought to get it through your thick skull that you and Ryan are dunzo. And because of that, your life is about to get awesome. You're going to let some boy who wasn't even good enough to stay with you, you're going to let him prevent you from actually reaching your dream?"

"No," I told her. I wasn't.

"What was that?" she asked.

"No!" I repeated.

She cupped her ear with her hand. "I can't hear you."

"I said no!" I yelled. Moonglow snorted from down below.

Mel grinned. "That's better. Now slap me some ace."

We high-fived. She brought out another beer from the cooler and tossed it to me and we clinked bottles over floating dust and summer sweat.

"So, back to my question…which one of them are you going to shag?"

I laughed. "Oh, Mel. You know me."

She watched me carefully, deep in thought. "Actually, I don't think *you* even know you right now. But you're about to find out exactly who Dawn Emerson is. And you might find that after being on a bus with some of the hottest, most virile men in the USA, you'll be coming back a whole new woman. And the only way you'll get there is by being shagged to death. Preferably by more than one man."

She finished that off by wagging her brows. I giggled, my face going uncharacteristically red. I knew there wasn't going to be any "shagging" going on, but I didn't doubt for a second that I was going to come back a whole new woman.

The question was: What kind of woman was I going to be?

❋ ❋ ❋

"First time flying?" the woman next to me asked.

I looked at her kind face, fear flashing in my eyes. My hands were gripping the armrests until they turned blue, the safety belt tightened across my stomach as far it would go. Gee, how could she tell?

I nodded, swallowing hard. Suddenly, I wanted nothing more than to tear off the belt, run down the aisle, and jump down the emergency slide. The bus back to Ellensburg had to still be waiting outside the Seattle airport. I could use my return ticket, hop back on, and within a few hours I'd be back in my father's arms and squeezing Eric to death. I'd never left home before. I'd never been on an airplane before. Today was full of way too many firsts and my queasy, panicking body wasn't having any of it.

On top of that, I was sad and already missing everyone. Mel was right when she said that my brother and dad would be fine with me leaving. But it didn't make it hurt any less. And it definitely didn't ease the pressure. That morning I saw the sorry sense of relief in my father's face. It made him look years younger. He was happy that I was going, knowing I was fulfilling a passion, and relieved that I'd be bringing home a check at the end of all of it. His salary as a repairman was barely enough to keep us going in this recession and it was peanuts compared to the farm when the cattle were grazing and the hay was growing. My contribution would help us out a lot, financially and mentally.

As for Eric, well I could tell he was putting on his brave face. But he could never fight the tics that came with emotion, and that's what eventually gave him away. Plus he was my brother. He was as close to me as anyone could be and I would have done anything for him. If he had opened his mouth and said, "Please, Dawn, don't go," I wouldn't have gone. But he hadn't, because he loved me too and he wanted to prove that he could take care of Dad, even if Dad couldn't take care of him. He told me to do good, to write every day, that he'd take Moonglow out on walks in the field to keep her active, and that he'd listen to Hybrid albums and send good vibes. I knew he would too. He was a good kid like that.

Then there was Mel. I'd never seen the girl cry in the eleven years I'd known her, but damn if I didn't see some extra moisture welling up in those big brown eyes of hers. Of course she had to send me off with a few extra things that she shoved in my suitcase. One of them was her favorite t-shirt, white with stars on it that said "Mel Rocks Your Socks." She had picked it up in Portland once at some funky shop and wore it at least once a week. She said she was giving it to me for good luck, "like a lucky Mel's foot—except a shirt instead of my foot."

She then proceeded to give me a blue dress with wide sleeves and a deep v-neck in both the front and back. I had only three dresses: a light cotton one that reached the floor, my tacky rodeo

31

queen one, and the one I wore to prom. Those definitely weren't coming with me on my trip and Mel knew it.

"You might have to look like a woman," she said with a wink. "I thought this was a bit rock-ish too."

I held up the dress against me. It would reach my knees at least but the top was a bit too risqué for my liking. But I thanked Mel anyway, brought her into a big embrace, and I was off on the Greyhound, looking down at the three of them as the bus left the station, wondering what I had gotten myself into.

I spent most of the bus ride earlier trying to busy myself and keep my mind occupied from the pangs of sadness that hit my heart, and the fright that fluttered around in my stomach as I took on the unknown. I decided the best course of action would be to prepare myself as much as I could for Hybrid. I started by looking back at what I had written, including the piece that examined the evolution of their sound.

Hybrid. According to Webster's, it is "anything derived from heterogeneous sources, or composed of elements of different or incongruous kinds: a hybrid of the academic and business worlds." In the music world, Hybrid is a bastard combination of sexual prowess, chugging guitars, and swaggering bass with delicate hints of country blues and Latino flavor. It is a mess of a band, who, with their upcoming third album, are already pushing the envelope with their energetic live shows and intense fearlessness.

Yeah, it was a bit cliché to have that dictionary definition, but whatever. Hybrid won me over with their sound, the way they took a band like Led Zeppelin and made it roll like a freight train. They wanted to take on anything—*anything*—and do it louder. Harder. Better. I loved them for that.

Sitting beneath the ominous shadow of the snow-capped Mount Shasta lies the Northern California town of Redding. There's not much to it. Dry, rolling hills spread lazily about on both sides of the interstate, dotted with farms and orchards. It's a slow pace of life here, good, honest and humble. So where the hell did the band Hybrid come from as they clawed their way out of Redding's dusty belly? How did that town produce the heaviest, most groundbreaking band to ever grace American soil?

I had often wondered that. That was one thing I hadn't seen in many interviews with the band—how everything really got going, what inspired them all as individuals?

To answer this we have to look back to where it all started. Imagine a fifteen-year-old Robbie Oliver strutting about in his parent's garage to Mickey Brown's thunderous guitar and Mickey's brother, Austin, on bass. On the lead guitar they had Bill Watkins, a skilled guitarist who was a friend of Robbie's father. They've even got a neighborhood kid on the drums just trying to keep up. Fast forward a few months, and the band has gotten rid of the neighborhood kid and put in Sage Knightly instead. Yes, little Sage started on the drums but it wasn't long before things were shaken up. Bill suffered a mild heart attack, and Austin Brown came down with a good ol' fashioned case of mono. Sage jumped at the opportunity to do lead guitar—not a far stretch since he was the key songwriter and could play any instrument— and Noelle Clark, Mickey's girlfriend, took over the bass. Soon, Graham Freed answered an ad in the Redding classified section, and they had a new drummer as well. This was the real start of Hybrid, a band that mixed genres and their own musicians.

My own obsession with the band started with Ryan, actually. We were into a lot of music together, and though his tastes leaned more towards the blues and country, he picked up Hybrid's first self-titled album on a whim while visiting San Francisco. There had been no radio play for the album at all, so no one had really heard of them. But for whatever reason, Ryan bought the record, took it back home to Ellensburg and played it for me in my room. I wasn't hooked right away. Sometimes it sounded too loud. Other times, too weird. But it got its claws in me, and pretty soon I was learning everything I could about the band.

Which, at the time, wasn't much. With no radio play, they also had no press. I'd written a fan letter to the address on the back of the record but never heard back. They were reclusive and mysterious. It made me love them more.

Then the second album, *Asteroid*, was released on Elektra Records and things exploded. Their first single, "Red Blues Sun" got airplay everywhere. It was the song for the summer of '73. They started touring and making appearances on The Midnight Special with their quieter numbers like "Pieces of Ash" and "The Deal Fell Through." Robbie and Sage became the focus of the band. Robbie for his extraordinary voice, his manic, monkey-like behavior on stage, and his foxy Californian good looks. Sage for being a 6'3" powerhouse of pure talent, the driving force behind the band, and the one code the press couldn't crack. Where Robbie loved nothing more than to talk about himself and the music (and the women), Sage never said much of anything at all.

I was going to have to change that.

The roar of the airplane engines coming alive shook me out of my thoughts. We had coasted up the runway and now we were headed for the sky.

I looked over at the lady next to me. She had a book out and was thoroughly engrossed, not paying attention at all to the fact that we were about to be launched into the air in a metal tube with wings. I had brought a book too, *Carrie* by some new author, but there was no way I'd be able to concentrate on it while 35,000 feet in the sky. I didn't even know why I'd picked that book as it looked kind of scary and scary stuff wasn't really my thing.

I wasn't sure if it was because I was thinking of the book, or because we were now in the air and I was terrified of us falling to our deaths, but an incredible chill passed over my body, causing every hair on my arms to stand up. My eyes had been squeezed shut for the last few minutes so I opened them to the circulated air and fluorescent lights.

The chill intensified.

In the narrow space between the seats in front of me was the shadowed face of someone staring in my direction. I could barely make out that it was a little boy, maybe around six years old. He kept his dark eyes on me. He opened his mouth to grin.

My breath caught in my throat.

It lasted only a second, only a flash of white teeth, but I could have sworn his teeth were fanged. Sharp as razors and entirely inhuman.

Then the smile vanished and the boy turned around.

I spent the rest of the plane ride with my eyes locked on the back of his seat. I didn't fear the airplane anymore—I feared something else.

It wasn't until we were getting up to get our bags that I got another glimpse of him. He was smiling, perfectly normal teeth, chatting to his parents, a cute young boy overall. He didn't look my way once, and by the time I was walking into the airport, dragging my carry-on behind me, I'd come to the conclusion that it was all in my head.

Why on earth had I just spent a couple of hours on an airplane focused on some random little boy when I had more pressing things to think about? Was it just a distraction for my mind? Because it had worked.

Now, as passengers dispersed in the arrivals terminal, I had to look for a man carrying a sign that said Dawn Emerson on it.

The man would be Hybrid's manager, Jacob Edwards.

The man who would take me to the band at the famous Red Rocks Amphitheatre.

The band who would become my shadow for the next few weeks.

I was hit by such a burst of excitement that I thought my heart was going to bounce its way out of my chest. My knees began to quiver, the handle of my bag starting to slip out of my clammy hands. Could I do this? I didn't even know where I *was*.

Denver, right, Denver, Colorado. I was Dawn Emerson in Denver, Colorado, having survived her first plane trip ever with a non-demonic little boy. I was thousands of miles away from home, standing in an airport full of strangers going back and forth. I was on the verge of something epic. It could go well, it could all go bad, but it was going to be epic in whichever way it went.

I was going to throw up.

I spied the signs for the bathroom and began to hurry my way there when I heard someone call out my name.

I stopped and forced the vomit to stay down. I tried to compose myself. Smoothed the fringe down on my shirt.

I turned around and looked. Over by the baggage claim was a tall, red-headed fellow holding a plastic sign that had my name on it. His eyes lit up at my gaze and he gestured for me to walk over to him with a quick shake of his head.

"You're Dawn, right?" he yelled, full-on Cockney accent. People in the terminal turned to look at us, perplexed at the ginger invasion.

I nodded, feeling like a deer caught in the headlights.

"Well hurry up and piss and get your ass over here, time is money."

Yes, he certainly did just shout that at me from across the airport.

I was a little too annoyed to piss or vomit now. So this was the Jacob Edwards, was it? What a rude dude.

I straightened my shoulders, gripped my bag tighter, and hurried off toward him.

"Dawn, nice to finally meet you," he said as I neared him. "I'm Jacob Edwards, but you can call me The Cob. Actually don't. I can tell I might like you and I only let buggers call me that."

Now that I was up close, I could see he was quite the brutal looking character. Oh, he was handsome in a peculiar way with a large sloping forehead and broad chin. His eyes were small and sparkling, a weird amber color, and his nose had been broken a few times. Freckles dusted the tops of his cheeks along with pockmarks.

This was the man who kept Hybrid under control. Given some of the rumors I had heard, I wondered how often he was able to do his job. Guess I'd be finding out.

A little thrill ran through my body at that thought, and I held out my hand. I needed to act professional, assertive.

"Nice to meet you, Jacob. Thank you for, you know, thinking of me," I said. He took my hand in his and gave it a bone-crushing squeeze. I had no doubt he could have broken it in two. So much for being assertive.

He held on to it for a few more seconds, looking deep into my eyes like he was testing my pain threshold or something. Then he released it and smiled. "It was nothing. Now let's get started. I have a cab waiting for us."

I couldn't help but feel shy while looking at him. There was something magnetic about his presence and it was hard to guess his age. His mannerisms and skin made him look older, but his eyes and smile placed him at about thirty. He was a beefy guy, wide at the waist, built like a tree. His knuckles looked fat and he had a bunch of gold rings on them. His suit was checkerboard and ugly.

He turned and started marching toward the door. I followed behind him, my long legs trying to match his, my brain lagging behind. I ignored the tingling sensation in my hand.

We burst through the main doors and into the Colorado sunshine. It was brighter here than at home, the air smelling fresh from the mountains. I immediately imagined Moonglow tossing up her white mane, Arab nostrils wide, soaking in the oxygen. This was horse country, a more rugged version of home.

But now wasn't time to be thinking about home. We had stopped at a cab that was running at the side of the road. Jacob tossed my sign in the trash (kind of a bummer because I would have liked to have kept that as a souvenir), then opened the door to the backseat, taking my suitcase from me with the other hand.

"Get in," he gave me a little shove toward the door. "And be careful, she bites."

She bites?

I got in and sat in the back of the cab, expecting to see a dog or something. Instead I saw the very unamused face of Miss Noelle Clark. Bassist. Girlfriend of Mickey Brown. An original member of Hybrid, and one of the hottest chicks in the music industry.

She was looking at me like I'd already tested her patience. Despite the dullness in her heavily-lined eyes and the tightness of her normally full lips, she was prettier in person than I'd seen in photographs and on TV. She was thinner than I imagined, but dressed straight out of a magazine spread, a headband on her head, her dark, wild hair trailing down her shoulders. She wore a slightly transparent black lace dress and tall platform boots. It was sexy and hard-edged all at once. She was one of the few musicians who could pull off the Alice Cooper look without being Alice Cooper.

And I was very aware that I was shoved in the back of a cab with her and staring at her blatantly.

"Hi," I said awkwardly. I wiped my sweaty hand on my cords and put my hand out for her. "I'm Dawn. I'll be—"

"I know why you're here," she said quickly. She turned her attention to Jacob who was just coming into the car. "Can we get a move on or what?"

Jacob shot her a look over his shoulder. When his amber eyes narrowed, he looked positively avian. "You don't call the shots, missy. You wanted to come along and along you came."

She sat back in her seat and crossed her arms, looking out the window with annoyance. "Had I known it would take so long, I would have sent someone else to get the alcohol."

I felt like I had to say something. "I'm sorry the flight was a bit late and—"

"And now," she added, still not looking at me, "I have to watch what I say because some groupie is in the car."

"Hey," I protested. "I'm not a groupie!"

The cab driver and Jacob exchanged a look and the car roared off. I was thrown back a bit and I made sure I was fastened in properly.

Noelle rolled her eyes but didn't say anything.

"I'm a journalist," I went on to say even though it didn't seem like anyone was listening. Jacob was grinning like a madman from the front seat, like he was really enjoying himself.

"You'll have to excuse Noelle here," he finally explained, tucking away those big teeth. "She's the girl of the group. You might be infringing on her territory a wee bit."

I gave him a funny look. Well why the hell did he want me to come on the road with him if he thought it was going to be a problem?

Never mind, suck it up, I told myself. I was obviously a bundle of nerves and taking things the wrong way. I'd win Noelle over sooner or later. She was just one tiny piece of the band, albeit a fairly formidable one considering the chill she was giving off with her cold shoulder.

I took a deep breath and gave them both a smile I hoped was charming and understanding. "No worries, we have plenty of time to get to know each other. Tonight I guess is all about settling in."

"Yeah, you have the easy part," Noelle said to me out of the corner of her mouth. Her arms were still crossed. "This is the start of our tour. I...fuck, Jacob, how long till the store?"

Jacob patted the cabbie on the shoulder. "Pull over at the nearest establishment, good sir."

The cabbie gave him an eye roll that rivaled Noelle's but did as he asked. Soon we were rolling into a generic-looking liquor store, all pale blue paint and gold letters.

Noelle sighed, either annoyed or relieved, then put her palm flat out toward Jacob. He put a few bills in her hand. "This is part of the room and board," he told me with a wink. "You're included, Dawn. Go in with Noelle and pick your lot."

I raised my brows at him. Noelle had closed her hand over the money and was out the door and walking fast toward the entrance.

"Go on," he said, nodding at her. "Give her a hand. And make sure she doesn't steal anything."

He looked serious, so I couldn't figure out if it was true or not. No matter, if the band tour manager wanted me to follow Noelle, bassist of Hybrid, into a liquor store, then that's what I was going to do.

I walked into the store, the air conditioning smelling like ice, and went over to Noelle who was perusing the vodka section.

"Looking for something in particular?" I asked. Sometimes I sucked at small talk.

"Maybe." She straightened up and glanced over at the cashier. His back was turned to us, arranging a display on the wall. She quickly unscrewed the cap off a bottle of Smirnoff and quickly chugged a mouthful. Then she wiped her lips, put it back on the shelf and grabbed the Grey Goose next to it. She repeated it all over again, keeping her eyes on the cashier but never looking the slightest bit chagrined or worried.

I was aware that my mouth was hanging open a little so I closed it. "Taste testing?"

She screwed the cap back on the Grey Goose.

"Jacob never gives us enough money, and I heard half the fucking venues don't even supply the kicks anymore. Fucking economy."

After she had her third mouthful of vodka, a relaxed glaze had come over her eyes.

"Hey, wanna be of help to us?" she said lazily, scooping three bottles of Smirnoff into her arms. "You go get the beers. A case of Corona. A case of Carlsberg. A flat of Heineken."

I was strong but if she thought I could carry all of that, she was crazy. And judging from the way she had moved on down the aisle and was putting mini bottles of booze into the tops of her boots, there was no disputing it.

Oh boy. What exactly had I got involved with here?

I made my way over to the beer fridges, aware that we could get totally busted at any moment and I would be guilty by association. I thought Mel could be a badass at times, but Noelle was taking the cake and enjoying every mouthful.

I took what I could to the counter where Noelle was waiting, seemingly impatient. She had the bottles of vodka, a bottle of Crown Royal, a bottle of Jameson, and two boxes of red wine. I hoped that was their booze for the week and not just the night. I knew Hybrid got in trouble sometimes for being disorderly, but I didn't think it was *this* bad.

It took two trips to get the booze out to the car, with Jacob sitting in the car watching us the whole time. I wondered if he hoped it would be some sort of bonding experience between Noelle and I. I couldn't tell you if it worked. As we drove off toward the amphitheater, which was a long drive out of the city, she went back to being quiet and sullen.

And I went back to overthinking things. As the realization that I was actually in a car with Hybrid's bassist and manager began to sink in, I started focusing on another problem—one that I could see becoming a shadow over this whole tour. Just what the hell was I supposed to write about here?

When I had called Barry back and told him I was on board with the idea, he barely gave me any ideas for the piece. He said it *could* run on the cover, which was unbelievable, but it really depended on what I came up with, what it was going to be about. The last thing I wanted was a poor version of celebrity journalism, talking about the shoplifting habit of their bassist. I wanted it to be about the music and I hoped that's where it was going to go.

I took in a deep breath and let my eyes drift over the mountain scenery as the cab climbed higher towards rolling red and green hills. I needed advice but I didn't have anyone to give it to me. Even if Ryan and I were still together, every time I mentioned writing, his eyes would glaze over. He loved the music part and loved sharing music with me, but I never had the impression he thought I was going to do anything great with it. My dad was a good listener when sober, but he wasn't one for advice. Mel's opinion would get me into trouble. Anything Jacob said would be biased, and Barry didn't seem like someone you could bug. Besides, I wanted to come off stronger than I was. The only person I could think of would be the young music journalist Cameron Crowe. The kid was only sixteen and writing genius articles for Rolling Stone. But he was famous now and in a class of his own. Not my class, not by a long shot.

I needed a mentor. Maybe I should have had one all along.

And now, I realized, I had been thrown right into the deep end. Alone.

Thank god I knew how to swim.

CHAPTER FOUR

It wasn't long before the cab rolled up to the Red Rocks Amphitheatre. My heart went pitter-patter over the sight of the famous red rocks flanking the sides of the natural arena, a desert-like oasis with the lights of Denver in the background. This was the place where The Beatles rocked in 1964, where Jethro Tull's sold out show a few years ago led to the "Riot at Red Rocks" and a five-year ban on rock concerts. The ban was apparently still in place; the only way Hybrid was able to play was because they were the opener for Pretty Mary and both of them were playing "unplugged" or acoustic only.

Still, by the looks of the fans who had already begun to ascend on the venue, an acoustic show didn't keep out the rockers. I had only heard about their acoustic only show on the ride over and I was totally intrigued by it. No wonder they had wanted me for the start of their tour; this was something that not many rock bands did, let alone one that gave Black Sabbath and Led Zeppelin a run for their money.

The cab was only able to get so far before we were met with the barricade that cut off the road from the backstage area. We climbed out of the car, armed to the neck with alcohol, and made our way toward the guard at the gate.

Jacob was talking to him, motioning his head in my direction.

"The other redhead is with us."

"Where's her pass?" asked the unsmiling guard. He was built like Andre the Giant, only Andre smiled a lot more.

Jacob sighed. "I don't have it on me. It's inside. I'll come show you later, okay, mate?"

"She can't come in without a pass. Rules."

Noelle rolled her eyes at the hold-up and quickly flashed her badge from out of her purse. She pushed past the guard and disappeared into the darkening area behind the stage.

Jacob looked back at me and seemed to be thinking.

A cool breeze came rolling down the cliff sides and mussed up my hair. I felt disheveled and stupid standing there with my arms wrapped around two cases of beer, being told I couldn't come inside like I wasn't good enough.

Jacob came over, set the flat down on the dusty ground, and pulled his laminated pass over his head. He placed it around my own neck, giving me a look. "I'd go and get it but I'm afraid you'll take off with everyone's beer. And if Mickey doesn't get his Carlsberg, he's gonna be right pissed. Try to follow Noelle. The band should be in their dressing room, if not the bus. And tell someone to come get me, please."

He gave me a little shove toward the guard. Shoving seemed to be his thing.

Suddenly I was full of panic. I couldn't go in alone! I was already getting flack and I wasn't even inside the venue yet.

"Who do I ask? Where do I go?"

"Are you deaf, woman? Get someone. Preferably from the band. You do remember what the band looks like, right?"

I nodded dumbly and found myself walking past the guard with Jacob's pass around my neck. I shot Jacob a look through the chain link fence. He gave me a "bye bye" wave, before plucking a beer out of the flat and opening it with a satisfying crack.

I turned around and tried to get my bearings. I was behind

the stage and it wasn't at all like I pictured. The road continued off to the side, where two large buses sat. Along the rock faces, multiple doors disappeared into it, all guarded by different men, checking passes for everyone. At the stage area, a few lucky souls were lined up along the side, while sound technicians fiddled with the board and roadies ran about with instruments.

I looked down at the pass that was resting on top of the case of Carlsberg. It said ALL ACCESS across it. If I wasn't so lost and nervous, I would have felt like doing a little kick of joy. All my passes before were either photo or media passes—I'd never had the coveted All Access Backstage Pass for anything before.

"Hey, those beers for me?"

I looked to my left to see a cute, smiling guy in a Sabbath t-shirt approaching me.

I smiled uneasily at him. "No, they're for Hybrid, and apparently Mickey will be pissed if he doesn't get his share soon."

I hoped I sounded cool.

"Good point," he said. He stood beside me and peered down at my pass. "Ooh, All Access. Aren't you fancy?"

I took a quick glance at his pass and found it to be hanging off the side of his jeans. I guess that was the cool way to wear it.

"You're apparently fancy, too."

He grinned. He reminded me a bit of Robert Redford, if Redford had a slight beer belly, tattoos, shaggy black hair, and a mustache. He held out his hands.

"Well, here let me help you. I promise not to drink any."

I let him take the Corona but kept the Carlsberg close to my chest.

"I'm Chip, by the way."

"Dawn."

"And so, Dawn," he said, "might I ask why you have Mickey Brown and Sage Knightly's beer?"

So the Corona was for Sage. Interesting. I think that was the most I knew about him.

And here went the spiel I'd have to repeat for the

45

month of August.

"I'm a music journalist for Creem Magazine. I'm going on the road with the band for this tour, and hopefully if I write a good enough story, I can get the band on the cover."

He raised his brow. "And are you a fan of the band?"

I grinned. "One of the biggest."

He returned the smile. "Well aren't they lucky. For once, they get a journalist who's a fan *and* she ends up being a hot chick on top of it."

That thing where I rarely blushed? It was happening again.

"I'm just hoping they won't toss me out of the bus in the middle of Kansas," I said, thinking of moody Noelle.

"No way. Anything goes with Hybrid, so as long as you keep the alcohol flowing and the coke powdered."

Now it was my time to raise my brows.

He stroked his mustache and looked chagrined. "Ah, fuck. I guess I shouldn't be telling you these things, should I? Hell, you're going to be on the road with us, you'd find out sooner or later."

"Us?" I repeated.

He nodded. "I'm the sound tech. I like to think I'm the best, but I'm really just the most loyal. Come on, let's get those boys some beers."

I looked back at Jacob on the other side of the fence. He was drinking his beer and talking to a few people.

"Jacob needs a pass too," I told him. "He gave me his."

Chip raised his hand in the air in dismissal and started walking toward the buses. "Jacob's The Cob, man. He can take care of himself."

I shot Jacob one last glance and then hurried after Chip, the bottles in the box rattling against each other.

He stopped in front of one of the buses, an aging forty foot behemoth of scuffed chrome and peeling green paint. The windows were tinted, but from the faint afternoon light coming in the other side, I could see movement inside and silhouettes. The vague drone of a stereo emanated from the closed doors.

"This is it. The Green Machine," he said, looking up at the bus with pride. "She's a piece of shit but we've decided to love her anyway."

He gave me a coy glance over his shoulder.

"You ready to meet the band and your home for the next few weeks?"

My mouth went all dry and I couldn't speak. I nodded slowly, my body caught in a net of apprehension. My fingers gripped the box of beer until it hurt, and I had the greatest urge to just run far, far away.

He let out a laugh, clearly amused by my attack of nerves, and pounded his fist on the bus door.

"Let me in, you fuckers!" he demanded.

The bus swayed back and forth slightly. The door proceeded to shudder and then eased open with a hiss of hydraulics.

He went up the first few steps, passing the beer to someone inside who I couldn't see properly, and paused.

"Are you guys ready to meet Rusty?" he yelled into the bus.

Rusty? I was Rusty now?

"Who the fuck is Rusty?" someone hollered back.

"It's that groupie chick," I heard Noelle say from inside.

I nearly dropped the entire case of beer on my foot. My fingers clung on strong with anger instead of nerves.

"Well, I don't think she's a groupie, per se…" Chip trailed off. He looked over at me. "Well, get on over here and say hello."

I took in a deep breath and willed my legs to move. Somehow my sneakers carried me to the bus door and I climbed up the stairs until I was at the top of them beside Chip.

I gave him an anxious smile then turned to face everyone in the smoke-filled bus.

I don't think I'll ever forget *it*, that feeling of having a band that you loved, the faces you gazed at in magazines, the ones who created life-changing music, staring back at you, and only you. It was almost too much to take in at once, but my brain did a commendable job of taking a snapshot of it as Bad Company's

"Rock Steady" provided the soundtrack.

Behind the empty bus driver's seat was a table with two benches on either side of it. Noelle and Mickey sat on one side facing me, Noelle in his lap. Her arms were draped all over her boyfriend, the quiet rhythm guitarist. He was of medium height, dressed in khaki green suede that was too big for him. I'd seen pictures of him with his shirt off and he was pretty thin and ripped with fine muscle. His eyes were dark and wary, his hair long, his beard and mustache adequately bushy.

Across from him and turning around in his seat to see me was Robbie Oliver. *The* Robbie Oliver. The Metal Monkey. The Spazz of the Stage. The Singing Seducer. And he looked just like I imagined he would. He wasn't the tallest guy, maybe my height, but he had a gymnast's body that he usually showed off in the tightest pants and undershirts. He had moves, he was flexible, and on stage he was a maniac. Off stage he had a reputation for being a lady-killer. From what I understood, he had a fiancé in California, but that didn't stop the rumors from flying.

And how could they not? Robbie had three things going for him: one, his charm—he was a gregarious man, full of snappy one-liners and quick wit. He was never rude to the press or to fans, even when they got too nosy or extreme. Two, his looks. Robbie was twenty-eight like most of the band and had that wonderful boy meets man appeal. His hair was a shiny and thick chestnut, the kind you'd see in shampoo commercials. It fell blunt across his forehead and longer in the back and nicely framed his sparkling blue eyes and dimples. He was somehow cute and sexy at the same time, and the sexiness came from three—the fact that he could sing the panties off of anyone. Any woman, anyway, and I was sure any man. Robbie Oliver was the man Mel waxed on about when we were going through the rock stars we'd like to shag list (I should not have to point out that the list was her idea and my only contribution was to nod and listen to her). She didn't like Hybrid's downtuned guitars, but she did love Robbie's soaring voice.

And here he was, shirtless except for an open sky blue vest that matched his eyes. And he was looking at me. Smiling.

It took all my energy to look away, and when I did, my eyes rested on Graham Freed. He was sitting at the front of a long couch, closest to me. Graham was an amazing drummer and one of the key aspects to Hybrid's success (in my opinion, anyway) but he certainly wasn't the most charismatic. Oh, he wasn't bad looking by a long shot—none of the guys in the band were anyone you'd find fault with. He had shoulder-length black hair and a thin beard and was covered in tattoos and strange piercings that made him look like a tribesman. He loved to admit his fascination with the occult, never really refuted the fact that he had ties to a Satanic church, and was just a general oddball. Of course, everyone knew the whole thing was bunk and it was just for show, but his opinions made him annoying. To me, Graham was always the disgruntled drummer of the band constantly vying for attention.

Except in this case, Graham looked like he didn't want any attention from me. In fact, I could have sworn he shuddered at my presence and his brows were knit in confusion.

I kept my eyes moving and settled on the last person on the bus. The person sitting at the end of the long couch.

Sage Knightly.

He was leaning against the wall with a book in hand, his long, black-jean clad legs sprawled in front of him. On his feet were his trademark flip-flops, his wide upper body in a wide-collared black shirt that was unbuttoned halfway, a peek of his scruffy firm chest popping through. Tattoos drifted out of the sleeves and onto his forearms. He was looking at me with all the intensity in the world, and in my numb state I couldn't read any expression on his face. His gray-green eyes were clear and piercing, framed dramatically by his low, strong brows. Black curly hair fell softly on his forehead and onto the sides. His dimpled chin was strong, his bottom lip was full with an upper lip that curved sweetly. His skin was bronzed and looked more exotic in person, alluding to his rumored Hispanic ancestry.

He was the man on my wall.

My musical hero.

My musical crush.

And he was on the bus, sitting there, right in front of me.

No, wait…he was leaving.

With a slight narrowing of the eyes, he finally stopped staring, and after giving everyone what seemed to be a disgusted look, got up and marched down the aisle toward me. He was so tall he almost had to duck down as went by. I leaned against Chip to get out of his way—Sage was built like a brick house and probably would have clipped my shoulder.

"We have your beer!" Chip yelled after him as Sage pushed past me and stomped off the bus. He didn't even throw us a backward glance.

I looked back at Chip, my heart racing, the urge to vomit teasing me. What the hell just happened there? Did I piss him off somehow? Already?

Also: Holy smokes, Sage Knightly just touched me.

Chip grinned. "Welcome to the band, Rusty!"

"You're not the guy from Rolling Stone," Graham said to me, sounding accusatory.

I looked at him, surprised. "Rolling Stone? No, Creem."

"I thought I asked for someone from Rolling Stone," he mumbled angrily. Wait, the drummer arranged for this?

"Who cares, she's hot," Chip said, putting his arm around me. "Come on, put down the beers, let's get the introductions over with."

I put the beers on the table, right in front of Robbie. Our eyes met and I immediately tore mine away, too many weird emotions going through me at once. I was bewildered, shook up, confused, and in disbelief.

"Nice to meet you, Rusty," Robbie said in his smooth voice. "I'm Robbie."

He smiled. I was turning into a puddle of swoon.

"Dawn," I corrected him and immediately felt silly for doing so. Robbie Oliver could call me Pooey-Poo-Poo Smelly Face if he wanted to.

"Rusty it is," he said, still smiling, still working out those dimples. He scooched over and patted the faded seat next to him. "Come, sit, regale us with your tales of Creem Magazine."

I made some sort of noise. Chip pushed me lightly into the seat and tossed everyone a Carlsberg, making sure Mickey got his first.

After I had gotten over the fact that Sage had just snubbed me, I was overcome by the girly, juvenile, dimwitted sensation of "Oh my god, I'm squished up next to Robbie Oliver. Oh my god, Mickey Brown and Noelle Clark are sitting across from me, drinking beer. Oh my god, Noelle won't stop glaring at me. Oh my god, how did this become my life?"

Thankfully I wasn't able to dwell on it for very long. Chip was shoving a beer in my hand while Robbie started rattling off the questions: How long had I worked for Creem Magazine, where was I from, what was my favorite band, what was my favorite Hybrid album, what was my favorite Hybrid song, and who was the best singer in the world?

Naturally I answered "you" to that last one.

He grinned and patted my hand. "That a girl! Great answers." He looked at Noelle, who continued to look unimpressed. "See, she's not a groupie."

Then he leaned into my hair and whispered into my ear, "Not that I'd mind either way."

I let out an awkward laugh. Was Robbie hitting on me?

"She's a groupie with a badge," Noelle shot in.

I responded with a look that could kill.

"Can I quote you on that?" I asked sweetly, finding my nerve. "Would look real good in the article."

She narrowed her eyes back at me and I heard Robbie suck in his breath.

Chip laughed. "Wowee, boys, I think we're going to have an

interesting few weeks."

"I wanted the guy from Rolling Stone," Graham muttered.

"No one cares what you want," Robbie yelled at him over my head. He then looked at Mickey. "Boyo, make your girlfriend behave."

Mickey shrugged and took a sip of his beer. "Whatever, man, Noe can do what she pleases."

"And what I please isn't here yet," she said. She leaned down and plucked one of the stolen mini liquor bottles out of her boot.

"Patience," Mickey told her and proceeded to roll a joint.

I didn't know what they were talking about, but I had a feeling it had to do with drugs. Before I could ponder that more, Robbie bumped me with his hip playfully.

"So what do you think, miss rusty journalist?"

I couldn't help but smile. He had a nice way of making me forget the people on the other side of the table. "About what?"

"Well, let's start with the bus."

"I told her we love the piece of shit," Chip added as he went to sit on the couch beside Graham.

"Piece of shit is right," Mickey said, not looking up from his joint. "It's only a matter of time before she goes off the road."

"Such pessimism," Robbie scolded him. He took a big sip of his beer before looking around, admiring it.

I did the same, if not just to take the pressure off of me. The table we sat at was small and kind of cramped, but would do to have a bite or play a game of cards. The carpet of the bus was this dirty green that matched the velour of the couch cushions. It probably sat three people comfortably and looked long enough that even the 6'3" Sage could stretch out on it. Above the couch were cupboards and a small stack of 8-track tapes and books. Further back, there was a closet, and then two bunk beds tucked into the side. Behind Noelle and Mickey was another set of two forward-facing seats, and behind that a tiny kitchen consisting of a mini fridge, sink, and one burner. I couldn't tell what was in the back but I assumed it was a bathroom and more beds. It was a nice bus…or it would have been in 1965. Now it was down at its heels, a victim of too many wild tours.

"Our driver's pretty cool too," Robbie went on to say. "He used to drive around Elvis. He has many stories. We have yet to get him drunk to hear them, but we have plans. Ain't that right, Boyo?"

Mickey nodded and lit the joint at his lips. After inhaling and passing to Noelle, he let out a slow puff of air that drifted off into the bus's already smoky atmosphere. "Yeah. If Bob doesn't have a heart attack on us."

"So why did they send you here?" I heard Graham say from beside me.

"Pardon me?"

"Creem," he explained, nostrils flaring slightly.

I gave him a look. His harping on about this was getting on my nerves.

"I don't know," I replied. "Jacob arranged this, why don't you go ask him?"

Okay. So chiding the members of the band that I was supposed to interview probably wasn't the best idea.

And then I remembered. I looked beside me at Robbie, still finding it unnerving that he was just inches away, our hips touching on the seat. "Speaking of Jacob, he's outside the gate. He gave me his pass because I didn't have one. He said he wants one of you to go get him."

Robbie shook his head and reached over for the joint dangling from Mickey's slightly shaking fingers. "Rusty, don't worry about The Cob. That's rule number one on the bus. Having Jacob around is like having a creepy babysitter who owes money to the mob."

"I swear Jacob is the mob," Mickey said in between coughs. "Even the names rhyme."

"That's brilliant," Robbie told him, blowing smoke in his face. "You should start writing lyrics for the band."

"Go fuck yourself," Mickey replied.

"I've tried. My dick was too big." Robbie leaned back in the seat, his legs spread open, knee bumping against mine. My goodness he had on tight pants.

I looked away and cleared my throat.

Noelle got off of Mickey's lap, making annoyed noises.

"I'll go get Jacob," she said, reaching for a pass that was hanging off a cupboard knob. She looked back at Mickey and he tapped the side of his nose.

"Could you two be any more obvious?" Graham said.

"Shut up, Graham," she retorted over her skinny shoulder and flounced down the stairs and out of the bus.

"You do drugs, Rusty?" Mickey said with glazed eyes.

I could feel everyone looking at me.

"I smoke a little dope from time to time," I admitted.

"No coke?" he asked.

I shook my head.

"Acid?" asked Chip.

"Quaaludes?" asked Robbie.

"No." I felt like I should elaborate with some excuse but there wasn't really much to say other than the fact that I didn't do hard drugs. I'd seen what my mother had gone through on prescription meds and that was enough for me.

Robbie put his hand over mine and squeezed it. It was warm, and his lovely well-formed fingers were delicate and soft. "Good for you. More for us then."

He took another toke of the joint then added, "But don't quote us on that."

"Yeah, maybe don't quote us on anything until we say when," Mickey mused, suddenly sounding concerned.

"You're just thinking about Noe. Your woman is going to get in trouble," Robbie said to him.

"No," Graham spoke up. "You're going to get us in trouble. You always do. Starting with hitting on the hack here."

I shot Graham another glare. Did he and Noelle make some sort of deal to tag team me?

Robbie took his hand away, looking chagrined.

"Sorry, I can be too friendly."

Chip snorted. "That's an understatement."

"I do mean well," Robbie continued, good naturedly. He looked over at Graham. "And I think you need to mind your manners over there. Oh wait, forget it. You don't even have a soul."

Clearly having enough of our company, Graham got to his feet with a sigh and looked down at us. "We all lost our souls when we joined this band. And despite what Mickey says, I think you should quote me on that."

He pointed at me, his nicotine-stained finger right in my face, then left the bus. Now it was just me, a buzzed Chip on his fourth beer, a stoned Mickey, and Robbie.

At least the atmosphere wasn't so volatile. I felt my body relax for the first time since stepping on the bus.

Or maybe it was the fact that the thing was now hot boxed.

Either way I took the opportunity to start setting some ground rules.

"Look, I'm sort of new at this going on the road with a band thing," I told them, trying to get my brain to think straight. I figured being honest couldn't hurt in this situation, or at least with these guys. "So I am not sure what the rules are about this sort of thing. I know I'm going to be traveling with you for most of the tour. I'd like to interview everyone separately at one point, and maybe do one together—"

Robbie sucked in his breath at that. I continued, my voice shaking with nerves.

"—and I'm also just going to absorb the atmosphere, the feeling of your shows, what life on the road is like, what life in Hybrid is like."

"Do we get to approve what's written?" Mickey asked.

I wasn't sure how to answer that. "Well...no."

Mickey shook his head and put the joint out on the table, adding to other burn marks. "I don't know man, whose idea was it again to have a journalist with us?"

"Graham," Robbie said. "But we all agreed. Even Sage."

"Actually, I don't think Sage ever did agree," Chip put in. He was now lying down on the couch, a beer balancing on his belly. "In fact, I think I remember him saying, 'You guys are all fucking idiots to think this wont fuck us royally' and then he threw a book at Graham."

Mickey let out a short and stupid laugh. "Oh yeah. Fucking Graham."

Robbie turned to me. "We think Graham had this idea that if he got this dipshit ass-kisser journalist from Rolling Stone, that he'd come and focus just on him. You know, this ass has got a wicked hard on for drummers or something."

I looked down at my hands. "Guess I kind of ruined that."

"You didn't ruin it, Rusty," Chip said. "It was Jacob's call in the end, and I'm sure getting a writer who's an actual fan of the band—the whole band—won't hurt us. Plus, like I said, you're hot."

I gave him a wry look even though he was watching his beer can rise and fall.

"Hot and smart," Robbie added.

"Dude, stop hitting on her," Mickey said.

"Why? Jealous?"

"If I were jealous, Noe would have both my balls in her purse already."

I cleared my throat. "So, just to be clear, I will be observing you all, but you can always ask for things to be off the record."

"Can everything be off the record?" asked Mickey.

I couldn't help but laugh. He really was worried.

"No," I said with a shake of my head. "I'm just saying…"

"She's saying watch what you say and try to keep your drug use hidden, you moron," said Chip.

"Drug use?" Jacob's booming accent rolled into the bus.

We all turned to see him walk onto the bus and up the stairs. He smiled down at me. "Thanks for coming to get me, Dawn."

"I sent Noelle!" I said defensively. I felt secretly delighted that we were behaving like chums already instead of strangers, like arguing with Hybrid's manager was something I normally did as part of Dawn Emerson's normal life.

"You should have sent a cat, it would have gotten to me faster," he said, taking a seat beside Mickey with a groan, like his bones were tired.

"Where is she?" Mickey asked.

"Oh, she and Graham took the flat of beer to the dressing room. You boys realize you can go hang out there too. Might be better since we're about thirty minutes away from showtime."

"Did you do soundcheck already?" I asked.

"Yeah, this afternoon," Robbie said. That disappointed me. I'd always wanted to see the band—any band, actually—during soundcheck. It was like an extra special, private performance.

"How did it go?" I asked.

Robbie shrugged. "It went…"

His eyes flew across the table to Mickey's and they exchanged an unreadable look. Finally Mickey looked at me.

"Noe can't play the bass unplugged so we have her doing simple notes on the keyboard. She's not too happy about it."

"And Graham is being a shit at keeping time on those fucking tambourines," Robbie added.

"And I have no idea how to get Robbie's voice so it doesn't overshadow everyone," Chip said with a sigh.

Jacob looked at me and smiled, opening his hands in surrender. "So you can see, you're about to witness one hell of a show."

"The only person who knows what they are doing is Sage," Robbie admitted.

"And me," Mickey put in. I caught the slightest trace of bitterness in his voice, and the quick look he shot at Robbie only added to it.

"Of course, you," Robbie comforted him. He turned to Jacob expectantly. "So, boss, should we go do this or what?"

"Take your time," Jacob said, twirling his gold rings around his thick fingers. "I've already got the money for us from the owner, so if you want to go at things half-arsed, be my guest."

"So passive aggressive, Jacob," Robbie chided him softly. "I don't think I like this side of you."

Jacob tilted his head and winked at me. "Just trying to keep the peace with the writer here."

Robbie put his arm around me and shook me slightly. "Good old Rusty, already keeping everyone on their best behavior."

When I got over the embarrassment and wanting to squeal like a girl at the fact that Robbie Oliver had his arm around me, I couldn't help but wonder—this was their best behavior?

How long would it be before I saw them at their worst?

CHAPTER FIVE

The rest of the evening went quite well. I didn't see the band at their worst (I knew that would come later) but I did get to enjoy one of the most memorable shows of my life. I guess they could have sat around and banged pots and pans and I still would have thought it was awesome just because I was there, and for once, I was special.

With the band getting ready for their acoustic set, I ended up following Jacob around like a lost puppy. I didn't mind it. There was something about Jacob that made people pay attention to him. He seemed to know everyone at Red Rocks and I didn't doubt he probably knew everyone in the music industry. With him I felt strangely protected, as if he had taken a shine to me, and it made me feel important. Though it was sad that all I wanted at times was for Todd or Ryan to see me, see how far I'd come. Todd because he'd shit himself with jealousy, and Ryan because I wanted him to know what he was giving up. He thought I was going nowhere? Well once he saw the article in Creem Magazine, the article I wrote, he'd see how wrong he was.

But that would have to wait. That evening I didn't even take a single note or recording. I was going to, bringing out my notepad as Jacob and I stood at the side of the stage, but he made me put it away.

"By the end of this tour, you'll be sick of the band and you'll have more notes than you can shake a stick at," he told me with his trademark wink. "Tonight, just watch and remember. Not as a journalist but as a fan. Take it all in, Rusty."

And so I did.

I placed my notebook and pen back in my purse and looked around me. Looked at where I was. I took in everything.

When you're on the side stage of the Red Rocks Amphitheatre, you might as well be on stage yourself. It's that immense and frightening. All you can see is a wall of people, staring down at you, watching your every move. Behind that wall are the stars, pinpricks in the emerging darkness. You have a succinct idea of what it's like to be wanted and adored, to have fans and music lovers alike hanging on your every action, revering you, expecting you to deliver. It's a strange mix of adulation and pressure.

Aside from giving me goosebumps from the sheer immensity of people in Hybrid shirts, lighters waving in the breeze, the side stage also gives you an in-depth look at the band. Obviously you'd have a better view from the very front, where gaggles of groupies and long-haired boys competed for space, but from the side I got to experience the band like few were able to.

For starters, you get an inside look at that moment before the band hits the stage. You can feel that incredible build-up and tension from the crowd as they wait impatiently for the band to appear. You can see the anticipation on their stoned faces, hear the excited talking, the stamping of feet. You also get to see the band behind the stage. What they do before they step out into the spotlight. In this case, Noelle and Mickey were in an embrace, Noelle obviously overcome with nerves. Graham looked bored at the prospect of handling tambourines while Robbie rubbed his hands together, jumping from one foot to the other, like an insatiable bunny rabbit. I had to wonder how much of that energy was natural and how much was drug-fueled.

Then there was Sage. He was a strong and silent presence. He stood at the back, watching over everyone, calculating mysterious things in his head. I had never seen Hybrid live except on TV, and I knew that Sage played with the cool confidence of a cat. But at that moment, it seemed like his confidence was wavering. It was hard to tell, seeing as I had to look over the soundboard, past Chip, random people, instruments, and sections in order to get a glimpse of him. It was dark and his face was cast in shadows half the time. But, as silly as this sounds, I felt this uncertainty rolling off of him. Like I was picking up on an unsaid vibe that something was off. Something wasn't right. Sage was worried and that wasn't the Sage I knew.

Then again, I didn't know Sage at all, except that he didn't seem to want me there.

To prove that point, our eyes met at one instance. I tried to smile. He kept staring right back at me, his full mouth in a hard line, his eyes glinting dangerously. I had told myself he was only rude to me earlier because he had other things on his mind and that I shouldn't take it personally. Now it seemed that what Chip had said about Sage not wanting a journalist among them was true. Sage didn't like me. He didn't want me there. It was personal.

I looked away and tried to bring my attention back to the atmosphere of the crowd, wanting to get sucked into the anticipation. The lights went dim, the audience erupted into applause, and one by one I saw the band leaving the backstage area to walk onto the stage, a spotlight shining down on each of them as they took their place.

Sage was the last on the stage, and as luck would have it, he was the closest to me, just off to the side of the soundboard and Chip. I tried to pay attention to the rest of the band, I really did. I tried to sneak glances at Noelle as she played at the keyboards, trying to hide her nervousness and shaking hands. I tried to watch Graham as he shook the shaker and beat at the bongo drums with just the required level of lightness. I tried to pay attention to Mickey as he flew through his chords with ease, each strum of the acoustic guitar rising sweetly from the stage. I tried to keep my eyes on Robbie as he struggled to keep his voice in check, his manic mannerisms to a minimum. I even tried to watch Chip as he mixed the sounds of the different mics, brows furrowed in concentration.

But try as I did, I could not keep my eyes off of Sage Knightly. I just couldn't help myself. Seeing this man on stage was like watching a lion prowl along the crest of his kingdom. He commanded respect even when he was seated on his chair with only an acoustic guitar at his fingers, and when he got up, the Mexican textile strap straining against his neck, every eye in the crowd followed his every stride. Normally Sage was a background figure, quietly commandeering the direction of the show, but tonight, with Robbie subdued, Sage became the star. Without a doubt, you knew this was the man who made Hybrid what they were.

I watched as his long fingers expertly picked along to complex and haunting solos. I watched the intensity in his eyes as they stared off into the crowd, calling on his talent from somewhere. I watched his tall frame, his large, rounded shoulders muscling into the heavier chords. I watched his flip-flopped feet tapping to some internal metronome.

And I watched a faint shiver roll through his body. His eyes snapped away from watching Robbie belt out "She Could Have Loved Me" and his vision made a beeline to the front of the stage. There, squished up along the barricade, was a strangely familiar looking woman: long white hair, pale face, feverishly gleaming eyes. As beautiful as she was, she gave off an immense feeling of dread that gripped my bones. Sage watched her as if hypnotized. The woman smiled up at him.

And in that smile I saw fangs. Her face transformed disturbingly with black holes for eyes, an elongated, wrinkled face of yellow-white, a wide gaping hole for a mouth, teeth protruding. A long tongue slid out, crawling with quivering insects. It licked its absence of lips, curled delicately along peeling skin. I heard noises deep inside my head: the buzzing of bees, painful wails, horrific chants that built up to immeasurable volumes. I felt horror, a terror so complete that I had one thought: I was going to die there on the stage. I was going to lose my soul.

I was going to Hell.

I was all fear and only fear, and that's what I would be for all my existence.

Then it all stopped. The amphitheater stopped spinning, the noises ceased and were replaced by an off-key guitar chord. It was Sage, losing his rhythm for one brief moment. His eyes had been too focused on the woman in the crowd, who was no longer demonic, just white-haired and ecstatic. Just a fan. Just a wannabe groupie.

I felt Jacob's hand on my shoulder and I jumped a mile high.

"Are you okay?" he asked, eyes dancing. He nodded at my hands.

I looked down. I was gripping the barricade between us and the soundboard like I was hanging on for dear life. My knuckles were dead white.

I couldn't speak. Jacob looked at me thoughtfully, assessing me. I couldn't get it together to ignore what had just happened. I felt like I had just tripped on the headiest of drugs. I kept looking back at the crowd, expecting that demon face again, but didn't see it. I watched Sage too and he was behaving off-balance, shaken. Could he have seen it too? Seen the impossible?

"You're overwhelmed," Jacob assured me, his eyes flitting between Sage and I. "It happens to the best of us."

His hand on my shoulder squeezed firmly. I nodded, slowly coming out of it. Yes, I fucking was overwhelmed.

"Set is almost over anyway, do you want to head to the dressing rooms and get something to eat?" he asked.

I shook my head. "No, I'll stay. I'm just…sorry, I don't know what happened."

I put my hand to my clammy forehead and looked back to Sage. He was back in stride, peeling off perfect licks. The pale woman was still there, now talking to a shorter girl that had the same perfect white sheet of hair cascading down the sides of her face. Everything was fine. It was better than fine. I was onstage with Hybrid.

"You're right," I told Jacob with an apologetic smile. My voice and body had stopped shaking. "I think I was just caught up in the moment. I thought I saw something that…well, that certainly wasn't there."

A flash of something dark went through his yellow, hawk-like eyes. Then they relaxed and he grinned with mismatched teeth. "I'd stay away from Graham's punch then."

I smiled uneasily back at him and focused my attention back on the end of the set. As expected, it went off without a hitch. Whatever had Sage all shook up earlier wasn't affecting him anymore, and when I thought about it, that was probably in my head too. They were tighter than ever. For their encore, the song "Wet Lips" was played as heavy as possible, with the band knocking over their chairs and Robbie jumping about the stage, wailing and hollering, as if they were all plugged in. The crowd surged and cheered and I knew the Red Rock owners probably thought another Jethro Tull riot and extension of the rock ban was on, but "Wet Lips" ended with Robbie on his knees, singing, as the lights went down. There was an eruption of applause, whistles and lighters waving, but the barricade held, everything was contained, and Hybrid gave their appreciative waves and stepped off into the darkness of the backstage.

I turned to the crowd and soaked up the accolades as if they were for me. Then, with a newly found smile on my face, I followed Jacob backstage, giving Chip a thumbs up for a job well done as we passed him.

The rest of the night was a bit of a blur. I can say this was completely my fault, as no one forced me to drink a fifth of Jameson.

Jacob and I had entered one of the doors built into the rock face and we emerged in a lounge area that ran along the dressing rooms. Hap Starts, the straggly singer of Pretty Mary, was just leaving his band's dressing room for the stage and gave Jacob an appreciative head nod. Journalists with media passes lingered about, picking at the spread of finger foods while normal-looking patrons, who I could only assume were friends and family, drank cheap cans of beer from the ice bins. Then there were the groupies, a gaggle of girls my age or younger who were drop-dead gorgeous—no special passes needed for them. They eschewed the food and chose to remain by Hybrid's door. They only moved when Noelle came out, her hair wet from a shower, her eyes cutting into them like a butcher knife. I could see why Noelle was paranoid about me being a groupie. I really had no idea that so many beautiful, albeit skanky-looking, girls were after Hybrid. I mean, Jacob had told Barry that the reason I was there was to lure in more women, though I suppose he meant more women "fans" not groupies. There was a difference.

Then again, I couldn't really blame them. When I got over the fact that they weren't about the music, it was no wonder they were after the band. Robbie had a reputation, and I'm sure he wasn't above turning down the occasional groupie. Same went for Graham; though he was a bit abrasive and scary in his weirdo faux-Satanist ways, some chicks would dig anything with a bone. Mickey was taken, but that wouldn't stop some girls from at least trying, and Sage, well, once again I had no idea about him, whether he was a man-whore or not. I had heard somewhere that he had been married at some point but judging by the lack of ring, I'd say that definitely wasn't the case anymore. Secretly, Sage's love life was one of the things I wanted to get to the bottom of. Did it belong in Creem Magazine? No. Did I want to keep the information for myself, and possibly Mel? Hell yes.

I wasn't sure what to do while the band was still in the dressing room. I assumed that people just sort of waited out here for them after the show and then they'd appear and everyone would party. I didn't belong with the heavily bosomed groupies, nor did I have the casual appearance of friends and family. Normally I would have said hello to the journalists but even they all seemed to know each other and they probably wouldn't have taken me seriously anyway. I was the odd one out and I plunked myself down on a single chair, a cup full of potato chips in one hand, and tried hard to look like I was busy.

"Rusty," Chip called out a few lonely minutes later, appearing behind me with a bottle of Jameson in one hand and another paper cup in the other.

I turned in my seat and looked up at him appreciatively.

"Hey, Chip. Good job with the show and all that." I know, I sounded like a total dork.

He shrugged and began to pour the whiskey into the cup, straight-up. "Went better than expected. Better than soundcheck anyway. Though I'm fucking glad we aren't doing any more of these unplugged shit shows. I'm not big on this experimental stuff. Stick with what you know, you know?"

He took a sip of the whiskey and handed the cup to me. I took it gingerly and looked at him for assurance.

He nodded at it, his eyes twinkling. "Pour vous."

"Oooh la la," I replied and took a tiny bit of it into my mouth. It burned the good burn and I tried hard to swallow it with ease. "I thought you guys were going to go into more of the experimental stuff though. I mean, Molten Universe really pushed some of the boundaries of your sound, you know. In a good way," I added.

He laughed, making himself look younger. He tipped the bottle at me. "You sound like a music critic, Rusty."

"I am a music critic, believe it or not."

He eyed the journalists. "You're not with your friends."

I shrugged, trying to play it cool. "I prefer to do my own thing."

"And you're not with the groupies either."

"Like I said."

"Do I hear a hint of jealousy in your voice?"

I looked at Chip as if he had two heads. "Me, jealous?

Of groupies?"

Oh, I wish that hadn't made me so defensive.

"They make no apologies for lusting over the rock stars."

Chip looked oddly serious when he said that and I had to wonder if he was taking a swipe at me. I wasn't jealous of the groupies and I wasn't lusting over any rock star. I mean, yeah I was obviously star struck—they were one of my favorite bands for crying out loud—and of course my eyes were drawn to Sage anytime I was near him, but that was different. That wasn't about lust, or thinking about Sage unbuttoning the rest of his shirt and undoing those heavy pants, that was…where was I? Yes. My feelings toward Sage were purely the admiration of his talent sort of thing.

Chip smiled at my inner argument and switched the subject. "So you like the experimental side of Hybrid?"

I took another gulp of the whiskey and handed the cup back to him. "I do. And it's organic, you know? It fits. No one is doing anything because it's a fad. No one is afraid they'll be branded hype by the corporate rock machine. You can tell that everyone is just branching out a little."

He snorted caustically. "If by everyone, you mean Sage. The waltz-like numbers and those horns and the steel guitar and Mexican bullshit, it's all him. If it were up to us, we'd stick with what made us big. We're loud and heavy. End of story. Sage pushed a little too much on this album and fuck if I know why. That is, of course, just my opinion and don't you dare quote me on that. Remember, I'm loyal, Rusty. I'm just the sound tech."

He took a drink, filled up the cup and handed it back to me. "Now if you don't mind, I'm going to go make the rounds, see what kind of trouble I can scrounge up."

He gave me a quick pat on the back and then took off toward the washrooms with the bottle of Irish Whiskey. He winked at the groupies as he passed them by and one of them responded by grabbing his ass.

I rolled my eyes. Why on earth would I be jealous of *them*?

And then the door to the dressing room opened and Robbie popped his head out. He did a quick scan of the room, glossing over me, then flashed his adorable smile at the groupies and quickly ushered them into the room. The door shut behind them.

Disappointment and anger competed for space in my belly. What was I, chopped liver?

I sighed, took another gulp of my drink, which was going down easier and easier, and decided if I couldn't (wouldn't) go hang out with the groupies, I would try my luck with my supposed colleagues.

I got up and made my way over to two loveseats where three people with media passes were sitting. One was an older dude with extremely long and shiny hair, a photographer, judging by the bag of equipment beside him. The guy sitting right across from him had a bowl-cut and that stuffy, uncomfortable posture that told me he was way out of his element and was probably used to reviewing John Denver. The other guy had on a Dust shirt and was busy scribbling notes. None of them looked up at me until I nervously cleared my throat.

"Hi, I'm Dawn. I write for Creem Magazine."

The photographer gave me an unimpressed look. "Oh look, another chick writing for Creem. Is it true that Kramer has all you broads in some sort of harem?"

The stuffy guy snickered at that while the Dust dude shot me a quick look, as if he could barely spare a few seconds away from his notes.

"No, I don't even live in Detroit," I told him, crossing my arms. It was a feeble argument. "Kramer just believes in the feminist movement, that's all."

I didn't even know if that was true, but there had to be some reason why Creem had quite a few women on staff. And no, it wasn't because they were part of his harem.

"Creem," the Dust dude mused as he took a break from his notes. "So I take it you're doing some sort of piece on Hybrid."

"Actually it's a fairly big piece," I boasted. "Might make

the cover."

He smiled to himself in a patronizing way. It made me want to rip his balls off.

"Lady, rock and roll is dead. That's what Creem keeps saying. Soon Creem will be dead too."

He went back to writing as if I wasn't standing in front of him, giving him the death glare of all death glares.

"A bunch of sick freaks, not even a real publication," the stuffy guy added. He looked at the photographer. "Have you actually read some of that smut? Even their so-called Messiah Lester Bangs writes like some horny teenager."

The photographer smirked at that and turned his head to face me. "I hope you write funny because funny is all that magazine seems good for. Would be nice if a band like Hybrid could get an actual serious article about them, not your getting drunk with the band, shooting stupid questions when you can, angle." He eyed my drink and then said, "Oops. Too late."

He looked behind him at the closed dressing room door. "Oh, and it looks like you're too late to join the groupie parade too. Better luck next time."

Maybe it was the whiskey. Maybe I was just so mad that all reason and thought left me. But I leaned down so my face was right in the photographer's blasé view and said, "I don't need luck. And I don't take advice from men who look like they belong in a Gee My Hair Smells Terrific commercial."

And with that I straightened up, put my chin high, pretended not to notice their gaping mouths, and gave them a grave "gentlemen," followed by a nod. Then I turned and strode right over to the dressing room door.

It was a gamble. I knocked on the door and didn't dare turn around and look at those pompous, chauvinistic assholes, and prayed that someone would answer and that someone would let me in.

Please, please, please, please, I thought, my heart starting to pound nervously in my throat. *Please let me in. Please don't be Sage.*

After what seemed like an agonizing eternity, the door opened a crack.

It was Sage. God damnit.

I stared pleadingly at his green-gray eyes. This was the closest I had been to him and it was taking all my control not to examine each plane of his face, each scruffy hair on his jaw.

"Hi, I was wondering if I could come in," I said, lowering my voice a bit so the journalists wouldn't hear me.

He narrowed his eyes thoughtfully. I heard girls laughing in the background and someone yelling "Who the fuck is it?"

Sage looked away from me for a moment and yelled back into the room, "It's Dawn."

"Who the hell is Dawn? You mean Rusty?" I heard Robbie say.

Sage's eyes came back to mine and I tried to look impassive, as if hearing him saying my real name, not a nickname, hadn't made my legs shake.

"I bet you think you're allowed everywhere," he said to me. Hi voice was smooth and low, like rich cream that sinks to the bottom.

"If I thought that, I wouldn't have asked," I replied and hardened my gaze.

He seemed to appraise me for a moment. He gave me a small smile that was more on the amused side of things, a few shades south of sincerity, and then opened the door wider.

"Come on in," he said. It was almost a challenge.

I tried not to look *too* grateful in case I lost some credibility, and quickly slipped in through the door. I gave the jerkasses in the waiting area one last look before the door closed behind me.

CHAPTER SIX

So, there is backstage and then there is *backstage*.

I was definitely *backstage*, a place where journalists only dreamed of going.

And well, me too. But for different reasons.

For starters, there was no shame here. I had to check mine at the door with everyone else's.

Robbie was sitting on the couch, dressed only in a towel, and with some very obvious tent-poling action going on. I quickly averted my eyes to the next thing, which happened to be one of the groupies, the one with the largest breasts. Breasts that were now on display. Her top was gone and she was sitting beside Robbie in only a thong. He was drinking out of a bottle of champagne with one hand and groping her breast with the other.

I think blushing was becoming second nature to me now.

Mickey was standing in the corner, also wearing a towel, talking to one of the other girls. Noelle was nowhere to be seen. And he wasn't just talking, but full-on leaning in, acting interested while the overly tanned girl had her fingers at the edge of his towel. Assuming Noelle would have a fit if she saw this, I kind of felt bad for her. She was nasty business, but still.

Jacob was leaning against the wall, talking excitedly and drinking out of what looked to be a medicine bottle. A girl with Cher-like hair and honeyed skin was listening to his every word. She didn't seem groupie-ish, but interesting nonetheless.

At the table, Chip and the other tanned groupie were snorting up lines of coke while Graham seemed to be getting a hand job at the same time by the incredibly spaced-out looking girl. The minute Chip saw me standing there, how I was watching them all in what must have been very apparent shock, he nudged the bottle of Jameson with his elbow.

"Hey Sage," he said, wiping his nose quickly. "Get Rusty some of this. She's going to keel over."

Sage walked over to the table in two long strides and snatched up the bottle. He gave Chip a disapproving squint before coming back to me.

He stepped up close, very close, so that his wide chest was inches away from mine, and his towering frame enveloped my whole view. I stood my ground, as tempted as I was to take a step backward.

Sage placed the bottle in my hand, our fingers touching. It was just for a second, a brush as light as a feather, but it rattled my nerves. I struggled to keep my eyes glued to his.

He lowered his voice. His breath smelled like beer and something fresh, like the ocean.

"Is my band just what you expected? Is this what you're going to write about?"

He was egging me on, daring me.

"I'm not writing anything tonight," I told him. I put on a mask of false confidence and took a swig of whiskey straight out of the bottle, matching the intensity of his gaze. "Tonight I'm just a fan."

"Just a fan..." he mused, scratching at his long sideburn, black hair against lightly bronzed skin. "Right. And then the next day? And the next day? Do you really want to document a band coming to its knees in its dying days? Is that what a fan wants to see?"

His voice was so low that he couldn't have been heard over Jeff Beck on the 8-track and the drunken cries of debauchery in the background. What exactly was he telling me?

I flapped my mouth helplessly for a few seconds, trying to figure out how to respond.

He leaned in even further, staring at my lips. I could see two strands of light gray at his temple, the absolute way his eye color matched the leaves of a sage plant itself.

"You're all the same you know," he continued, almost whispering now. His eyes met mine, mesmerizing orbs through his long curling lashes. "You're just like those girls over there. Just like those pricks outside. You take and take and take and say you want to be a part of it all but you're really here to witness the fall. Be a part of history. Say you saw it happen. I know what it's like, Dawn. In a few more years, no one will care."

Halfway through Sage's speech I was struck by a few words he slurred, and when I stopped trying to make sense of whatever the hell he was talking about and noticed the way his body swayed and how his green feline eyes were glazed, I realized that the rumors of Sage being a drunk were at least a bit true. Not that I was judging; I was the one drinking Jameson straight out of the bottle.

"I'm afraid I don't know what you mean," I told him, finally taking a step back. I had always dreamed about my first conversation with Sage, but I never imagined it would go like this; full of hostility and drunken ramblings, with half-naked, fucked-up people in the background.

Even though I had just left them that morning, my heart suddenly ached for my brother, for Dad, for Mel, even Moonglow. Things had seemed so much easier and innocent back in Ellensburg.

"Are you thinking about running away?" Sage asked, seeming to read my mind, his voice louder now.

I took another swig of Jameson, something I knew was quite unwise, and straightened up, making myself as tall as God made me.

"I don't run away from anything," I told him. "Sorry, you can't get rid of the hack that easily."

I thought I saw a glimmer of appreciation in his gaze but that was quickly lost when Jacob interrupted us.

"For Christ's sake, Robbie!" Jacob boomed from across the room. Sage and I turned around to see the commotion. Before I looked away, I saw Robbie, fully naked and sprawled out on the couch, getting head by the also fully-naked chick. Everyone else was watching, even laughing, as if it was some sort of game or part of their nightly entertainment. Maybe it was.

All I knew is my hand was covering my eyes and I was peeking through my fingers trying to find the door out. My favorite band managed to go from onstage musical heroes to backstage-perverted-idiots in the space of an hour. To be honest, I was disappointed, like to the point where it hurt.

And a little sketched out. Couldn't ignore that feeling.

I made it to the door just as Chip asked, "Where is Rusty going?" and Jacob chided Robbie over acting like a monkey in front of the journalist. It didn't matter, I wasn't staying. Me and the bottle made it out into the clean (and seemingly pure in comparison) waiting area where the journalists and minglers were still hanging about.

I wasn't about to deal with them either. I felt alone, scared, and scarred. I went for the bathrooms and once inside the women's one, all mirrors and bright orange walls, I made sure the stalls were empty and plunked myself down on the can.

I don't know how long I sat in there, just taking small swigs from the bottle, staring at the floor and the tips of my boots that carried marks and scars from my barrel racing. It could have been ten minutes, it could have been an hour. Maybe everyone was looking for me, maybe no one was at all. Maybe I'd be forgotten and left behind, a castaway in the Red Rocks Amphitheatre. My only consolation was that I had just enough money on me to get a flight home—that was one of the stipulations from my dad. It was our savings, everything we had, and I hated to think I'd spend it on a flight from Denver to Seattle. That was one of the many reasons why I knew I wasn't going anywhere. We may have gotten off to a weird and rocky start, but I was touring with Hybrid and that was the end of the story.

The door to the bathroom creaked open, snapping me out of my drunken daydream. A girl came in, sniffing hard and obviously crying. I watched as her feet came into view under the stall door. Tall black platforms with feathers on them. Noelle's après show shoes.

I waited for a few awkward moments, trying to debate whether I should make my presence known or not. But I was sure that Noelle knew she wasn't alone in the bathroom, and I might as well let her know it was me before she started shooting up heroin or eating babies or whatever fucking crazy things this band normally got up to. I still couldn't get the picture of Robbie getting his dick sucked out of my mind, and was a bit disgusted that my brain kept fixating on it.

I opened the door and peeked out, catching Noelle's sad reflection in the mirror. She wasn't doing anything scandalous, just trying to apply mascara to her eyes that were already shedding the stuff down her cheeks in black rivers.

"Are you okay?" I asked quietly, carefully, like she was a young filly I was about to break.

"Why don't you mind your own business," she snarled, but her attempt at looking mean failed and she shut her eyes to two big, fat teardrops, her mouth curling in an ugly grimace.

I paused, unsure of how to deal with her. Mel was my closest female friend and normally so unemotional and brave (aside from that morning, of course). My mother had been depressed my whole life, either crying herself silly or stoned off of prescription drugs. I had nothing in the middle. No stereotypical female teacher or mentor to go by.

I had a feeling Noelle was a lot like me though. She looked hard on the outside but the shell was frail and easy to crack.

I went back in the stall and pulled out a few rounds of toilet paper, wadded it up, and placed it in her hand.

"Here, this is softer," I told her. "The paper towels will just make your face red."

She nodded painfully and brought the tissues up to her face, wiping away the black tears. I stood beside her, leaning back along the counter, not in any hurry to get her talking. The last thing I wanted was to be seen as a nosy journalist. I just wanted to *be*, and to be distracted by someone else's feelings other than my own.

After a few more sniffles and when her breathing calmed down and she wasn't shuddering, she opened up.

"The guys said you were in the dressing room," she said, folding the wet, blackened tissue over in her hand.

"That I was."

She shot me a shy look. "You know it's not like this every night."

I shrugged. "Honestly, I didn't know what to expect. I have zero expectations now."

"I'm not trying to make excuses," she said, clearly about to make an excuse. "But it's always kind of wild the first night of the tour. You don't understand, we were all really nervous about this show. We all thought it was a lame idea to begin with, but Sage thought it would be good for us. Whatever."

A wave of defensiveness rolled off her and she turned to face the mirror again, examining her tired, sad, make-up smeared face. She was so pretty, even when she had been put through the ringer.

"Hey, you're Hybrid," I explained. "You're one of the next big things, if not the big thing right now. You're, like, the heaviest band out there and you seem to be groupie central. It's okay if things get wild. I mean, look at Zeppelin."

"Yeah," she said with an edgy laugh. "But there are no pretenses in Zeppelin. We got to open for them once. I saw how they operated. It's all on the table, you know? No one is pretending anything. Page doesn't try to be someone he's not. No one tries to get their girlfriend out of the dressing room, no one pretends that they aren't fucking random sluts when they clearly are."

She spat out the last words like they were rotting in her mouth.

"Does...did Mickey and a groupie hook up?" I asked, not knowing the delicate way to put it.

She laughed again, the black eyeliner sinking into her crow's feet. "You're going to have a hell of a time with us, you know that don't you? Bet you didn't think your article on Hybrid would turn into a juicy expose."

She was right about that. Me with my small-town, idealistic views of rock and roll. I knew debauchery existed but not in a world that I could ever be a part of. Now Noelle had brought up a great point. I wanted to write this article to bring Hybrid to the world, to earn respect for myself and the band. If what I saw tonight was an indication of anything, the article was going to come across as a tabloid, celebrity scandal fodder.

Now we both found ourselves sighing and looking at our reflections in the mirror. I was startled by my own appearance—I looked older and just as tired. My red hair was frizzed out to the sides, and my beige, suede, fringed top was speckled with spilled whiskey. My high-waisted jeans were covered with potato chip residue where I had wiped off my hands. My face didn't look as rock and roll as Noelle's, but the mascara I put on earlier had smudged underneath my eyes and my lipstick was long gone. So much for trying to look pretty.

"Ugh," she said, giving herself one final look. "I'm going to the bus. I think we're leaving in the next half hour, so I'd book it soon if I were you. That's if you still want to join us. I won't blame you if you leave. I would."

I gave her a questioning look. "Are you in cahoots with Sage now? As I told him, I'm not running away."

She opened the door to the washroom and shot me a wry look over her skinny shoulder. "We'll see."

She left, the door swinging in her place. I sighed again and ran the tap and splashed a bit more water on my face, trying to fix myself up before bed. Speaking of bed, I had absolutely no clue where I'd be sleeping. On the bus? Where? Was there room? Were we staying in a hotel? Or driving all night? There were so many questions, and at the moment, any answers were beyond my capability.

I eyed the half drunk bottle of Jameson, wondering if they'd get mad if I left it behind, and proceeded to slurp water out of my cupped hands. I heard the door swing open again and looked up, expecting to see Noelle.

My heart seemed to stop pumping.

It wasn't Noelle, but the tall, thin and deathly pale girl from the crowd. The one that looked familiar. The one with the long sheet of white hair.

She was standing in front of me, dressed in a pure white dress that hugged her every curve. Up close I could see her hair was the palest shade of blonde and as straight as a ruler. Her face and skin was an enviable, creamy sort of pale, like full-fat milk. Her nose was long, her lips plump and perfectly formed. Her eye color itself was lavender—a full-on, opaque mix of purple and pink—and her eye shadow was an iridescent gold that seemed to move and shimmer on its own, like it was a living, breathing thing.

She was eons from the face I had imagined in the crowd. And yet, there was something not right about her. Something about her gave me the absolute chills. Perhaps it was the way she didn't seem to blink.

She smiled, normal, straight teeth, and pointed at my face.

"Your nose is bleeding," she said in a voice that sounded metallic bouncing off the tangerine bathroom walls.

I quickly put my hand to my nose and lifted it away. Ripe blood shone from the side of my finger.

I'd never had a nosebleed in my life.

I gave the girl a quick smile.

"Thanks," I told her, reaching for the paper towel.

The girl reached out with her own hand and grabbed me around the wrist. Her hand burned, like it had been forged in fire. She smiled again, and in my shock, I did nothing as she took a step closer, her pale purple eyes focusing on mine. What kind of drugs had she done to get her eyes like that?

"You only get one warning," she said. Her grip on my wrist tightened. I stared at her, dumbfounded. "Get out now, while you still can. We can still give you a few more years."

Somewhere I found my tongue. It was almost lodged in my throat.

"What are you talking about?" I eked out. What the hell was with people tonight?

"I shouldn't even be warning you. But let's just say I'm a fan too."

I blinked. "Obviously. I saw you in the crowd. You're backstage."

"This is about *Sage*." Her grip wasn't getting looser.

"I still don't know what you mean," I told her, gathering up some strength. "And I'd like it if you let go of my arm."

She did, with great reluctance.

"As you wish," she said, smiling like nothing weird at all had just happened. I could feel the blood still trickling out of my nose. I quickly snatched the paper towel and put it to my face.

She brushed past me, nicking my shoulder in the process. My skin burned from the contact. She stopped in front of the mirror and cocked her head at her reflection. I watched her carefully. I could have sworn that for one split second, her reflection didn't match up, like her face in the mirror was more to the left than it should have been, and her eyes were looking at me when they should have been looking at herself. She still hadn't blinked.

Shit. This was the last time I was ever drinking Irish Whiskey.

"I'm going to go now," I found myself saying. I started backing away toward the door.

"Do as you like," she said, not looking at me. "And you can tell Sage that he can't run anymore. We will always find him. Always."

Whatever, you crazy stalker, I thought and quickly disappeared out into the hallway. I could hear music from near the dressing rooms, and as I shuffled down the brightly lit corridor, I noticed the Hybrid door was still closed. The journalists were all gone as were the random tag-alongs. I didn't want to spend an extra second in that place, so I booked it out the main door and headed straight for the bus. The air was cooling rapidly at this high elevation and the night was filled with the sound of Hap Starts and Pretty Mary at the stage. Roadies, crew, and security were still milling about, but I focused on the bus and shut them out. I just wanted to sleep and let this night be done.

The door to the bus was open and a faint light was coming from inside. I climbed up the stairs and saw Noelle standing in the aisle, brushing her teeth. Her makeup was washed off and she was dressed in a thin nightshirt. She looked young and vulnerable.

"Hey," I said, still feeling wary around her.

"Hey," she replied. She spit the toothpaste into the kitchen sink and rinsed off her toothbrush.

"So," I said, making my way toward her, looking down at the couch. "Should I just crash here or?"

"Do you want to sleep tonight?"

"Ideally."

She beckoned me with her finger. I came toward her and she pointed at the top bunk across from the kitchen. "I'm sleeping below, you can sleep up top. I don't feel like shacking with Mickey tonight, and you don't want to sleep any place that someone could either puke on you or pass out on you. Trust me. It happens."

I gave her a grateful smile and snatched up my duffel bag. I went into the tiny bathroom, the last time I would see it remotely clean, and got ready for bed in boxer shorts and a small Black Sabbath t-shirt. By the time I climbed up into the top bunk and got settled beneath a cheap sleeping bag, I was out like a light.

I didn't wake up when the rest of the band got in. I didn't wake up when the bus roared to life and we started our nighttime journey across America.

I only woke up once, at four in the morning, when my wrist and shoulder started to sting and burn, like they had been licked by fire.

CHAPTER SEVEN

I was dreaming about my mother just before I woke up. I was sixteen again and wandering the fields behind my house. There were holes in the ground that moles had created, only these ones seemed fathomless and got bigger the more I walked toward the distant hills. I kept walking though, until my mother's sing-songy voice soared out above the waving grass. I turned to see her. The farmhouse was gone, as was the barn, and it was only her. She was as pretty as always, with long red hair that gave off an angelic glow as the sun hit it, like a rusty aura.

"Dawn, I must leave you," she said.

"Don't go anywhere, I'll be right back," I told her. I turned around and kept walking, my feet struggling to find footing in the grass. I tried my hardest not to look at the holes for I felt I would fall into them if I did.

"It's all over. There's nothing left for me," her voice teased at my back.

I kept going, tossing over my shoulder, "I'll be right back. Don't worry, Mom."

My mother was the queen of crying wolf. She'd been threatening us with this and that since the day I was born.

Then she said "I'm sorry" in a tone of sincerity I never heard from her. It made me stop and look back.

The farmhouse had returned and it was in flames behind her. She was standing there with my father's razor blade in one of her hands, covered in blood from the sticky, deep cuts she made in both wrists.

"I'm sorry," she said again, heartfelt and anguished.

I could scarcely move in my horror. Then I found my legs and began running toward her, jumping over the holes and side-stepping them.

I was so close to reaching her, my arms outstretched to grab her wrists and soak them with my shirt, when the ground opened up. A hole became larger at the last second and I was airborne, falling down into a darkness that was lit from the bottom by a fire's angry light. As I fell, I looked up. My mother was standing over the side, her blood dripping onto my face.

"I hope you don't see me again," she said, before the fire swallowed me whole.

* * *

I woke up in a cold sweat, my heart beating rapidly as the remnants of the dream lifted out of my head, and with the uncanny feeling of someone breathing on my face. It smelled rank, like menthol cigarettes, coffee and mothballs.

I held my breath and managed to pop an eye open. Staring back at me were the citron-tinted eyes of Jacob. His pupils resembled a reptile's for a split second but as my eyes adjusted from their sleepy fuzz, they went back to round pinpricks.

"You're alive," he said dryly, and another burst of odor wafted my way. I was lying on my side in the top bunk and he was just tall enough to have his head at my level.

I scrunched up my nose and moved my head back. "What time is it?"

He pulled out a pocket watch from his ugly jacket and gave it a quick glance. "Ten in the morning, Rusty. I thought you might want to join us for breakfast."

Ten already? I leaned over and poked my head out of the bunk. The bus was deserted and the early sun was streaming in through the dusty windows.

"Where are we?"

"Just east of Lawrence, Kansas, if that means anything to you. It means nothing to me."

Kansas. It sounded so far away and oddly exotic to my sheltered ears. The bus really had been going all night long.

He patted the edge of the bunk. "Well, hurry your lazy arse up then and get in while the getting's good." He pointed out the window. "We'll be just in there. Want me to order you anything? Orange juice? A wholesome glass of milk?"

I gave him a tepid look. "Coffee, please, and lots of it."

"That a girl," he said with a grin. I always expected Jacob to have gold teeth glinting in his mouth. He turned and started moving down the aisle. I began to get off the bunk, hanging my body rather ungracefully until my feet found the bunk below.

He had stopped at the doors, watching me with amusement. "You know, I hope you don't take last night the wrong way."

Right. Last night. I wiped away the lewd images before I had a chance to dwell on them. I pulled down at my Sabbath shirt and stared at the leftover messy bed on the couch, avoiding his eyes.

"They're a metal band," he continued, his voice more grave. "They like to have a good time. It's normal, Rusty. You'll get used to it, eventually, and if you don't, well…try loosening up a bit."

I snapped my head up to give him a dirty look but he was already out of the bus. Right, like I was the one that needed loosening. I was just fine, thank you. It was the band and their careless manager that needed some tightening.

I got dressed quickly, not wanting to keep the band waiting, and put on a pair of white hot pants and a simple red and white striped tank and denim vest. The shorts were the most scandalous thing I owned, and I felt like showing them that I wasn't as uptight and prudish as they seemed to think.

The moment I stepped off the bus and into the hazy sunshine, I immediately felt better. The weird interaction with Sage's stalker and my disturbing dream were swept away as I looked around at the surrounding flat fields of golden soybean punctuated by aging grain silos. It was hot already, the oppressive heat of the Midwest giving central Washington a run for its money.

The diner itself was one of those popular truck stop joints, quietly charming in its simplicity and spinning neon sign, with semis and camping trailers lining the outer edges of the half-empty parking lot. I stepped inside and immediately spotted the band. With their long hair and young bravado, they stood out like…well, like a bunch of rock stars. The patrons, worn out truckers and passive middle-aged couples, were on the edges of their padded vinyl seats, watching them like one watches snakes at the zoo.

They had taken up two booths, with Noelle, Mickey, Graham, and Sage at one and Robbie, Jacob, and a small, hawk-faced man I presumed was the bus driver at the other. Jacob saw me and motioned at me to come over and take a seat beside Robbie.

Just great. I felt like I could never look Robbie in the face again.

I sighed and sucked it up and made my way over. I stopped at the end of the booth and smiled at the bus driver. He was an older man, maybe late sixties, with a shock of white hair and a bad comb over. He wasn't, however, frail in the slightest. He had a scarred cheek and twinkly blue eyes that promised a load of scandals and stories.

"This is Rusty," Jacob said, as if he were some proud father—who'd forgotten my actual name. "Rusty, this is Bob, our driver and the driver of all drivers."

"Nice to meet you, Bob," I told him, totally conscious of Robbie's eyes at my back, not wanting for the attention to be taken off the driver. "I hear you used to drive The King around."

He chuckled and slurped back some coffee before saying,

"If you think you can get secrets out of me, you're dead wrong."

"Bob will take those to the grave," Robbie piped up. "I've tried."

I flashed Robbie a vague smile without looking at him fully and sat down next to him.

"You're not as charming as you think." Bob pointed at him. "Noelle, however..."

Noelle craned her head around from the booth behind us. "What's this about what?"

Jacob pushed an empty cup toward me and filled it with coffee from a steaming pot. "Nothing you need to hear, Noe. Your ego is already too big for your britches."

She breathed out through her nose in annoyance and turned back around in her seat. Across from her, Sage looked up from his coffee and our eyes met. He looked tired but strangely vibrant, like he only needed passion and nerves to coast through life. I didn't want to look away, so I held his eyes until he was the one who gave up and fixed them on his coffee cup, as if he could find all of life's answers there.

"Did you have fun last night?" I felt Robbie whispering into my neck. I looked over at Jacob who was watching me as he always did, a wry smile dancing on his cracked lips.

"Not as much fun as you had," I said spitefully. I couldn't help it. It was inevitable.

I finally looked over at him, his cornflower blue eyes just inches away from mine. How could someone so fresh-faced and California-kissed be as depraved as he was? Right now, with his white teeth, dimpled chin, and wavy chestnut hair, with no signs of drug use or lack of sleep in his eyes, he looked like the poster boy for posterity. In other words, not at all like a fucked-up sicko who liked to fondle breasts and get his dick sucked for the enjoyment of his bandmates. I had a hard time believing it even happened at all.

He smiled and I caught a wave of remorse or embarrassment in the way his head ducked briefly. "Sorry about that. I forgot you were in the dressing room. We're not used to having girls there. Normal girls. Professionals."

I heard Noelle clear her throat loudly from the other booth. He ignored her. "You know how it is though. You just gotta go with the flow."

Sage snorted. I looked at him sharply, unused to the sound of amusement from him.

"What?" Robbie challenged him.

Sage stroked his chin and looked out the dirty window toward the resting tour bus, her green paint looking extra faded in the sun.

"What, nothing," he said. "If anyone's going to go with the flow, it's you."

"Well, if you stop the flow, you'll be called a cock-blocker," Robbie shot back.

"That's a new one," Sage mused. He slowly took his eyes off the window and looked right at Robbie, straight-faced and unflinching. "God knows what would happen if you'd put your cock away for two seconds. Maybe you'd get some real work done."

I sipped my coffee and watched the two leads as they traded barbs across the tables. It was enthralling and I wished I had brought my tape recorder with me.

Robbie laughed but it was mean and forced. "Oh, I see. I see. Sage, the one whose name means wise, thinks he's the sage one. As always. Can do no wrong unlike the rest of his band, I mean his *minions*."

"Boys," Jacob barked, his eyes hardening. "Can you try keeping your issues in your pants where they belong? It's morning. I have a headache the size of the USSR, we have a journalist sitting at our table, and there's another show tonight. A real one, none of this pussy-footed acoustic shite. Let's please talk about something else. Bob, you pick the topic."

Bob looked unconcerned, I guess as every rock and roll bus driver should.

"So do you think Nixon's going to get impeached?" was

Bob's contribution.

"Fuck Nixon," Robbie said. That sunny look of his had disappeared.

"Many want to," Bob noted.

I could tell Robbie wanted to keep fighting with Sage but the guitarist wasn't having any of it. The diner waitress had stopped at their table and she was busy taking his order, her eyes darting at the band with apprehension as she jotted it down.

Bob and Jacob got into a light discussion over whether the full Watergate tapes were going to be released, with Mickey jumping into the conversation every few minutes with his pro-Republican stance. When the waitress made her way to us, I ordered toast and two poached eggs, while Robbie refused to eat anything.

"I'm not hungry," he said through grinding teeth. I could feel the energy oozing out from his pores, and I knew why he was such a manic mess on stage—it was the only place his frustrations could come out.

When the waitress finally left and the political conversation was getting more heated than I would have liked, Robbie decided he had enough stewing and excused himself. He bolted out of the diner, his hair flowing behind him, and disappeared around the corner. No one took any notice except for Jacob, who watched him out of one eye with a calculating gleam to it. Then he continued berating Mickey for his backward thinking.

I munched on my toast, and after eating an egg, I had enough too. It felt awkward and stifling in the diner and too many customers were watching our strange company.

I excused myself from the table and went out the doors after Robbie. I didn't know why really, part of me was still put off from his behavior last night, but I was curious as a cat to see one of the best singers in the world down on his luck. Call it morbid curiosity.

I found him smoking and leaning against the stucco walls, just out of the intense sunlight that was steadily building up power by the second.

"Robbie?" I asked timidly.

He managed a smile when he saw me. "Hey."

I walked over to him, glad I was wearing Keds and not my platform heels—I was just his height. He seemed to notice and straightened up a little more.

"Are you okay?"

He shrugged and gave me a sheepish smile. "Oh, fine. This is normal, just breakfast with the family, and you know how it is on family trips."

I leaned against the crackled wall too, enjoying the coolness at my back. "The trip just started."

He puffed on the cigarette then offered it to me. I didn't smoke, usually, but I thought I'd be polite and have an excuse to stay in case he remembered I was a journalist.

"Yeah. It's like this when it starts. All of us getting used to each other again."

I put the smoke to my lips and barely inhaled. "I thought you all lived in the same town. Redding, right?"

Robbie laughed. "Redding. Fuck no, Rusty. You ever been to Redding? I got out of there as soon as I could. We all did, except for Graham who bought a weirdo hermit shack by Lake Shasta. Everyone else lives in Sacramento. Geez, aren't you a journalist?"

I looked down at the ground and handed the smoke back to him. "I know. I read so much stuff about you before I left, I think it was information overload."

"Aw, that makes sense," he said. His eyes watched the cars coming and going on the nearby freeway. "I guess this is a lot to handle for a small-town chick. It's still a lot to handle for a small-town boy. I still pinch myself, you know? Like this might be taken away at any moment. Like my life has been leased to me."

"Can I quote you on that?" I asked hopefully.

He shrugged. "If you can remember it. If your brain thinks it's worthy. That's why I never do interviews if I'm being taped. I like that you guys have to take notes. When you take notes, you forget the bullshit and remember the good stuff."

I didn't even have my notepad on me at the moment and my shorthand was atrocious. But I nodded anyway and tried to store Robbie's words away in my head. *Like my life has been leased to me.*

"So you don't all hang out in Sacramento," I said, bringing the conversation back around.

He shook his head and blew smoke out of the corner of his mouth. "No. We used to. Sage and I were best friends. I guess we still are. But he's been busy. Like, really busy. This last album ate him up from the inside."

"You can tell. It's excellent."

Robbie shrugged again. "I guess. I'm not too fond of it, I think some tracks are too soft, but what can you do. You heard Sage in there. He's always right."

"That's what you said."

"It's all I know," he said sadly. He passed the smoke back to me and flashed me a cover-worthy smile. "But that's life. That's part of being in a band and I'm grateful for every day I'm with these crazy fuckers. It's just hard being in a relationship with five fucking people. I have enough trouble with one relationship."

"Your fiancé?"

"Cheryl," he corrected me. "She's lovely but it's hard. She doesn't trust me on the road."

"Gee, I wonder why!" I stamped my foot.

"Hey, Redwood, we have an understanding. When I'm on the road, I'm a free man. If she had a problem with it, I wouldn't be...well...you know. Whatever you saw last night."

"Speaking of," I began, wondering how much I should say, "are all your groupies so loosey goosey?"

"Hey, they don't come to our shows for the music," he joked.

"I don't mean *easy*," I said. I looked around me as if I shouldn't be talking about it. The parking lot was empty of living souls and the cars on the highway rumbled to and fro. "I mean as in nuts. Crazy stalker type nuts."

His mouth twitched and he took the cigarette back from me, taking a final puff before throwing it on the ground and crushing

the butt beneath his boot. "Uh, well, there are a few girls that…
might have mental issues."

I leaned in closer to him. "Yeah? What do they look like?"

"Well, they're hot."

I rolled my eyes. "Don't tell me you slept with mental cases."

He looked shocked. "No. Look, I don't need to get involved
with a psychopath, and these chicks are clearly psychopaths. But
anyway, if you must know, they aren't after me. They like Graham
and Sage. They follow them around on every single tour."

"Is one of the girls tall and thin with long white hair and
purple eyes?"

"I don't know about her eye color but that sounds like Sonja."

"Sonja?"

"You'll know if you met her."

"I think I might have."

He regarded me carefully. "Did it feel like you had your soul
sucked out of you, like she drained every essence of your being
and you were left with nothing but a shell?"

I looked at him askance. "Maybe. The girl I met was in the
bathroom, and yeah, I don't know about the soul sucking per se,
but she was very strange. She told me some crazy shit that didn't
make sense, then said she was coming after Sage."

He nodded. "Oh yeah, that's Sonja. She's the crackpot
ringleader of the GTFOs."

"You mean the GTOs?" I was thinking of Girls Together
Outrageously, which was a more or less respected and nearly
professional groupie outfit led by Miss Pamela, Jimmy Page's
muse (who charmed him, along with Jim Morrison, Mick Jagger,
and a million other men).

"No, the GTOs are lovely ladies. We call these chicks the
GTFOs—or Get the Fuck Outs."

I had to smile at that, despite being riveted to everything
Robbie was saying. "So who else is in this, what was it,
crackpot group?"

He listed off his fingers. "Sonja The Soul-Sucker. Terri the

Know-It-All, who, by the way, pretends she's a music journalist too. Don't fall for it. She's not. And Sparky. She's the short round one. You'll see them again, unfortunately."

"And they're stalking Graham too."

"Yep. And for some reason, I guess cuz Sparky's all pro-Satanic cult, Graham likes to have them around. Keeps his damned and needy soul feeling wanted. He usually goes off with them and they leave us alone, though I shudder to think what they're doing."

I made a disgusted face, not wanting to think about it either. "Graham's a bit of an odd one, isn't he?"

A dark expression momentarily clouded his face. "Odd is an understatement. Sometimes he can get a little scary…"

I frowned at that, ignoring the skin prickling feeling at the back of my neck and was about to ask Robbie what he meant when we were interrupted.

"What are you guys doing? Get your arses over here!" Jacob boomed, poking his ginger head from around the corner.

I shot Robbie an apologetic look. "Sorry if I got you in trouble with the boss."

"Oh whatever, we pay his salary," he said dismissively. "I'm glad you talked to me. And again, I'm sorry about last night. I'll try to do my, um, wheelings and dealings in private."

"Thank you," I said, and we made our way back to the bus, feeling like a couple of kids who sneaked off of school property.

❊ ❊ ❊

The bus ride was ripe with tension. You could feel it coming off the ugly walls and bouncing on the fake wood cabinets. Sage and Robbie weren't talking. Actually, Sage wasn't talking to anyone, and had decided to go lie down in the back.

I decided to get cracking on my journalist thing and get some interviews down before we arrived in Kansas City, but my results were as flat as the passing landscape. Noelle was back to being a pissy, spoiled brat, Mickey was trying to coddle her and gain her forgiveness, and kept shooting me a look as if I was the one who forced him to hook up with a groupie the night before. I felt I got enough out of Robbie that morning and didn't want to push him, and Graham flat-out told me I could only interview him between 2AM and 3AM. Total bullshit but he was sticking to it.

"It's the dark hour, when my mind is at my sharpest," he told me with total lack of irony in his voice.

I heard Robbie groan to himself and knew the rest of the band was pretty fed up with his faux-Satanic ways but Graham seemed to fully believe it.

We pulled into the auditorium around noon and I was relieved to see Chip and the rest of the roadies there, having traveled in two large Astro vans. I was also relieved to see a stack of payphones outside of the building. I had forgotten to call my father the night before to let him know I landed okay, and I was itching to make a call to Mel and fill her in on everything that was happening. Not talking to someone other than a band or crew member was killing me inside.

My father didn't answer so I left a quick message telling him and Eric that I was fine and the band was taking good care of me. I called Mel next, plunking in the last of my stack of coins, but she wasn't home either. Her mother seemed glad to hear from me though and said she'd pass on the message that I was fine and that I missed her. It was true, too. I did miss Mel and her snarky attitude on life. Not that I wasn't capable of sarcasm myself, but it was nice when you felt like you had someone else on your team that you could compare notes with. I didn't have that with Hybrid, and that was something I was just going to have to get used to, hopefully sooner than later.

When I hung up the phone, I spied Sage leaving the Astro van with one of his guitars in hand. It was black, sleek, and sexy, just like the man himself, and his intricately tattooed forearms bulged as he handled the musical beast. I shook my head lightly, snapping out of my strangely lustful daze, and decided to take my chances with him.

"Sage?" I ventured carefully, walking toward him. He had seen me coming and seemed to be forming excuses in his head already.

"What is it?" he asked, barely glancing at me, walking off toward the backstage doors leading into the building.

I trailed after him. "How are you feeling?"

The question surprised him and he slowed down a bit. "How am I feeling?"

"You seemed a bit snappish at breakfast," I said. "Last night too. Thought maybe you have an object lodged up your ass or something. Something a doctor should remove."

I couldn't believe I just said that. Neither could Sage. He didn't just slow down, he stopped and gave me an incredulous look. "Excuse me?"

Way to go Dawn, I thought. *As if he couldn't hate you more.*

I licked my lips and tried to smile. "Well, do you?"

He seemed speechless. This probably wasn't good.

But then, he did something I hadn't expected.

He smiled.

And then he laughed. It was short and brief, but genuine and made the dimples stand out on his scruffy cheeks. It was the best sound I'd heard all year.

Then he shook his head and continued walking off toward the auditorium, strumming his guitar as he went, leaving me with a view of a tight ass in tight black pants.

What I had meant to do was ask him when a good time to interview him would be. I totally messed that one up.

I watched him go for a few beats, then I decided to give up on him for the day and try again tomorrow. Tonight I was going to concentrate on the music and just the music. If the band wanted to play hard to get with interviews, fine (and if I was going to bungle up some interviews with my big, fat mouth, fine). That didn't mean I wasn't going to observe and then compose the best damn live show review. Ever.

I shuffled back to the bus, gathered my purse, my notepad, my tape recorder, and the venue's All Access Pass, and went to go catch Hybrid's soundcheck.

CHAPTER EIGHT

I discovered that although I got a perverse sense of importance and satisfaction standing at the side of the stage with Jacob and all the other privileged people, the best place to see the band, any band really, was to be in the crowd with the rest of the fans. Though I was closer to the band on the side stage and had a great viewpoint for watching Sage work the guitar or Graham pound away on the drums like a man possessed, it felt removed and distant, like I was merely observing them. I wasn't part of the experience. So fifteen minutes into Hybrid's monstrous set, I excused myself from Jacob's stoic company and made my way down the stairs at the side of the stage and into the Kansas City crowd.

I let the human tide, ebbing and flowing toward the stage like multi-colored water, take me, and within seconds I found myself squished in the middle of the floor, in between two metal heads who only stopped banging their heads to take a hit of pot. I was in my element here, and though I got a few curious glances at my All Access Pass (which I did wear a little too proudly), people paid attention to the band. And so did I.

The acoustic set from the night before was a nice change, but this show was the real Hybrid, a living breathing band that aptly mixed Sabbath-like downtuned licks with a dash of Jim Morrison lyrics and the funky, blues groove of Muddy Waters. During that show I forgot all about the talk I had with Robbie earlier, or the unexpected sass I delivered to Sage. I was just a fan, always a fan, a worshipper who talked to God in her head but fell to her knees at church.

There were lights and smoke, from the stage and from the audience, and Robbie and Sage gave the crowd everything they had. They were dueling against each other, pushing themselves for glory, and by that act, pushing each other. They were both winners here with Robbie leaping into the crowd like a soaring Messiah, making love to the microphone pole, telling the world his secrets with the deepest of growls; and Sage slinking along the sides, surging forward to join his equal, then disappearing into the shadows of the stage, giving the audience only a glimpse of his blistering fingers and the incinerating peels of sound he demanded from his guitar.

It was an epic, flawless, tingling-deep-in-my-belly type of show. I took notes between songs—just the feelings flowing through me or descriptions of the audience. Their enthusiasm built me up at times, and when a solo threatened to bring the crowd to its knees, I was sinking down, down, down with them, tears in my humble eyes.

It was a high unlike any other, a wave of perfection and human unity. It was all the purple prose in the world. It was magic.

Until I had a beer thrown in my face.

It happened near the end of the show, during one of my favorite songs, "A Loss to Win." It wasn't an accident. I was standing there, mouth agape at Robbie's power, when I felt someone sidle up to me. I barely paid them any attention until I noticed their eyes flowing up and down my body and settling on the pass around my neck. They burned there, and I could have sworn my chest flared up with heat.

I took my eyes off the stage where Sage and Mickey were

serenading each other with their strings and looked down. A short girl with Rod Stewart hair, dyed black as coal, and giant boobs was staring at the pass. I could have sworn she licked her lips, which were lined with dark red lipstick. She was dressed head to toe in black and her eyes were dark and soulless.

"Can I help you?" I asked unsurely. I didn't feel like getting into an altercation, but I was at least taller than she was and a good deal lighter where it mattered.

"Can I have your pass?" she asked sweetly. She finally ripped her eyes off my chest and looked at my face. I shuddered internally. She looked crazier than I originally thought, and I immediately knew who I was dealing with—Sparky, one of the GTFOs.

"Um, and who are you?" I knew to handle the wannabe devil worshipper with care but I was annoyed I had to deal with her during a song I had been waiting for.

"Someone who deserves it more than you, bitch," she answered. One of the metal heads in front of us looked behind him to see what was going on, and upon seeing her, he shot me a "good luck with that" smile and turned back around.

I put my hand to my pass and clutched it in my hand. "I don't know who you are, sorry. This is my pass. I'm a journalist."

I put my attention back to the stage and prayed she'd go away.

She sidled closer and reached out with her hand, attempting to close it around mine.

"Give me your pass!" she screeched like a jungle monkey.

I was flabbergasted but quick to act, and I backed up into the crowd, feeling their hands at my back, supporting me for the meantime. "Holy fuck, what's your problem, you psycho!?"

"You don't deserve it, you fake fan. You know nothing about him and I was here first," she said coming forward, her black-nailed hand outstretched like some crazy fucking witch.

I put my palm out to stop her, and for some reason it did. But it didn't stop her from taking the cup of beer that she had in her other hand and throwing it in my face.

"I'll see you in hell," she snarled and stormed off into the crowd, amused concertgoers parting for her like the Red Sea. I watched her go, speechless and shaking with adrenaline as the warm beer soaked me.

"Whoa, chick is tripping," said one of the metal heads who had been holding me. Now that I was able to stand, his hands were at my ass and copping a feel.

I shrugged him off and gave him a dry "thanks" as I shook the rivers of beer off my arms.

Chick *was* tripping, but I didn't think it had anything to do with drugs. Though who really knew in this day and age. I patted down my wet hair and carefully wiped the smelly, cheap draft beer from my face and under my eyes, pulling up my tank top to do so. The metal head stared at my bare stomach with glazed lust, and I decided it was a good a time as any to get my ass off the floor. My favorite song had ended and Hybrid's spell had been broken by a groupie witch.

I pushed my way through the sweaty crowd, Noelle's basslines rumbling beneath my feet, and climbed the stairs to the backstage area. There were a few people in front of me so security was busy grilling them about their passes or lack thereof, and over their heads I could make out Jacob at the very edge of the side stage as it sloped toward the back, talking to a young girl.

He didn't look too impressed with her and was making shooing gestures with his hands. The girl waved her pass in his face and pointed at the stage and the show in progress, but Jacob just shook his head, not budging over whatever they were arguing about. The girl looked like a replica of Sonja, with the same pale hair and skin, just a bit shorter and with bigger hips. When she finally gave up and walked away, her nose beaked sharply in the profile and I caught a flash of violet eyes. I had a feeling that was GTFO numero three, Terri the Know-It-All.

Finally I was let through by the stocky gatekeeper with a close inspection of my pass and a pitying glance at my drowned rat appearance.

"Christ on a cracker," Jacob exclaimed as I slogged toward

him at the side stage. "What happened to you?" He sniffed me. "You fall in a pint?"

"Something like that," I said with a sigh. "Hey, who were you just talking to?"

His mouth twitched in a grimace. "Oh, the usual riff raff."

"Robbie told me about the GTFOs."

Jacob shook his head with annoyance and started fiddling with the rings that adorned his fat fingers. "Of course he did. Robbie's jealous that Sage and Graham are getting all the attention and he has to deal with normal groupies. He doesn't get the crazies. Makes him feel left out."

"What did that girl want? Was it Terri?"

"I don't pay attention to their names," he said calmly, twirling a big gold ring around. "She did mention you though."

"What? Me? I've never met that girl."

He cracked a smile and lifted his shoulders back, looking down at me slyly. "She knows you though. Says you're a wannabe music journalist and can't be trusted. Says you're just a groupie in disguise, and that she's the one who should be writing the story."

"Are you serious?"

He shrugged. "I'm always serious, love. For what it's worth, this Terri as you say, has an actual media pass. She writes for someone, though I wouldn't be surprised if it was a private magazine out of her parent's basement, judging from the looks of her."

I crossed my arms, not liking this at all. "So what else did she say?"

"That was pretty much it. You know, it's just girly grade school stuff, tattle-taling and all that. Don't worry, Rusty. I can tell when someone's sucking up to me and spreading the nasty stuff for ulterior motives. I'm the manager for crying out loud. That's my job."

I wiggled my mouth in thought. "I don't like it."

He patted my shoulder. "No one likes it but it comes with the territory. Did you think you'd be able to interview the band

and not score the wrath of other writer fans or groupies? Judging by the beer shower you just took, I'd say you know now."

He walked off toward Chip at the console. "Welcome to groupie high."

✱   ✱   ✱

"You're looking a little tired, Rusty," Robbie said, peering at me with concern. I was sitting across from him at the table, trying to drink a glass of water while the bus trundled along the rough highway toward Minnesota. "Was I snoring?"

"Nah. I just didn't sleep very well," I told him truthfully. After the show was over and I was glancing over my shoulder every second, expecting to be ambushed by Terri, Sparky, or Sonja, we headed right back to the bus and a just waking Bob got us out on the road. Everyone was in great spirits but extremely tired and it wasn't a very lively night. I had stayed up for an hour or so playing cards with Mickey and Noelle while the rest of the band went to bed early.

The top bunk was now officially mine as Noelle and Mickey were back to taking over the full bed in the back and Robbie decided to camp out beneath my bunk. Graham and Sage took over the other bunks toward the back and Jacob had a permanent claim on the couch. I guess it was the best place for a steely guard dog to be.

There's something very comforting about sleeping on a bus; the drone of the engine and the sway of the roads make you feel like a baby being rocked to sleep. The confined space of the bunk helps too. But for whatever reason, I tossed and turned all night and the only reason I knew I had gotten any sleep at all was because I remembered my dream quite clearly.

I'm not sure if it's because Jacob had mention high school earlier, but that's where my dream took me. It wasn't even a dream in a sense because I merely relived a moment that had already happened. I was in grade eight, during Mrs. Hoolahan's gym class. Normally I loved gym—I was very athletic and was ace at most sports, except for badminton since I had a reputation for breaking birdies and throwing rackets. It was after a game of soccer where I had scored the winning goal. It wasn't a big deal since most of the girls didn't give a shit about sports, but it made me happy and the popular set hated to lose. They taunted me as usual afterward, calling me flat, a surfboard, and a boy. One of them asked me if I had a secret penis and if that's why none of the boys liked me. I guess I was tired after the game and just plain sick of the same girls always bullying me and calling me names. So, I punched the girl—Tiffany, of course her name was Tiffany—right in the face. It shocked me and I immediately regretted it, especially when I saw the blood pour out of Tiffany's fair nose and I was consequently suspended for a few days. My parents didn't really care, and because my mother, at this point, was beginning her downward spiral, my dad was grateful for the extra help on the farm. I couldn't tell if they were even disappointed in me, but it didn't matter. I was appalled by my violence and growing short temper, and I made a vow to myself to keep my anger under control.

Maybe last night's altercation with the GTFOs triggered repressed feelings of injustice or something, but I woke up from the dream feeling angry, grumpy, and ready to lash out.

Robbie leaned back in his seat and lit up a cigarette. The blue smoke drifted through the hazy air of the bus and I absently followed it as it curled around Graham and Mickey sitting at the couch. Mickey was scribbling into a notebook. Graham was staring right at me in some sort of unfeeling gaze. When his eyes finally came into focus and recognized mine, he flinched. Then a cold, cold smile spread across his lips. His dark eyes sparkled like shiny buttons and I quickly averted my eyes before I asked him what the hell he was looking at. Like I said, I was grumpy.

Luckily by the time we got to St. Paul, Robbie was hell bent on getting me out of my mood. Once we parked at the venue, he grabbed my hand and my purse and pulled me off the bus.

"Where are we going?" I asked him, trying to hide the excitement in my voice. Day three with Hybrid and the fact that Robbie Oliver wanted me to go with him somewhere still lit up my insides.

He let go of my hand, much to my dismay, and gestured off in the distance. The city of St. Paul looked bigger than I had expected, with a charm that reminded me a bit of Ellensburg. "I don't know, man. I'm just sick of the bus. Let's go get fucked up and throw stones across the Mississippi."

I could have done without the fucked up part, but the famous river at least piqued my interest. We walked away from the venue for a good ten minutes, Robbie babbling about how much he disliked Mick Jagger and how he thought Page had been better off with the Yardbirds. None of it was very good interview material, unless Robbie wanted to start a pissing contest with Jagger, who was clearly such a big enough star that he wouldn't care, but I let him talk anyway. The boy was a bundle of energy and obviously one night of jumping around like a rabid dog on stage didn't do much to dissipate it.

We seemed to be getting away from the river, and the afternoon heat was stifling like a thick, wet blanket that coated my arms and made my hair frizz out like a porcupine. Robbie told me he knew a person in the area and that he had to say hello for a couple of seconds. We stopped outside of a modest walk-up and he quickly disappeared up the stairs. I stood on the sidewalk, watching the normalcy of a town I'd never been to. Kids down the corner sat at a lemonade stand, while young moms pushed strollers down the cracked asphalt, waving a fan at their faces. The sun beamed down on me with such intensity that I knew I'd have a new crop of freckles on my nose by the end of the day.

Minutes later, Robbie came skipping down the stairs, taking them two at a time. He clapped his hands together and his hair shone in shades of amber and mahogany in the sunlight. "Well, shall we head back?"

"What about the river?"

He did a little jig. "Oh right, to the river!"

"Unless you think we'll miss soundcheck."

"Those fuckers can soundcheck without me. Sage usually fills in." He shot me an artful glance as we started down the street. "Have you ever heard him sing?"

I shook my head, wondering why he was looking at me like that. "No, just in backup."

"He's good. I mean, he's not me."

"Of course not. You're Robbie Oliver, a Golden God."

"No, that's Robert Plant. I'm a Silver God. Almost as precious and not as bright. But Sage, he's good. Very low. Bassy. Gets you here." He reached over and squeezed my stomach.

I squealed and ran away from him a few steps, nervous laughter at my lips. I watched him shyly, keeping more than an arm's length away.

"You sound fond of him, even though you guys argue."

"Like I said yesterday, Rusty. He's the head honcho. He calls the shots and you hate him for it but you're stuck with him. He's like my dad in a twisted way, and he's only twenty-seven. Well, actually twenty-eight. His birthday is in a couple of weeks."

"That's cute that you remember his birthday."

"You're cute," Robbie said. He made another grab for me, holding me by the arm, and brought me to his chest.

And that's how I first found myself in the arms of a famous singer, his eyes sparkling playfully in the heavy sunlight, his sweat-tinged hands on my skin. For a second I wasn't sure if he was just going to stare at me with that smile on his face or if he was going to kiss me.

He didn't do either. He dropped my arm and whispered, "You're a college student, right?"

I nodded, holding my breath.

He bit his lip and his eyes looked up as he dug his hand into his pocket and fished around. He brought out his hand, opened his palm, and my eyes followed to a few pills marked Lemon 714.

"You're used to ducking out, right?" he asked.

I didn't understand. "You mean from class?"

That made him pause, his eyes searching mine in wonder before he let out a hearty guffaw.

"You're kidding. Oh, Rusty, Rusty, Rusty. Ducking out, man? You know, with ludes? Soapers? Motherfucking Lemon Sevens?"

"Yeah, I get it," I snapped.

"Well that's what these are, Redwood. Ludes for me and ludes for you. Let's get lewd and rude together." He opened up my hand and placed the pills in them.

I didn't do drugs and I certainly didn't do drugs with rock stars. Rock stars who certainly didn't need drugs.

"This shit is going to get you too fucked, Robbie. You have a show tonight."

"You have no idea what you're talking about," he said lazily. He popped one pill in his mouth and swallowed it down dry. "You drink. You toke. Loosen up. Join the band."

"I'm not with the band and never will be with the band," I admitted. It came out more bitter than I would have liked. "And I need to stay sharp. And so do you."

"Oh, come on. I need fun!" He sounded like a little boy who didn't get his way, and actually started to look like it when he stamped his feet a few times. "I thought you were different from the rest of them."

"Them?" I cocked a brow at him.

"Everyone," he said exasperatingly. "You're a fan. You're supposed to be fun. We feed you and you feed us. It's a two way street, groovy mama."

I sighed. I was never a pushover when it came to peer pressure, but I hadn't dealt with Robbie Oliver before. My willpower was powering down. Fast.

"Fine. I'll do it."

He let out an amusingly girlish yelp.

"But," I warned him, raising my finger in the air. "You have to promise me that this isn't going to royally fuck me up. I'm a virgin…at this sort of thing. I can't be making a fool of myself. I really, really can't."

He picked the pill off my hand and ran his fingers along the bottom of my lip until it tingled. "Don't worry now. You won't be worrying later."

He placed the pill on my tongue and I swallowed it.

CHAPTER NINE

Robbie wasn't kidding when he said I wouldn't be worrying about it. It was a slow start and it didn't really kick in until we were back at the tour bus and the band was just finishing up soundcheck. But when it finally hit me, it was with a delicious bang.

I was hanging out in the backstage area where all the drinks and food had been set up, all fold-out tables and metal chairs, picking at some vegetables and dip that tasted like it had been left out in the sun for too long. Suddenly I felt immeasurably…good. The top of my head started to tingle and pretty soon my fingers felt too numb to even grasp the carrots properly. I gave up on them and sat back in the chair that earlier felt hard and uncomfortable and now felt like it was crafted from a marshmallow cloud.

"Rusty?" a Cockney accent rang out.

I slowly eased my head in its direction and saw Jacob standing there, staring down at me with apprehension.

I couldn't speak but that was okay. I gave him a lopsided smile.

"Oh dear," he muttered to himself and looked around. The rest of the band was who knows where. In fact, all I could remember was carrots and dip—who knew how long I'd been sitting alone.

Finally, Jacob said, "Robbie put you up to this, didn't he? That cunt."

His harsh words shocked me but didn't stop the flood of warmth through my numbed limbs. It was the weirdest sensation. Wonderful.

"It was Quaaludes, wasn't it?"

I found myself nodding.

"How many did you take?"

I held up a finger and finally managed to say, "I'm okay. I feel good."

"Of course you feel good. That's not the point. You need to have your wits about you, Rusty. That's why you're here."

You always said I should loosen up, I thought lazily to myself.

"How can you protect yourself when you're just sitting here, staring stupidly at the wall like some ignoramus?"

"No one will hurt me," I told him peacefully and gave him another smile. I wasn't afraid of his boys. I wasn't afraid of anything. I told him so.

"I don't think you understand…it doesn't matter," he said. "You just sit tight and don't go anywhere."

I did as he said. At some point later, as people passed me in the hall as clouds of dust, Jacob appeared again, soaring above me like a rough angel. He grabbed me by the arm and hauled me to my feet. I couldn't feel my feet! They were gone and I had to look down to make sure they hadn't been chopped off by an invisible goblin.

"Easy now," he told me. His strong grip on my arms felt good too.

He brought me through a heavy door to the side stage, and to my stupid surprise, I was met with a blast of sweat, heat, and noise. There were fans screaming at the band—they were already playing. The music hit my ears in a weird delay, but once it found them, the notes wiggled their way into my brain like a happy little worm.

I leaned against Jacob, minding his weird smell of mothballs and coffee, but loving the feel of his large firm body beside me. It was hard keeping my eyes focused, but when they did, they went to Sage and Robbie. Speaking of Robbie, there he was, fine as anything. He wasn't as manic as usual, but he was sensual and slow and I wanted a part of it.

Time was behaving badly, and within what seemed like minutes, the show was over and everyone was heading back to the dressing rooms. I loitered outside, splayed on the chair while strangers ignored me and drank the band's beer. The effects started to wear off, but only enough so that I was able to stand on my own two feet without collapsing to the ground in a pile of mush.

I felt both bored and content and was making my slow saunter over to the dressing room when the door opened and Robbie emerged. His face lit up like a light bulb when he saw me and it made me giggle.

"My rust-colored woman," Robbie said, ignoring a few pretty girls who had been hanging out in the corner of the lounge waiting for him. He grabbed my head between both his hands. "You must come with me."

He took me out of the venue and outside, where we spilled into the gated parking lot like a walking river of bones and blood. The stars were high above, looking heavy in the moisture-laden heat. We walked over to the tour bus. It was empty and waiting, sitting like a metal beast.

It was a blur what happened next. I was pressed against the bus, the cool chrome setting my bare skin to tingles, and Robbie's hands were in my hair and on my arms. It felt good, too good, and all I could think of was sex. My sex. His sex. All the sex in the world.

Then his lips were on mine and his tongue was in my mouth and I had a horrible feeling deep in my gut that this was wrong. Even my brain tried to shout rational things like, "This is a mistake. You're both on drugs. You're a journalist. He's Robbie Oliver," but my body wanted him. The drugs wanted him. And from the way his hands were unzipping my jeans right there in public in that open, dark parking lot, he wanted me too. What Robbie wanted, Robbie got, and I was suddenly no different from any of the other girls.

His tongue slid over my neck like honey and I leaned back against the bus, letting that honey trail trickle down into my shirt where he pulled my breast out with one hand and started swirling around my nipple. I moaned loudly, not caring, only feeling, and didn't bat his other hand away when it slid between my open pants and my stomach. His fingers reached for me, playing with the soft hair between my legs, before they found my clit and started rubbing. I moaned again until he brought his head up and shoved his lips against mine. I couldn't ask for the feeling to end. I couldn't ask him to stop.

But someone else would.

One aching second he was there at my mouth, the next there was nothing but air on my lips and tongue. My eyes flew open and saw Sage's hand pulling Robbie back at the shoulder.

"What the hell do you think you're doing?" Sage growled.

Robbie tried to push him away weakly. "Whatever man, you cock-blocker."

Sage shot me a look, sussing me out. I was suddenly aware that my breast was popping out of my shirt and that my pants were undone. Somewhere in the back of my head I knew I would be embarrassed later on. I made a slow attempt to cover up while Sage gave Robbie a shake.

"You can call me a cock-blocker all you want, but getting the journalist high and taking advantage of her isn't usually in your repertoire."

"She's fine, she wants me," Robbie said casually and with a few slurs.

"She's not. And you're not," Sage sniped and pushed him away toward the venue. "Go find Jacob, he wants to talk to you."

Robbie stumbled off like a fawn just finding its footing. I watched him go, trying to gather my thoughts and senses. Things were wrong. I had just done a very bad thing and my brain was too slow to catch on.

Satisfied that Robbie was on his way to Jacob, Sage set his sights back on me. His eyes glinted like a silver leaf in the night.

"You said you wouldn't run away," he said, his voice low and husky. The sound of it made my nipples hard and I knew his eyes flew to them for just one instant. Forget Robbie, if Sage had wanted me right there and then I would have been all his.

He tilted his head to the side, thinking things over. I wondered if he knew what I was feeling; he must have known that the drugs had me ready and willing. But whatever he thought, he didn't say. Not about that.

He took a step closer to me, putting one hand against the bus and leaning on it, like the school stud against a locker. My lips parted as I watched his, the wicked curve of his mouth that led to dimples that sometimes appeared.

You could make love to me against this bus, I tried to say. *I won't mind.*

But somehow, I didn't say it. What he had said earlier was just coming around in my lude-addled brain.

"I'm not running away," I said throatily. "I'm still here."

He smirked. "Are you, Dawn?"

He patted the top of my head gently with his hand, his expression melancholic. "Are you here? Right now? There are different ways to run away and I know them all. Whatever you run from will always find you."

I couldn't make sense of it. "I took some Quaaludes."

"I know you did," he cooed like a father calming a crying baby. Then his face grew serious. "But here's the thing, Dawn. This band is my family. It's pretty much the only family I have and it's my job to keep them functioning as long as possible. When I fail, they fail and we all fail. There is no later. There never was. Later is something that's used up with the lazy belief that there's always a tomorrow. I do what I can now, while I can. And this includes keeping everyone in line. Robbie doesn't need this complication in his life. The last thing this band needs is for one of us to get mixed up with a journalist. We're all given a certain amount of time and all I ask is for my time, our time, to go smoothly. Do you understand?"

Somehow, I did. I nodded meekly.

"You know I don't want you here," he continued, the rolling wave of his voice balancing the harshness of his words. "It's nothing personal. And I also know you aren't about to go anywhere. You're tougher than that. Or maybe just damn stubborn. I'm making as much peace with this as I can. So if you're going to be here, with us, you'll need to function too. This isn't a great start."

"I'm sorry," I said, my eyes breaking away from that dusky green. Whatever sexual, sensual urges the drugs had been piling up in my loins were now dissipating fast.

He leaned back and removed his arm from above my head. "Don't be sorry. Just work with it. I don't care who you screw or when you screw them, but I think *you* do. You just don't remember."

I nodded again and tried to pull myself off the bus. He put his hands on both my shoulders and brought me up straight. He kept them there, warm and strong, and leaned down a little to look at me at eye level.

"Are you going to be okay?" he asked.

"I think I need to go to bed," I said.

"All right, hold on."

He kept one hand on me to keep me steady, and with the other he pulled a pair of keys from his black pants and stuck it in the bus door. After a few twists and turns of the stubborn lock, there was a click and the door opened with a loud groan. He gave me a quick smile.

"In case you're wondering, if Bob's still sleeping at his hotel, I always have an extra set of keys."

He came over to me and guided me up the stairs, one step at a time. I leaned a little into his body and was overcome by his smell of fresh ocean and pipe tobacco and the immediate urge to sleep.

"Come on, you're almost there," he said as my eyes began closing. I walked a few steps more and began to fall toward the lower bunk. He caught me in his arms and they wrapped around me with strength.

"I don't think that's a good idea, especially when Robbie comes back on. I love the bugger, but when he's on ludes, he's going to try and hump everything, even the gear shift. No offense, of course."

None taken, I thought.

"Do you need to go to the bathroom before you pass the fuck out? I can hold you up but if you want me to do anything else, you're on your own."

If I wasn't fucked up out of my tree, I would have thought Sage was trying to be funny. But I shook my head *no*, and the next thing I knew, Sage was lifting me in his arms and somehow depositing me up on the top bunk. He did it effortlessly and I felt like I was sinking down into a warm mass of feathers.

"Sleep tight," I heard him say. "We'll be on our way soon."

His words rang throughout my head as I was pulled deeper and deeper into the dark chasm of sleep. I was almost under, almost in my dreams, when the bus shook slightly.

My eyes opened carefully and I expected to see Sage standing by the bed. But there was only the faint light from above the couch next to the bunks, casting long shadows around the bus. I was too tired to raise my head off my pillow and look around, but I had the eerie, unsinkable feeling that I wasn't alone on the bus.

Someone else was with me.

I opened my mouth to call for Sage but a faint noise stopped me. It came from the bunk below. I held my breath and listened.

It was a weird wet and slopping sound that was punctuated by the bunk shaking. In my drugged head I imagined a pile of bleeding guts and an animal rooting through them and wolfing them down in thick, drooling gulps.

I felt frozen in a weird panic, trying to figure out what it could be and trying to battle the now steadily encroaching sleep. Before

I could look over the edge of the bunk and look, as terrifying as that prospect was, the bunk shook a final time and something solid fell out of it and slapped onto the floor. The last thing I heard was the sound of something wet and heavy being dragged, and the last thing I saw was a long, low shadow passing along the walls, heading out the bus door.

Sleep claimed me before I had the chance to scream.

CHAPTER TEN

Dear Miss Melanie,

How are you doing, honey child? I keep calling you and missing you, but your mom mentioned you met a "nice young man" and well, I guess that explains it. That's all she told me though, so don't worry about your mom spilling pervy details (not that I think you'd tell your mom all about your love life, but since I'm not there, I can't imagine who you're spilling the beans to!). But anyway, RIGHT ON!!

It's hard for you to get in touch with me on the road and I don't know when this letter will reach you, but I can tell you that on August 13th, I'll be staying in Nashville for two nights at the Hermitage Hotel (SUPER LUX!!). Most of the time though we just sleep on the bus, so this will be so much fun and I can't wait to hear your voice—I hope you call! Ask for Rusty (don't ask!).

I've been fine. It's been a weird trip, that's for sure. At first I was so shy and nervous around these guys, and not all of them have been very nice. I gotta be honest. Noelle was an outright bitch at first, but she's warmed up a teeny bit. Well, she's not glaring at me as much, and she's stopped calling me a groupie, and she actually gave me a pretty good interview yesterday. Mickey is kind of quiet and I get the feeling he doesn't really care about me one way or another, but I don't mind. Graham is an ass. When he's not setting off by himself on some "business," he's reading cult-like textbooks. He likes Aleister Crowley just like Jimmy Page does, but at least Page is sincere with his black magic and stuff. Graham just seems like a poser, always wearing black and acting like a creep. And he knows I am on to him, that's why he's always glaring at me or being weird when I'm around. I get the feeling he wants me to be there, but I worry him just the same. The rest of the band doesn't even pay attention to him and neither do I…except when I have to interview him during 2-3 AM in the morning. What a loser! I'm NOT looking forward to that.

There's Jacob, the band manager. He's an enigma. He's like tall and large; he reminds me of a British boxer turned gangster and should have gold teeth. He's very rough around the edges and just last night at Chicago's show, he punched a rabid fan in the head for coming after Robbie with a pen (I guess he thought it was a penknife?). But I like him for some reason. He looks after me like a surrogate father, in a way, and he seems to know way more than he lets on. Sometimes I think he's Merlin.

Robbie…oh dear. I can't wait to get you on the phone so I can spill the real details. He is as charming and gorgeous as you would think. He's easy to talk to…or he was. He's kind of distanced himself from me after the other night. Mel, I did a real dumb thing. REAL DUMB. I don't know if there was something inside me that needed a rebound to get over Ryan or what (and it worked, because I haven't thought about him in days), but let's just say drugs and tongues were involved and leave it at that. Seriously. You wouldn't believe it. I hang my head in total shame.

What makes it worse is that we were caught by Sage himself. Sage Knightly. You know I've always had a soft spot for him, and being here with him on the bus has only made it worse. At first he was pretty pissed that I was here, but he's coming around. He told me that, in not so many words. He's very distant from me and keeps to himself a lot but there is no question he is large and in charge. And MEL, HE IS LARGE! Don't get your head in the gutter, I haven't touched him and don't plan on it (Dawn is no longer allowed to touch rock stars!), but he is large in form (super tall, super amazing smile, crazy strong—I'd embellish but you'd get the wrong idea—tattoos that are hotter in person made up of tiny snakes and Day of the Dead type stuff…speaking of, it's quite apparent he's of Mexican blood somewhere. Though his eyes are that light green/gray color, his skin tone is very olive in real life, and I caught him reading a book in Spanish once). Anyway, rambling, he's also larger than life. I hope to interview him at some point, but every time I work up the nerve, I either say something snappy or I don't say anything at all. I don't know what that guy is doing to me, but I don't like it.

What else? Well there are some crazy groupies that the boys call the GTFOs (not to be confused with the GTOs, and by the way, pretty sure Robbie has done the deed with Miss Pamela), and they are nuts. One is a journalist and is trying to get me in trouble with the manager by spreading lies and being a jealous bitch, the other threw beer on my face, and the other, the "crackpot ringleader," is called Sonja and I swear she's a witch. Or maybe I've just been hanging around Graham for too long.

As for my writing…eh…it's coming along. I wrote a long concert review for the story yesterday on the bus ride to Chicago. I've got some notes on Robbie (though he won't let me use a tape recorder) and Noelle. I'm actually writing this right now on my knee as I head toward Creem's office. YUP, I am in Detroit and I'm about to see the big boss himself, Mr. Barry Kramer. It's sort of unofficial, they knew the band was playing in town, and asked Jacob to send me over. So I'm in a cab and sort of sweating to death of nervousness. Wish me luck!

It feels weird being on the road and so out of touch with the world. I heard Nixon got impeached! The economy is totally sinking into a recession! There could be wars going on and I wouldn't know about it! The only inkling of the world at large that I have is when Bob, our bus driver, stops to fill up the bus and complains about the gas prices. But at the same time, it's kind of nice. Now if only I could just buckle down and start writing some genius stuff.

I love and miss you and hope I see your smiling face soon!

Dawn.

Future Editor of Creem Magazine

"Could you pull over the next time you see a post box," I asked the cab driver as we zoomed up suburban Detroit's bumpy streets. "I need to mail a letter."

"No problem, mama," the cabbie answered back. I folded the letter to Mel and stuck it in a stamped envelope and sealed it shut. Then I sat back in the ripped cab seats and watched the world go past, trying to keep myself occupied.

Detroit was huge and more sprawling than Seattle. It wasn't pretty by any stretch, not even close to the Emerald City, but it had its own vibe and sense of malaise. Cars were made here, and according to the headlines I'd caught from gas station newspapers, as the economy crashed so did the auto plants. You couldn't see it in the faces of the kids as they played on the streets in threadbare clothes, but you saw it in the adults as they stared blankly at their neighbor's foreclosure signs on overgrown lawns. The black population was huge but even Mel wouldn't have fit in. She was too cute and full of smiles. The folks here stood on the street corners with suspicious baggies, eyes full of hate and defeat as my cab rolled past them. It was a hard luck city, and I had to wonder why Creem decided to set up office in the land of motors.

We drove past a post box, but before I had time to point it

out, the cabbie said, "Too dangerous for a white lady like you." When we finally did find a box, he ran out to mail the letter and left me in the cab. I had been away from the band and the safety of the tour bus for a half hour, and though my cabbie seemed like a good man, I had never felt so alone in the world. One tall redhead in a world of real life problems that would put any spoiled rock star's to shame.

As the cab trundled along the streets, I tried to sit back and relax. Now that the letter was out of my hands and on its way to Mel, my mind was free to wander and that wasn't always a good thing. It wanted to get nervous about going to Creem, meeting Barry and discussing the work in progress...which so far hadn't been much work at all. I felt beads of sweat forming underneath my palms and a shakiness in my lungs from my building nerves. Oh boy.

I kept my eyes focused on the city rolling past, trying to ignore it. When we stopped at a light, I looked over at the brown Cadillac next to us. There was a woman in the backseat holding up a bundled baby and cooing to it. I couldn't help but smile. Even though I couldn't see the child's face because of how it was swathed, the cute way the mother was bouncing it up and down and the sheer joy on her face made me feel warm inside.

I watched as the mother brought the baby in closer for a kiss.

A long, inhuman tongue protruded from the infant like a waving tentacle. It licked the mother's nose, slopping around her face.

I felt the skin at the back of my neck tighten. My arm hairs stood on end. My breath was gone.

The mother smiled at the child as the tongue slinked back into its head. Then she slowly, deliberately turned her head toward me. She smiled again. Her teeth were red with blood and it dripped down her chin. As she kept that frozen grin on her face, the infant's tongue came back out and wiped it all away. Blood spilled down its pulsing, wet length and into the baby's blanket.

I hadn't noticed I was screaming until the cabbie slammed on the brakes and I was jerked against the seatbelt.

"What the hell, woman?" he yelled, giving me crazy eyes in the mirror.

I looked back out the window at the Cadillac. It was already ahead of us and turning down a street. I couldn't get my thoughts together, couldn't feel my limbs. What the hell was happening? Did I really just see that?

I gulped for breath and shook my head. "Sorry. Thought I saw something."

The cab driver didn't look too convinced.

Finally we reached the Creem office and I tipped my cabbie handsomely for getting me there in one piece. He gave me a funny look, a little glad to have me out of his cab, and took off down the street. I couldn't blame him. I was simultaneously a nervous wreck over meeting Barry and a paranoid nusto who was seeing baby demons on the street. I had to get myself under control and fast.

Here I am, I thought, standing in front of the rather plain building on Cass Avenue. The rest of the buildings on the street were rather quaint and Victorian looking, but Creem Magazine's headquarters looked totally rock and roll in that "I'm not trying hard" way.

I took in a deep breath and tried to keep the waves of nausea at bay, and made my way up the stairs to the front door. I almost reached it when the door flung upon and Lester Bangs stepped out.

I nearly had a heart attack. Here was my hero, Lester, in all his mustached, aviator sunglasses glory, wearing a dirty t-shirt with a rainbow on it that did nothing to hide his potbelly.

"You're the kid? The chick? The kid chick?" he asked, talking a mile a minute. I noticed he still had one foot in the door.

"I think so?"

He waved me over. "Come on, come on. It's not safe out here for a girl like you."

I couldn't tell if he was making fun of me for being a country bumpkin or what, but he quickly ushered me inside. He closed the door behind me and set about turning as many locks as possible.

"Rough neighborhood?" I asked.

He let out a shy, "Heh heh heh," and when he was done, he turned and ran up the narrow stairs, calling over his shoulder, "we had a break-in a few days ago. We're getting the fuck out of here."

I ran up the stairs after him, noting the smell of smoke and incense in the air. When I got to the landing and turned the corner, I was faced with a neat and tidy teak desk and the round, smiling face of a woman in her early thirties. She exuded both welcoming and no-nonsense qualities about her, and her multiple bracelets shook as she reached out to shake my hand.

"I'm Maureen," she said. The phone beside her rang, rattling in its receiver.

"Mother Goose," cut in Lester, winking at me.

"Maureen, I'm Dawn," I told her. "We spoke on the phone."

"I speak to everyone on the phone, dear. Go right in, Barry is waiting for you." She reached across her desk and smacked Lester on the arm. "Be nice to this one."

"I'm nice to all the ladies," Lester told her but she was already occupied on a phone call.

Lester gently touched my shoulder like his contact would set me off, and steered me around the corner of the desk and cloudy, plastic partition until I was in an open-planned office. It was like a small city, with cluttered desks lining the outskirts and narrow corridors between them. Papers were flying everywhere, caught in a dirty breeze that rolled in from an open window, a breeze that did nothing to clear the thick haze of tobacco and pot smoke that hung in the air like a mass of thunderheads. The office was pretty much empty except for a man and woman who wrote side by side in the back of the room, she on the phone taking notes, he clacking up a storm on his Underwood typewriter. The walls were dotted with Robert Crumb cartoons, signed records, concert photographs, and magazine covers. It was chaos and heaven all at once.

"Barry's in here," Lester said, taking me to a closed office and rapping on the door.

"Just a minute," said a voice from inside. Lester looked at me and smiled, all puffed cheeks. For such an abrasive and iconic writer, he looked like nothing more than a giant child.

"Have you ever spent months, years, looking for a certain record?" he asked me in a lowered voice, looking like he was confessing a delicious secret. "You know, the b-sides and the shit you can't find anywhere?"

I nodded and didn't have to think long. "Yup. The UK version of *Let it Bleed*. Finally found it in a secondhand store in Olympia."

He smiled even wider, then tried to look serious. Lester's face didn't *do* serious. "You'll do all right here, kid."

Then he left me, moseying back to his place at whatever desk was his, while the door to the office opened and Barry poked his head out, eying me warily. Bowie's "Width of a Circle" drifted out from a giant record player sitting on his bookcase.

"Dawn Emerson?" he asked. "Come in."

I gave him a quick smile and stepped into his office, taking a seat across from his desk. He came around and flopped casually down in his chair with a sigh.

"So you're Dawn...or is it Rusty now?"

Barry wasn't exactly like I pictured. I would have thought he'd have long straggly hair and a rampant beard, but he was clean-shaven and wearing a button-up shirt. He was older than I assumed too, maybe in his mid-thirties.

"Just Dawn," I told him, silently cursing whoever had come up with that nickname. Jacob, probably.

"So, Dawn...tell me how it is."

I launched into a short recap of the last few days on the road, made easier since I just had to recite it all for Mel in the letter. I tried to keep out the boys' bad behavior but Barry was smarter than that and wanted to hear everything. I told him about the backstage blow job antics and Robbie on ludes. I left out the part about me being high and fooling around with him, and for that I felt like a bit of a traitor.

Barry didn't seem too surprised at any of it and leaned back in his chair thoughtfully. "So are they treating you right?"

"Oh yeah, everything is fine. They've all been lovely. Of course, well, not Graham as you know. But most of them."

"He's an odd one," Barry remarked. "But every band has its dillhole and that's Hybrid's. It could be worse."

"I guess so," I said with a shrug, hoping I seemed cooler about it than I was.

"So that's it." He got up and went to the record player, flipping the LP over. "Nothing else really going on?"

My eyes followed him, confused. The acoustic jangle of "Running Gun Blues" began to play; *I count the corpses on my left, I find I'm not so tidy.*

"I'm not sure what you mean?"

"Oh, I guess you don't. It doesn't matter. You have a few more weeks."

I pursed my lips in puzzlement.

He noticed and continued. "The Cobb...I mean, Jacob, he had told me that this tour was going to go down in history and that's why you needed to be there to record it."

I snorted. "I don't know why Jacob would tell you that. Granted, I'm not queen of the road, or even the highway, but...I really don't see anything historic about it. What else did he tell you?"

He sighed and flapped his hands and came back to his seat. "That was it, really. He sounded so sure of himself, I guess he thought he needed to sell the band to me. But, who cares man, we would have loved to run a piece on Hybrid anyway. Jacob's got a reputation for stretching the truth."

"And breaking people's noses," I added.

"That too. Well, that settles that. Just keep doing what you're doing, Dawn. Keep organized, keep your eyes open."

I got the impression he wanted me to leave and started to get out of the hard chair. "Do you need me to mail you some of the pieces I've written so far?"

I don't know why I asked because I really didn't have much to send. I hoped he wouldn't call my bluff.

He didn't. "I trust you, Dawn. We'll get it all sorted out afterward. After all, the band is paying for you to be there, not us. So, you know, do what the fuck you like!"

It probably would have made me feel better if Barry had told me to work hard and turn in some glorious piece of writing, but it seemed that the editor of Creem didn't really have the highest of hopes for me or for this so-called tour that was going to go down in history. What a crock of shit.

I gave him a grateful smile and said those famous of famous words, "You won't regret this." Then I stepped out of his office and into the bullpen. The two writers in the corner were laughing with each other and smoking, paying no attention to me. Lester Bangs was nowhere to be seen, like I had only dreamed him up.

I went back to Maureen and got her to ring a cab for me. I asked her about some of the writers like Patti Smith, who had gone on to form a band, and Mike Saunders, who coined the phrase "heavy metal" a few years before, and she was a little more enthusiastic about my time with Hybrid, confessing that she had a crush on Mickey.

"Don't tell Noelle that," she added before snatching up the ringing phone. "We need more women in rock."

❊ ❊ ❊

If you asked me, sometimes there were too many women in rock. And I didn't mean Noelle, who was an anomaly in her own right, or the female music critics like Lisa Robinson (whom I wished I had seen at Creem). I mean the groupies.

Hybrid's groupies.

And in particular, the GTFOs.

After I caught a cab from Creem's office back to the venue, I was immediately thrust into the show with a new determination.

Even though the tour wasn't shaping up to be uniquely memorable in anyone's eyes aside from my own, and definitely wasn't going to go down in history, I wanted to do the best job I could. So, as I did in St.Paul, I went back into the crowd and tried to capture the show from the view of the fans. The longer I was on the road with the guys, the less I felt like a fan and the more I felt like one of them. A jaded Dawn was the wrong Dawn.

By this time, after several shows in a row, I was getting a bit used to their sets, and knew exactly what numbers were coming next and found it easy to organize my show thoughts. I used most of my time to watch the band from different areas of the venue and tried to pick up the flavor of the crowds. The Detroit crowd was absolutely nuts and the hardest and toughest group I'd seen so far on tour. Drinks were spilled, people were crowd-surfing, stomping on each other, pushing and shoving. It was an angry bunch, but the kind of anger that gets fueled by beer and hard times. Rock and roll was Detroit's outlet and I finally understood why Creem chose the motor city as its headquarters.

But in all of this musical chaos, there was a glowing constant. The tall white body of Sonja, who stood right before the stage, dressed in a long white cloak that never seemed to get an ounce of dirt, sweat, or cigarette burns on it. In fact, the men and few women around her seemed to keep their distance as much as they could, despite the squeezing and crowding of everyone else on the floor.

I was on the floor too, to the side where the ground sloped up a bit, and I watched her closely. She was swaying slightly with the music, her pale thin hands grasping the rail in front of her, her vibrant eyes focused right on Noelle. She watched her like she was trying to bore a laser through her head.

Hybrid began to play their sludgier cover of Sabbath's epic "Children of the Grave" and it opened with only Noelle's plucky bassline. It was at that moment that she decided to look up, perhaps feeling Sonja's intense, heat-filled stare, and she looked absolutely startled, her eyes shining with surprise beneath her heavily shadowed lids. Noelle's surprise continued to her fingers, where she messed up a few lines and was unable to get back into it until Graham came down with the drums and Sage and Mickey launched into the famous riff.

It was one of those screw-ups that was unfortunately noticeable, but no one in the audience cared after a few beats as the driving sound caused the human waves to crash against each other.

Noelle noticed though, and Noelle cared. After the show, she went straight for the bottle of Smirnoff in the backstage lounge and started gulping it down like water.

"Hey, leave some for us," I said jokingly, putting my hand on top of it and bringing it away from her mouth.

She shot me the nastiest look, the kind that usually preceded a few tears.

"Stay out of it, Red," she snapped, so I let her guzzle it down until she had a coughing fit and started leaning against the wall for support.

I looked around the backstage area. The guys were heading into their dressing room and laughing with each other, followed by some Detroit-based groupies whom I hoped were normal. Mickey didn't even pay me and Noelle any attention, nor offer his girlfriend any words of consolation, which I thought was a total dick move. Only Sage, the patriarch, came over.

"Everything all right here, Noe?" he asked in a low, smooth voice. His eyes darted to mine for a second, then returned to her scrunched up face. This was the closest I'd been to him since the whole ludes fiasco, when I was so fucked up I imagined a monster was on the bus.

"I don't want to be here anymore," Noe said, spitting out her words. "I'm sick of this, I'm sick of everyone!"

"Okay," I placated her, trying to smile and calm her down. "Where do you want to go?"

She took another swig of the vodka before Sage expertly plucked it out of her hands.

"Hey," she protested, reaching for it.

Sage placed his hand on her shoulder and firmly held her in place. "You can have this back, but you have to share it with us. You can go wherever you want tonight, but Dawn and I are coming with you."

I raised my brows at him. *We are?*

He ignored me and leaned closer to Noelle, tipping up her chin that ran wet with a few tears until she was meeting his eyes. It was amazing how much power he had over them all. Then I caught the softening of Noelle's expression and a subtle parting of her full lips, and I realized maybe he had more power over Noelle than I thought. She had transformed into an embarrassed, shamed rock star into...well...she kind of looked like a girl in love.

I looked away, feeling like I had stumbled upon some weirdly intimate moment.

"You up for going out, Dawn?" he asked after a few beats.

I turned my head and shot him a quick smile. Noelle was wiping underneath her eyes and trying to suck things up, and his expression toward me was expectant. Almost pleading.

If Sage wanted me to go out on the town with him and Noelle, I wasn't going to say no.

"Of course," I told him. "Where are we going?"

He clutched the vodka bottle tightly to his chest and surprised me.

"The Motor City," he sang in a voice that sounded like he ate a pack of cigarettes and washed it down with gasoline, his best John Lee Hooker impression. "The Motor City is burning."

CHAPTER ELEVEN

It was all sorts of interesting being squished in the back of a cab with Sage and Noelle. None of us had opted for the front seat, and he wanted to give Noelle the window in case she felt like vomiting, so I was in the middle and leaning up against him.

To be honest, I never wanted that cab ride to end. There was something deliciously romantic about being in the dark of a moving vehicle, feeling a virile man's arm brush against yours, his hip flush to your side, as you watch the city lights move past. Detroit wasn't burning but my heart was starting to, licks of flames that threatened to one day consume me.

We were silent in the back and we all passed around the bottle of Smirnoff like little teenagers. Our cab driver either didn't notice or didn't care. It was probably the latter. Only near the end of the ride did he start chatting up Sage about the best Detroit bands like MC5 and Alice Cooper. I listened with interest, never getting to hear Sage talk about the music he liked. He had as much passion for Iggy and the Stooges as I did for Hybrid.

Sage had asked the driver to drop us off at a little dive bar on the western outskirts of town. It was a strange neighborhood, the city meeting the suburbs, but Sage said he'd been there once before and that the owner gave musicians free drinks.

We settled into the bar. It was surprisingly crowded given its location, a mixture of blacks and whites, middle class and lower class. The jukebox was playing jazz music, there were bowls of nuts on all the tables, and tacky Christmas lights lit up the ceiling. The air was perfumed with the smell of rum, smoke, and cheap cologne. It was kind of perfect, just the type of place you'd end up with a rock star.

We took our seats at the bar, a cold piece of carved copper, and Sage ordered us all a round. We had left the vodka behind in the car, and we were all sufficiently buzzed. Well, I was buzzed. Sage seemed large and in charge and Noelle was steadily getting wasted. Several times I had to keep my hand at her back so she wouldn't fall off the stool. Soon, we had the bartender serving her virgin drinks.

"I can't believe I screwed up," she mumbled into her hands, making it almost impossible to understand her.

"Honey," I said, even though I'd never called anyone honey before. It felt right and I rubbed her back gently. "Who cares? That's what makes live music so great. You recovered. No one noticed."

I turned to Sage for support. He only gave me a little nod, a motion for me to continue. I wondered how often he had to play the consoling role here.

"Everyone noticed," she wailed. "It's the most important part of the song!"

That wasn't really true, but I could tell Noelle didn't want to hear any sort of reason. So I just said, "Yeah it sucks, I'm sorry," and she continued to whimper into her drink that was only lime and water.

I sighed and brought out my small notebook from my purse. I thought about asking Noelle if she saw her but I thought it might bring on another whine, so I kept my mouth shut and started flipping through the pages.

"Too dark to see, isn't it?" Sage asked, delicately popping

some cashews in his mouth. I tried not to stare at him chewing, at his strong jaw as it went to work. It was ridiculous how he made me feel when he was so close and I had a few drinks in me. He was only eating for crying out loud.

I quickly averted my eyes to the stack of bottles on display behind the bar.

"I can see in the dark," I told him.

"Really?" he asked, munching away. He paused. "What else can you do in the dark?"

Okay. What?

I looked at him with wide eyes. "Sorry?"

He laughed, and once again his dimples transformed his rugged, strong face into something almost beautiful. I watched him, mesmerized, before he said, "I'm just joking, Dawn."

Damn.

"I didn't know you could joke," I said, pointing at him with the straw of my drink.

"I try and mix it up. It never lasts very long."

"The tall, dark…" I almost said handsome, "silent type gets boring does it?"

A wash of sadness came over his eyes, turning them dark in the low light.

"A little laughter every now and then makes you feel alive."

Boy, was he ever Broody McGee.

"Has anyone ever compared you to Mr. Rochester?" I asked innocently.

"Will you guys shut up and stop flirting?" Noelle slurred from my left.

I didn't dare look at Sage, though I knew his face was still downturned and contemplating the Mr. Rochester comment. *Thanks for the awkward moment*, I thought to myself, silently cursing Noelle.

"I don't feel well," she said and started to lean too far off the stool.

"Noelle," I said in alarm, reaching for her.

Sage was quicker, and he was out of his seat and holding her up before I even got off my stool.

"She going to be okay?" asked the bartender.

Sage nodded, putting one of her skinny arms around his wide shoulders.

"She's just had a rough night. Ring us a cab, will you?"

The bartender nodded and we found ourselves outside the bar in the quiet and balmy Michigan night. Normally the idea of being somewhere different again would have given me a special, satisfied feeling but I had to admit I was a bit worried about Noelle.

Seeing as walking was a chore for her, I helped Sage bring her to the curb and we sat her down together.

"Not exactly how you thought you'd spend tonight," I said to him over her head.

"No, I pretty much knew this was coming," he said with a hint of a smile. His eyes glowed in the wash of a streetlamp. "Noe doesn't take hardcomings easily."

"She just screwed up," I said, aware that we were talking about her as if she wasn't slumped over between us. "No big deal."

"Everything's a big deal to Noelle," he admitted. "I'm sure she gave you a different side of her during the interview, but this is the real her. Drunk and ashamed."

I was quiet for a few moments before I spoke up. "That's kind of sad."

"She's just people. We all are. Just because you're in a band doesn't mean you stop having human problems. Fame, money... that doesn't fix those things. Those things will always find you."

"And who are you?" I asked softly, knowing I'd seen the drunk side of him.

He slowly brought his eyes around to look at me. They narrowed in thought. "I guess you'll find out when we talk."

"We're talking now," I said.

"This isn't the interview."

"Why not? Are you so different when you're being held

accountable?"

"Accountable," he said with a short laugh. "That's quite the big word for Creem Magazine. You sure they know what it means?"

Now it was my time to get prickly. "I don't get you."

"No one said you had to," he said casually. "I'm not some puzzle to be solved."

But you are, I thought. I didn't have any good rebuttal to that, so I just looked away and hoped the cab would come down the street.

"Besides," Sage continued in a lighter voice, "you don't interview the guitarist of a heavy metal band when the bassist is passed out on him. That's so cliché."

I rolled my eyes.

"So let's talk about you instead," he said.

"Me?"

"Yes. You. The redhead with the beautiful brown eyes."

Butterflies swirled in my stomach at that.

"Come on, tell me about Dawn Emerson. Where were you born?"

"Ellensburg, Washington. Home of the rodeo."

He smirked. "And were you ever part of the rodeo?"

I cleared my throat and said defiantly, "Yes, actually. Every year. And I win every year."

I shot him a sideways glance and saw he was staring at me, mouth agape.

"Well, go on," he said, wide-eyed.

"I do barrel racing with my horse. Moonglow. This was supposed to be our last year. We've came first or in the top three in the last seven years I've been doing this."

I was totally prepared for him to laugh. He looked stunned. Then impressed. "Why is this supposed to be your last year?"

I shrugged. "I don't know. I'm getting old or something."

"You're, what, twenty-one?"

"Yeah, so?"

"That's not old."

"Then I'm over it. People grow out of things."

I knew I was sounding defensive. The truth was, the fact that I was getting over the whole rodeo and racing circuit scared me. I liked to hold onto the way things were, even the shitty things. And I knew it made my dad proud. It always had, even in the toughest times.

"That's true. People do. They change. So what will fill the void?"

I laughed quietly. "You know what? I have no freaking idea, man."

"Not music journalism?"

The funny thing was I always thought it would. But now that I was on the road and living it, I wasn't feeling fulfilled. I was feeling confused.

"I don't know…maybe. I hope so."

"Do you love music?"

I looked at him askance. "Of course I love music."

"Maybe that's enough then," he said. "Just to love it."

I chewed on my lip and thought about that, my eyes drifting over to Noelle's hunched over back and the black lace of her scratchy shirt.

"Can you play music?" he asked, his voice getting lower, like he was afraid of disturbing me. "Like an instrument? Can you sing?"

"I can play guitar," I admitted. "I can sing a little too, but I'm not very good."

"Will you play for me one day?" he asked huskily. He leaned more toward me. "Will you sing for me?"

My cheeks heated up at the prospect.

"I don't know…"

"And something original. I'd like to hear something from your heart."

I smiled in amusement. "That's borderline corny, Sage Knightly."

"Perhaps I'm secretly borderline corny then. This is off the record, of course."

"Oh, of course."

"You do that for me, and we'll be even."

I raised my brows. "I wasn't aware we had a score to settle."

That look of melancholy blazed in his eyes again and he let out a puff of air. "I know you weren't."

"Why…" I began but couldn't finish.

He smiled shyly. "I'm vague again. Sorry."

"I just never know what you're talking about. I get that you didn't want a journalist here on tour but come on. It's not that bad. It's not even historic like Jacob said."

His gaze snapped to mine. "Jacob said what?"

I was a bit put off by his sudden change in demeanor. He went from corny to intense in two seconds flat.

"He said, well, he *told* Barry Kramer at Creem that someone needed to cover this tour because it was going to be historic or go down in history or something like that, and that I should be the poor sap to document it all."

Sage frowned and looked away. The silence around us was heavy, punctuated only by the occasional cry from inside the bar and the hum of jazz music.

He cleared his throat. I expected him to elaborate on why he seemed so shocked about what Jacob said, but instead he started to get to his feet. "Can you watch Noe for a second? I'm going to see if they can call us another cab. The bus will leave without us."

I doubted the bus would leave without the bassist and lead guitarist, but I did what he said and brought Noelle up next to me while he disappeared into the bar, his flip-flops echoing in the night.

While I waited, Noelle stirred and began to mumble out sentences.

"The demon," she said, her head swinging between her knees.

I leaned in close. "What was that, Noelle?"

"It's that demon in white, always in white." Her voice became higher and clearer.

I looked back at the bar and wished Sage would hurry it up. If I knew any better, he was probably inside having a few shots. Noelle was really losing it and scaring me at the same time.

"She wants me. She wants me," she repeated. It sent chills up my arms.

I rubbed her back and whispered, "Who wants you? Who is the demon in white?"

She began to whimper and rocked back and forth with more force. "I saw her. Every night I see her. She gets in my thoughts. It gets in my head. She keeps coming."

Suddenly her head sprang up and I thought my heart was going to bound out of my chest. She looked straight at me, totally sober, a pure fear sparkling in her blue eyes.

"Sage did this. He did this," she alleged in a raw, throaty voice. "He brought this on us. On me!"

My breath became ragged, the goosebumps marching along my arms.

"What did he bring?" I choked out.

She collapsed against me, and I caught the words, "monsters, monsters, all of them" coming from her lips.

Just then bright lights appeared on the street and I let out a huge breath of relief when I saw the cabbie sign on the roof.

The door to the bar swung open and Sage ran out. Before I had a chance to digest what Noelle had told me, he was at our side and lifting Noelle to her feet like a ragdoll. He waved at the car and shot a look at me.

"Aren't you coming?" he asked.

I stared at him, dumbfounded and kind of scared. What the fuck was Noelle just talking about? Sage brought this? Brought what?

"Dawn, are you all right?"

I finally found the strength to ease myself off the curb and I gave him a quick smile. "I'm fine. Let's go."

The cabbie didn't look too pleased at having to give a ride

to a drunken invalid and initially refused, but Sage stuck an extra wad of bills into his hand and that seemed to turn him around.

Once in the cab, Sage and I were engulfed in an awkward silence. At least it felt awkward to me. He smelled like whiskey so I was right about him going back in the bar and drinking, and he seemed to be lost in his own little world. Meanwhile, I went over what Noelle had been saying. Most of it was just the drunken rantings of an upset rock star, but some of it made sense. For one, she mentioned the woman in white and it was too much of a coincidence for her not to mean Sonja. But calling her a demon? Unless she meant that figuratively and I wouldn't put it past Noelle to call every woman out there the spawn of Satan.

Plus, whatever Sage brought upon all of them was pretty much everything. He was the boss, the genius, the real voice. He made the band what they were. He brought everything to Hybrid and without him there would be no band.

As for the monsters…well, that could have been figurative too. Monsters of the music industry. Groupies. Journalists. The band. Everyone was suspect, not just actual monsters. There were no such things as monsters.

But I couldn't deny the icy fingers that clamped around my chest the moment she uttered those words. I couldn't help but think of the noises that came from underneath the bunk that night I was on drugs, the sick, insect-like shadow I saw on the walls before I passed out. Of course, that was the answer: I was on drugs. That was the easy explanation. But it didn't explain this uneasiness and fear that never seemed to go away.

I looked up at Sage, his face half in shadows, half lit up in the amber glow of a passing light. It was odd to still want him after the weirdness of tonight. Maybe it was the prickles at the back of my neck or the fact that he was still a very mysterious, sensual man who was crammed up beside me in the dark. Maybe it was that I had listened to his music while lying on the floor of my bedroom for hours on end. Maybe because at heart I really was just a lowly little journalist, a college student who had no real reason to be there. Maybe it was all of those things. It didn't really matter.

Carefully, like I had the power to ruin everything with one touch, I rested my head on his meaty shoulder. It twitched, briefly, as I caught him by surprise. Then he relaxed back in his seat and I knew this was okay, if just for the ride home.

I closed my eyes.

CHAPTER TWELVE

One thing about staying on a tour bus is the lack of hygiene. Not that anyone was beginning to stink, except for Graham, but that's because he kept rubbing weird oils all over himself. But I found it frustrating that the hot water was almost always gone, so I was left with giving myself a sponge and water bath in a room the size of a closet. Thank goodness for dry shampoo, best invention of the 1970s.

My head was deep in the fruity smelling cloud of powder when I felt someone come on the bus and saw Mickey heading for the back room.

I poked my head out of the washroom and looked over at him. It was a cloudy, hot day in Philadelphia and he should have been inside doing soundcheck with the rest of the band.

"How's it going?" I asked, trying to rub the dry shampoo out of my head.

He paused when he heard me, his hand deep in a leather satchel.

"It's going," he said. Then he resumed searching for something. Seconds later he pulled out a small bag of weed. He stared at me with a defensive expression, like I was going to lecture him on drug use or something.

It occurred to me that now was the perfect time to get my Mickey interview and I knew just the way to do it.

"Aren't you supposed to be with the band?"

He frowned. "Not really. I'm too hungover to do the soundcheck. A tech is checking it for me."

"Do you mind if you smoke a bit of that with me?" I asked, making my eyes big and pleading.

"Uh...okay," he said, a bit taken aback. "I was just going to go for a walk around the building. Nothing special."

I grinned. "That's perfect! Give me a second."

I quickly ran a few drops of patchouli oil on my hair to tame the frizz then grabbed my messenger bag that had my notepad and tape recorder in it.

We left the bus, and as we strolled, I pretended that Mickey didn't make me feel extremely awkward. He was the hardest one out of the bunch to read and the one guy I felt like I never really knew. Well, unless you counted Graham. But I tried not to.

We rounded the corner, away from the backstage area, before Mickey lit up. We stopped near a loading dock and took a seat on the cement steps. The dark clouds above us looked ominous and the heat they were trapping below was stifling.

After Mickey took a few puffs, he passed it to me. I took only the smallest bit, needing to keep a sharp mind. I wanted, needed, him to open up and he was always more jovial when he was high as fuck.

A few minutes of increasingly comfortable silence flew past before I asked, "Do you mind if I interview you now?"

He snorted, smoke coming out of his nose. "Aw, man, Rusty. This was your plan wasn't it?"

"I'm just trying to make you comfortable," I said, raising my hands in peace.

"Well, you did that all right. Okay. Fine. Ask your stupid questions."

So I brought out the tape recorder and the notepad where

I had already made a list of "stupid" questions and started the interview. It was hard to be as professional as I should have been, considering I was high and laughing half the time. But Mickey was laughing too.

At least he was, until I started asking the serious questions.

"How's your relationship with Noelle?" I searched his face. The reason he was so hard to read sometimes was because he hid beneath so much facial hair. It made his expressions subtle and made him look much older than he was.

"Noe..." he started. He sighed and scratched absently at his beard. "Noe is my everything."

"How do you explain the groupies then?" I knew it was a bit of a rude, not to mention personal question, but my interviewing tactics had gotten bolder these days.

I wasn't surprised by the dirty look he gave me.

"What is that supposed to mean?"

"I mean..." I began, trying to say it properly, "you're in a relationship with the same woman for years. You're childhood sweethearts. Yet it's kinda obvious that you hook up on the road. I'm just curious as to how your relationship survives that."

He fell quiet, his sharp eyes searching the empty lot in front of us. I swallowed hard, hoping I didn't piss him off too much and waited with bated breath for him to say something, anything.

Finally he gave me a gentle smile. "I think being part of the band is the hardest fucking thing in the world. I wouldn't have survived this long if it wasn't for Noe. She's been my island since the beginning. Is she perfect? No. You see me sleeping around with the groupies but she's no angel either. Oh no. But I still love her and that's a love that doesn't go away. I know I'm not perfect either. We make our imperfectness work. If she asked me to change, I'd change for her. And she'd change for me. But we love each other too much to ask for anything more than just staying alive. Rock music, you know, bands, all this shit. It kills you. The industry kills you. Your bandmates might even kill you. Sometimes I get the feeling like this whole thing, the band, the tour, everything, I feel like it's a big joke and one day we're going to get it, and we're not going to be laughing. But Noe's part of the joke, too. So I go forward and so does she. That's how we survive. Because we have each other."

I didn't think I'd ever heard Mickey talk that much and I quickly checked my tape recorder in a mild panic, hoping it was working. It was, the wheels were turning, and I did a dance of joy inside from having just snagged a wealth of pull quotes from that one long, surprisingly heartfelt ramble.

"That's kind of beautiful, Mickey," I told him.

He held my gaze steadily. "It's the truth. Beauty or not. I love Noelle. She loves me. Noe and I aren't typical but we love and we make it work. You need love in a business like this. If you don't have love, then none of this means anything."

He put the joint out on the ground and stuffed the roach into a pack of cigarettes.

"You mind if we go back now?" He asked, getting to his feet. "I feel like a rat missing soundcheck like this."

He pulled me up by my arms and I smiled gratefully. "Thank you. It was nice to hear you speak."

"Anytime you wanna smoke a little something something, you know where to look."

I took that as a very welcoming sign.

I pressed the stop button on the recorder with a satisfying click and we walked back around the building until we were near the bus and the back doors again.

"Hey, Rusty," Chip hollered at me, sticking his head out the backstage door. "Phone's for you!"

I stopped in the middle of the parking lot and looked back at Chip.

"Who is it?"

Though unlikely, Mel or my brother could have found out what venue the band was playing at. I hoped it was them saying hello, but part of my chest froze up with a burst of worry. What if it was Dad? Maybe he got drunk and hurt himself or choked on his own vomit. What if Eric was beaten up at school and was in the hospital. What if—

"It's Barry Kramer from Creem!" Chip yelled back.

Okay. That wasn't so bad. But I had a feeling Barry didn't call you if he had good news...unless the band was going to be on the cover.

Fixating on that positive, I gave Mickey a small smile and ran across the lot, my humidity-challenged hair flowing behind me.

"Thanks," I told Chip and ran over to the payphone inside the backstage area.

"Dawn here," I said into the receiver.

"Dawn, it's Barry," he said through the line.

I swallowed hard. "Yeah. Hi, Barry, what can I do you for?"

"Oh, not too much. How are you?"

I scratched nervously at my head. "I'm good, good. Tired."

"And the band?"

"They're...you know. Good. Being themselves. Noelle got pretty drunk after the Detroit show, and out of sympathy, Mickey was plastered on stage the next night in New York. But I just got a good interview out of him, so there's that."

"I know about the New York show, I read the review in the Times," he said absently. "But that's not why I'm calling."

I scratched harder. "No?"

"Dawn...I'm playing a hunch here. Just a feeling. Normally I'm not sticking my honker in our writers' business, and hell you're not really *our* writer anyway, but I kind of like you and I just wanted to give you a heads up."

He paused and I couldn't think of anything to say.

"We've been getting some letters here at the office about you."

"About me?" I asked with widening eyes. The scratching stopped.

"Yes. I don't know who they are from and there's no return address, but they've obviously been written by some sort of fan with an agenda."

"Well, what are they saying?"

"That you're a fraud. That you're crazy and were a stalker and a groupie and all that usual shit that women like to sling at each other."

"Terri," I whispered, thinking of when she was talking to Jacob.

"As I said, I don't know her name. But this girl *thinks* she has it in with the band and the manager. She acts like she's with them, that's she's been the number one fan from the beginning. That she gets special privileges. That normally isn't any reason to call you like this, but based on the fact that I've got twenty fucking letters here from her, I'd say we've probably got a nutter on our hands. And by that I mean *you* are dealing with a nutter on your hands. I just want you to stay safe, Dawn."

Once I found my voice, I told him about Sonja, Terri, and Sparky.

"It's probably one and the same then. All bands get them and they all can't be Miss Pamela, queen of the groupie scene. But take it from me, I've been in the music journalism business for the last five years, and before that I knew more about the scene than anyone else. Sometimes fans aren't well, and the weirder and heavier the music is, the more likely they'll attract the unstable ones. Music gives birth to obsession and obsession can lead to… just watch yourself, you dig?"

"I dig," I said. "Thanks Barry."

I hung up the phone and looked around me, suddenly afraid again. I was alone under buzzing fluorescent lights, and still tired as anything. The pot had made me want to pass out but there was no way I felt like napping by myself on the bus. I shivered, totally creeped out, and made my way over to the stage to watch them finish the rest of soundcheck. I didn't want to take any chances.

✿ ✿ ✿

For the Philly show, I pretty much became Jacob's shadow. Wherever he went, I went, like a redheaded Tweedle-Dee and

Tweedle-Dum. Only when I had to go to the bathroom did I leave his side, and that's when I tagged along with Noelle.

She was nicer to me since the night in Detroit, and I'd thought she felt embarrassed or something. I never brought up the stuff she said to me about the supposed "demon in white," but there was something different about her now, like she was more aware of things around her. I was jumpy because of what Barry had told me, but so was she, and she had been like that ever since she came out of her hangover on the way to New York. She was wary, afraid, and meek. Mickey certainly noticed her change and was beating himself up over it, blaming himself for not being supportive and all that jazz. It was true, of course, but I didn't think that's what was wrong with Noelle. She was frail at heart, but by the time the second show in NYC rolled around, she wasn't looking ashamed anymore—she was looking haunted. The fear that never left her eyes worried me, and even when I thought she'd catch on that I was tagging along with her to the washroom every time, like a couple of gals at a nightclub, she didn't mind. I think she was just as scared as I was.

But were we scared of the same thing?

Eventually Jacob noticed something was going on. Or he'd always noticed and had waited for the right time to bring it up. With normal Jacob flavor, it happened to be a few minutes before the show.

"Tell me what's on your mind, Rusty," he said dryly as we stood at the side of the stage. He was running a nail file underneath his fingernails and flicking out the dirt.

"I got a call from Barry today."

"Oh?"

"He said he'd been receiving some letters about me."

"Oh?" he repeated, a bit more interested.

"If I didn't know better, I'd say that Terri or one of the other Get The Fuck Outs is behind it. It kind of gels with what you said back...well whatever city that was in. That it was groupie high school."

His golden eyes remained on his nails. "Oh yes, ain't that the truth, love."

"So, that's going on. I'm mildly freaked out." I crossed my arms, feeling a chill.

"I can see that. I don't blame you. Do you think these girls are…dangerous?" he said the last word like it was laden in silk.

I gave him a weird look. "You tell me! I've just learned who they are. You've dealt with them longer."

He exhaled sharply through his nose and finally looked me in the eye. His red hair flamed under the stage lights, giving him a hellish aura. "Everyone has the chance to become dangerous. If the right weather patterns are created, if the right feelings are invoked…feelings of injustice. Jealousy. Feelings of being owed something they believe they have a right to have. To…collect. We all have it in us to become a danger, either to others or to ourselves. It's only a matter if the right clouds are brewing. Certain clouds will create a storm."

"And?" I egged him on impatiently. "What clouds are brewing? Are these groupies dangerous or not? Do I need to start sleeping with a switchblade underneath my pillow?"

A slow smile spread across his rough lips. Then he shrugged and turned his attention back to cleaning his nails. "Couldn't hurt, could it?"

I mulled on that cryptic comment for a while and tried to pay attention to the show as Hybrid wowed the Philly audience. But I couldn't. I had this weird feeling like time was running out—probably a by-product of hanging around a pessimist like Sage who seemed to act at times like there was no tomorrow.

When the show was over and everyone was sweaty and exhausted to the core, I went to the bathroom with Noelle. While she was in the stall doing her business, I examined my face in the mirror. I had dark circles under my eyes and the nice tan that had dusted my skin during the heat of summer was dwindling. Thanks to late nights and never-ending bus rides, I was on my way to having a skin tone as appealing as a cadaver.

I sighed and blew a strand of hair out of my face.

"What's up?" Noelle asked, flushing the toilet and coming up beside me to wash her hands. She was looking tired too, maybe even worse than I was. She'd lost a lot of weight in the short time I'd known her and she'd already been skinny to begin with. Her striped sailor dress with a ripped hem hung off of her and the flowered headband she wore made her look like a wilting stalk.

"I'm just…tired," I said truthfully. "You?"

Her eyes faltered for a second, then she straightened up and eyed herself in the mirror with a hardened gaze.

"Just tired."

I felt like Noelle and I were dancing around the same subject—the same fears—but I had no idea how to approach her about it without sounding like a loon. I wouldn't even know where to start.

"I have a question," I started, trying to plan out my sentence. "About some of the groupies the band gets."

Her eyes dropped from her reflection, and she cast her gaze to the ground with lowered lids, listening.

"I think you know—" I began, but shut my mouth as soon as the bathroom door swung open and one the girlfriends of someone in Grand Funk Railroad, the band that Hybrid had opened for that night, came in. She shot us a defensive look at first but relaxed once she recognized Noelle. She gave her a shy smile and went into the stall.

I looked back to Noelle to tell her we'd talk about it later, but she was already leaving the bathroom, like she was trying to escape the subject. Given the way Mickey sometimes was with groupies, I couldn't really blame her. I followed her out the door and into the hallway. The lounge at the end was bumping tonight with tons of lucky fans and media personalities around to see Grand Funk, but by the bathrooms it was quiet and eerie.

I saw Graham leaving the lounge and heading toward us, presumably going to the boys' bathroom which was further away. Noelle and Graham didn't even acknowledge each other as they passed and he sure wasn't about to look at me. But, for some stupid reason, I thought I could get to the bottom of something tonight.

"Graham," I called and trotted after him. He wasn't much over six feet tall but he covered a lot of ground with his long, tattooed legs that were poking out of his black workman shorts.

He didn't stop and neither did I. I reached out for his shoulder just as he was about to go in the bathroom.

"What?" he snarled, whipping around to face me with hate-filled eyes. I never liked being this close to him. His skin was tight and pale, almost waxy. He was considered handsome and dark by some girls, but all I could see was a black cloud billowing deep behind those dark eyes, always watching, always spiteful. An upside down crucifix hung from his necklace, swinging along his tattooed collarbone. Always playing the part. Wasn't he?

I swallowed hard and took a few steps back. "I just wanted to ask you a few questions."

"Can it wait till I'm done pissing?" he snarled.

I nodded, a bit scared. I didn't know what I'd been thinking, ambushing him just before he went into the washroom.

He shook his head, cursing me I was sure, or damning me. He went toward the door, his hand out to push it open.

"I just wanted to know about your psycho groupies," my lips said before I even had a chance to think. Talk about poking the bear.

I clamped my mouth shut but wasn't prepared for what happened next. In a whirl of black and limbs, Graham spun around and grabbed me, his nails digging into my arms. The next thing I knew I was being slammed against the wall and he was holding me against it. His body was strong from years of wielding drumsticks and I didn't have a fighting chance to get loose.

"What the fuck is that any of your business?" he growled, his face mere inches from mine. His breath smelled rotten. His eyes flashed from within, going from a dark brown to a burning red, like it was being lit from the inside. I held my breath in fright.

"You don't even know why you're here," he uttered slowly in

a raspy, wet voice and brought his face even closer. The back of my head where it hit the wall began to throb and my arms ached from where his grip cut into the muscle. "But I do. You better forget about this story and go home. You aren't going to save him. You're not going to save any of them."

"Let me go," I said, squirming. His eyes began to go from a lit red to all black, and his pupils began to widen until his eyes were one deep hole from corner to corner.

"What the fuck are you?" I cried out, feeling horror spreading through my lungs and heart, seizing me, paralyzing me.

"A debt collector," he snarled through a mouth that began to widen to a gummy, shark-like grin, his skin cracking along the edges, blood dripping down toward pointed teeth.

Around the corner we heard the door to the bathroom open, and I took that opportunity of distraction to push Graham back enough to knee him straight into the balls.

When I was nineteen, I was attacked on campus by some potential rapist or mugger. I fought him off the best I could, but it wasn't until I kicked him right in the junk that he fell to the ground in pain and I was able to run off and call the police. I was counting on that reaction.

Graham did not fall to the ground. He didn't even register any feeling except surprise. And amusement, because the demonic fucker just smiled even more. I was living a nightmare.

"What the fuck?" Sage's voice boomed down the dark hall and in seconds he was shoving Graham off of me. Before Graham had a chance to react, Sage punched him right in the face. Graham's normal, nasty face. Whatever thing I thought I'd seen was gone and now Graham was on the ground, clutching his nose that was dripping blood on the linoleum.

Sage turned to me, holding my arms..

"Dawn, what happened? Did he hurt you?" he asked frantically. A vein pulsed on his tense throat.

I shook my head no, then yes, then no, and feeling a torrent of tears building up inside me, I shrugged Sage's hands off and ran down the hallway, leaving him behind to yell after me then say to Graham, "You fuck, what did you do to her?"

I pushed my way past the crowd in the lounge, getting a few looks of concern and sympathy. I looked like nothing more than a girl who was tripping or crying over a rock star's rejection, and in seconds I burst through the back doors, past security and all the way into the parking lot. The bus was the last place I wanted to be, so I booked it past the main security gate, my vision blurry with tears, and ran out into the open road, where a few late concertgoers were trying to find parking on the grassy curbside.

I ran blindly for a few meters and then collapsed underneath a cherry tree. I was lucky the venue was a bit out of the city and I didn't have to face too many curious passers-by. I leaned back against the tree and let it all out, everything that had been cooped up in my heart for the last week. The fears, the shame, the feelings of inadequacy, the confusion. The feeling that I was in way over my head, alone on the road with no one I could really trust. Everyone seemed to have an agenda, and I was the only one open and honest about mine. I was scared, scared to the bone. I was scared about failing. I was scared of the unknown. And I was scared I was slowly losing my mind. There was another two weeks left of the tour. How on earth was I going to survive? When was I going to throw in the towel?

I cried, ugly and bawling, for who knows how long. I didn't come up with any answers. I just missed my dad, my brother, and Mel more than anything in the world and felt an ache spread in my stomach.

"Hey," I heard a voice say in the darkness and the sound of flip-flops that followed.

I looked up and wiped my eyes,. Sage stood above me for a looming second before he crouched down to my level. He looked me over with quiet concern, then took his hand and stroked my hair softly. "I've been looking for you."

I closed my eyes and leaned back against the tree. I felt him sit down and lean against the tree beside me. It would have been a funny sight for a concertgoer, the guitarist of the opening band sitting on the side of the road with his trademark open black shirt and flip-flops.

"Do you want to talk about it?" he asked.

I shook my head.

"Can I talk about it?"

I shrugged, too tired now to care.

"Graham...," he started. He paused, trying to find the words. I opened my eyes and turned my head to look at him. He was plucking grass out of the ground and tossing it at the road.

"Graham wasn't always like this," he continued. "When we first started out...he was an answer to...he was a really good drummer and we needed a good drummer. I think...I know, actually...that the moment I got on guitar and the moment we got Graham on drums was the moment Hybrid really began. There was no stopping us. And...I felt in debt to Graham. He was always an oddball. Rough around the edges, didn't have too many redeeming qualities to be honest. But he worked well with us as a whole. He kept to himself and when it came time to do his job, he did it well. He was never one to get hooked on drugs. He was never late to rehearsal. He was as steady as a drummer should be. He certainly was no Bonzo."

He paused and gathered his thoughts. The headlamps of a passing car lit us up with garish light for one second before plunging us into obscurity again.

"He was interested in the occult since high school. None of us took him seriously. Then as Black Sabbath and Alice Cooper got more popular, he started to indulge in it more. He wanted to make it his thing. He believes it..."

"Do you believe it?" I whispered.

He furrowed his dark brows. "I don't know what I believe anymore. If there's black magic and white magic, this is one big gray area."

"Is he human?" I asked.

Sage snorted loudly and shot me a bewildered look. I suppose that sort of question deserved it. "Is he human? What…of course he's human, Dawn. He's someone I wouldn't mind punching in the face again, but he's human. He's a human being. Why? What happened between you guys?"

I sighed, feeling a little bit stupid. Part of me wanted to believe that I saw his face contort into that of a demonic hellbeast, and part wanted to blame it on paranoia, stress, and sleep deprivation. "He…got all angry and like threw me against the wall and got all up in my face. I just asked him about the groupies. I may have called them psychos."

"That doesn't matter," Sage said angrily. "They are fucking psychos. And the only reason they never leave is because he keeps inviting them around. Do you know how many times during the last tour I discovered he had given them All Access Passes?"

"They're after you too, you know," I told him.

His eyes hardened like steel. "Believe me, I know."

He looked off at the auditorium as the reverberation from Grand Funk filled the air, his jaw wiggling back and forth. A light breeze came along and softly tossed up his black curls.

"What do you want me to do?" he said, his voice flat and emotionless.

"What do you mean?"

"He has no right to put his hands on you like that. No right to talk to you like that. If you want him off this tour, just give me the word and I'll do it. Believe me, I'll do it. It would be my pleasure."

His offer caught me off-guard. He would kick a lifelong member of the band off the tour…if I asked? He'd do that for me?

I watched him carefully, trying to see why he'd do it. "You'd have no drummer."

"We can always get another drummer," he said with a dry laugh. "We're one of the more popular bands on the road right now. We could probably even get someone big to fill his shoes."

I should have said yes. I should have asked Sage to get rid of Graham. But there was that nagging doubt in the back of my mind that I was just a girl and I was overreacting. If Sage kicked Graham off the tour for someone like me, well that would indeed go down in history. I couldn't ask for that weight on my shoulders.

"Don't kick him off," I told him.

He didn't look happy at that prospect. "Are you sure?"

"Yes, just…make sure he stays away from me. You can bet I won't be doing his interview anymore."

"So you're staying?" he asked, sounding surprised.

"I'm not going anywhere."

"Dawn…" he warned.

"Sage," I retorted. "I don't run away. Remember? You said things have a way of finding you anyway."

He watched me for a few moments and his closeness brought about the smell of pipe tobacco that he kept rolled up in his shirt pocket, the tobacco I never saw him smoke. He exhaled, a sigh of acceptance.

"That may be right. But that doesn't mean I have to like it." His expression grew serious and he leaned a few inches closer to me. In the dark, beside me on the grass, he was more brooding, more manly, more mysterious than ever before. Another breeze wafted over us, smelling like foliage and heat, and tousled his hair ever so lightly. Once again my body became electric with nerves, and my lips tingled at the idea of being kissed. It was hard not to think about that when his face was so close, his lips so full, his eyes sexual and somber all at once. I loathed myself for feeling this way.

"Dawn," he said gravely. "I want you to promise me something. Promise me that the first sign of things getting… fucked up…weird…too much…that you'll go home."

I opened my mouth to protest, to tell him things were already fucked up, weird, and too much, but he went on.

"Just listen, please. I know you hate the idea of going home, but you've caught a lot of shows, spent a lot of time on the road, you've interviewed most of the band. You've really got everything you need."

"I haven't interviewed you," I pointed out. "And you're the most important piece of the puzzle."

"I'm the most broken piece of the puzzle," he spat out. He quickly composed himself and tried to smile. It didn't reach his eyes. "If I give you an interview soon, will you think about packing it in? That doesn't mean you're quitting, it just means you're done."

"Why do you want me to leave so badly?" I asked, stung.

Silence swamped us like the thick humidity.

Finally he said, quiet and husky, "I have too many things to worry about. I don't want to worry about you."

"You don't need to worry about me," I told him. I smoothed down my hair and shirt and put on a sober face.

"You're stubborn and you're scared," he said, smiling just enough to make his cheeks rise, dimples found in the scruffy two-day beard on his face. "It's a dangerous combination."

"I hear the world's a dangerous place," I replied.

He got to his feet and held his hand out for me. I returned his smile and put my hand in his, relishing the strength and warmth as he closed it over mine and pulled me to my feet.

"Come on," he said, pulling me along. He let go of my hand when he was satisfied I would follow. "Let me go have another word with Graham. I plan on breaking every bone in his body except his arms and legs. Hybrid needs those."

We walked back to the auditorium in a comfortable silence. In my head I kept repeating what Graham had said to me when he had me pinned up against the wall.

"You can't save him. You can't save any of them."

CHAPTER THIRTEEN

I woke up to a weird slurping noise in the middle of the night, followed by a shaking of the bunk. I had my curtain drawn across, but even then I knew it was entirely dark on the bus and that it was in motion. I heard Bob at the driver's seat, shifting gears as the bus climbed the hills that cluttered around southern Virginia.

I held my breath, listening for that slurping sound again, terrified of the monsters, real or imagined. Then I heard a sucking noise, followed by a groan. I'd heard that groan before. It was Robbie, in the bunk below.

I drew back the curtain and poked my head over the side. In the dim light I could see Robbie. Well, I saw parts of him. He was 69-ing with a rather porky-looking broad, her giant ass pulled apart by his hands, the white skin of it shining in the bits of passing light from the highway.

I gritted my teeth in anger and fell back into bed, putting the pillow over my face. I was dealing with Graham being an abusive asshole, potentially dangerous groupies, and shadowy Sage, and yet Robbie was still Robbie and managed to sneak some random chick on the bus for the journey down to the Charlotte Music Festival. I wished I was so carefree and clueless.

By 9AM, most of the people on the bus were up, except for Graham, thank god, who slept in the latest since he went to bed the latest. I knew Sage had given him a talking to last night when we returned to the venue, and I was glad I got to bed without having to face him. One look under the night sky and I would have sworn he was turning into a monster again.

I hopped off the bunk and got my first look at the smuggled groupie. She was sitting next to Robbie at the table, across from Noelle and Mickey, drinking a cup of freshly brewed coffee. She wasn't as large as I had originally thought, just soft and curvy, the type of body I could easily have if I didn't watch what I ate. She had honey blonde hair and green eyes and a cherubic face that wasn't very sexual or cunning at all. She looked nice, and she was wearing one of Robbie's t-shirts, stretched across her breasts. She caught my eye as I walked over and gave me a demure smile.

Behind the eating booth, Jacob sat on the bench flipping through newspapers. He spoke to me without looking up. "Someone better introduce Rusty."

Sage was lying down on the couch with his eyes closed, a book on his chest, his shirt raised enough so that I could see trails of dark stomach hair snaking down toward his pants and hand-tooled belt. I tried not to stare and looked back at the new girl.

"I'm Dawn," I said, trying to push both my thoughts about Sage and my anti-groupie feelings away.

"Don't listen to her," Robbie spoke up with a cheeky grin. "Her real name is Rusty. Rusty, this is Emeritta."

Over the next hour, as the bus rolled through the trees toward the festival site on the banks of the Catawba River, I learned that Emeritta was actually a pretty cool chick. She was from Boston and was a huge fan of everything loud and gritty. She loved MC5, Sabbath, Vanilla Fudge, Iron Butterfly, and most of all, Hybrid. She gushed to Robbie about how his yapping howls in "Freedom Run" made her think of a dog in heat, and that the first time she saw them live, she almost came. She said it in a fit of giggles, which was quite endearing, and her own face went pink at her frankness. Most of all, Emeritta was kind and really listened to you when you were speaking. It made me feel a little ashamed for branding so many groupies a slut. I mean, yeah she slept with Robbie and I had a feeling she slept with a lot of rock stars, but a slut is a name you give a girl you don't like. I liked Emeritta and was happy she was coming with us to Charlotte...and any other place after that, depending on how quickly Robbie discarded her.

By the time the bus was pulling up to the festival and lining up with all the other tour buses, the band had found their newfound energy and everyone was getting pretty excited. Graham only came out of the back room near the end, and to his credit, he stayed as far away from me as possible. I caught Sage shooting him wary glances from time to time but Graham took on a very hangdog, meek appearance. I, however, didn't believe it for a second. I could still sense that black violence rolling around in his soul...if he even had one.

I could tell this was going to be a special show by the amount of whiskey and Bailey's Jacob was pouring into his coffee. The festival was still sleepy this early in the afternoon, but the breeze of the river was deliciously cool and the air was swamped with a sensual headiness, punctuated by the sun that shone high in the sky and sparkled off the trees. The backstage area wasn't some dingy dressing room or cramped lounge, but a bunch of mobile trailers scattered about in a pastoral setting behind the big stages. All of us, including Emeritta, walked through the grassy field now turned a miniature town of musicians. We passed trailers marked for Earth, Wind & Fire, Deep Purple, and The Eagles. We saw the wide-mouthed Steven Tyler of the band Aerosmith having a beer on his trailer steps, and spotted Bob Seger and Randy Bachman chatting up a few gorgeous blonde women.

The Hybrid trailer was just as big as the other ones, and our neighbor, who was playing an acoustic in his doorway, was none other than Ted Nugent. Even Sage was impressed and immediately went over to introduce himself.

Despite the ups and downs and nagging sense of doom that

permeated my thinking as of late, the festival was turning me around. It was impossible not to smile, and I was glad Emeritta, someone as star-struck as I was, was there with me. We both took many walks together up and down that grass alley between the trailers, trying to look into windows (subtly, of course) and listen to what music was coming from what trailer. It was what I imagined Hollywood was like.

While we did our rounds in the steaming sun, squealing at the hello we got from a killer-mustached Jon Lord, I got to know Emeritta a little better. Now that she wasn't surrounded by one of her favorite bands, she was more forthcoming.

"So what do you think about the other groupies out there?" I asked, trying to convey sincerity.

She laughed and tucked her hair behind her ears in a nervous gesture. "First of all, we hate that term. I know Zappa and Miss Pamela made it all cool and stuff, but I'm just a rock lover. A lover of rock. I love with my ears and my body."

I nodded, trying to figure out how not to insult her further. "I guess groupie doesn't have to be a negative term though."

"No, it doesn't, but I know the way girls like you say it."

I raised my brow but let her go on.

"You seem to forget all about the women's movement. We're free to love who we are and when we want to. A lot of us just happen to love rock stars. It doesn't have to be bad. The bands love us. Everyone should be happy, don't you think?"

"Sure," I mused, seeing her logic. We sat down at a splintered picnic table along the fence. You could hear fans on the other side, trying to see over it or find a knothole to look through. I felt immensely cool, a feeling I thought I had lost. I relished it.

"See," Emeritta said, beaming at me. "You love too, just differently. I know how you feel because I feel the same way right now. It's far out. And when I'm with the men, I feel far out then too. But ten times more. You haven't hooked up with anyone from the band?"

I hoped I wasn't blushing. The last thing Emeritta needed

to hear was that I hooked up with Robbie. It was something that made me feel dirty and ashamed, and though she probably wouldn't have cared, *I* cared.

"No," I lied. "That's against the journalism oath."

"They make you take an oath?"

"I took my own oath. Thou shalt not touch rock stars."

"Tough oath you got there. I'd last five minutes. I heard that the first female journalist who went on the road with Led Zeppelin got raped by Bonzo."

"That's just a rumor," I dismissed, knowing the fabled story. "Bonzo's just a drunken teddy bear."

She grinned, her teeth small and crooked on the bottom.

I rolled my eyes but smiled. "Let me guess, you slept with Bonzo."

"No, I didn't. And I know he didn't rape anyone. He just got super feisty with the journalist. He gets like that. He did, however, fuck me with a champagne bottle."

I nearly burst out laughing. "Okay, I just met you, Emeritta. I don't need to know all your details."

She shrugged, clearly unfazed. "It's a pity you took your oath. Wouldn't Sage be fun for a night?"

I couldn't help but glare a little. "I wouldn't know."

"Oh, me neither," she quickly said, showing her palms in peace. "Sage isn't the groupie type. I've heard the occasional hook-up story, and I think he was with Miss Pamela for a while, just fuck friends, but he's the unattainable lone wolf of the rock circuit. Just in case you were thinking about it."

"Well I wasn't." I was really starting to hate Miss Pamela and her ways. If I was being honest with myself, I was jealous.

"You ladies want a beer?" a voice called out.

We looked over to see Randy Bachman walking toward us with two Coronas in his hands. He had an affable way about him, one of those non-threatening musicians, which I guess they all are when they're from Canada.

He stopped by our table and handed us both a beer, which

we accepted graciously. We made small talk for a few minutes while I tried really hard to be professional and not gush about The Guess Who, knowing he probably didn't want to talk about his ex-band.

After he left to go join Fred Turner, I shot Emeritta a look.

"You thinking about him?" I joked.

She shrugged again. "Not at the festival, but he's kind of cute. Why not?"

There I was back to not understanding her mentality. We finished our beers and began the hot walk back to the trailer, the grass tickling my bare legs. I realized she'd never answered my original question.

"So, back to this, what do you think about the other groupies...rock lovers...out there?"

She seemed to chew on that for a bit. Literally chewing on a piece of her blonde hair.

"It's a dog-eat-dog world, that's what," she admitted with downcast eyes. "At the beginning, girls were a lot nicer to each other. It was all about the music and we were all in it together. Then the groupie scene kind of exploded thanks to that stupid Groupie movie. Now you'll find girls who pretend to be your friend. You know the ones who say things like, "How are you, darling, I heard you had a flood in your neck of the woods, I was thinking about you and hoped you were okay," or something else said out of fake concern. But they only say that shit when you're in public and there's lots of people around to see it, and then they go and talk behind your back. They only want people—musicians and famous people especially—to think they are oh so nice while they go and spread rumors about you when you're not looking. That's what I think about other groupies. No one helps or loves anyone anymore. It's every *fan* for themselves."

I was surprised to hear her rant like that, but there was a sense of relief to her face, like she hadn't been able to confide in anyone for years. I was slowly but surely finding out that all the fun parts of the music scene weren't exactly as they seemed.

* * *

Given that realization, when we got back to the trailer I wasn't too surprised to find Robbie doing a line of coke with Jacob and Noelle, the white stuff sorted out on the faux-wood dinette table. None of them looked ashamed and just continued to snort the stuff up using a twenty-dollar bill that Jacob had provided. Jacob, who was wearing a yellow and brown suit despite the heat, gave me one of his "I am what I am" looks and carried on.

I tried to ignore the disgust I felt (they had a festival to play, shouldn't that have been enough excitement?), and I walked into the rear of the trailer and flopped down on the cheap green couch beside Chip who was lying down and drinking a can of Pepsi. Sage, Graham, and Mickey were nowhere to be found. I heard Robbie offer Emeritta a hit but she refused, saying she never did hard drugs. I liked her even more after that.

Hybrid's set was on the second biggest of the three stages, with the coveted sunset slot. I was going stir-crazy in the hot trailer, and convinced Chip to explore the festival with me and catch some lesser known acts (Emeritta and Robbie disappeared into the back room of the trailer, so there was no point waiting for her). The rest of the band seemed to want to stay on the bus with that one measly rotating fan. I'd later figure out that they were nervous and hiding. Playing to a crowd that's not specifically there to see you was always a challenge to them, a band that too easily judged their talent by the crowd's reaction.

Chip was good company and knew a lot more about some of the bands than I did and loved to flex his "I know everyone" muscle. We drank beer and enjoyed the sunshine, mingling with other roadies and sound techs as well as the general public—scruffy-bearded men and women in flowery dresses. There was an overall stench of marijuana and body odor in the air, though the occasional breeze wafted by carrying the smell of hot dogs, dirt, and river water. The Catawba River was the place to be in between sets, and we sat by the muddy banks, watching a bunch of stoned hippies run into the water naked and shrieking.

As fun and carefree as the setting was however, that didn't stop me from glancing around every chance I got. I was looking for Sonja, Terri, or Sparky, my eyes fixating on every pale blonde or spiky-haired brunette I saw. I wondered if they were here, hiding and waiting, and if they were, what they would do to me. Of course, there was a big chance they wouldn't do anything— their bark could have been worse than their whorish bite. But I wasn't going to take any chances; Jacob didn't tell me they *weren't* dangerous, and Sage, in all his vague glory, was definitely leaning toward that option too. Maybe it would just be name-calling and hair-pulling (which I would win at), or perhaps something worse. I shuddered a bit at the thought and Chip mistook that for a chill and put his arm around me.

"Is my Rusty doing okay?" he asked, steering me back toward Hybrid's stage. He was going to have to set up and check the levels soon. The sun was low in the sky and the air temperature was dropping to a more tolerable level.

I smiled awkwardly but let him keep his arm there. Chip was harmless, and I felt like a little extra protection couldn't hurt.

Hybrid went on to an electric and moody atmosphere. The sky was darkening, a mixture of bright reds and purples as the glowing sun began its descent toward the horizon. Bats appeared, flittering above the crowd's head, followed by the flowery, cooling smell that comes with dusk after a hot day. I spent the first few songs at the side stage, gawking at the members of REO Speedwagon before Emeritta dragged me down into the crowd where we could experience the show as it was supposed to be seen.

I didn't know why Hybrid was nervous at all, or if perhaps that tension made them play that much better, but it was the best show of the tour. Absolutely. Determined to knock the socks off of the crowd, they gave it all they had. Robbie strutted around like a peacock, wailing into the mic like his life depended on it, his tight pants, open fringed vest, and winning smile causing the women to shriek and fan themselves. Sage and Mickey worked with each other, walking right up to one other during the harder parts, like a riff-off, only they were smiling for once and enjoying it. From my viewpoint I couldn't see Graham and for that I was glad, but I could hear his monstrous sound and that was enough for me. The only one who seemed off-kilter was Noelle. She held her own with a nervous, hunched over stance, and a few times I was certain she was going to mess up, but she pulled through and so did the band.

It really was a prime example of the band's energy and musicianship. They introduced a never-played before cover of "Purple Haze" which made the crowd go bonkers, and they ended with "Wet Lips" which they extended from three minutes to fifteen, jamming without a care in the world. I looked at the dude next to me, and he had his eyes closed, moving to the unpredictable beat, his face lit up with a spacey smile. I heard murmurs spread through the audience, things like "far-out," "cool city," "awesome," and "best set of the festival." Hybrid wowed their fans and earned new ones in the making. Troubles aside, I was honored to be a part of it. The band really had me on a roller coaster ride.

Finally, Hybrid was pretty much forced off the stage and REO Speedwagon took over, probably wondering how they were going to top that. Emeritta and I made our way through the clustered, intoxicated crowd toward the backstage gates when Sage came out of them, heading toward us.

"Robbie's looking for you," Sage said to Emeritta. Beads of sweat rolled down the sides of his head, his black curls sticking damply to his skin. His coal-colored shirt was soaked through and it clung to every well-formed muscle. I had to wonder how on earth Sage managed to keep up a body like that when he was playing music all the time. Did he do sit-ups and bench presses in his sleep?

Emeritta grinned like a girl in love and gave me a sly (almost *too* sly) wave before skipping off toward the gate, her giant boobs swinging from side to side.

"She's great, isn't she?" I commented. I looked up at Sage who was watching her go with amusement.

"As far as groupies go, yes, she's great."

"I thought bands loved groupies."

He gave me a funny look. "When you deal with the psychopaths, you get burned out on groupies as a whole. Want to go listen to some good music and get a hot dog?"

I was startled by the invitation. "What, now? Don't you want to shower?"

He lifted up his arm and sniffed. "I think I smell better than most people here. Don't tell me Miss Emerson is afraid of a little sweat."

Was there an innuendo in those words? I couldn't tell. So I did what I normally do in these situations: I laughed nervously.

"Besides there's an act here I don't want to miss. Ever heard of Tom Waits?"

I thought about it and we slowly made our way back into the crowd, toward the food vendors. People stared at Sage as we walked past, not believing their eyes.

"Yeah, I've heard of him. Haven't listened though. Doesn't seem like my kind of music, and I don't know, debut albums aren't always the best."

He scratched at his sideburns, green eyes glowing incredulously. "That's where you're wrong. To really understand music, to love it for what it is, you have to be open-minded and go into everything thinking you might find a new part of yourself. It can only make your heart bigger."

Now it was my time to give him an incredulous look. He was being borderline corny again and yet…I was eating it up.

We stopped to get our hot dogs, people in the line moving aside for him like he was an ice-breaking ship. A few of them told him how wicked the show was, others gawked, a few looked at me with interest, and others shot me dirty looks. I threw back my shoulders and stood proudly beside him. I was the journalist and he was the subject and this was his kingdom. When we got our dogs, mine piled with extra relish, he took my hand in his and led me through the mob toward a smaller stage. My skin vibrated at his touch, like static or musical waves.

He didn't let go of me until we found a place at the back of the crowd, everyone hushed together in front of us, strangers in the dark. The stage was small and dimly lit with red and yellow lights. Despite my height, I could barely see Tom Waits and his ragtag band, but I heard them. Not at first, I was too wrapped up in having the hulking Sage standing right next to me, his hand by his side, so close to my hand that now felt cold without his touch. But after a few choruses of "I Hope That I Don't Fall In Love With You" I really *heard* him. His raw voice was subtle, the composition simple, but it grabbed me. I looked up at Sage and he was already staring at me with a knowing smile in his eyes. I held them for a few seconds, lost in the specks of gray-green that shone through the darkening sky.

He was the first to look away. He eyed the stage. "Can you see?"

I shook my head and tried to step up on my tip-toes. We were too far behind the crowd and the stage was too low and small. "It's okay though."

He glanced beside him then patted at his round shoulders. "Want to come up here?"

"What, on your shoulders?"

He grinned and shrugged. "Yeah, why not? Everyone else is doing it."

The idea of a 5'9" girl sitting on a 6'4" guy made me want to laugh. We'd be the brontosaurus of the festival. The acid trippers would see us and freak the hell out.

But Sage was asking me to sit on him. There was no way I would turn that down.

"Okay...sold," I said, trying to fight the grin that threatened my face.

He crouched down on the grass, ready for me to climb on top. I bit my lip and went for it. I put both legs on either side of his head, totally conscious of him being engulfed by my bare skin and hot pants. He wobbled a bit and grabbed my legs with his arms.

"Are you ready?" he asked. By now the people in front of us were turning around and watching us with drunken interest.

"Go for it," I told him, grabbing onto his head. His hair was so unbelievably soft, and I let my hands get lost in it, thankful that it was thick and I had lots to hold onto.

When I was eleven, my father took me to the Ellensburg Fair. They had camel rides and I begged him to let me go on one. You get on the camel when it's lying on all fours on the ground and you hold onto the hump for dear life while the handler gets the camel to rise awkwardly to its feet. There's a few terrifying moments where you're certain you're going to go flying head over beast, but then you're rising up into the sky like a queen.

That's what it was like when Sage straightened up. I yelped and held onto his head and hair for dear life, yanking it back more than he would have liked, certain I was going to come crashing down on the crowd around us, who were watching us in a daze. But I managed to stay on and when Sage was steady, I felt like James Cagney—"Made it! Top of the world, ma!" There were a few polite claps from around us and one guy said, "Right on!" so I wasn't the only one impressed.

"Areymdojffhh," Sage mumbled.

"What?" I asked, leaning down. I then realized my thighs were gripping the sides of his face so tight that he wasn't able to speak properly. I loosened them and apologized.

"No problem," he said, taking in a deep breath and tightening his hold on my calves. His hands were deliciously firm. "I asked if you were okay."

"I'm great," I said. For once, how could I not be? I was high in the air on the shoulders of Sage Knightly, watching over a hushed and attentive crowd while Tom Waits sung to the crowd.

163

He was sitting down by his piano, an acoustic guitar in his arms, an interesting looking man that packed the same kind of beast-like heat as the man under me. His voice was emotive and raw.

"So goodbye, so long, the road calls me dear
And your tears cannot bind me anymore,
And farewell to the girl with the sun in her eyes
Can I kiss you, and then I'll be gone."

I closed my eyes and let the words and music wash over me, feeling the taught shoulders beneath my legs and his soft hair that tickled my thighs. The night air was thick and humid, everything slowed down and sensual, yet my heart was ramming against my ribcage a million miles a minute.

"Though I held in my hand, the key to all joy
Honey my heart was not meant to be tamed."

Sage shifted beneath me. I put one of my hands back into his thick hair and left it there, pretending I needed to hold him. It took all my willpower not to start playing with it.

"I guess you don't do this very often," I told him, my voice cracking slightly.

I couldn't see his face but I could feel him smile. "No. Usually my head's turned the other way around."

My body flushed from the top of my cheeks right down to my loins. I was suddenly very aware of the pressure on my clit as the blood started to pool there and throb against his head. Sage had just put some incredibly erotic images in my head, and within seconds I was transformed into a hormonal mess. This wasn't good at all. But my body had other ideas and it made my mind conjure up a fantasy of Sage lying me down in the tall grass, amongst the concertgoers, ripping off my shorts, and licking me from the inside out.

As if he sensed the lust permeating from me, he began to run one hand up and down my calf, very softly, very slowly, while still keeping me aloft.

We stood like that for the remainder of the show, his strong fingers stroking my skin, still hot from the sun, while I squirmed uncomfortably, fighting the urges that were building up inside me. Having a man's head between your legs wasn't the best time to start wondering what he looked like naked, if his cock was as large as it seemed to be when he was wearing tighter pants, if his ass and legs were just as sculpted as his upper body. I was never like this when I was with Ryan, but Ryan had never been a man and with him I'd never really been a woman. I wanted to feel like a woman now, and with the one man who could do it for me.

This was getting ridiculous. I attempted to bring up a neutral subject.

"So how did you learn of this Tom Waits fella?"

He tried to shrug. It was hard with me up there.

"He's on the same label as us. They gave me a copy of the album, and after one listen I was hooked. Fucking hooked. I just...I wish I could do something like he does, you know? He doesn't care. I've seen him so many times and he just doesn't care what mold he fits into. He's as honest and authentic as they get."

It was weird to hear Sage wax poetic about someone else. Like he envied him.

"Can't you do the same?"

He laughed, quietly. "I've tried. That's what Molten Universe was all about. One last attempt to do what I want."

I raised my brow. "One last attempt?"

He cleared his throat. "I mean, it hasn't gone over well with the band. Critics love it, but the fans are a bit iffy, I can tell. They don't want us to play the new tracks live, they want the old tracks. They want what we are known for. If I branched out and did stuff on my own...oh, I doubt the fans would follow me."

"I'd follow you," I admitted.

Silence. Tom Waits went onto dulcet piano tones.

Finally he said, "Thank you, Dawn. I really should be happy for the support I do get...it's the curse that comes with success, I suppose. At first you want anyone, just anyone, to listen to you.

Then you get that anyone, you get mostly everybody, then you want the critics to pay attention to you. Then you get the critics, but it's not good enough. You want more. You want to push the boundaries and damn if the world decides to not watch."

You'd think I wouldn't be able to relate to the gripes of a rock star, yet I could. Deep down inside it was about being validated. I needed my own validation as much as he did.

We elapsed into pensive thought and watched the remainder of the show. He never stopped stroking my leg.

CHAPTER FOURTEEN

After Tom Waits played to a quiet close, I reluctantly climbed off of Sage's shoulders and onto the soft, dewy grass below.

"Thanks for that," I said, suddenly feeling awkward in his presence. It probably had to do with the increasingly naughty thoughts I had during the concert, like my libido was being woken after a long hibernation. Or maybe for the first time ever. I could still feel his calloused hands on my calves.

He gave me a small smile, one that barely pulled on his lips, and nodded at the main stage. "Want to head back? See how everyone else is doing?"

"You don't want to meet Mr. Tom Waits? I'm sure you can arrange that," I pointed out.

He shook his head. "It's dangerous to meet your idols. You'll always be disappointed."

I chewed on that as we made our way back to the main stage. It was getting late and the last act was going on to a packed crowd. We didn't really notice anything was amiss until we saw the flashing lights coming from the trailers and a group of people at the security gates trying to see what was going on.

A terrible, sinking feeling dropped in my stomach. This

wasn't good. I knew it.

Sage and I exchanged a panicked look. He grabbed my hands, and in moments we were running through the crowd, trying to fight our way to the gate. The closer we got, the more chaotic the scene. There was an ambulance on the other side, parked outside of our trailer. Through the chain link gate I could see a bunch of people standing around it. Anguished cries filled the air. In the distance was the eerie sound of another emergency vehicle.

Once we managed to get past the onlookers and the head-up-his-ass security guard, we broke into a run straight for the Hybrid trailer. Musicians, big and small, famous and not, roadies and special access people were all huddled around, talking gravely to each other. I ignored them and we made our way to the open door where medics and first aid officers were milling about.

"What's going on?" Sage asked a medic, the terror in his voice squeezing his vocal chords.

"Are you part of the band?" he asked, blocking the door.

I could tell Sage wanted to say, "I am the band!" but before he could Mickey's voice rang out from inside.

"Sage! Let him in, he's our guitarist."

The medic looked chagrined as we pushed through. I could tell he wanted to stop me from going in but decided against it.

I wished he had stopped me.

I wished I could scrub clean my eyes from what I saw next.

In the middle of the floor was Emeritta. She was lying on her back, arms sprawled above her. Blood pooled beneath her nose. Her once alive and alert eyes were rolled back in her head. She was pale as death. She was death.

I put my hand to my mouth and felt everything go in slow motion. It wasn't a sudden sense of loss or grief but a shocked unfeeling, like someone had applied a numbing agent to my heart. There was Emeritta, dead on the floor of Hybrid's trailer and all I could do was blink. Finally I took a seat at the table beside Noelle who was watching everything with a dazed expression. I couldn't tell if she was high or in the same boat as I was.

Mickey was in the corner of the trailer, his arm around Robbie who was crying. Seeing tears flowing from the bloodshot eyes of one of the more affable men around delivered a jab to my insides, causing my breath to hitch. I hated it when men cried. It reminded me too much of my father.

"What happened?" Sage cried out.

A first-aider pushed him back as he tried to get to Robbie.

"She overdosed," the first-aider said.

"That's a lie!" Robbie cried out. "She never touched the drug. I left her to use the bathroom. I was only gone a couple of minutes. She wouldn't have used it. She was against drugs!"

He collapsed into a fit and Mickey had to calm him down again. Sage was absolutely bewildered as he looked between Robbie and the body on the floor. For all intents and purposes, it looked exactly like Emeritta had overdosed, but I too heard what she said to Robbie earlier, that she didn't do hard drugs. Perhaps that was just a front and she was an addict deep inside. Maybe she wanted to do it to impress Robbie. There was no way of knowing.

The police didn't look at it that way. The minute they showed up, shoving their way into the trailer, you could tell they were itching to arrest a few rock stars. Even though the festival was packed with likeminded people, most people in the South weren't at all accepting of long-haired rock musicians. At one conservative diner we stopped at it was a scene straight out of Bob Seger's "Turn the Page": *You always seem outnumbered; you don't dare make a stand.* You knew the cops were going to make hell for Hybrid, just as they made hell for Zeppelin years before.

The first thing they did was grab Robbie and Mickey and haul them out of the building for questioning. Despite Noelle's cries of protest that she and Mickey weren't even around when it happened, they weren't going to let the shaggy-haired, bearded Mickey out of their grasp. They almost got Sage too, one cop asking if they should question the "half-breed hippie" until the medic told them he and I had just showed up.

Sage's face flared with indignation—whether it was because he was called a hippie or a half-breed, I don't know—but he couldn't do anything, and if he tried, he'd be questioned too. So we could only watch while two members of Hybrid were taken away and only he and Noelle remained. Soon the cops cleared out everyone who wasn't a coroner or a paramedic, and we found ourselves surrounded by the local media and questioning onlookers. Sage refused to deal with anyone except for Jacob, who took him off into the darkness to talk. One reporter with a camera in tow tried to approach them, and Jacob grabbed the woman's microphone and tossed it on top of Ted Nugent's trailer.

I stayed behind, trying to blend into the black surroundings. By now all the musicians had retired to their own areas, perhaps paranoid of impending drug searches. I found no comfort in the gossip of the people who remained, talking about Emeritta like it was inconsequential for a groupie to die, like she had asked for it. I had only known her a day but it still burned deep inside. And if I was being honest with myself, something just didn't sit right. Though it was totally possible, I didn't believe she had actually died of an overdose. It was too bad you couldn't convince people on your own gut feeling.

I hugged myself, feeling the humidity shift to chilled air. I had nowhere to go, so I wandered around the back of the trailer, trying to compose my thoughts. It was too fresh and her body was still inside the trailer—it was going to take a long time before the reality of it all would sink in. I remembered what had happened when I found my mother dead in the bathroom all those years ago—I was in a delirious stupor for weeks. The blocking mechanism in my head was busy at work again.

I was alone in the dark back here. Or so I thought. The crime scene investigator's flash caused light to burst from the tiny windows, and in one illumination I caught the face of Graham standing at the rear of the trailer, a few paces in front of me. In that flash I saw his pale face smiling gruesomely. It went black again, and in the next flash, he was gone.

* * *

It was lucky we didn't have a show the next day, seeing as we had to wait around in Charlotte until Robbie and Mickey were released from custody. We all slept on the bus—Bob had parked it in an empty department store parking lot on the outskirts of the city since Sage wanted us off the festival property and as far away from it as possible.

No one slept well. The bus echoed with deep swallows, sighs, and the occasional murmur. Ironically, the only person who did seem to sleep was Graham. But after seeing him smiling in the dark like that, nothing about him surprised me anymore.

I tossed and turned all night, staring up at the roof, trying to come to terms with things. My heart and my brain were having a battle over what to focus on. My heart ached for Emeritta, and her death was hitting me harder than perhaps it should have. Part of it was just the shock, the other part was the loss of someone I really liked. Then my brain came in and started dwell on the hows and the whys. And when all was said and done, it wanted to think about Graham. The goateed man sleeping on the couch, snoring heavily, seemingly unaffected by any of this. It wanted to think about the things he had said to me, that he was a debt collector. It wanted to think about what I saw when I looked at him. That image of his face contorting into one of a monster's rolled over and over again in my head. It didn't matter how many times I told myself I imagined it, that it was a product of stress and lack of sleep and repeated exposure to very loud music. I kept seeing it. My brain wanted to tell me something.

It turned out that by 10AM, Robbie and Mickey had been released, but we didn't pull up into the police station until noon. They both climbed onto the bus, solemn and embarrassed. Robbie looked like he had been to hell and back, with puffy eyes and sallow skin. Mickey seemed on edge, eyes bloodshot and buzzing with indignation, fingers tapping wildly on his knee.

I made them some instant coffee and gave them bananas

and crumbly muffins to munch on. As the bus roared out of the city toward Georgia, Jacob decided to call a meeting. I sat in the booth, my knees curled up to my chest, feeling more like an onlooker than anything.

First we heard from Robbie and Mickey, what had happened to them in jail. They told their stories over and over again to the police, with cross-examining from all angles. Robbie had to lie and tell them they were just fooling around in the trailer before he went to the bathroom. If he admitted at all that he had used drugs or supplied the drugs that she ODed on, he would have been in some major trouble. Those cops were looking for any excuse to lock rock and roll hippies away. He then told us the truth; that after he came back from the bathroom—and he had been in there for ten minutes having the coke shits—he found Emeritta on the floor. The drugs were nowhere to be found, presumably all in her system, and even the cigar tube he kept the drugs in was gone.

"Well isn't that a bit weird?" Noelle spoke up. "I didn't see it anywhere in the trailer."

"I know," said Robbie. "I can't even think straight. I know, I *know* I left her with the cigar case. It was right on the table damnit. I trusted her because she said she didn't do drugs. When I came out and found her there…well, maybe the tube was still there and I didn't see it. I wasn't looking for it. How could I when there was a fucking dead groupie on the ground!"

"She wasn't a groupie," I said bitterly. Everyone turned to look at me. I brought my gaze to the tops of my freckled knees. "She was a lover of rock."

"Anyway," Robbie continued, "maybe she had it in her hand. I don't know. But when I look back I don't remember seeing it."

"I think the cops took it," Mickey said.

"If the coppers took it, they would have questioned you about it," Jacob pointed out. He was leaning against the kitchen, his burly arms folded.

"So where is it?" Noelle pondered.

We all fell into silence and shrugs.

"Does it matter?" Sage asked, bringing his eyes around to meet everyone else's. "The girl is dead. It's not directly our fault, but it wouldn't have happened had it not been for us."

Robbie glared. "Thanks Sage, real supportive."

Jacob sighed. "What Sage means is that it's all done. And to be honest, we're lucky that we're all sitting here on the bus. And I mean all of us. This could have been a lot worse."

I snorted angrily. "How could it have been worse? A girl fucking died in our trailer!"

"Oh, it's your trailer now," Mickey cut in. "Since when are you part of the band?"

I narrowed my eyes. "I'm not, but it doesn't mean it's not affecting me. Seems I'm the only one who actually liked the girl."

"You didn't even know her," said Noelle, rolling her eyes.

"I think we should cancel the Atlanta show," Sage said quietly. That got everyone's attention.

"What the hell?" Robbie cried out. "We're not cancelling anything."

"Robbie, you were just released from police custody," Sage warned. "A girl is dead because of us. I think it's more than the right thing to do."

"Screw your right thing to do!" Robbie got to his feet and stood in front of Sage who was sitting on the couch. He leaned over and got in his face, steely blue eyes against chilled green ones. "If every band had to cancel their shows because a groupie died, no one would ever go on tour!"

"Sit down," Sage ordered with a keen sense of calm.

Robbie threw his hands up in the air. "I'm not going to sit down. No fucking way I'm going to sit down because for once, you're not acting in the band's best interest."

"It's true," Graham spoke up. I wasn't the only one surprised to hear him; he had been silent this whole time.

"What?" Sage snarled. His gaze locked on Graham's head like a laser beam.

"I said," Graham said louder, raising his head and meeting

his challenge. "Robs is right. We can't cancel the show. We've never had a strong pull in the south. The last time we were here it was weak city. We cancel, we miss out. I thought a pessimist like you would realize we won't have a second chance."

Sage shook his head, his eyes searching the ceiling of the bus as if he'd find some comfort there. "I don't believe this. Guys, come on. You know I'm not taking this lightly."

"Well maybe you should," Mickey said, while Noelle jabbed him in the side with her bony elbow. He swatted her hand away and nodded at Robbie and Graham in some unspoken agreement. "I mean, if we don't go on, it's like the cops won. Her death would be in vain."

Oh for crying out loud, I thought to myself. I was so close to losing it on them but I bit my tongue. Hard. Until I tasted blood.

Sage threw me an uneasy glance before he focused on Jacob. "Jacob, talk some sense into these boys."

Jacob was polishing his teeth with the edge of his polyester jacket. He waited until he was done and satisfied before speaking. "I've always believed the best way to run a band is in a democracy. Let's take a vote. All in favor of cancelling the Atlanta show tomorrow night raise your hand."

Sage and Noelle raised their hands. Mickey appraised her with disappointment but she refused to look at him and kept her eyes on Sage instead. I raised my hand too, knowing someone would say something about it.

Jacob was the first. He gave me a polite nod. "Sorry, Rusty, I'm afraid it's up the band only."

I put my hand back down, knowing it wasn't my place but still feeling rejected all the same.

"All righty," Jacob carried on. "Now who is in favor of playing tomorrow night?"

Graham's, Robbie's, and Mickey's hands all rose up. Jacob took it all in, making little noises of agreement under his breath. "Okay, well the majority seems to have spoken. We're playing tomorrow night. End of story."

"You're an ass," Sage said simply.

"Oh, dear Sage, you can say it. Don't be shy. I'm a cunt," Jacob said unapologetically. "But I'm a cunt who's been in this game a long time, longer than you all, and though it would be a nice gesture to cancel the show for a groupie that no one here really seems to care about, it would be fatal to us as a band. For once, Graham has a valid point."

Graham looked pleased with himself, if that was possible.

Jacob continued, "We need to conquer the south. Lynyrd Skynard, Allman Brothers, southern rock has a brilliant pull down here and we need to grab them before they get burnt out. And anyway, we deliver a nice little statement to the media tomorrow about the dead bird, it gives us free media exposure and a nice sense of mystique that the local kids will go nuts over. There's always a way to turn that frown upside down and that's what I'm here for. I'm the manager. I manage so we always come out on top."

CHAPTER FIFTEEN

The drive to Atlanta wasn't very long and by the time nightfall rolled around, Bob had brought the bus into a small motel outside of the city. We were staying at an incredibly expensive hotel in Nashville, a splurge since we were playing two shows there, so our digs in Atlanta had to be inexpensive and there was no way anyone could tolerate being on the bus with each other any longer. After the whole vote, no one really seemed to be speaking and it was yet another awkward bus ride.

I was greatly looking forward to the fact that I had my own room. I didn't care that the shag carpeting had a peculiar, sour smell or that the sink was filled with rust stains. I loved the fact that I could unpack my duffel bag and I had a door to close and buffer out the band.

I lolled around in the room, taking a luxurious shower (the shower on the bus officially had no hot water anymore), stretching out on the bed like a starfish, and reading snippets of the *Carrie* book I brought. When it was getting a bit too weird and spooky, I put it down and wrote a letter to Eric. I would have called, but the long distance rates on the crackly motel phone were exorbitant.

When that was all done, I tried to pen some music-oriented

prose but my brain was coming up blank. Everything I wrote was wrought with purple doom like I was subconsciously more distraught over the situation than I let on. Everything was weighing on me heavily.

I closed my notebook with a sigh and lay my head on the itchy beige bedspread. It was only nine o'clock and too early to go to bed, but soon my eyes were closing like heavy curtains.

I wasn't sure how long I had been asleep for, or if I even was, but my eyes snapped open to a weird metal sound emanating from the bathroom. To my utter surprise, the light in the motel room was out and I was engulfed in pitch blackness. The only light I had was coming from the bathroom door. It was closed and the light spilled under it like a garish sheet.

I held my breath, slowly propping myself up on my elbows. My mouth was dry. I tried to listen and think at the same time. How did the light go out? Did I leave the light on and close the door after I had my shower? It was plausible but it didn't sit right; I was used to conserving electricity in my house and turning off lights was like second nature to me.

Clink.

There it was again. The sound of metal on porcelain, like someone had dropped a razor in the sink.

My heart nearly stopped at that, then slogged through my chest like it was stuck in mud.

I listened harder, ignoring the fright that was building steadily in my chest, my eyes watching the light under the door as if I expected to see a shadow appear at any moment. It seemed rational. When it never came, I gathered up the nerve to get off the bed. I blessed the muffling properties of the shag carpet and crept forward until I was at the bathroom door.

I held my breath again, willing my body to not have a heart attack. I put my head to the door, and as softly as possible, laid it upon the wood.

I heard nothing. I waited.

A click shot through the layers of wood to my ear.

The light from underneath the door switched off.

I was now in total blackness. And I wasn't alone.

I had no time to think. I whirled around, ready to run out the door, when I was met with an immense front of frigid air that blew at my face and hair.

"Do you remember me now?" a calculating voice echoed in the cold, coming from right in front of me.

I let out a yelp, panic squeezing every bone in my body, and somehow managed to make it through the pitch black room to the door. My fingers slipped clumsily on the knob a few times before I managed to grasp it and fling the door open, feeling nothing but immense dread nipping at my heels, like a hand reaching for me in the dark.

I ran outside, sweat chilling on my skin. The motel was one level and L-shaped and I was at the more isolated end, surrounded by dark trees and a path to the small pool, the only thing that was really lit up.

I went straight there, wanting to be as far away from the room as I could be and around as much light as possible. From the pool you could see the clerk in the motel lobby and the trucks and cars roaring past on the distant highway giving a sense of safety and comfort; life was going on and sane people were out there.

Still, I scampered to the other side of the pool area so I was facing my door—which was wide open—and the rest of the motel and leaned against the white guard rail that went around the glowing aqua water. I sucked in my breath, trying to calm down.

This wasn't a matter of hallucinating anymore. Someone had been in my room...someone was still in my room. Maybe I was confused and thought the voice was coming from another place, but the fact was that though I could blame the bedroom light going out due to a burnt-out bulb, it was too much of a coincidence for it to happen to the bathroom one. Besides, I *heard* it. I heard the click that happens when you flick off a light switch. Someone had turned it off. And they had done it mere inches from me. I had been a sitting duck.

Or something turned it off. I quickly dismissed my wayward thoughts. Dealing with a "someone" was bad enough. It could have been anyone, a hitchhiker or someone creepy coming in for the night. Maybe I had fallen into a deeper sleep than I thought and some pervert had broken in and had been in the bathroom getting ready for….

I shuddered. I had to get help before I drove myself insane, and was about to run over to the motel office when I noticed I wasn't alone at the poolside.

Across from me there was the faint red glow of cigarette embers. Someone was sitting on the poolside chair smoking. I squinted at the shape, feeling panicky all over again, and saw eyeballs glinting, a reflection from the waving pool light. They were smoking and watching me.

"Hello?" I called out softly. "Who's there?"

The shadowy figure barely moved and they certainly didn't say anything. The cigarette glowed again. I peered at it, trying to block out the light from the pool and focus on the person. The more I stared, the more it began to resemble a woman. I saw long pale limbs stretched out on the vinyl chair, a white face, and long dark hair.

"Noelle?"

There was no response. Even though I felt extremely unsafe and needed to go tell the motel clerk what had happened, if it was Noelle sitting there in the dark, I couldn't just leave her.

I slowly walked around to the pool gate and pushed it open with an eerie groan. I shot a look over to my room, still waiting for someone to walk out of it. I kept one eye on it and approached the smoking figure as one approaches a snake. I considered the burning cigarette a warning rattle, and she was coiled and ready to strike.

I was only a few feet away when my eyes adjusted and the light from the pool became clearer.

It was Noelle. I kneeled down beside her, nervously glancing between her and the open door. She was smoking as if she were on autopilot. Her eyes were dry and staring blankly forward. Her skin took on a greenish tone from the light.

"Noelle," I whispered. "Are you okay?"

She didn't answer. I looked back at the door and put my hand on her knee. It was clammy and cold to the touch.

"Noelle, we have to go. There was someone in my room just now, and I think they're still there. I have to tell the motel clerk. Come on, it's not safe to hang out here."

I attempted to pull at her arm but she was rigid and unyielding.

"Please," I said firmly.

She finally looked at me, her head turning my way like it was on creaky hinges. Her eyes glowed spookily as she appraised me.

"Do you think that's going to help?" Her voice was as soft as the breeze ruffling her hair.

"What?"

She puffed deliberately on the cigarette.

"Noelle? Please." I pulled on her a little more.

She laughed coldly.

"It's too late. They're here."

A bead of sweat trickled at the back of my neck.

"Who is here?"

"I told you. The monsters. They've come for us all."

My mouth went dry and I had to swallow a few times before I spoke. "Noelle, please, you're scaring me. I'm already scared. Just come."

She shook her head slightly.

"You go and tell whoever. They won't find anything. They hide themselves too well. But they're here. And soon they'll be inside you. They'll be inside me very soon. They want to take us all. We're owed to them."

Debt collector, Graham's voice whispered inside my head. I suppressed a shiver.

"Please," I tried again. My voice cracked. "You can tell me more later, Noelle, and I'll believe you, I will, but you have to come with me."

"I don't care if you believe me," she remarked flatly. "It's already too late."

I took in a deep breath, trying to figure out my next course of action. Noelle was obviously as high as a kite and talking nonsense. So why was she scaring me so much?

"I—," I began to say but stopped when my heart went dead cold. Noelle's expression was frozen in absolute horror, eyes wide, mouth open in a silent scream.

With fevered breath, I looked over my shoulder to see what was causing the terror on her face.

On the other side of the quiet road that went past the motel was a woman in white. She was staring at us, eyes black pits, white hair flowing in the breeze. It was Sonja.

But the more I looked at her, the more she wasn't Sonja. She was almost a ghostly apparition, partly transparent, and leaking black fluid out of her mouth as she smiled.

I looked back at Noelle. Her expression hadn't changed. She was stuck, a portrait of mind-numbing terror. A silent scream that never ended.

My eyes volleyed back to the woman in white.

She was no longer across the road.

She was standing on the curb that bordered the parking lot. The parking lot that sloped toward the pool. Just feet away.

Her eyes were bleeding black pools that promised a wealth of revulsion.

I didn't know what to do. I couldn't breathe. I couldn't speak. I couldn't move.

Then I heard Noelle, her voice bursting through like a siren.

She started screaming and thrashing on the lawn chair, her voice rising high into the air, a scream that personified all that everyone feared.

I put my hands on her shoulders, trying to calm her down and prevent her from hurting herself, and threw another glance over my shoulder, expecting to have to fight off Sonja as well.

But she wasn't there. The road was empty. The darkness was

all consuming.

Within seconds, the clerk came running out of the motel and the doors to various rooms opened. Suddenly everyone from Jacob to Mickey to random motel guests were gathered around, trying to figure out what was going on.

Mickey flew to Noelle and tried to get in her face to calm her down but Noelle screamed like she had never seen him before in her life. Sage went to her side and tried to steady her but she thrashed violently against them both.

"What happened?" Mickey screamed at me.

Everyone looked at me but I couldn't even speak.

Jacob put his meaty hand on my shoulder and gripped it hard, the rings digging into my bone.

"What happened, Dawn?" he asked with a glint in his eye.

I shook my head, my tongue thick and stupid. Next the tiny motel clerk with the hairy ears was at my side asking the same thing.

I was finally able to say, "I don't know. She was sitting here alone and then she just started screaming."

I could tell Jacob knew I wasn't telling the whole truth but he let it go. I went on, "I was in my room earlier and someone had broken in."

"What?" someone in the crowd cried out over Noelle's wails.

Frenzied whispers erupted among the motel patrons.

"It's true," I said to the hotel manager. "I fell asleep, and when I woke up, the lights in my room were all out and someone was in my bathroom. The light was on. I heard them in there. Then they turned off the light and I ran out of the room. I ran all the way here and saw Noelle and then she just started screaming."

The clerk looked extremely puzzled, shaking his head in disbelief. I didn't know how else to describe it. They both seemed like two unrelated incidents but I saw Sonja just as Noelle had. Could it have been her in my room?

My eyes made their way back to Noelle. Mickey was trying to calm her but wasn't having much luck. Sage had a hand on her arm, holding her down, but he was looking at me. His expression was entirely unreadable.

The manager sighed. "I better go call the police and get an ambulance here too."

He ran off into the office.

"Aw, Christ," Jacob swore. "This is all we need."

I couldn't help but glare at him. "I thought you liked bad press."

His eyes narrowed into venomous yellow slits. They seemed to go from avian to reptilian in a single blink.

"I think you're going to need to tell me the truth soon," he whispered into my ear.

I moved my head out of the way. "I am telling the truth. Take it or leave it."

He chewed on his lip for a moment, searching my face. "I'll take it. For now."

He left my side and went to go help Sage and Mickey.

I felt Robbie sidle up to me.

"Was there really someone in your room?" he asked. His shoulders were hunched and it looked like he couldn't take any more punches from life.

I nodded, my eyes automatically darting over to the door. If it really had been a person in my room, they were probably gone now thanks to Noelle's distraction. But I was starting to think it was just as likely that it had been Sonja, or one of the other GTFOs. Someone who wanted to fuck with me.

"I think..." Robbie trailed off.

"What?"

He started laughing to himself, like he remembered a funny joke. I watched and waited until the maniacal laughter stopped and he composed himself. He was still a lesser version of the rock god I used to know.

"Do you feel it?" he asked quietly, his eyes darting around.

I leaned into him. "Feel what?"

"It," he said. "Something. Like something has a hold on us.

Like…."

"Like?"

He shook his head and gave me a twisted smile. "I bet you never expected any of this."

I frowned at his change of subject. "Did you?"

"Yes," he answered plainly and didn't elaborate. I didn't feel like pressing him. I didn't think it would do me any good.

We watched Noelle for a few minutes until the police and ambulance arrived. The police immediately came to me and barraged me with questions. I could tell Jacob was hoping they wouldn't bring up Emeritta's death, but the Atlanta cops weren't stupid and they'd already heard all about it. Naturally they believed that Noelle was on drugs until the paramedics seemed to dismiss it.

Maybe it was because I was a female and a journalist, but the cops were easier on me than they were with Robbie and Mickey, and I wasn't brought in for further questioning.

They went to the motel room to investigate my side of the story, and though they found the bulb in the bedroom had burned out naturally, there was a razor in the sink that hadn't belonged to me or anyone else. There was no sign of a break-in, so whoever had been there had come in when I wasn't aware. That freaked me out more than anything, knowing that someone had been in my room and I was lying there asleep and totally helpless.

Noelle still wasn't responding to anyone, so she was strapped down into a stretcher and shoved in the ambulance. Mickey and Jacob went in the ambulance with her, leaving me, Sage, Robbie, Bob, Graham, and a load of frightened guests.

"So," Robbie said, looking at us. "Who's up for sleeping on the bus?"

No one argued, not even Graham, and we gladly locked ourselves in the vehicle and attempted once again to get a good night's sleep.

Once again, a good night's sleep never came.

✻ ✻ ✻

The next morning Atlanta was under a deluge of rain as the remnants of an early tropical storm came in from the Gulf Coast. It was hot and sticky inside the bus, the windows all closed to keep out the incoming water that flowed down the planes of the bus like miniature waterfalls. No one had slept and with two nights of sleep deprivation, emotions were running high. We munched sugary confectionaries and strong coffee that Bob had snapped up from a local café, happy just to have our mouths occupied.

I explained what had happened as many times as I could and the guys kept asking me the same questions as if I'd say something new next time. I left out the part about Sonja being across the road knowing that would be dismissed as a trick of the eye, but I mentioned the monsters.

I tried to not make it obvious that I was watching Graham as I told them all. His expression didn't change at all, not even when I brought up Noelle saying "We're owed to them."

"What does that mean?" Robbie asked.

I shrugged and looked at Sage. He was sitting on the couch, staring at some blank spot on the wall. He hadn't said a word all morning and I had to wonder what on earth was going on in that head of his. I hoped he wouldn't shut down too. The band needed him more now than ever. I *needed* him.

"It means Noelle is nuts," Graham said, rapping a drumstick against his leg.

I shot him a disgusted look. "How can you say that?"

"How can you not say that?" he countered. "Go and listen to what you're saying and tell us those are not the ramblings of a crazy loon. Fuck, we all know Noelle's a weak chick. She always was. Even, I don't know, five years ago. We all thought she'd grow out of it and get some balls or something but she never did. And Mickey just let her do whatever she wanted. Drugs, other men," his eyes shot to Sage in a brief exchange, "booze, whatever the fuck."

I wasn't stupid. I made the connection and it immediately

made sense. Sage and Noelle had slept together at some point. That would explain their somewhat strained relationship and the way she seemed to look at him at times with puppy dog eyes.

Or the way she used to. Now there was no knowing what was going on with her. And there was no way in knowing what was going on with me. That last thought chilled me to the bone. I had to wonder how long Noelle had thought she had monsters coming after her. Had it started out for her the same way it started out for me? Was that the path I was going down? I was already hiding things from everyone: what Graham had said to me, the demon faces, seeing Sonja in the darkness. I kept it to myself because I couldn't bring myself to believe it and I knew no one else would. But maybe Noelle had been doing the exact same thing.

If she had pulled me aside a week earlier and told me what she'd seen, would I have believed her?

No. Of course not.

A few hours later, Jacob returned to the bus. We all jumped in our seats at his knock and Bob reluctantly opened the door, expecting monsters to follow him up the stairs.

"Christ it's raining as fuck out there,'" Jacob said, shaking his jacket off, water flying onto the floor. He threw it onto the bench in a wet sop and looked down at us like a teacher inspecting his pupils. We sat there, watching him, waiting.

He let out a despondent sigh and rubbed his face. "Okay, folks. Here's the new development…."

With grim lines across his face, he proceeded to tell us that Noelle wasn't coming back anytime soon. The doctors couldn't find out what was wrong with her. There had been no sign of drugs in her system, at least nothing more than residual amounts. She didn't even test positive for alcohol so the doctors could only say it was most likely a combination of stress and lack of sleep that led to a nervous breakdown. Given that Emeritta had just died, there was a very strong chance that Noelle had been in a state of shock and this was how her body was dealing with it. They were hopeful she would eventually snap out of it, but they were going to keep her under observation for a few days, and after that, she'd probably be sent back to Sacramento to be with her parents. He said that he'd already spoken to them and they were flying out to Atlanta as soon as possible.

Jacob went on to say that Mickey offered to take care of Noelle, but seeing as they didn't live together in Sacramento and her parents pretty much thought Mickey was the world's worst influence, they weren't having any of that. Which led to the next part.

"Unfortunately," Jacob said, looking at Robbie and Graham with unease. "We're going to have to cancel the show tonight."

"Obviously," I said.

He looked at me sharply. "Obviously, yes. Thank you, Rusty."

"Just tonight?" Graham asked.

"Well…I don't know. I'm afraid it's time for another band meeting."

Everyone looked at me. I raised my brow.

"Is that my cue to leave?" I asked.

Jacob nodded at Bob. "Both you and Bob should probably go and stretch your legs."

I looked at the downpour outside and exchanged a look with the stoic bus driver. Seriously?

"Hey, she can stay," Sage said.

"Why, you're not done sucking up to your little buddy yet?" Graham spat out, smashing the drumstick against the seat.

Sage glared at him. "She can stay. She's pretty much one of us now."

I felt vaguely flattered.

Graham laughed viciously. "She will never be one of us. She wasn't even supposed to be here in the first place."

"Yes, yes," Jacob chided him, "you wanted the guy from Rolling Stone. We heard it a million times before. Well, it's Creem magazine, baby. What better place to record the shitshow of the century."

I pursed my lips, thinking that over. Shitshow of the century.

A tour that went down in history.

I was suddenly aware that everyone except Sage was looking at me expectantly.

"Come on, Rusty," Bob said, getting to his feet and slipping on a jacket. He pulled out a golf umbrella from underneath the couch then opened his arms for me, gesturing to the door.

I let out an angry breath of air and went to join him, not even bothering to give the band one last look before we opened the bus doors and walked out into the rain like a pair of rejects.

We were still in the motel parking lot, so Bob and I walked through the mounting puddles and up a block until we got to the café. Despite the coverage, we looked like a pair of drowned rats and we plunked ourselves down on the pink vinyl booths.

"Don't take it personally," Bob said in his ragged voice, smoothing back his white hair. "If I never fit in with another band, I'll be one happy fucker. They can ruin you, ya know?"

"I can see that," I told him, smiling tiredly at the telepathic waitress who plunked two mugs and a pot of coffee on the table.

He took a sip of his coffee and smiled. "Oooh, damn that's good." He then placed the mug down and folded his hands in front of him. "You know, I've been on a lot of tours. Hell, I've been doing this for most of my life. I couldn't even begin to tell you about half the shit I've seen. Not only because I've been sworn to secrecy, because I have...The King had some strict waivers. But because I've blocked it out. Or I've just refused to believe it. But this band...this band, Rusty...something is not right."

A shiver ran up my spine. I knew it wasn't just the wet clothes. "You feel it, too?"

He leaned back and thoughtfully spun his mug around.

"I don't know what I feel, exactly. But whatever it is, I've felt it from the start. I'm not into supernatural, hippie-dippie mumbo-jumbo shit. I'm not the god-fearing man I used to be. But there's something with us...almost like it's on the bus with us...that hasn't let us go. I know that doesn't make any sense but the reason I'm telling you is because I know you can feel it too. These things…these aren't coincidences. I've been around enough to know when to call a spade a spade. It's almost like the band is cursed…and it's only going to get worse from here on out."

Cursed. That almost made perfect sense. Or it would have, had the idea of a curse not been so ridiculous. I was as much into the hippie-dippie mumbo-jumbo as Bob was and my journalistic mind was constantly trying to find reason and logic.

"Curses don't exist," I said reluctantly.

"But what if they do? It would explain some things. This feels like more than a string of bad luck. First that girl dies, rest in peace. Then Noelle has a mental breakdown. Could one thing be the result of the other? Sure. But I don't buy it."

"Me neither," I said. "But if it's a curse, someone had to have cursed us. Who would do that?"

He raised his brows. "I couldn't tell you, Rusty. But I can tell you I've heard some pretty weird shit at night on the bus when everyone is asleep."

I tried to ignore the goosebumps on my arms. "What shit?"

"Graham," he said soberly. "He rarely sleeps. He only sleeps when the sun comes up and then it's only for a few hours. I've never seen anyone get by on such little sleep before and so consistently."

"What does he do? Just lie there?"

He nodded. "Oh, he lies there. On his back. Staring up at the ceiling. And he chants things. Very weird things. You can barely hear him, but sometimes I really try and listen. He's not chanting in English, you can bet your mother on that. It sounds like Latin to me, but then I'm a pretty ignorant soul."

I leaned in across the table and lowered my voice. "Have you ever seen him do any of that Satanic shit that he's always talking about?"

Bob smoothed back his hair again and seemed to think. "I can't really say. Maybe chanting in Latin counts. I've seen him always talking to this equally freaky girl."

I straightened up. "Was she blonde?"

"No," he said. "And I know who you're talking about, the GTFOs. No, I haven't seen the blondes around. They aren't allowed on the bus at any rate, strict orders from Jacob. This girl is a bit on the chunky side, really short, nasty haircut."

"That's Sparky, she's one of them."

"Interesting," he mused. "Well, anyhow, I've only seen her a few times. She kind of stands off in the distance, and like Graham has some stereo receiver in his head, he gets up and goes off the bus and meets her. They disappear for, oh I don't know, maybe ten minutes, and then he comes back alone. He doesn't seem any different. I always assumed he was getting himself serviced."

I grimaced at the thought. "When does this usually happen?"

"In the middle of the night."

"What?" I shrieked. People in the café turned to look at me. I gave them a sheepish look and lowered my voice. "What? In the middle of the night? How?"

"I stop at a gas station to fill up or a truck stop for food and she's usually there."

"Well, don't you find that fucking weird!?"

"Look, Rusty, of course I find it weird. But these are rock stars. They all have their weird quirks. And having scary chicks show up at gas stations you stop at isn't that unheard of. Especially when they're following the bus."

Alarm bells rang in my head. "They follow the bus?"

"Sometimes. Fans, groupies, they're all obsessed. It doesn't matter what band."

I sat back in the booth, feeling floored and disturbed at the same time. All this time I assumed that if I didn't see the GTFOs, they weren't around. But they were and it was something as simple as following the tour bus. Now I knew for sure that I had seen Sonja the night before. And she'd done something to Noelle, something horrible, to get her to freak out like that.

Suddenly I felt very vulnerable. Were they still around? Were they hiding out in the rain, waiting for our next move? I wiped a hand at the window, smoothing away the foggy condensation, but seeing only the gray daylight and wind-scattered downpour outside.

"I hope you'll keep our talk just between us," Bob said. "I don't know how much longer this tour is going to go on for, but I don't want to get booted off the job because they think I'm talking hocus pocus. I've got a big mortgage back home and a wife that looks up to me, and gigs like this are hard to come by."

I nodded absently, not even sure what I was going to do with our talk.

"If I were you though," he continued, "I'd consider going back home soon. You're a beautiful young woman and you've got a good brain in that head. I'd hate for anything to happen to you."

I eyed him carefully.

"Do you think something will?"

"It's rock and roll, Rusty. Anything that can happen, will happen. Even the impossible."

I took little comfort in that and had my first sip of coffee. Bob was right. It really was damn good.

CHAPTER SIXTEEN

Bob and I left the café just as the rain was starting to let up. I took that as a sign. I don't know what kind of sign, but a sign that some sort of change was happening. As creepy as our conversation had been, talking about it with Bob strengthened me somehow and made me feel like I wasn't alone. The band might have been in one camp, but we were in the other and in this case it wasn't a bad thing, especially if the curse nonsense turned out to be true.

Back on the bus, the mood was somber and tense. It turned out that the band had decided to continue on with the tour. They would get a replacement bassist to cover for Noelle starting with the Nashville show and hopefully that person would fit in well enough that they could replace her for the rest of the tour.

"What's Mickey going to say about it?" I asked.

Jacob twirled his rings with downcast eyes. "Knowing Mickey, he won't have a problem with it. He loves Noe and all but he loves music more. Sad fact of most musicians, ain't that right boys."

Robbie grumbled while Sage stared at Jacob thoughtfully, as if he was figuring something out. Jacob felt his eyes on him and, without looking up, grinned very slowly, like an afterthought.

Seeing as the band wasn't going to be playing, Jacob made

Bob drive the bus to an office center and he got in touch with the promoter of the Atlanta show. Then he, Robbie, and Graham started the long process of trying to telephone as many bassists as they could think of. I stayed with Sage on the bus, both of us surrounded by a weird hush of unsaid words and mixed feelings. He had gone through so much in the last twenty-four hours, I wasn't even sure how to act normal around him anymore…if there ever was a normal between Sage and I. The Tom Waits show seemed like a lifetime ago. We seemed like different people then.

After maybe twenty minutes, Sage got up off the couch and stretched, his arms reaching far above his head. I tried not to stare at his stomach and the hint of defined abs that momentarily peeked out underneath his black western shirt. My hormones didn't seem to understand the bigger picture here.

He glanced down at me and I quickly looked away. I knew he caught my staring and I prayed that the flare I felt on my cheeks wasn't translating into a blush.

"Do you want to get out of here?" he asked.

"Where do you want to go?"

"Anywhere that serves copious amounts of liquor."

I nodded, thinking that sounded like a most reasonable plan. We left the bus, relieved that the rain had stopped, and let Jacob know we were going to be at a bar down the street.

"Which one?" Jacob asked.

"The dirtiest," Sage replied.

He wasn't wrong. It felt like we walked forever, but eventually Sage spotted just the right place. A neon open sign stuttered, one window was boarded up with wood in place of fixing broken glass, and a wall of motorbikes was lined out front. Inside we were met with a bevy of heavy-set, pock-marked gentlemen and hostile glares. I was glad that Sage's hair wasn't that long and that the visible tattoos on his arms gave him some sort of street cred. I hoped that his mixed heritage skin wasn't going to cause any problems.

We sat down at a hard wooden booth and proceeded to

drink, starting with a pitcher of beer while Steppenwolf played on the stereo. We didn't speak much until we were starting another pitcher and I figured Sage's tongue would be looser. So far he seemed so wrapped up in his own thoughts.

I cleared my throat and adjusted my seat. "So, you're part Mexican, right?"

He didn't look surprised or annoyed at my question, though I thought he would have, considering he never really talked about himself in interviews.

"Is this part of the interview?" he asked.

I shook my head, but I was silently cursing myself for failing to bring along the tape recorder. Though, from a moral point of view, interviewing someone when they were drunk wasn't exactly fair anyway.

"My mother was," he said. His eyes drifted over to the pool table where two bald men in leather vests and spider web tattoos were racking up. "She moved up to Redding when she was sixteen to do farm work with her mother. I think they worked at every abusive shithole in town until they finally found my father. We had an apple and apricot orchard at the time. It wasn't the biggest but it was still more than my dad could handle by himself."

I was secretly thrilled that he was opening up to me. "So your mom and dad met because she worked for him?"

He smirked. "Not quite the fairytale story, is it?"

"It kind of is. I'm sure the life of a laborer isn't the best," I said, thinking of the poor men I saw bent over in the hot Ellensburg fields.

"No, it's not. My dad took care of his workers very well but he was one of the rare ones. They were so grateful. Maybe that's why my mother married my dad, I don't know. Their life back in Magdelena was pretty shitty from what I understood. Then my grandfather died and they had nothing. My mother, grandmother, and uncle snuck into the US, crossing the Rio Grande, swimming for their lives just like in the movies. My uncle was older and decided he wanted to live in Arizona. He had some friends there, and if you can believe it, he wanted to start a Mariachi band. But my grandma had dreams of the Pacific Northwest. They were heading up to Washington but Redding was as far as they got."

He took a few big chugs of beer and I watched him intently.

"Anyway, my mom and dad fell in love. My grandma died a short while later. Maybe she had an idea of what was to come. I don't know about Ellensburg, but Redding is a small place. Aside from Mount Shasta and the lake and the agriculture, there's nothing going on there. People talk. People are close-minded. When they discovered my father was dating, and then marrying, a Mexican, they made their lives hell. This was the 50s and that kind of shit wasn't heard of. My father was beat up a lot. When I was younger, I was kicked around by the other kids. I may have had green eyes but my skin was dark enough to be different, especially when I was young. And my mother…one night she went out to get groceries. She never came back. I was eleven years old at the time and just getting into music and my world came crashing down. She was attacked in the parking lot of the grocery store, just beside her car. Beaten to death by a bunch of racist fucks."

I knew my mouth was open but I couldn't find the strength to close it.

He avoided my eyes and stared down into his beer, watching the bubbles with vague interest.

"They never did find out who did it. I never told anyone this but…it made me afraid. I feel so…ashamed…that I stopped talking to my uncle. I stopped listening to Mariachi records. I stopped speaking Spanish. My only saving grace was meeting Robbie one day after school. I was fourteen, he was fifteen. We both loved Iron Butterfly and Elvis. The rest is history."

I chewed on my lip. I knew the rest thanks to band interviews, but I also knew deep down that wasn't the whole story. But now, of all times, wasn't the time to press him.

"I'm so sorry," I said softly. I reached out and put my hand on his. He brought his brooding eyes up to meet mine and I nearly got lost in them.

"So that's me," he said, voice low and rough. "What's Dawn's story?"

I removed my hand.

"I don't have much of one," I told him, giving him a carefree smile. He didn't buy it. His eyes narrowed until they were two green slits.

"Not used to having the tables turned on you, are you? Always the interviewer, never the interviewee."

"Something like that."

"Well, we already know you're a soon to be ex-rodeo champion and you're not sure if music journalism will fill the gap."

"I guess."

"So tell me about your father. You do have one of those?"

I prickled a bit at that. "I do. He's a good man."

"You sound hesitant. What does he do?"

I paused. "He works at a farm equipment repair shop."

"Respectable blue collar job."

"He used to raise cattle. And then Timothy hay."

"So you're a farm girl through and through."

"And you're a farm boy through and through."

He raised his glass at me. "Here's to us then. Any other similarities?"

My eyes fell to the wood table, distracted by the graffiti from rebellious patrons.

"My mother is dead."

I saw his shoulders go slack out of the corner of my eye.

"Saying sorry doesn't really help, does it?" he said quietly.

I shook my head and held back the tears. I rarely talked about my mom and it definitely wasn't a good idea when I was half-cut and dealing with everything else I had been dealing with.

He didn't ask how she died and for that I was grateful. Suicide comes with a side of anger and guilt that I wasn't ready to deal with.

I glanced at the cracked clock on the wall.

"Should we head back now?"

"Do you think we've ignored our problems long enough?" he asked silkily. "I don't. I'm not even close to being done yet."

I didn't protest too much when he ordered us another round.

* * *

By the time Jacob showed up at the dive bar, we were good and drunk. Not belligerent but definitely not sober. Sage and I had stopped talking about the intimate subjects and waxed on about music instead. It was wonderful to shoot the shit with him, someone who really knew what they were talking about and didn't judge me for saying I still liked Jim Morrison, even though he was a giant buffoon. We almost forgot all about our problems at hand: the fact that the tour might be cancelled, that Noelle was in the hospital, that a young girl died the other day, that Graham was turning out to be more serious than I gave him credit for, and that dangerous groupies were following our tour bus. Yup, almost forgot all about those.

It turned out that once Chip and the other roadies in the equipment van found out about the cancelled show, Chip knew of the perfect replacement for Noelle. He was right when he told me he knew everyone in the business. One phone call later and we had a twenty-three-year-old guy called Fiddles, who had toured with Boz Scags, all lined up for Nashville.

With that all settled, we found another motel in the Atlanta area for the night. This one had better security and was closer to the hospital for when Mickey would join us. Everyone would be sharing rooms too, not only to save costs, but because everyone was still a bit freaked out and on edge. Jacob and Bob got one room. It looked like Robbie was going to pick Sage, but Sage wasn't a dummy and volunteered that I stay with him. I suppose he didn't trust Robbie and he certainly didn't trust Graham. I was glad for that, but also flushing on the inside from the potential awkwardness of sharing a room with someone I had thought about naked.

I caught the sly looks on Robbie and Jacob's faces as I picked up my duffel bag from the motel lobby and Sage and I made our way to our room, weaving up the stairs. It was on the upper level, overlooking the tour bus. Jacob and Bob were on one side of us, while Robbie and Graham were downstairs. I wanted him as far away from me as possible.

Sage flicked on the light switch. There were two beds (which was good, right?) with ugly orange bedspreads, an avocado green carpet, and faux wood paneled walls. A shiny desk and two chairs were in the corner and beside it was a small fridge.

We exchanged a look full of drunken glee and I made a beeline to it. Inside, it was fully-stocked with cookies and alcohol.

"I guess we won't have to leave the room," I said, before I realized how sexual it sounded.

I snapped my head around to look at Sage. He was sitting on the edge of the bed and smiling lazily at me, long legs splayed.

Uh oh. I avoided looking at his crotch and made a mental note not to get too plastered.

I tried to act casual. "So, what would you like?"

"Anything strong and fast," he said, raising a brow at me, a smirk tugging at the corners of his thick lips. I knew he was baiting me, that he wanted me to come back with some kind of sexual repartee along the lines of "is that the way you like it?" but I decided that playing that game when we were both drunk and drinking was dangerous. I already had enough danger.

I threw him a few mini bottles of bourbon, then got some glasses and disappeared around the corner with an ice bucket, looking for the ice machine. I kept a wary eye on the bus and the street, expecting to see the GTFOs or any suspicious vehicles, but so far there was nothing out of the ordinary. I couldn't wait to be out of Atlanta.

When I returned, Sage had sucked two bottles dry and brought his acoustic guitar out of the case. I put the glass of ice on his bedside table and plunked my butt down on my bed. I motioned to the guitar strap with the Mexican pattern.

"You haven't shunned everything about your heritage," I pointed out.

He strummed a few chords. They gave off a melancholy air that filled the room. "I decided I wanted to be myself while I still had the chance."

"I think we always have a chance," I said.

He gazed at me. His eyes were slanted down at the corners, a sign he was getting drunker. "Tomorrow is one of the many things you can't count on."

I wrapped my arms around my legs. "Boy, you really are Mr. Optimistic, aren't you?"

My attempt to make light of things didn't work. He ignored me and began to play a song. It was something haunting and beautiful, a waltz. I had never heard it before and I was caught up in a swirl of emotions as the sad melody wrapped around me.

He sung in a low, bourbon-soaked voice that made the hairs on my neck stand up and my insides melt into putty.

I hung there dreaming as she strangely cried
I hung there watching as she seemed to die
And she survived and I feel like I'm dying

When he finished, I was momentarily speechless.

"That was beautiful, Sage," I gushed when I found the words. "What is that? A new song?"

He smiled gently. It made his eyes dance. "Actually, it's a very old song. I wrote it before I joined the band."

"You were so young!"

He looked bashful for a second, then reached for his drink. "I was a dramatic kid. It's hokey."

"It's really not," I told him, watching as he poured two more mini bottles into the glass and downed it. I felt a trickle of unease at the amount he was packing away. He was a large man, but we'd drunk a lot all day, and it was now dusk and he was showing no signs of stopping. I regretted giving him so many bottles.

"You're not drinking," he said to me, slurring a bit. He

took off his guitar and laid it on the bed beside him, handling it like a baby.

"I'm pretty drunk as it is," I said, but the clarity in my words betrayed me.

He shot me an annoyed look. "You're judging me."

I shook my head. "I'm not doing anything, Sage."

"Exactly. So give me whatever is left in there." He nodded at the fridge.

I shook my head again. "We've had a rough few days, we should probably take a break."

It happened in the blink of an eye. He lunged across the gap and pushed me down onto the bed by my shoulders, his incredible weight on my body, hips crushing into my hips. He pinned my arms above my head. His face was inches from mine, lips curled angrily, wired eyes searching my wide ones.

"You say that so easily," he growled near my lips. "A rough few days. Is that what you think this is? Just a rough few days?"

"N-no," I stammered. I didn't fear Sage. But I feared men when they had too much to drink.

"I thought you were different, Dawn. The only one on this tour left with a heart and soul." His eyes flared with indignation.

"I am different," I protested, so conscious of the proximity of his mouth to mine. I stopped squirming and let his hands hold my arms to the bed. If he wanted to feel powerful, I was going to let him. But I was going to get what I wanted too.

"You have no idea what I've been through," he told me. His demeanor softened and his grip on my wrists loosened. He still kept his face as close as possible.

"I have some idea. But I'd like it if you could tell me the rest."

"Are you here to make me feel? Is that part of the plan?" he sneered delicately.

I blinked at him. Feel? Feel what?

"I don't know why I'm here, Sage," I admitted, getting angry. "And that's the god damn fucking truth. I'm here because Jacob wanted me here. Jacob wanted someone to cover your band going down in history. Well guess what, it is going down in history. For fuck's sake, people are dying and losing their minds and I'm losing my own damn mind every day I'm here. And I know you keep telling me to leave, and maybe I'll end up doing that. But while you're questioning my motives, I'm wondering what the hell it is that you're not telling me. Or any of us. Because none of this is normal, Sage. It's not even close, and I know, I *know*, that you know a hell of a lot more about what's going on than any of us. If there is a plan in all this fuckery, Sage Knightly is the one behind it."

I was so angry, I almost spat in his face. He balked a bit at my rush of words, then frowned, thinking it through. He was still so close and I was just at that point where I was going to do something really stupid, like kiss him, just to get him to stop staring at me.

His gaze dropped to my lips. His own parted slightly, his lower lip full. I bet it was soft and easy to suck on. My breath became slower and labored, my body tense, not knowing what was going to happen next. The air was thick and buzzed around us, like it too was waiting for movement.

"Tell me what you know," I whispered. The tip of his nose brushed against the tip of mine. I felt his very hard erection press firmly into my thigh.

He closed his eyes, his lashes long and black against his golden skin. I closed mine, inching my lips closer to his. They barely touched, just a hint of sensitive, wanting skin on skin. I was about to arch my back and press my lips firmly against his, invite his tongue to play with mine, when he suddenly got off me.

I sat up in surprise and watched him as he walked over to the window. He leaned against it, watching the sky fade from light gray to dark purple.

Did that all really happen? I put my fingers to my lips. I was so close to kissing him. I felt him, how large he was, how much he wanted me. Now he was across the room, miles of distance between us, his focus elsewhere.

I sat there for a minute, swallowed by awkwardness and the ugly bedspread. Then I brushed off the rejection and went to the fridge. Screw everything I had just said. I was getting drunk.

I cracked open a can of Pepsi and a mini bottle of rum and made myself a quick drink. I was just taking my first sip when Sage spoke.

"Have you wanted something so badly that you would have done anything to get it?" he mumbled, his muscly back still to me. "Like, the kind of want that leaves you on your knees and asking for someone, anyone, to answer your prayers?"

I took in a deep breath. "No."

But the truth was, after my mother had died and my dad was waking up in vomit every morning and Eric was coming home with shiners, stuttering and crying his eyes out, I did fall to my knees and pray. It wasn't even to God in particular. I was out in the field behind the barn, walking and wishing for something better than what we had. It was such a violent, desperate need that I was shaking as I asked for my mother to come back, for my father to stop drinking, for Eric to lose his Tourette's. I wanted to be someone, someone important. I wanted to be revered, I wanted to be respected, I wanted to be loved. I wanted it all so much that I remember thinking I would do anything for it. I would give anything for it.

The next thing I remembered was waking up in the field just as the sun was coming up.

"Do you know the story of that song Crossroads?" Sage went on. His voice was flat.

"By the blues guy?"

"Robert Johnson."

"I think so. He sold his soul to the devil in exchange for success. It happened at the crossroads."

"Do you believe that?"

I put down the drink and gave Sage my full attention. "Well. No. It's just a song."

He let out a small laugh. "Of course it's just a song. You

know Robert Johnson was only twenty-seven when he died. He barely had any success."

"Then the devil was a liar. I wouldn't expect anything less."

"His success came later."

"Then he should have been more specific."

"Some say he didn't even sell his soul. He just made a deal. And it wasn't with the devil himself."

"Either way, I'm sure it wasn't a very sound deal."

He shrugged.

"I'm turning twenty-eight next week," he remarked, finally turning around to face me. His skin was ashen, eyes tired. "Joplin, Morrison, Hendrix, Johnson. They all died at twenty-seven."

"Do you think they all made deals with the devil?" I asked. My next question was, "Did you make a deal with the devil," but I didn't ask it. I just let it sit there on my tongue. It was easier that way. Then it wouldn't be real and no one would have to deal with answering it.

"And I said, 'Hello, Satan, I believe it's time to go,'" Sage sung softly by way of an answer. He scratched at his sideburns and reasoned, "I doubt Morrison would have made any deals."

"Why not? He died rich and famous."

"He died alone," he argued. "The hopeful bargainer will always ask for love."

"He had Pam."

Sage smirked and flopped down on the bed, almost landing on his guitar.

He mumbled into his pillow, "Pam loved him. I don't think he loved Pam. Finding someone you truly love is much harder than finding someone to love you."

Spoken like a true rock star.

In a few minutes he was snoring away. I sighed and walked over to him. I took off his flip-flops, filled a glass of water beside him, placed a few Aspirin there too, then got myself ready for bed. I wondered if Pam ever felt like I did. Based on what Sage had just told me, I decided she did.

CHAPTER SEVENTEEN

"You guys are looking a little rough," Jacob commented. He couldn't disguise the childish glee in his voice.

Sage and I were sitting at the table as the bus headed to Nashville. I don't know about Sage, but I was having a hell of a time trying to keep down the greasy eggs and bacon we had for breakfast.

"We're fine," Sage assured him, chugging back orange juice straight out of the carton. He had told me that a carton of OJ and three ibuprofen were enough to kick the hangover out. I settled for one pill and a glass of juice and so far it wasn't helping. I certainly wasn't built like a rock star.

I could feel Jacob's gold-tinged eyes on my face. After Sage and I emerged from our rooms this morning, the others made no attempt to hide the fact that they thought we screwed around. To my surprise, even Graham looked happy at the prospect and none of them would believe me when I said Sage passed out at 9PM mumbling about Jim Morrison.

Mickey was on the bus with us, his eyes and mouth drawn into pensive lines of worry. Noelle was still under observation for another day but her parents had arrived and made it very clear that they didn't want Mickey around. According to him, she was catatonic, not recognizing anyone, not even him. It was like she completely shut down. The doctors were still hopeful that time and being in a friendly, familiar place would bring her around. We were hopeful too, but I had this dreadful feeling that tugged in the recesses of my heart, like it was a hope in vain.

I wondered if Sage felt the same way. He didn't show it. After opening up to me last night, after our almost intimate encounter, we were back to the friendly but distant rock star and journalist relationship. That was fine for the time being though. I needed to interview him over the next few days so I could get it over with and head home if I wanted to. It wasn't an option at the moment but I wasn't about to rule it out. A lot of what Bob had said ran around in my head like it was on spin cycle.

Nashville presented new problems in terms of having to play after all the recent negative attention the band had been receiving. Add in the fact that they had a new bassist to contend with, and the stakes went up. Yet, I was looking forward to it. Mainly, I was looking forward to hearing from Mel. I crossed my fingers beneath the table and hoped she could get a hold of me.

Nashville was as exciting as I had imagined. There was so much music and soul in the atmosphere that it was immediately addictive. It was like you could feel the presence of every musician who had passed through or honed their craft there hanging in the air like the thick humidity.

We all settled into The Hermitage Hotel just after noon, giving us a few hours before soundcheck. I had my own room once again and what a room it was. In fact, it was the nicest room I had ever been in. It had plush carpets, creamy walls, and expensive wood furnishings that gleamed. No semen-stained bed sheets for Dawn Emerson anymore!

I was only in my room about ten minutes, just enough time to take off my hot bell bottoms and put on a pair of denim cut-offs and a ratty Stones t-shirt, when the phone rang. I leaped off the bed and my heart followed suit. I snatched up the phone on the second ring.

"Hello?" I cried out breathlessly.

The dry voice of the operator came on. "Dawn Emerson? You have a call from Melanie Jones. Please go ahead."

The line clicked and Mel came through. "Bitch!"

I nearly cried at the sound of her voice. "Mel!"

She laughed. "Aw, hey Dawn chicka, oh my god it's so good to hear you."

"I know! I was so afraid you didn't get my letter."

"Oh, I *got* it. Child, we have to talk. Robbie! What the fuck happened with Robbie Oliver!"

It felt kind of stupid rehashing what happened with Robbie. Not only did it feel ages ago but there was nothing exciting about it anymore, not when compared to what had been going on. But I didn't really want to get into the heavy stuff with Mel. I knew she'd worry about me.

So I told her exactly what happened, all the details of the ludes' night.

"Anyway," I finished, "it was no big deal. We're cool."

"He better be cool or I'm going to come down there and kick his ass. Speaking of coming down there…I'm coming down there!"

I was stunned. "What?"

"I booked a flight for the San Antonio show. I have a cousin down there I can stay with, he's cool."

"Oh, Mel…"

"What? Don't you dare tell me you don't want me there, bitch. Because I will cut you. After I hug you first, of course."

I rubbed at my forehead.

"No, it's not that. Of course, I want you here. I want more than anything to see you. But, I don't know, it's really not as fun as you'd think, Mel."

She laughed. "Look, I'm not looking to hang out with the band. I'm not trying to be all cool. I just want to see you and see the show. That's it."

"Have you heard what happened?"

"Yeah, I fucking heard. It's all over the radio here. A chick dies, now Noelle's ill? What even happened with her? The press just says she's sick but they won't say what with."

Demonfever, I thought to myself.

"We don't actually know. Things are pretty heavy here."

"I bet they are. That's why you need me there. I know how you get, Dawn when other people are hurting. You turn into a mother, always taking care of everyone else, sticking around, making sure everyone's going to be all right. That's what you're doing, isn't it?"

"Not really." And that was true. I couldn't take care of those boys if I tried.

"Bogus, Dawn. You totally are. And what's my job as your lovely African princess sidekick? It's to kick your freckly ass."

I couldn't help but laugh. I knew there would be no convincing her. Mel was coming to join me on tour, and there was nothing I could do about it. I tried to be happy.

"All right, there's no stopping you," I relented.

"You got that right, sister. Now I better go before my ma kills me for the phone bill. I love you, lady."

"Love you too," I said sadly.

"See you in Texas. Yeee haw!"

We hung up and I heard her voice still in my head. I sighed and got off the bed. I looked at myself in the ornate mirror that hung above the polished desk. I looked hardened, my hair resigned to the eternal fuzz of humidity. It seemed like every time I got a glimpse of myself, I was looking less like Dawn and more like some other girl. No, not girl. A woman.

Whoever I was turning into, I had to be brave and I had to be strong. I wasn't about to let some scary groupies and superstitions stop me from doing my job. I still had an article to write, one that would finally garner me the respect I craved, the importance I needed, and I had to stop getting sidetracked. Yes, Emerrita was a tragedy and Noelle's condition was sad, but I had to find that thread of journalistic hardness somewhere inside me. I needed to stop feeling with the band. Mel was right, I was becoming too focused on them and how they were feeling. I was getting too close. I needed to become that impartial player once more, and I'd start by treating Sage like a subject and not a friend. And certainly not someone I constantly thought about getting in the sack.

Even though from the way he handled me and the feel of his cock on my thigh, he promised to be a very passionate, rough ride.

"Snap out of it!" I yelled at my reflection. "Do your damn job."

The Dawn in the mirror looked surprised. I took that as a good sign.

* * *

The first show in Nashville went off without a hitch. Hybrid played at a tiny venue right downtown and the place was packed to the doors. Robbie started off the set by saying some heartfelt words about Noelle, though Jacob made sure that any mention of Emeritta was zipped. Then the band launched into one of their most powerful and energetic shows yet. It was good to see them back in the game, and I could tell they needed the show to let out all that they'd been feeling since the festival performance. It was raw and emotive and the crowd called them back for three encores. They played until they were absolutely exhausted.

Even Fiddles, the new bassist, kept up nicely and had a nice presence without being too flashy. Jacob looked pleased to the gills, and I could see the money signs dancing in his head as concertgoers stuck around after the show, snapping up Hybrid t-shirts and albums until they were all gone. Everyone likes a sob story and any press was good press. Jacob was right about that.

The next day in Nashville we were set to play at an outdoor venue just outside of town, headlining for a psychedelic band called Electric Duck Bath. We had the whole day free for exploring or doing whatever, so I chose to accompany Bob on his personal tour around the city. He'd been to Nashville with musicians so many times it was like his second home, and he was a very enthusiastic host.

To be honest, I also went with Bob because I wanted to distance myself a bit from the band. After the show last night, I went straight to my hotel room to compose a review and then I went to bed. I didn't want to party and I didn't want to socialize. I wanted to be the journalist, and who better to hang around with than the only other person who wasn't part of the band?

Between old guitar shops and tiny cafes where we scooped up Moonpies and RC Cola, Bob and I danced around the topic of curses. I asked him if he thought Sage knew something about all of it.

"Assuming what you say is true," I added, licking the sticky marshmallow off my fingers.

"I would think so," Bob reckoned. "But I don't know. If we're talking about Jacob though, I'd say yes."

"Why is that?"

He shrugged. "He's the manager. Managers know everything. And all of this is working out to the band's advantage, don't you think?"

I stopped in my tracks. A piece of crumbled cookie nearly fell out of my mouth. "You think Jacob is behind all this?"

"No," he quickly refuted. "I don't. The Cobb has a reputation for being mean. But I don't think he'd ever hurt another person. Well, another girl. Well, a girl that was harmless."

"But?"

"You can tell there's a but, eh? Well, he's a smart man. Too smart. Too conniving. I wouldn't be surprised if he knew what was going on."

"But what is going on?"

"I don't know, Rusty. It could be anything. It could be nothing. I'm an old bus driver and I ramble sometimes."

"Well I'm a young journalist and I don't think you're rambling. I guess we'll just have to wait and see."

He gave me a grave look with his sprightly blue eyes. "If this does turn out to be more than just my rambling and throwing around frou-frou ideas, I don't think either of us wants to wait and see."

I nodded, hearing what he was saying but not finding the strength to keep going, keep touring, keep wondering.

* * *

The outdoor venue was nowhere near as nice as the one Hybrid played the night before, or even the Charlotte festival. It was pretty much a concert on a farm. Instead of soft fields of grass, it was a mixture of weeds and dirt. Instead of a glorious stage, it was a rather rickety old thing made out of rough wood. The whole thing may have been going for some backwoods, redneck kind of charm but it just came across as cheap and dirty.

The crowd was a weird mix too.

"It's like every Pink Floyd fan is out there," Robbie remarked from the side stage as we watched Electric Duck Bath finish their set. "Where the hell are the Hybrid fans?"

"Maybe we rocked them too hard last night," Chip commented.

Robbie made an annoyed sound. "Ugh. This is going to be one of those 'we have to win you over' shows."

I smacked him lightly on the shoulder. He jumped.

"I thought every show was supposed to be one of those shows."

He pointed at the crowd. They were young kids all swaying their muddled heads and waving their lighters to the band's spaced out moon music. "Do those kids look like they're about to be won over? They're about to fall asleep in an acid coma."

"Weren't you in an acid coma just recently?" Chip remarked. "Or was that Quaaludes?"

I smiled bashfully while Robbie glared at him. "Just make us sound good, Chip."

"Got it, boss."

"Where's boyo?"

"Right here," Mickey mumbled from behind us. He was still pale and sullen—I hadn't seen him smile in days.

Robbie went over and put his arm around him. "I don't know what you and the Sage one are planning on doing, but I'm going to be cranking up my furnace tonight. I mean, I'm going to be a monkey from mars. I'll win these spacey fucks over if it kills me."

"Be careful what you wish for," Graham said, walking past us toward the drums that the Duck Bath's drummer was now vacating.

Robbie frowned at his pithy remark and turned his attention back to Mickey. "Anyway, just so you know. Try and stay out of my way."

Mickey finally looked amused. "Have I ever been in your way, Robbie? I might as well be wallpaper."

I decided to let the band set up and plot their course of action and headed out into the crowd. They were right, it certainly was different, but there were a few metal heads among the hippies, and everyone looked like they were there to have a great time.

I made my way toward the back of the crowd to escape all the dust that was being stirred up, wishing I had worn my cowboy boots instead of sandals. I stopped at the side, grateful for a cooling breeze that chilled the sweat on my forehead. I felt like I'd been sweating for two weeks straight.

"Nice shirt," said a boy who had sidled up next to me. He was skinny as anything, all legs and arms and thick glasses. His hair hung down to the middle of his back and braces shined on his teeth.

I looked down at the Bad Company shirt I had snagged at their show and smiled. Any fan of my type of music was a potential friend.

I learned his name was Aaron and he was from just outside of Memphis. He was there with his brother who wanted to see Electric Duck Bath, though he was more of a Hybrid fan himself.

"I heard they can wail," he told me as if he had some

insider information.

I smiled agreeably and made sure my All Access Pass was still tucked in the back pocket of my shorts. At first it was fun to wear it like a badge of honor, but now I just wanted to blend in with everyone else.

Hybrid got off to a high-powered start. I guess Robbie convinced them to start with the cover of Children of the Grave to whet people's appetites and it worked. All the metal heads, sans me and Aaron, made a beeline to the front of the stage and started pushing against the feeble barricade.

I was just about to remark to Aaron on how boisterous the crowd was when my heart nearly froze. There, to the side of the barricade and by the stage, was Sonja.

She was standing there, watching me. I could barely see her through the crowd, but I could feel her eyes on me, the immense feeling of dread, sinking, drowning dread, like I was being submerged in thick black tar.

Aaron said something to me but I couldn't hear him. All I could do was focus on Sonja.

Then she was no longer alone. Sparky and Terri had joined her, the first time I saw them all together. They followed Sonja's haunting, terrible gaze until they were all looking in my direction.

"Do you see those girls?" I asked Aaron, not caring to hide the pure panic in my voice.

"What girls?"

"By the stage, to the left of it. The two blondes and the black-haired one."

"I see one blonde and one black haired one," he said. "They look pretty freaky, man."

I looked up at him and saw he was squinting in the right direction.

I turned my head back to the stage and saw that he was right. Now it was only Terri and Sparky. And they were starting to walk my way.

"Oh fuck," I yelped.

"What, what?" asked Aaron. "Do you know them?"

"Oh my god," I whimpered, my heart coming to life with a thump. "Oh my god."

I looked around me, wondering where I could go. The right side of the crowd was my only option. If I could run through the audience, I could make my way to the side stage and get there before anything could happen. In a mob of moving people, I was an easy target. At least on stage I was in open view, and even though I had my doubts about Jacob, I still knew he would protect me to the end.

At least I hoped he would.

"What's going on?" Aaron cried out in confusion. Terri and Sparky were closer now, violet and black eyes glowing supernaturally.

I shot him a terrified look. "Whatever you do, Aaron, stay away from those girls. They are bad, bad news. I have to go."

I left him and started pushing my way through the crowd, trying to get to the front. I was panicking, sloppy, and nearly fell a few times as acid-trippers freaked on me and chauvinistic metal heads tried to grab me. I didn't want to look behind me to see if Terri and Sparky were coming my way—I knew they were. I could feel them, hot on my heels, like heat-seeking missiles from Hell.

I almost made it to the front of the stage, the hotly contested property in any popular show, when I saw Sonja. She stood between me and the guard who stood at the side stage entrance.

She smiled at me, coyly, her eyes a vivid lavender which was just as creepy as the black holes I saw in her face the other night.

I looked up at the stage to see if the band had noticed, if they could see her, but Robbie was jumping around like he had a fire under his ass and no one else was paying attention. At one point Mickey looked down at me and gave me a nod of recognition but it was like he didn't see Sonja at all. I looked at her translucent, thin body and saw no type of pass on her. No one should have been in this area except photographers and there were none at this particular show. The security guard at the stage wasn't even paying her any attention. I started to wonder if I was the only who could see her.

Then Sonja raised her chin defiantly and exchanged a heavy look with someone over my shoulder. I felt two pairs of hot hands close around my arms and I didn't need to turn around to know who it was. I was caught.

Sparky and Terri dug their nails into me, puncturing my skin with a fiery stab, hot blood running down my arms, and they began to drag me away from the stage. I screamed and I kicked but no one paid me much attention.

That wasn't the only thing that made my skin tighten with terror.

Sonja walked toward the stage and, before shooting a smug smile my way, disappeared under it.

She walked right under the stage and was gone.

That couldn't have been good.

That wasn't good at all.

And while my brain was trying to process what I saw, I was getting further from the stage. A few people stepped up to me and asked what was going on but Terri and Sparky said I was suffering from a bad acid trip. I opened my mouth to tell them it was a lie but no words could form. It was like one of those dreams where you try to scream and you can't. I couldn't utter a word to save my life.

And I was trying to save my life.

I was almost at the back, near the paddock fence that led into deep, oaky woods, when Sparky's hands came off of me.

I looked around and Terri's hands came away too. Suddenly I had dropped to the ground, landing on my ass on the hard dirt.

Aaron was standing above me with a similar looking kid I assumed was his brother. They were standing between me and the GTFOs and they weren't mincing words.

"You get the fuck out of here before we call security," Aaron sneered through his braces. Sparky made a hissing sound and made another move for me but Aaron's brother put out his hand

and held her back.

"We have brown belts in Tae Kwon Do," he warned. "And I've been waiting to go all Bruce Lee on a couple of chicks."

I tried to catch my breath and got to my feet. I took a proud stand behind them.

"Now it's three against two and I'm a fan of Bruce Lee too," I threatened with false bravado. "Oh look, I can talk again."

Sparky and Terri exchanged a look before Sparky hocked a loogie my way. I ducked just in time and it landed on the dirt with a steaming hiss. Yeah, these chicks were totally normal. Not Satanic at all.

"Enjoy the rest of the show," Terri snarled, and together they disappeared into the crowd.

Aaron and his brother turned to look at me and I could only give them a smile of relief and thanks before I remembered it wasn't over yet.

"There's another one," I cried out. "She went under the stage."

"What?" one of them asked but I had already started running. Sonja wouldn't have been under there with that disgustingly smug look on her face, unless...unless...

I was halfway back to the front when it happened.

At first there was a terrific, inhuman groan, followed by confused looks from the band members and hushed words of bewilderment in the crowd. Then the stage began to buckle. There was a crackling sound, like fireworks, and the scaffolding above and behind the stage began to twist and snap just as the ground beneath the band's feet began to splinter like broken toothpicks.

I screamed and tried to push harder through the crowd, who were also panicking. The scaffolding collapsed straight down, slamming into the stage and taking a bit of the first row as well.

It was pure chaos. People were running everywhere, screaming, crying. I was pushed back and back with the incoming tide, further away from the place I needed to be.

When I was finally able to ride it out, when the mass of

people stopped pressing against me, I was able to run toward the stage, the only person who, along with fire trucks and paramedics, was just arriving at the scene. Their red lights and sirens echoed in the night air, a too timely sense of déjà vu.

The security guard emerged from the stage, holding his ripped off shirt to his head where it was bleeding profusely.

"Stay back, miss, please."

"I'm with the band!" I screamed. I fumbled for the pass in my pocket, showing it to him just as Fiddles and Graham emerged from the wreckage, looking dazed but uninjured.

"Where are the rest of them?" I screamed, breaking out of the security guy's grasp and getting in Graham's face. I was ready to blame this whole thing on him and the fact that he was unscathed didn't help either.

Graham just ignored me and walked off. He'd probably blame that on some sort of post-accidental daze. But Fiddles, god bless his weirdly named soul, grabbed hold of my hand and brought me back to the stage, which was more or less a pile of ruins and broken equipment. The huge banner that said Hybrid and Electric Duck Bath was flapping in the wind at the bottom, and we heard a few groans. As we lifted the banner off the ground, we saw Robbie lying on his side, gritting his teeth in pain.

I dropped to my knees and touched him on the cheek. "Robbie, are you okay?"

He nodded painfully. "My wrist. I think it's broken. Something hit it."

I smoothed his golden hair from his face. "Hang tight. I'm going to check on your brothers."

The security guard was soon on my tail, staying with Robbie as I climbed onto the rest of the stage.

"Sage? Mickey?" I cried out, my eyes searching the collapsed areas where they should have been.

"We're okay," came a voice to the back. I looked up and saw Sage and Mickey's head poking up. They were off the stage, completely behind it and standing on the ground.

I let out the breath I was holding in.

By the time I picked my way through the stage rubble, the paramedics were busy treating people. So far, somehow, it just seemed to be Robbie with a banged up wrist, the security guard, and two concertgoers who were treated for minor injuries. It looked far, far worse than it actually was.

I dodged the reporters who had gathered around the scene. I wondered how they had gotten here so fast and if there was some sort of journalist convoy that was following the band around just like the GTFOs. Only they were the reporters not the destroyers. I had come to the very weighty conclusion that the psychotic, demonic girls were the cause of everything that was plaguing the band.

And I had a feeling it wouldn't come as a surprise to either Sage or Jacob.

With those new thoughts forming in my head, I ran around the collapsed stage looking for either one of them, wanting answers, but neither were around. I did run into Aaron and his brother, whose name was Dave, and I practically fell to my knees in praise of them. I think they were pretty stoked to have saved a young lady and played it off, but nonetheless, I gave them my name and told them if they were ever at a Hybrid show to tell security that Dawn Emerson had sent them. I didn't know if it would work, but I wanted to give their brave hearts just a bit of hope.

I climbed on the tour bus and saw Mickey and Sage sitting in the near dark with silent, grim expressions on their faces. I looked at Bob.

"Where's Jacob?"

Bob sighed. "He's probably going to be a while. The promoter of the show is blaming him and the band for the stage collapse. He says Robbie's bouncing around caused it all."

I shook my head but was unsure how much I should say. Bob shot me a warning look and I decided to keep my mouth shut for the time being. We were almost sure that Sage wouldn't bat an eye about our curse theory—and if he did it was a well-rehearsed eye—but Mickey most likely had no idea. And he had already gone through too many traumatic events for one lifetime. Poor bearded dude deserved a medal.

I moved to the back and plunked myself down beside Sage.

"Can I talk to you?" I whispered in his ear. He still smelled like that sweet pipe tobacco, a scent I would forever associate with weakening knees.

He seemed to think that over. Then he whispered back, low voice and hot breath on my skin. "Can we talk tomorrow? I'm having a hard enough time thinking as it is."

I nodded. Even though Sage might know something, he was still the leader of the band and still human. His thoughts were obviously with Robbie, hoping that one of his best friends, if not his best friend, was going to be okay.

I must have fallen asleep where I was, because when I woke up, my head was on Sage's shoulder and Jacob was just coming on the bus. Robbie was behind him.

There were a few claps and I realized that Graham and Fiddles had joined us on the bus too.

"It's just a sprain," Jacob announced. His eyes glinted, unreadable. "He'll be able to play in New Orleans tomorrow, isn't that right, Robbie?"

Robbie nodded and raised his wrapped wrist in the air. "And the show goes on."

I felt Sage stiffen up next to me. It lasted only a second. But it was enough to tell me that we'd be talking tomorrow no matter what happened. We were lucky. If things had gone the wrong way there would be no show to carry on.

CHAPTER EIGHTEEN

"What happened to your arms, Dawn?" Fiddles asked with his crooked brown eyes.

I had just rolled out of the bunk and was rubbing my eyes at the murky daylight that was filtering in through the dirty windows of the bus.

Oh right, my scabby, cut arms. The places where the GTFOs had made their presence known.

Even though the band knew all about them, I held back on filling them in on what happened to me. Everyone except Sage.

"The crowd got pretty crazy," I replied casually.

Close to New Orleans, we pulled into a diner off the main highway. It was white and intricate, like a small version of a plantation house, and the parking lot was bordered by waving sweet gum and magnolia. It was the perfect place to grab Sage's arm as we got off the bus and lead him toward the shade of a towering oak.

We stopped by the rough bark, eyeing each other like we'd been separated for months and weren't sure where we stood.

"We have to talk," I said, letting go of his arm.

He smiled and my heart melted. "Are you breaking up with

me, Dawn? I thought things were going well."

I couldn't help but smile in return. I quickly composed myself. "What happened last night?"

He frowned but I didn't believe his confusion for a second. "The stage collapsed."

One of my eyes began to twitch. "Aside from that. You didn't see or hear anything strange?"

If he was surprised by my question, he didn't act it. He calmly folded his strong arms. In the swampy setting around us, the snakes tattooed on his forearms took on a whole new realism. "Please elaborate."

"I will. And keep in mind that I know what I'm about to say sounds ludicrous but I'm past the point of caring. I'm past the point of most things now."

He nodded, his full pink lips pursed in anticipation.

I ignored them and went on to tell him everything that happened at the concert. I didn't fill him in on the backstory, about what I saw with Noelle, or my talks with Bob, but I told him everything else.

When I was done I could tell it was taking time to sink in. A range of emotions flashed in his eyes and his chest heaved as if breathing became a chore. He bit his lip like if he didn't, the truth would spill from his mouth.

Acting on that and nothing else, I swear, I took a step toward him, closing the gap, and reached for his lips with my hand. I put my fingers on them softly, and said, "Whatever it is you're not telling me, I think I deserve to know now. Whether I'm just an annoying journalist to you or something more. Or something less. I'm still a person. And, believe it or not, I care about your stupid band. I care about you."

He grabbed my wrist with his hand. He stepped closer, so his face was right up to mine and said in a lowered and smooth voice, "You do deserve to know everything. Even the things that I can't come to terms with. But not now. Not here. This isn't the place."

I looked around me at the green lawns and swampy

surroundings. We were about to board the bus and head into the city of voodoo, the city of New Orleans. If Sage said whatever he had to tell me needed to wait, I believed him.

"Okay," I said, shoving my finger in his face. "But before the show and after the show, wherever you are, I'm going to be there. You're going to tell me what the fuck is going on and after that, you're going to give me my god damn interview."

I thought he was going to lick my finger for a second. Instead he said, "Deal."

We made our way back to the diner, grabbed a bite to eat, and were back on the road. The road to answers.

*   *   *

I stayed true to my word. I pretty much became Sage's shadow, following him everywhere he went, my tape recorder tucked firmly into my messenger bag. He tolerated me, barely, and I never pushed him for answers. I just waited and made sure he knew I was waiting.

The band was understandably jittery when it came time to perform. Robbie was hopped up on painkillers for his hand, something he was happy about considering he usually paid a lot for the same pills off the street. Everyone else was double-checking the stage every five minutes. Luckily the venue was small, sturdy, and fairly new.

Despite that though, barely anyone showed up. It was the most timid, lackluster, and small crowd I'd seen yet on the tour. I would have thought New Orleans and its occult and black magick leanings would have brought out the fans and music goers with morbid curiosity, kind of like a car wreck, but that wasn't the case. People were scared of Hybrid and stayed away. There were maybe fifty people there, tops.

The band looked scared of themselves too. They played subdued and with an air of defeat. Robbie went through the motions, containing himself (the drugs probably had a hand in that), and even Graham's drums sounded faint. It was a sad, sad show, and as I stood on the side stage with the increasingly mysterious Jacob, I could see the lines of worry on each and every band member's foreheads.

I had thought about asking Jacob some more pressing questions about Graham and the GTFOs but judging from the swears that spilled out of his lips every five minutes and the hate-filled glare in his eyes, I decided against it. Whether he had something to do with it all or not, he was the band's manager and for once wasn't able to manage everything. There was no doubt that a lawsuit was going to follow from the stage collapse and there was certainly no way the band was going to make a profit from the New Orleans show. Things were slowly spiraling out of control. Maybe Jacob didn't care about needless deaths and mental illnesses, but he did care about money and now it was finally hitting him where it hurt.

When the band was finished and slogged off the stage with heavy hearts and shoulders, I walked to the backstage area to go wait for Sage. There was more than one dressing room for the guys, so Sage had taken one for himself and I sat on the chair outside, waiting patiently. I only left his side for a few minutes when I had to go to the bathroom and when I came back, the door was still closed.

One of the other dressing rooms opened and Mickey came out.

"Hey," I said to him, almost tempted to call him 'boyo' as the others did. "Did you see Sage come out?"

Mickey finished buttoning up his plaid shirt and shrugged. "I haven't seen him."

He started to walk off.

I called after him. "Mickey. I know I haven't had the chance to tell you this, but I'm really sorry about Noelle. I liked her you know."

He twitched for a second and stopped. He looked at me over his shoulder.

"Don't talk about her like she's not coming back," he said. His eyes held mine for a brief second and I could see a wealth of sadness in them before he disappeared around the corner.

I sighed, feeling lost and stupid, like I overstepped my bounds, and sat back in the chair for a few moments. Finally I got up and rapped lightly on the door.

"Sage? Are you in there? It's time."

I put my ear to the door and listened. I heard something from inside the room, like a chair being pushed back.

"I'm coming in," I said. "You better cover up what you don't want me to see."

Was it wrong to hope he wasn't covering up anything? I nearly drooled at the thought. I wiped my mouth cautiously then opened the door.

It was empty. What I could see of it anyway. It was obviously never meant to be a dressing room and had an extra room that was separated by half a wall. There were stacks of chairs and old PA equipment spilling out from around the corner.

That's where I heard the noise again, followed by the sound of a chair being pushed back.

"Sage?" I ventured again. I walked toward the noise, wondering what he could be doing back there. I wished the light from the middle of the room reached far enough, but most of the chairs and equipment were lost in shadow.

I was nearly at the wall, ready to peak over the side, when I heard another noise.

One that made my blood run cold.

It was a wet, slopping sound, like something slimy and heavy was being dragged along the tile floor, heading in my direction. I had heard and seen the shadow of the same thing on the bus, and I was in no hurry to see it again. In my head I pictured a giant earthworm with two legs, dragging its slimy gray segmented body along, leaving trails of goo and blood, a round mouth filled with rotating teeth, open and ready for sucking.

I almost vomited from fright.

"Dawn?"

I gasped and whipped around, startled to see Sage standing in the doorway, rubbing a towel at his curls.

His eyes narrowed. "What is it?"

I looked back at the wall. The noise had stopped. That was probably the only chance we were getting.

I turned and ran toward him.

"I think we need to get out of here," I said, grabbing his forearm. My fingers barely fit around it. He didn't budge, his eyes on the back of the room.

"Did you see something?"

"I didn't see something, I heard something," I told him, panic rising in my voice. I tugged on him again. "And if you know what's good for you, you're not going to stick around and let it show itself to you."

He bit his lip, almost as if he was deciding whether to explore it or not. He looked down at me, a knowing twist to his lips.

"Is it something bad?"

"Sage," I said, pulling him closer, keeping my gaze steady. "It's the worst."

He nodded quickly. "I thought it might come to this."

We scampered out of the room and slammed the door shut.

"Should we warn the others?" I asked, nodding at the other dressing room.

He shook his head. "If we tell them not to go in there, they'll just go in there."

We crossed the hall and he knocked on the door. "Guys?"

"Do you know what it is?" I whispered.

He gave his head a slight shake. The dressing room opened and Fiddles popped his head out.

"What's up, my good man?"

"Dawn and I are going to meet a friend of mine," Sage told him.

This was news to me.

"It's like, getting late, man," Fiddles said.

"We won't be too long. And if we are, hold the bus. This is very important."

Fiddles shrugged. "All right, catch you later."

He went back in the room and Sage was walking fast toward the exit. I ran after him, my bag bouncing against my thigh.

"Where are we going? I thought I was going to get some answers."

"We're both going to get some answers."

He opened the door and we stepped out into the humid night that smelled of coffee and gasoline. I'd always dreamed of visiting New Orleans, having some beignets and wandering around the French Quarter, reveling in the atmosphere. Of course life had different plans for me and I soon found myself in the back of a dodgy cab with Sage as he read out an address from a business card.

I snatched it from his hand and peered at it in the light.

"Mambo Maryse," I read out loud. There was only the name and an address. "What on earth is a Mambo?"

"Someone who hopefully can help us."

"Help us?"

He gave me a grave look. "Sorry, Dawn. You're in this now, too."

I looked at the cabbie who was eyeing us suspiciously in the rearview mirror. "Do you know what a Mambo is?"

His eyes grew wide and he shook his head vigorously. "No man, no I don't want any part of this. No part. I'll drop you on the corner of the street and then you'll have to walk."

Sage scrunched up his forehead with his hands. "Whatever, just get us as close as you can."

I wanted to throttle him and demand he tell me what was going on. But getting answers from Sage was like pulling teeth, and he had a fear of the dentist.

I sat back in the seat and tried to compose my thoughts that were flying all over the place. It didn't do me any good. I couldn't come up with any conclusions. I had no choice but to wait until we met this Mambo Maryse.

CHAPTER NINETEEN

Twenty minutes later the cab pulled to a stop at the end of a deserted street. We had left the city a while back and the land had changed from built-up and bright to dark and spacious. This street bordered what looked to be swampland, maybe a bayou or a river. Dark, depressed trees waved their long leaves in a building wind. The houses facing them were scattered apart with messy lawns and rusting trucks in the driveways. I suddenly wished we had stayed back at the venue, but with that horrible sucking creature in the dressing room, that wasn't much of an option either.

The cabbie didn't waste a second and took off when we closed the doors, the wheels spinning.

"Didn't even have a chance to pay him," Sage muttered as it disappeared in the distance.

That wasn't good.

He looked warily down the street we were on where the faded streetlamps stopped The houses down that dark way looked old and forgotten, almost swallowed up by the wild vegetation.

"Looks like we'll have to head down that way for a bit."

That also wasn't good.

We walked, keeping a vigilant watch around us for anything

out of the ordinary. We passed one house where an old lady sat in the shadowy porch chair, swinging with the breeze, not moving an inch. I had to wonder if she was dead or alive.

"Can you at least tell me how you knew about this person?" I whispered.

"My uncle," was his answer. "He's good for this sort of thing. You meet a lot of strange people when you're in a traveling Mariachi band."

"Unlike a traveling rock band?"

"Stranger."

When we finally found the house with the right address, I was quite surprised to see it was the most well-kept house on the street. It was dark and small with a red glow from the windows and beads instead of curtains. There was a tended garden with flowering plants that smelled heavenly. We went up the stony path to the front door and, after taking a steadying breath, Sage knocked on it.

We waited, listening.

"Are you even sure anyone is home? Is she expecting you?"

He gave me a look indicating I needed to shut up. So I did.

We waited some more, and he was about to knock again when we heard the slide of the peephole. After a few beats, as if the person was deciding whether to open the door or not, we heard many locks being undone and finally the door opened.

The woman was lit from behind with that eerie crimson glow. I couldn't really see her face, but she was short with pulled back dark hair.

"Can I help you?" she asked in a full-on Creole accent.

"Hi, I'm sorry to bother you so late," Sage began.

"Late is all relative. What do you want?"

I eyed Sage expectantly. *Yes*, I thought. *What do you want?*

"I got your card off my uncle. You met him once when his band was here, the Mariachi Seven. His name was Felipe Gonzales."

"He sounds very Mexican. I think I recall him."

Her head turned in my direction briefly. I smiled faintly

before her attention went back to Sage. "But you didn't answer my question. What do you want?"

"I need your help with a hex removal."

I don't know what I expected Sage to say but I didn't expect that. The woman, however, just raised her brow and calmly said, "All right. Come on in."

I followed Sage inside the house. The woman pulled on the string of a table lamp and I was able to see her more clearly. She was pretty and surprisingly young, maybe thirty at the very oldest. Her eyes were small and dark, skin smooth and pale, eyebrows full and expressive. She was wearing a long African looking tunic made up of oranges and browns. She stood in front of us and clasped her hands together.

"I am Mambo Maryse," she announced. "Please tell me your names."

"I'm Sage Knightly," he said. "This is Dawn Emerson."

"Are you a couple?"

"No," I said quickly, perhaps protesting a bit too much.

She nodded, clearly noticing.

"Do you have money up front?"

Sage was caught off-guard. He paused and pulled out his wallet from his dark jeans. "I've never done this before, I don't know how much."

"I charge by the half hour," she answered simply. "Fifty dollars. A genuine hex removal will take at least an hour. We will have to investigate the problem first, then I'll have to make a potion specifically for you."

Potion? I looked around the room and noticed how normal it all looked. Just the neat and tidy, albeit dark, home of a single woman.

She noticed me staring.

"My office is downstairs." She waited until Sage gave her a hundred dollar bill then she turned gracefully and made her way down the narrow hallway. "Come with me, please."

We walked down a short flight of narrow red lacquered stairs and then we were in her office. This was more like it. It was dark, the walls were a lush purple color, and books, tomes of all sizes, were piled high on dark wood bookcases. There was a little table in the corner that looked like it belonged at an herbalist's, piled high with strange jars, liquids, and powders. There was also a kettle and bags of tea, which I assumed were for tea leaf reading. In the middle of the room was a round table with two chairs on either side with an honest to god crystal ball on it as well as a pendulum and a stack of cards. Two white candles burned brightly in a silver holder.

Instinctively I grabbed Sage's hand. He gave me a squeeze and held on tightly.

Mambo Maryse brought over another chair from the side of the room and put it at the table. She nodded at it.

"Here, sit down, please."

We did so. The candlelight flickered ominously on her face as she studied us.

"I would like to hear what is going on. Why do you think you're being hexed? From the beginning, if you will."

I kept hold of his warm hand. He steadied himself with a deep breath and launched into it.

"I don't really know when it started. We've just had a lot of bad luck lately. Especially on the tour. I'm a musician like my uncle. I'm the guitarist in a band called Hybrid, a bit of a hybrid of sounds: metal, rock, and blues. Anyway, a few months ago, someone broke into our rehearsal space and stole all of our equipment."

I looked at him in shock. I hadn't heard any of this.

He continued, his eyes watching the flames dance. "It was a lot of money. Aside from my acoustic which I kept in my house, everything was lost. We weren't even going to do a big tour for Molten Universe—that's our new album—a lot of the songs don't translate well live and we just wanted to get on with recording the next one. But now we had no instruments and no money. On top of that, album sales weren't as strong as the last

229

two. So we had to do this tour. We needed to earn our keep. And then things started getting, well, weirder. I had this feeling like I was being followed everywhere I went. My dreams were about fire and monsters, things you'd see in the movies. I couldn't sleep anymore and I was worried about the tour. I just had this terrible fucking feeling like it was all a big mistake. Then Graham, our drummer, had this great idea of getting a journalist to cover the tour. Our band manager agreed and found Dawn here."

The woman's eyes flicked to me briefly then went back to Sage. I noticed she was watching him closely, almost in disbelief.

"Dawn can attest that the tour's been crazy. I don't know if you follow the news, but we had a girl, a fan, die from a drug overdose in our trailer a few nights ago. Then our bassist went batshit crazy and she's being treated in a hospital. Last night our stage in Nashville collapsed, though thank god no one was hurt. Tonight there was barely anyone at the show. We're losing money now and we're going to get sued over the stage collapse."

She squinted at him. "That's it?"

He looked puzzled and laughed nervously. "Well, what more do you want?"

"And you think there is a hex on you? Who do you think would do that?"

He shrugged and exchanged a look with me. Mambo Maryse was watching me closely now.

"I think I would like to hear from Dawn here. She seems to have a different story than you do."

I opened my mouth to say something but she continued, "But first I would like the truth to compare it to. And though I believe what you say has happened to you, is happening to you, I don't believe you're being honest with either me or your friend. Or perhaps yourself."

She put her hands on the table, palms up.

"Put your hands in mine."

I let go of Sage. He seemed nervous. Terrified, actually. I didn't like seeing him terrified. He was supposed to be my rock.

He was certainly built like one.

"What are you going to do?" he asked tersely.

"I'm just going to hold your hands. That's all. I will see if I can get a reading off of you. If not, I will use ceromancy." She winked at me, the first show of humor. "That's just reading candle wax."

"Do it," I whispered, kicking him lightly under the table. She wasn't going to bite. At least, I hoped she wouldn't.

With great reluctance, Sage laid his hands in hers. They were so large and dark compared to her small, pale ones. She gripped him lightly and closed her eyes.

We watched as she sat there, motionless at first. Then she began to frown and twitch. It got worse and I wondered if she was having a seizure of some sort. It reminded me of my brother on rough days.

Finally, she grew completely still. Sage and I leaned forward, holding our breaths, watching her closely.

Her eyes flew open. They were completely black from rim to rim.

I stifled a scream. We were too scared to move.

She spoke in a thick and raspy metallic voice. "You, fool. Did you really think you could get out of the deal? We told you the conditions and you agreed. This is your fate, Sage Knightly, this is the fate you chose."

Then the woman closed her eyes, twitched once more, and shot up out of her chair, her eyes back to normal and filled with fright. She pointed at him, hand shaking.

"Get out!" she cried. "You get out of here! Your lie could have cost me!"

"What's going on?" I scrambled to my feet, nearly knocking over the chair.

Mambo Maryse shook on the spot. "You may invite a demon into your life, but you do not invite a demon into my home!"

"Demons?" I cried out.

Sage refused to move. He stared the woman down.

"I'm not leaving until you tell me what to do! I paid you!"

The woman pulled the bill out of her robe and threw it on the table. "You take your money and get out. You knew this wasn't a hex. You lied!"

"Sage, what the fuck is she talking about!?" I screamed, my focus swinging between the two.

"Tell her," she commanded. "She deserves to know what you dragged her into."

"Hey, I didn't drag her into anything!" he yelled, coming around the table toward her, a towering man on a mission. "My manager did!"

The woman stood her ground. In all the fear and confusion, I was impressed.

"Your manager is part of it! Didn't you question it? You knew you made the bargain, you knew it."

"I was only fifteen!" he bellowed, his voice booming across the room. Utter anguish contorted his face. "I wanted a better life! I shouldn't have to suffer for it!"

"But you have been. You knew this was coming. You're going to lose everything that was given to you."

"So how do I stop it?!"

"You can't," she told him. A flash of sympathy clouded her eyes. "You can't stop it."

"Would someone tell me what the fuck is going on here?" I yelled, throwing my hands up in the air.

She looked down at the ground. "You need to leave. Both of you. Sage, I suggest you fill her in while there is still time. You're only twenty-seven for a few more days."

My eyes widened.

"I'll go," Sage said, defeated. He eyed the bill on the table but didn't pick it up. "But please, tell me what I can do to save any of the others. They shouldn't have to suffer because of me."

"I said there's nothing you can do. You made a deal with black forces. Almost with Satan himself. There is no getting out of it. Your only hope is the code."

"Code?"

Her mouth jerked briefly with dry amusement. "A moral code. They only take what is owed. Nothing more and nothing less. You need to think about exactly what the deal was. What it is you asked for. That's the only place you'll find answers. I can't give them to you."

I exhaled sharply through my nose, trying to keep my frustration and anger under control. The woman was being kind and giving us this much.

I put my hand on his arm. "Come on, we need to go."

Sage sighed and gave me a quick nod. We left up the stairs, leaving Mambo Maryse behind to start cleansing her office, chanting and waving smoke around.

Neither of us bothered to call a cab from her house, so we walked down the dark, quiet street in silence. I waited for him to speak. I knew if I started, I'd end up crying or screaming or hitting him. I didn't do well when frustrated. I didn't even know where to begin.

We were turning onto the main road when Sage finally spoke.

"I'm going to tell you everything," he said quietly. "You might not believe me. But it's the truth. You might hate me. But it's the truth."

"I'll try to keep an open mind," I said. After hearing monsters in the dressing room and seeing another entity speak through our medium, there wasn't much I wouldn't believe. I was as willing as they got.

"When I was fifteen, I went camping with Robbie and his family. They were outdoorsy people. My dad was always working on the farm so I didn't have that many chances to get away. And I liked Robbie's family. They always welcomed me. They had what I once had. So we went to Lake Shasta. It was the usual spot for people in the area. It's beautiful. Warm. The lake is full of fish, this unbelievable green-blue, and the banks are this rich red earth. We stayed on one of the many peninsulas that jutted out into the water. Robbie's parents in one tent. Me and Robbie in the other.

"I woke up in the middle of the night thinking that someone was calling my name. Part of me thought I was still dreaming. I got up and realized I had to pee anyway. I left the tent, not waking Robbie, and walked through the darkness. The area there at night is pretty spooky. It's alive with creatures. I saw the calm eyes of a gray fox as I walked down the path toward the lake edge. Some animal growled and moaned across the shore.

"I didn't think Lake Shasta was sacred in any way. It's a manmade lake, after all. So I pissed in it as teens do. Then I put my ass down on the ground and started to cry. I remember feeling so distraught, so helpless and alone. I guess years of not dealing with my mother's death caught up with me. I had so much want inside, ripping me apart. I had just joined the band with Robbie but I was the drummer. I wanted to be more than that. I saw Mickey and his girlfriend Noelle. I was jealous. I was a scrawny little shit back then, and unfortunately I was in love with Noelle and she'd never given me a second look. We were poor too, and my dad was struggling. Things were just bad. And to a fifteen-year-old, it was life-threatening.

"I don't know how I just lied there, crying on those muddy banks, my pajamas totally ruined by the clay. I remember thinking I'd need a new pair and that my dad was going to be furious.

"That's when the splashing started. I looked at the lake and…there was a woman walking out of it. She was totally naked. Long pale white hair, even when wet. She was the most gorgeous thing I'd ever seen and at that point I'd been looking at a lot of Robbie's nudie mags.

"Obviously I thought I was dreaming. I'd told myself that it was all just a dream for a very, very long time. But I know that's not the case anymore.

"I got to my feet and the woman walked toward me, leaving no footprints behind. She had brilliant light gold eyes that seemed to glow from within. I asked her who she was. She told me her name was Alva and that she could give me whatever I wanted.

"I didn't believe her but then again I thought it was a dream.

How the hell could it not be a dream? So I asked her, "What do you mean, anything?"

"She said she was magic and that if I wanted to make a deal with her, she would give me anything my heart desired. Smart boy that I was, even in a dream, I asked her what the catch was.

"She smiled and said there was no catch. That this was a loan. I would tell her what I wanted and she would give it to me for a certain amount of time. When the time was up, they would take back everything that was given to me.

"I asked who "they" were—she said she didn't work alone. She made the deals and she had others making sure that all sides of the bargain were upheld. This, in her words, meant making sure my desires were fulfilled, then later, making sure they were taken from me."

Debt collectors, I thought.

"It sounded like a pretty good bargain to my young mind. Not that I believed a second of it. But for a dream, it made sense. So I told Alva what I wanted. I said, "I want to rich and famous. I want to be really good at guitar and to be known for my songwriting skills. I want respect from my bandmates, everyone except Robbie because he already respects me. I want to find someone to love, and when I do, I want them to love me back."

"So Alva stuck out her hand. We shook on it. It felt our hands were being fused together. The lake began to bubble and boil like a hot tub, steam started to rise, as did dark shapes from the water. I saw monsters skulking around in the clay, giant earthworms with teeth. Alva's eyes went from pale gold to tar black and when she smiled her face turned into a demon's.

""You'll be seeing us soon. Enjoy your twenty-eighth birthday," she said in a voice that sounded exactly like what came out of Mambo Maryse.

"Then it all went black. When I woke up, I was still on the banks of the river and the sun was just creeping over the mountains. Birdsong filled the air. It was nearly impossible to think it was anything other than a dream.

"Shortly after, the guitarist fell ill and I took his place. Turns out I was brilliant at the guitar, more so than I used to be. After that, Graham joined and pushed our sound to another level. Success came slowly but surely. My father was injured in a minor car accident but ended up winning a huge settlement. When I left school, I fell in love with the most gorgeous woman I had ever seen. Soon she fell in love with me and we were married. I had respect. A bit of fame. A bit of fortune. I had everything.

When I was twenty-five, my wife decided she'd had enough of me. She asked for a divorce and took half my money. After that I fell in love with a model. She died a year later, slipped in her bathtub. Freak accident. Then I had a brief affair with Noelle while she and Mickey were on a break. I don't need to tell you what has happened to her. Money started to disappear. I wanted to push myself on Molten Universe, but the album didn't quite do it. My twenty-eighth birthday is around the corner, Dawn. Everything else will be taken."

I had been so busy listening, absolutely enthralled and horrified, that I hadn't noticed how far we'd walked. We were approaching the city again and the chances of getting a cab were on the rise.

Sage stopped and put his hands on my shoulders.

"Do you believe any of that?" he whispered.

I nodded, even though it sounded too outrageous to be true. I mean, I know I just said I had an open mind but…this was pushing it. I could believe demons and curses, but I had a hard time thinking this was because of a bargain he made with a woman called Alva nearly fifteen years ago.

Well, a demon called Alva and her minions of debt collectors. And just like that, everything made sense again. Or at least it tried to make sense. I felt like I had an ill-fitting puzzle board and I was pressing really hard to get the pieces to fit.

"How do I come into it?" I asked, my voice soft. I was scared to hear the answer.

Sage took his hand and ran it down the side of my cheek, his fingers gently stroking my skin. Goosebumps of desire competed with goosebumps of fear. Maybe they were one and the same.

"I'm so sorry," he whispered, resting his forehead against mine, his eyes staring absently at my lips. "I forgot to mention. One of the things I asked from Alva was that our last tour go down in history and that the story be in every magazine and newspaper. Everyone on earth would know the story of Hybrid."

I flinched.

"So you can see why I didn't want you on this tour. If no one was there to write about it, no one would care. I really didn't want this to be our last tour."

I swallowed hard, breaking out of his grasp. "We need a cab. Then I need a drink. And maybe some of Robbie's painkillers."

"It's a lot to take in," he admitted.

I laughed caustically, feeling like I was losing my mind. "It's a lot to take in already. It's too bad there's more to come."

We walked for a bit longer until we caught a cab. I was trapped in my head, just reeling, unable to come to terms with what was going on. Bob hadn't been far off with his ideas. I just didn't know what the hell I was supposed to do with the information. Convince everyone else to cancel the tour? Tell Bob to get out while he could? Oh god, Mel was meeting us in San Antonio tomorrow. I was going to have to do everything in my power to make sure she was safe.

Once we were back at the venue, we were met with a bunch of angry people. I felt like yelling at them all and asking them if they had any idea what the bigger picture was here. But I couldn't.

I also wanted to do something to Graham, anything. If my instincts were telling me something, it was that he wasn't even part of the damn band and never was. He was only there to make sure the contract was fulfilled. He probably wasn't even human.

And Jacob. The man who wrangled me into this mess. I had a few words for him but they had to wait till morning.

I climbed onto the bunk in my clothes, feet aching from the walk, head aching from the revelations. I fell asleep, hoping I'd live to see the sunrise.

CHAPTER TWENTY

I missed the sunrise but I did wake up, which was a major bonus. I hadn't died in my sleep and the bus hadn't careened off the road in some horrible accident. I was alive and so was everyone else. No one was very cheery, of course, as the bus made its way through strong sunshine and flat, dry desert on the way to San Antonio. The rest of the band was hung up on the dismal showing of the New Orleans show.

I was hung up on the fact that Sage made a deal with the devil and it seemed like everything was going to be taken from him—and from us—over the next few days. Two different things to worry about but each was valid in its own way.

When the bus pulled into a remote diner for breakfast I took the opportunity to grab Jacob.

"Can we have breakfast in here? Alone?" I asked him.

He frowned but didn't ask why. "All right, love. I guess one of the boys can bring us back something to eat."

"No problem," Bob spoke up. They all piled off the bus, stretching to the fresh air and sunshine. Sage was the last to leave and he was giving me a look, either the "don't you want me to stay?" eyes or the "what the hell are you doing?" stare but I gave him a quick shake of my head, my hint to leave me and Jacob alone. He obliged, dragging his flip-flops.

After they left, Jacob picked up the kettle. "I suppose some more coffee is probably needed, am I correct?"

"You are."

He made us both a cup and plunked the coffee creamer on the table for me. He eased himself into the booth, had a sip, then gave me a very insincere smile.

"I have a feeling I'm not going to like this," he said.

"Only if you have a problem with being honest."

"Rusty, I'm as honest as they come."

I cleared my throat and stared him down. And who was 'they' anyway?

"There's a very small chance that you'll think I'm crazy. Or that Sage is crazy. Or that I'm crazy for believing him. But I have to tell you anyway because I believe it's the truth. And I believe you already know about it. I just want to make sure we're on the same page."

A small smile twitched on his lips, his eyes flickering with uncertainty. "Go on…"

I started at the beginning of the tour and touched on every single thing. Everything. The GTFOs, Noelle, Graham, the stage collapse, what happened with Sage last night. *Everything*.

When I was done explaining, the coffee was cold and I was out of breath. I glanced at the diner, hoping they weren't coming back soon, and brought my expectant gaze to Jacob's.

He was smiling at me. "So what do you want me to say?"

I looked at him askance. "I don't know…anything. I mean, you're involved. The mambo said so."

"Well if the mambo said," he said jokingly. He leaned back in his seat, resting one arm along the top of it.

"So you're not?"

"I'm not involved. That's not my job."

"What's your job then?"

"I'm the manager. I manage."

"So you don't believe me."

"Believe you? Rusty, I know everything that you've told me. I've seen it too. I know exactly what's going on and I've known for a very long time."

My mouth dropped open. "How…how is that possible?"

"How is any of this possible?" He gestured at the bus. "It just is."

"What are you?" the words barely escaped my mouth.

"Nice choice of words there. Are you insinuating I'm not quite human? Perhaps a demon like Graham? No, I'm human. I am now anyway. I made my own deal."

"I don't follow you."

"There are others like me, Rusty. We're intermediaries. Some of us are guides. Some of us are guards in another place not unlike this one, a place called the Thin Veil. Some of us are managers in the most literal sense. We are referees. We uphold contracts to make sure things are fairly played out."

"But you're a famous tour manager!"

Jacob shrugged. "This isn't my first rodeo. Anyhow, all of us Jacobs are allowed to trade in our given occupations for a chance at mortality. It's called 'going rogue'. I chose to stay here. We are all given that choice, but we give up immortality for it. That's Jacob's price. After Hybrid falls apart, I'll still be around, God willing of course. I'll manage another band, hopefully some boring hippie shit."

"And you're all called Jacob?"

He nodded. "We are the Jacobs. But we can take whatever name we want if we go rogue. So far I'm sticking with Jacob. It suits me. It's so very biblical."

"Are you an angel?" I asked, knowing how stupid that sounded.

He laughed, full and hearty. It shook the bus. When he finally calmed down, he wiped his eyes and sputtered, "Oh my bollocks, Rusty. No, I am not an angel. I'm not good nor am I bad. I'm just here, trying to keep the playing field even. Of course if I can manage things in my favor, I'm going to. I'm the manager. It's what I do."

I looked down at my coffee and put my head in my hands. "I don't believe any of this."

"No, I don't blame you."

"Does Sage know?"

"I'm sure Sage has always suspected. But he's never said anything to me."

"Does Graham know?""

He nodded. My throat went dry. "So we're all fucked."

"Oh, I wouldn't say we're all fucked."

"Are they going to take Sage's soul?"

"They might try. But that's not part of the bargain. As Miss Mambo said, they are very literal. That's the only good thing about demons. But if Sage kills himself because he's lost everything he loves, that's fair game."

I narrowed my eyes at him. "How can you be so blasé? People are dying."

"That's life. It's not my fault. Sage is the one who made the deal."

"He was a teenager."

"Another reason to fear the youth."

I sighed, blowing a piece of hair out of my face. It was all too much. My eyes flew to the window where I saw the boys leaving the diner, Bob holding two Styrofoam packages for me and Jacob.

Shit. I had so much to talk about and barely any time to do it.

"So you're going to just let it happen," I said.

"If you haven't noticed," he hissed, leaning in. "I'm trying hard to make sure the band ends up on top. Sage didn't give me much wiggle room."

"And me. What happens if I just leave?" I asked.

"You can try. But you won't be able to. It's too late. You had your chance to leave, we could have brought another person in."

"You chose me though! Why? Why me of all people?"

He shrugged. A pause. Then, "I thought a fan should be

241

around for the end."

The door to the bus opened, the boys' voices coming in.

"Am I going to die?" I quickly whispered.

He smiled. This time it was melancholic. "I really hope not."

♣   ♣   ♣

I woke up lying in a field, surrounded by a purple and red sky. A farmhouse was on fire in the distance and the thunderous sound of galloping hooves filled the air, even though no horses could be seen.

"Get up, Dawn," a voice said from behind me.

I rolled over and sat up. My mother was lying in a bathtub full of dark red tar, submerged up to her neck. Her arms were splayed over the sides, dripping thick clumps of tar onto the dry grass. Each time a clump hit the ground, the grass steamed and hissed.

She was watching me with a serene smile on her face.

It pissed me off.

"What are you doing?" I yelled at her. "Stop smiling at me."

She didn't listen. She showed teeth as her grin spread.

I got to my feet and walked over to her. The earth shook a bit.

"Mom, please, this isn't fair."

She started to laugh, the sing-song maniacal laugh she would do when Dad tried to take her to a doctor appointment, the real crazy one that suddenly disappeared the moment someone tried to diagnose her. Then she was normal again, laughing only on the inside and the doctors thought we were the crazy ones.

"This isn't funny!" I screamed. Now her head was back and she was howling away. I stormed right over to the tub, leaning over the revolting tar and getting in her face.

"You left me! You left me to take care of Dad and Eric. You didn't even bother to stick around! You left and I had to do it all. I had to sacrifice everything! All those times Ryan invited me away with him and his family and I couldn't go. The times Mel did. I couldn't go. I always had to stay, I was stuck. You killed yourself because you're too weak and you left me here! You chained me to this place, you gave me a burden I never wanted to carry. You should have been here. You should have been a mother!"

She stopped laughing abruptly and focused on me like she was seeing me for the first time. Her eyes shone with clarity.

"You got away now, didn't you? Where's your chain?"

Then she looked down at my legs and she laughed again, all tenderness gone.

"Oh, there's your chain."

I looked down at my legs. My ankles were wrapped in heavy metal chains that went straight into the ground.

The ground that was now shaking.

I looked at my mom. She was still laughing and her bathtub began to sink into the earth, as if it was made of tar too.

And I was going down. All solidity beneath my feet disappeared and I was sinking straight through the earth. I raised my arms, trying to free myself and gain leverage, but there was nothing I could do. I was stuck. I was chained. I was sinking.

I looked up, gasping, but my mother was gone. Sonja was in her place, black leaking holes for eyes and a demonic mouth.

Sonja reached into the tub and pulled out my mom's arm, flesh cut open at the wrist.

"See you in a couple of days," Sonja said.

The last of the earth swallowed me.

＊　＊　＊

I heard the scream before I realized it was coming from my mouth. Sage was at my side, shaking me lightly with one hand, gently touching my face with the other.

"Hey, it's okay," he said. His voice was soothing but his clear eyes were scared.

I sat up but he caught me halfway and pushed me back down. He looked above my head. I was lying on the lower bunk and had been close to bashing my head into the bottom of the top bunk.

My mouth was dry. I couldn't stop shaking.

"What happened?" I said in a panic.

"You're all right. You ate your breakfast then you fell asleep. You looked exhausted."

I nodded meekly, feeling waves of terror wash through my veins.

He leaned in closer and smoothed my hair behind my ears. "I'm here. You're going to be okay."

I almost burst into tears. "How can you say that? We're not going to be okay."

"We're not going to let anything happen to you, Dawn," he said with quiet determination. His jaw pulsed angrily. "We'll do whatever we can."

"We?"

"I talked to Jacob. He told me what he told you. I'm a bit of an ass for not picking up on it...but what was I supposed to think? My manger is a supernatural scorekeeper?"

I couldn't even find that funny.

"I don't want to die," I whispered. I didn't want to sink into the earth, into the mouths of demons. But I knew, I knew that's what was going to happen. And it was going to be worse than just dying. I'd go to Hell.

He put his face right up to mine, his eyes were blazing. "I am not going to let you die. You hear me? I won't let that happen. No matter what."

Tears pricked at my eyes. He ran his finger under them. "No matter what," he repeated.

I wanted more than anything to believe him. He was watching me, looking at me with such passion and intensity. I knew he was going to fight for me. I wanted to give him a reason.

I put my hand behind his head, my fingers soaking in the soft curls, and brought his lips to mine. His were hesitant, but just for an instant. Something in him let go. I could feel it in his lips, the way they parted, trying to take all of me in. I could feel it in the hard frenzy of his tongue as it fucked the inside of my mouth one instant then teased the delicate rim of inner lips in another. I could feel it in his hands as they grazed the tips of my breasts through my thin tank top, my nipples aching to play.

Then whatever let go in him, let go in me. I grabbed him hard around his face and together we whimpered, our mouths hot and wet, not moving fast enough, like we were running out of kisses or air or time. There was so much urgency in our needs as he ripped the shirt right over my head and my small breasts bounced for him. He was on them without hesitation, licking them with his hot, wide tongue like he was forming whipped peaks. I moaned, not caring anymore and threw my head back, enjoying the feeling of his rough fingers as they pinched at my nipples, trailed down my neck, and squeezed hard around my waist.

His mouth still flicking my breasts until they hurt from pleasure, he let his hands wander south, taking in the feel of my skin like he was never going to feel another woman again. He unzipped my shorts and pulled them off, flinging them somewhere else in the empty bus. My underwear was plain pink and I expected that to disappear too but he kept them on and breathed hotly on them, his lips pressed firmly around my rapidly swelling ones. The teasing was making me delirious and I writhed on the bunk, unable to take it.

He finally pulled the underwear off, tossed it aside, then took a firm hold of my hips with his strong hands and pulled me out toward him at an angle so my legs were open and I was bare for him, hanging off the edge of the bunk.

"God, you're beautiful, Dawn," he murmured.

I raised my head to see if he was talking to me or my crotch. But though his face was slowly sinking south, tongue teasing the edge of his mouth, letting me know what was in store, his eyes were focused on mine. A green and gorgeous intensity that seemed to see right through me, into places I never knew were inside.

I propped myself up on my elbows, letting my head hang back, my long hair pooling on the bed. Sage started by running his tongue down each hip, over my sensitive pelvic bone, then down into the folds of skin which were already wet and throbbing for him.

He went at me, over and over again, the same steady licks, building up in layers of tension. My legs shook with impatience and I bit my lip to keep from crying out. The slow, almost complex way he teased me was torturous. I wanted nothing more than to come.

I could tell he did too. But he wasn't new to this game. Most rocks stars weren't. Just as I was at the breaking point he stopped. I raised my head, breathless and fuzzy-headed. He was standing in front of me, his shirt having just come off. My eyes focused on his bronze body, the sculpted muscles that defined every ab and every hard curve of his chest. His tattoos went all the way up his arms and disappeared over his swimmer's shoulders. I briefly wondered if the body of a god was one of the things he had bargained for as well, then I decided he was just damn lucky with genetics. It was some other kind of deal when you had a face like his, a body of an Olympic swimmer and…

I watched eagerly as he undid his silver-plated belt and let his pants drop to the floor.

…A cock that looked beautiful. Dangerously beautiful. Its immensity wasn't surprising given his size, but it still scared me momentarily. I had only slept with Ryan. I wasn't a small girl by any means but I was pretty sure that if Sage rammed that hard, throbbing dick inside of me that I would break in two. That death still seemed preferable to whatever the demons had in store for me.

I bit my lip in trepidation and he returned the motion with a sly smirk.

"Are you ready for me?" he whispered.

What was I supposed to say to that? I've always been ready? I'll *never* be ready for that thing?

I swallowed hard and kept my mouth shut as he slithered back over and dropped to his knees right in front of me. He took his rigid cock in his hands, stroking it lightly for a second, before he dipped the head into my mounting wetness and began to rub it against my clit in long smooth strokes, all the while never breaking eye contact with me.

I was growing frustrated. I wanted nothing more than for him to at least try and break me in two. That was all I had wanted, subconsciously or not, for the last couple of weeks and he was finally here, naked perfection, and being an actual cock tease.

"Please," I moaned without thinking.

He grinned. "That's all I needed."

In a flash he reached over and grabbed me hard around the waist and pulled me onto the floor of the bus. The he flipped me over so I was resting on my forearms and yanked my ass up into the air. I didn't mind. After years of horseback riding, I was proud of that tight ass.

Evidently so was he. He gasped with pleasure as he ran his hands along, even teasing a finger between my cheeks until it found the sweet spot again. With one hand firmly around the small of my waist, he guided himself into me. It was slow at first and I gritted my teeth together at the pain. He continued to tease my clit with his slick fingers though and soon I was begging him to come at me harder.

He did. He plowed into me, spreading me wider until I thought I might split. Then he came at me faster and faster, harder and harder, all to the same rhythm. It was that damn internal metronome again, the man had a perfect sense of timing and wasn't missing a single beat. His fingers were busy too and I relished the full feeling I had from my blood pooling in one place. His light cropping of chest hair tickled at my back, reminding me of the very large rock god who was on top of me.

He rode me this way until he couldn't hold on any longer. His fingers expertly rubbed me until I started to shake into a frenzy of hot fireworks. I started moaning, calling out his name, not caring who heard. I came violently. He did the same, his balls hitting hard against my ass, his grip on my waist turning into a stranglehold. He cried out, moans of passion shaking us and making our eyes roll back into our heads.

I collapsed on the floor, feeling like an old woman and a new woman at the same time. He joined me, dazed and breathing heavily. He wrapped his arm around me and pulled me closer to him. We were spooning on the dirty floor of the tour bus. It was damn near poetic.

When I caught my breath I turned over and looked at him. He looked at peace—it was the first time I had ever seen him look that way.

"I had no idea you thought about me like that," I whispered sincerely.

He cracked a smile. "I know you didn't. It made it that much more fun."

His smile slowly left him, the curves of his expressive mouth turning down. "Dawn," he began. "I'm sorry if this didn't happen sooner. I wish that we had more time. I wished it didn't have to be this way, to have these reasons, how I kept you at bay, but I still must protect you and—"

Before he could continue, the door to the bus shuddered open and Chip stepped onto the bus.

"Hey, Rusty," he called out, coming up the steps. His mouth dropped when he saw us. "Jesus, whoa, holy moly. Wow, sorry I…"

We were too stunned to cover up.

"Have you heard of knocking, Chip?" Sage asked testily.

Chip continued to stand there. "Well yeah, but normally I'm like invited to join in and stuff."

He gave me an expectant look. I rolled my eyes.

"Only in your dreams, buddy," Sage snarled. "Now get out."

Chip covered his eyes with one hand. "Okay, I'm just here to tell you that there's some crazy black chick looking for Dawn. She's hot but she's kind of terrifying. She already grabbed my junk."

"That's Mel!" I exclaimed. "Tell her I'll be right there. But don't tell her how you found me."

"I won't," Chip replied, but he was smiling and peeking at me through his fingers.

Sage pointed at the door. "Get out or I'll throw you out. With my dick."

"Sheesh, okay, I'm going, I'm going," Chip stumbled blindly down the stairs and out the door.

I rolled on my back and looked up at Sage.

"Always something," I remarked.

He smiled and got up. Still naked. Still beautiful.

He grabbed me by my arms and hauled me to my feet. I was a bit unsteady and my legs were trembling. It was going to take me quite a while to get over this ride. It was as rough and passionate as I had imagined.

We both slipped our clothes back on, me feeling more shy than he was. I grabbed my bag off the top bunk which had an extra pass for Mel inside.

"Come here," Sage murmured. He came up to me and pushed the hair off my face and ran his thumb over my lower lip. He gave me a quick and sweet kiss.

"Thank you for that," he whispered. I didn't have to be a genius to pick up on what he was really saying. That could have been the last time—for both of us.

I smiled sadly then wrapped my arms around him. He returned the embrace, squeezing me hard. He kissed the top of my head.

"I'm glad you didn't run away, Dawn."

"Me too."

I sighed into his chest and we stood like that until time was wearing thin.

"You go get your friend and bring her back here," he said, pulling away from me. "I want to meet her."

"And she wants to meet you," I grinned. I turned and skipped out of the bus.

It wasn't until I was outside and in the golden hazy Texas afternoon that I remembered what I had planned. I had to protect Mel at all costs and I was already thinking of bringing her back to meet the band. One round in the sack with Sage and my mind was all over the place.

I decided a quick meeting wouldn't hurt. Then she and I would do our own thing during the night. I focused on that and scampered across the parking lot toward the main security gates.

CHAPTER TWENTY-ONE

I heard Mel before I even saw her, giving sass to the security guard. I spied her through the chain link fence, my heart beating loud in my chest, and waved her pass at the guard.

"She's legit," I told him. "This is her pass."

He sighed, unfolded his bulky arms, and opened the gate. Mel ran toward me like a tiny little rocketship made of boobs and butt.

"Dawn!" she cried out, throwing her arms around my waist. I reached for her, squeezing her hard.

I broke down. I started bawling right there, holding Mel to me as tightly as I could.

"Dawn, whoa, what's going?" she exclaimed into my chest. She tried to pull back but I wouldn't let her. The tears wouldn't stop coming and I didn't care who saw. I felt like I didn't even have the strength to stand anymore.

"Holy shizz, child." She patted my back. "It's okay. Let it out."

I probably cried for ten minutes straight. Without me even realizing it, she had moved us over away from the guard and the hopefuls and placed us on the other side of a station wagon. I fell onto my ass and stayed there until the sobs dried up.

When I was done I felt as dry and empty as a husk.

"I'd ask if you are okay but you're obviously not okay," she remarked, folding her legs on the hot asphalt. "I've never seen you cry before."

I nodded and wiped underneath my nose and eyes. I was a mess through and through.

"Do you want to tell me what's going on?" she asked carefully. "You don't have to if you don't want to."

To borrow a phrase from Jimmy Page (who borrowed a phrase from Jake Holmes), I felt dazed and confused. I shrugged. "I don't even know anymore."

"Okay, don't freak, man. Relax. I'll talk. I'll let you know about the stinky pervert I had to sit next to on the plane. But first…"

She reached into her flower-dotted purse and pulled out a joint.

I gave her a wry look and leaned back against the car door. "How did you smuggle that on the plane?"

She beamed cheekily. "I'm good at distraction."

She brought the joint to her lips and lit it up. She took a hit then passed it to me.

"I'm sure you're up to your eyeballs in this," she said through a cough.

I took it and puffed back, shaking my head. "I've had too much to deal with."

"Dude, grass makes your problems easier to handle."

"Not my problems."

She sighed and took the joint back. "Okay, well let me tell you about how things are back in Ellensburg."

She told me about her new man and how good he was in the sack. She said she thought she was in love and wanted to have his babies one day. She said she was debating about going back into nursing for another year, but decided to stick it through. She told me that her brother crashed the Gremlin one night and it's totaled. He's okay though and he said he's going to get a sexy muscle car next but Mel's not allowed to borrow it. It felt good to listen.

"What about Eric and my dad?"

"Eric's okay. He looks happier. He told me this chick he likes that turned him down before has been calling him and wanting to do homework together when school starts. So who knows what that's about. But he's happy. And your dad is great. Really. Eric said he stopped drinking cold turkey."

"What?" I cried out, nearly choking.

"Totally legit. I saw him a few times. Sober as a nail. He threw out all the booze and your house looks clean for once. I mean, really clean. Grass is mowed."

"He never told me any of that," I said absently.

"Well, you know how it is for alcoholics. He probably thinks you wouldn't believe him. But so far, he's doing good. I like it. I bet he'll be like that when you get home. Oh, and Moonglow is fine. Eric's actually been riding her. Just in the field though."

The news felt so good that the feeling was surprising. Like I had forgotten that things had the ability to get better. Maybe not for me, but for my family. I nearly started crying again but the pot was at work in my system and helping me distance myself from the situation.

"So, you wanna tell me what's going on with you? I mean, you said some stuff on the phone and it sounds all heavy but... what's really happening, Dawn?"

I opened my mouth to speak but no words came out.

"Okay," she drew out. "Let me rephrase that. Did you sleep with Sage yet?"

I blushed furiously.

She smacked my leg and exclaimed, "I knew it! I could smell it on you."

"You can smell it on me?"

She grinned. "When I was hugging you, yeah. Your chest smelled like cologne and man tongue."

"Oh come on."

"Truth. Anyway, tell me how he was!"

"Mel, I don't even know..."

"That bad, huh?"

"No! He was...it just happened. I haven't even had a chance to process it yet."

"Did you come?"

"Did I ever." I couldn't help but smile at that admission. She joined me and soon we were both giggling like schoolchildren.

When we calmed down she asked, "What's he look like naked? Tattoos everywhere?"

"No, just on his arms and shoulders and down his back a bit. I couldn't really see because he had me flipped around."

"Oh man, I wish I had popcorn. Big dick?"

I grinned and didn't say anything.

She nodded, smiling slowly. "Right on, child, right on." Pause. "So do you love him?"

The question caught me off-guard. "What?"

"Hey, I'm just asking. You do or you don't."

"I...I don't think I do. Do I?"

"Beats the fuck outta me. Does he love you?"

I shook my head adamantly. "No. I don't think so. I don't really think he can love anyone. Or he doesn't want to."

"What if he does love you? Would you marry a rock star?"

I gave her a dry look.

"What?" she protested. "I want to plan a rock star wedding, what is so wrong with that? Oh my god, it would be so brilliant! You could accidently invite Ryan and that creep who works at Big Ears with you and—"

"Mel, let's drop it."

"Okay, but I'm just saying it would be cool. Of course you don't have to get married if you don't want to. You're a fine, independent young woman. Look at you, child, you're living the dream."

"I'm living the nightmare."

"Oh come on. It can't be all that bad."

I took in a deep breath, steadying my nerves. I leaned over and pulled her sunglasses off her eyes so I could look into them.

254

"Mel, I'm going to tell you something and I want you to listen and listen good."

Mel's face fell. She snatched the glasses from my hand and put them on the top of her head. "Dawn...you're kind of scaring me."

"You're about to get a lot more scared," I warned her with as much sincerity as I could express. "I need you to just listen to me. You're not going to believe me and that's alright, I don't expect anyone else to. I just need to talk. I need someone to know the real story—someone who's not part of it."

And I chose that point to take my tape recorder out of my bag. Mel's brows shot up.

"I'm going to record this just in case."

"In case of what?"

"You'll know by the end."

So, for the third time in as many days, I rehashed the entire Hybrid tour. As with Jacob and Sage, I didn't leave out anything. Mel wouldn't believe me, but she was my best friend and she deserved the whole truth.

When I finished, I sat back and waited for her reaction. I wasn't nervous. I was planning on her telling me I was bat-shit crazy.

It took a while for her to speak. It surprised me that she looked a bit frightened. The whites of her wide eyes positively glowed against her skin.

"Dawn," she said slowly. "You're not part of a cult, are you? Hybrid's not secretly the new Manson family or something?"

"No and no. Well...Graham might as well be."

"And you haven't been meditating in weird barns or drinking weird punches or doing drugs, have you?"

"None of the above."

"Your name is still Dawn Emerson?"

"That's what the press pass says."

"Huh," she said. She fell silent for a beat and dug another joint out of her purse.

"Mel?"

"I'm thinking." She lit it up, crackling burning papers, and took in a deep breath of smoke before rubbing the joint out on the ground.

"Oh, just tell me I'm nuts, Mel."

"Bitch, you ain't nuts. I believe you."

My brows rose to the heavens. I had to shield the overbearing sun with my hand to get a better look at her. "What, are you serious?"

She nodded quickly. "I do. Dawn, you've never lied to me. Except when you told me that you hadn't been kissed before Ryan came along because I know Doug Campbell got you in a closet at Sheena Meister's party. And when you lied and said you weren't in love with Sage just now. Those were the only two times. I know you aren't lying about this."

I paused. "So you believe me in the sense that you believe that *I* believe what's going on."

"I don't even think you believe what's going on."

"Sometimes I don't," I said with a sigh. "So what do you think?"

"I couldn't tell you. Except that you have to stay with me and my cousin for a few days and you need to get off this tour. Like, now. If I didn't think it would break your heart to leave Sage without saying goodbye, I'd suggest we leave right now and forget about them. Never look back."

"But you believe me? You believe that Sage Knightly made a deal with the devil? And now they are coming back to collect before his twenty-eighth birthday and I may or may not be included in those terms and conditions?"

"Yup." And I could see on her face that Mel was serious. And why wouldn't she be? When we became friends back in Ellensburg, we both took a lot of flak for it. At first her mother didn't trust her hanging around a "honky" white girl, always suspicious that I was going to turn on her daughter. She came around, of course. As for me, I was personally called a bunch of negative words that made my skin crawl, all because I was a white girl with a black friend. But through it all, we stuck together. And she was still here, all these years later, sticking with me when I needed her most.

"Dude, I love you," I cried out, tears threatening my eyes again.

"Dude, I love you, too. But I'm serious about getting you out of here. I'm sure my flight out won't be packed. We'll get you a ticket in the morning and this will all be over."

"But it won't be."

She leaned over. "But it's not your problem. Think about yourself. And your dad. And Eric. And your horse. And me, of course, Melanie Jones."

I nodded, knowing she was right.

She patted my knee. "Okay, writer girl, how about you introduce me to your rock star sex god?"

❋ ❋ ❋

I always thought my best friend was one of the coolest chicks on the planet. And when I say cool, I mean cool as a cucumber.

She was not cool when she met Hybrid. Not in the slightest.

But that was to the benefit of the band. They were smiling and cracking jokes like it was day one of the tour all over again.

First, Mel practically fainted when she saw Robbie, and when she recovered, she started jumping up and down and hugging the poor bastard. I'll always remember seeing her wrap her dark legs around his waist and him raising his injured wrist high in the air, trying to keep it out of her way.

With Sage though, she was totally the opposite. She giggled demurely and coyly and Mel doesn't do demure.

At one point on the bus, while she was in the midst of reveling among rock gods, she whispered into my ear, "I've been watching closely. Sage has gotten at least one boner just from looking at you."

I decided after that I wouldn't talk to her until her perverted mind was under control and she stopped staring at Sage's crotch. It was probably my fault he kept staring though, since I had slipped on that blue dress of hers that she had originally given to me to wear on tour. It was one hot number and a nice change from my jeans and vests.

But the way Mal acted around me, I had to wonder if she really did believe in the deal Sage made. To her it was just fun and games. But I had to remind myself that when someone throws something absurd at you and then plunks you in a room full of famous rock stars whose music you love (because that makes a huge difference), you're going to giggle at those rock stars. It was like if someone came up to me and was like, "Hey, my friend Mick Jagger is actually a woman and the gender-confused leader of a Satanic cult," and then in the next frame they were like, "Oh and here's Mick Jagger," I'd probably forget all about that first sentence and start drooling on Mick's shoes.

Mel didn't lose her enthusiasm during the show either. Hybrid had never played San Antonio before and they weren't sure how western Texas was going to take them, but they actually pulled it off. There was a definite drop in numbers compared to the other shows on the Molten Universe tour, but it was a lot better than New Orleans and that's all the band needed for them to play with a little more verve.

Being with Mel and seeing the show through her eyes gave me a new appreciation for the music all over again. With everything going on, it was hard to see Hybrid the way everyone else saw them. Just an awesome metal band who made awesome music. I needed that step away from being Dawn Emerson. I needed to know what the band was capable of doing to other people, and looking at Mel as she stood beside me on the side stage, moving her ass to the music and grinning like a fool, I remembered that Hybrid still knew how to rock.

Then the fact that this was going to be their last tour, their last album, hit me like a ton of bricks. There was nothing as heartbreaking like one of your favorite bands breaking up. It's like they are breaking up with you. Those bands, you plan your life around them. You plan vacations around concert dates. You save babysitting money for records. You live for those days when Creem magazine arrives in your dusty mailbox and you frantically flip through it for any information on your favorites. The bands, the musicians that you love, they love you back. And when they quit, when they fall apart, when they die—they ruin that future you thought they'd always be a part of.

My eyes were filling with tears again near the end of the show. Understanding, or at least anticipating, Mel put her arm around me and hugged me. Even Jacob shot me a sad smile which made my heart break even more. He was no longer putting on a brave face. This was really going to happen. This band was really over.

When the show was over and everyone was relocating to the lounge, I pulled Jacob aside and told Mel to go on through and drink all the band's booze.

"You know we're having some budget cutbacks, Rusty," Jacob remarked as he watched Mel sashay backstage. "Booze ain't cheap."

"Look, Jacob. I think I'm going to leave with Mel on her flight out of here."

He didn't show any expression nor did he say anything for a few beats, he just blinked. "Dawn…"

"You know I'd do anything for this band. Tonight, I mean, I know it. I love them. Warts and all. I love them, all of them, almost. But…I have a dad at home. He's been having a rough time, well, forever, and he's finally getting better. I have a brother with Tourette's Syndrome that I look after. They need me. They need me to be alive. My mother killed herself when I was young and I've been the mom ever since."

Jacob nodded and stroked his chin, letting me continue.

"I even have a horse. I have Mel, too. I have a future. I have things I don't want to lose and people who don't want to lose me. I know you said it's too late but I just can't accept that. As much as it fucking stabs me in the gut to leave the tour, I have to. I won't write the article in the end. It's not worth it."

He was silent, golden eyes searching the ceiling of the venue, lost in thought. Finally he lowered his head and smiled weakly. "I'm sorry, Dawn. You can't leave."

"But why not?" I stamped my foot like a child. "What could happen if I did? Who is going to stop me, you?"

"No, not me," he said calmly. "I would love to see you leave, Rusty. Like I said before, I like you. But that's not how this works. This is out of human hands now. Your fate has been decided."

"So tell me. Give me one good example of what's going to happen to me."

"If you fly out with Mel tomorrow, your whole plane will go down."

I was startled. "But…then I'd be dead. Who would write the story?"

"They have ways of working that out."

"But if they do—"

"They are demons, Rusty. Demons. They want you dead and dragged to Hell above all else. They want all of us dead but they can only do what they can do. The contract will be fulfilled."

"So why don't they kill me now? Get it over with and get some other writer."

He let out a dry, sad laugh. "Because what is the fun in that? They are like cats with a mouse, batting it around. Just because you don't see them right now, doesn't mean they aren't out there. They know what they're doing."

"But the code…"

"Yes, the code. But we are still at their mercy. Why do you think I'm here, for Christ's sake? I make things fair. If I wasn't around, I don't think there would even be a Hybrid anymore."

I grabbed onto Jacob's arm. "So help me. Help me escape."

He shook his head vigorously. "I can't."

"Why not?"

"I just can't. Look, I'm sorry, I really am. All I can say is the longer you stick around me, the longer I will do my best to keep you and everyone else in this band alive. But the minute you walk away, I can't help you. My duties are to Sage first, then to you. He has to come first. This is his contract. Yours will come later."

I gave him a funny look. "What do you mean mine will come later?"

He smiled and twirled around his gold rings. "Dawn Emerson. Stay with me. Stay with Sage. Why do you think I went out of my way to choose you?"

"You said because it should have been a fan to write the story."

"I chose you partly because I thought maybe a girl like you would give Sage something to live for when everything is taken from him. You're hope. So, write about the band and live your destiny. I promise we will do everything to protect you. But the minute you leave, I can't help. And you invite the danger of destroying everyone you love and know. I'm sorry, love. But you're stuck with us."

My heart thumped loudly in my chest, like it was just remembering to beat.

I swallowed hard. "But what do I tell Mel? She won't leave without me. And she can't stay here."

"I'm sure you'll know the right things to say." He patted me on the shoulder and disappeared into the darkness.

❀ ❀ ❀

After Jacob left, I spent a few minutes on the stage staring out at the empty venue, ignoring the roadies who were packing up behind me. I wondered what they'd do after Hybrid was no more. I wondered if they'd get other jobs in the industry. I wondered if they'd care if the band ceased to exist.

I wondered exactly how the band would end. Would there be a massive fight? Would Sage pick it with Robbie, destroying his relationship with him for the sake of destiny? Or would it end in something worse than that? Would the next stage collapse consume us all? Would it end in flames? That last thought struck a familiar chord in me and I remembered seeing that man back in Ellensburg, Ted with the beige Bug and his arm in a sling. He told me I wouldn't be able to save Sage and that it would all end in flames. I remembered seeing a white-haired girl in the backseat and I wondered how long the chess pieces had been set in motion and where my spot on the board was. Where was Dawn going to be moved next?

I sighed, hating myself for what I had to do next. Just like Sage might have to do with Robbie, I was going to have to sacrifice my relationship with Mel in order to save her.

I took in the view from the stage one last time and headed back into the backstage area. I had left Mel with Sage, knowing she'd be safe, but when I walked into the dressing room where everyone was hanging out and drinking like they hadn't a care in the world, The Guess Who's "No Time" aptly playing from the speakers, he was nowhere to be seen.

And Mel was talking to Graham. Scratch that, she was sitting beside him on the couch hanging on his every word.

I marched right over to her and stood in front of her until she finally looked up.

"Hey, Dawn," she said brightly.

Graham stared straight at me and sang in a high falsetto along with the song. "No time for the killing floor, there's no time left for you, no time left for you."

I shot him the nastiest stink eye that I could and grabbed Mel by her hands. "I need to speak with you."

I pulled her up and started to drag her towards the door.

"Ouch, Dawn, chill out," she cried, but I didn't stop until we were outside the dressing room.

"What the hell are you doing with him?" I sneered.

"What? He's harmless."

"Mel! He's a fucking demon, he is the opposite of harmless!"

She rolled her eyes.

"See!" I exclaimed, pointing at her viciously. "You don't believe me. I knew it."

"I do believe you," she argued. "But it's harmless to just talk to him. What's he going to do to me in there?"

"He can do plenty. He can get in your head. Look at what happened to poor Noelle."

She folded her arms and gave me a twisted smile. "I just got here, first of all, and Noelle was weak to begin with."

"You didn't even know her!"

"And you did? Come on, Dawn. Anyway, what am I supposed to say to Graham? Don't talk to me, I know you're a demon? You think that would be the better solution?"

I sucked in a deep breath and let it out slowly, trying to calm my aching heart. It didn't really matter about Graham. There would be no more of it.

"Look, Mel, I've decided I'm not going with you back home. I'm staying here."

She frowned. "No, you're not. You're getting the fuck out of here."

"I don't want to."

She sighed and let her gaze drop to the ground. "Man, I get it. You do love him. I know it. You don't want to leave him. I really get it, but you just have to…get over it. If everything works out later, maybe you can reconnect or something. I don't know. But I do know you're not staying with this band anymore."

I crossed my arms and said in my calmest voice, "I am not going with you, Mel. I have made up my mind."

She glared at me. "Dawn…why would you stay after everything you've told me? You're coming with me or I'm staying here with you."

"I don't *want* to go with *you*, Mel. And you are definitely not staying here. You can go back to your sad life in Ellensburg if that makes you happy. These are my people. I belong with them. Not some small-town hick like you."

Mel's face fell as I speared her with my words.

"This isn't you talking," she whispered.

I laughed richly. "This is me. This is the real me. This is the me I was supposed to be. Did you seriously think I'd come back to Ellensburg after all of this? I'm somebody now. You're still a nobody in a nobody town. You think I'd go back to that shithole with the likes of you? My god, you're so fucking backwards, Melanie."

She was so startled and so hurt. Her face contorted angrily. Anger was always Mel's first line of defense when she was hurting inside. And I had known *exactly* what to say to hurt her the most.

"You're being a bitch," she spat at me. "A fucking mean bitch."

Sage chose that time to walk toward the dressing room. He stopped before going in, looking at the both of us, perplexed.

Mel fixed her glare on him for a second before turning the weapon on me and looking me up and down. She was about to get nasty. Real nasty.

"A bitch and a major slut."

I rolled my eyes, pretending I wasn't bleeding inside.

"Oh," she continued with false surprise. "You don't like being called a slut, do you? A whore. Now the tables are turned, aren't they Miss Always Judgmental? Well, that's what you are now. You've become all those girls you look down on. Just some stupid slut who thinks she's better than me because she spread her legs for some mid-level rock star who's probably slept with everyone she's condemned."

Sage took a few cautious steps toward us, hands out, brows furrowed. "Hey, what is going on here?"

"Oh fuck you," Mel said. Then she looked at me again. "And fuck you, too. I knew it was a mistake to come out here. I knew you'd probably changed and gotten a big head. Glad to see I was right. You can stay here with your lame ass honky band and go straight to hell for all I care. You think you're better than me, after everything I've done for you? You don't even deserve my worry."

And at that, Mel spun around on her heel and marched off toward the exit. The minute she was gone, I fell to my knees in pain. Swirling, stabbing pain that ripped me apart. But the tears wouldn't come. There was nothing in me left.

Sage crouched down beside me, peering at me with concern. He put his hand on my shoulder but I shrugged him off.

"What happened?" he asked softly.

"Just go away," I muttered, closing my eyes.

"Angel, I—" he started.

"Angel!" I laughed bitterly at his term of endearment. "Get the fuck away from me."

"Dawn."

"Go!" I screamed at him, my eyes burning. "This is all your fucking fault! You did this. You did all of this!"

Now Sage's face crumbled slightly, his eyes awash in regret. "I was so young."

"You were an idiot. Still are."

I don't know why I was being so vicious to Sage. I guess I figured if I was going to turn into a complete bitch, I might as well sever all the relationships I had. I was probably burning away the bridges that tied Sage to me as his last point of hope. But I didn't care. I just didn't care anymore.

When he didn't move and didn't say anything, I glared at him, pushing and pushing.

"Your stupid, selfish mistake has cost you everything good in your life. It's cost the lives of innocent people. How does that make you feel, Sage, knowing you've destroyed so much in order to have so little?" I breathed heavily, waiting nervously for him to strike out at me in some way.

But he didn't.

He brushed the hair off my forehead and planted a kiss there.

"I'm carrying this burden just as I've carried it every day since I was fifteen. You're going to live a long and happy life, Dawn. I promise you this."

He stroked my cheek sadly, then got to his feet and walked into the dressing room. I was left on the floor, dying inside.

CHAPTER TWENTY-TWO

The drive from San Antonio to Phoenix was one of the longest of my life. I was so trapped in my own head, wallowing in my own misery that I couldn't sleep. I just sat at the table watching the bus's headlights shining on the dark, open road. I knew Graham was also up, lying on the couch, but he didn't say anything to me. I started to question my sanity, how I could just sit there with an actual demon close by. Maybe it was because Graham had so many sad, pathetic human qualities that it was hard to imagine he was anything but human. But I remembered what his face looked like that one time, and the creepy vibe, like tendrils of underlying horror, that came off of him was pretty hard to ignore.

It was probably two in the morning when Jacob came over to me and gently placed my notebook and pen in front of me.

"Write, Rusty," he told me in a hushed voice. "Write the story you were born to write."

I looked at him and then at Graham. Both of them were staring at me with otherworldly intensity. One leaning toward darkness and death. The other promising safety and light. Both of them wanted me to write the article to fulfill the terms of the contract so Sage's request could be completed. And I wanted to write the article for the same selfish reason I had in the first place: I wanted respect. I wanted to be admired. I wanted the world to know I was a writer.

I picked up the pen and started to write.

❋   ❋   ❋

I woke up with my head on the table, the pencil leaning out of my hand. I couldn't remember when I had fallen asleep but I had written several pages of the article already. It was probably all shit, but in my sleep-fogged brain, I was proud.

I raised my head and looked around. The bus was rolling down the desert highway, red rocks and craggy, cactus-dusted hills spreading as far as one could see. It was hauntingly beautiful in its bareness.

Bob was at the wheel as usual, humming along to the gentle strumming of Led Zeppelin's "Going to California." Graham was snoring on the couch. Everyone else in the bus still seemed to be asleep. It was quiet and the early morning light spread through the windows, enveloping everything in a hazy warmth. I felt strangely optimistic, considering what had happened the night before. The way I had hurt Mel. That terrible look on her face. But the optimism was usually a side effect of having written something I'd been putting off for a long time. It was the high that came from conquering procrastination.

I got out of the seat and stretched, then whispered good morning to Bob and set about making coffee and a bit of breakfast with the leftover eggs and bacon that were in the fridge. Nothing works like the smell of bacon and the sound of Zeppelin to get everyone on their feet. *The children of the sun begin to wake*, I sang along in my head.

Soon I was dishing out more food than I had. Robbie, Mickey, and Fiddles were hung over, which was actually nice to see. It meant they were back to their partying ways and things were feeling normal even though they very much weren't.

Sage sat next to me at the table and Robbie raised his brows at us, eating his eggs gleefully. "So a little birdie told me he caught you two banging on the floor yesterday."

"Fucking Chip," I mumbled, while Sage just glared.

Robbie shrugged and shoved bacon in his mouth. "Hey, dudes, I don't care. Good for you. You know Sage here needs to get laid more. So uptight, brother!"

Sage shook his head in amused annoyance. I could tell he was going to miss being with Robbie when all was said and done. So many years, so much blood between them. Robbie with his joy and insecurities. His voice. I hoped he would come out of this okay. If the demons left him alone, Robbie could go on to become one of the best singers the world had ever known.

"What the hell is that?" Jacob asked.

We all turned to look at him as he stood in the aisle, his eyes focused on the road ahead. I craned my neck around Robbie and peered through the windshield.

In the far distance where the golden haze met ragged cliffs, a gigantic, all-encompassing dust cloud was rising on the horizon. It was so big it almost curved with the earth, and it was growing bigger—and closer—by the second.

"Looks like a dust storm," Bob remarked. He shifted gears and the bus began to slow down.

"That's a dust storm?" Robbie exclaimed. "It looks like the fucking apocalypse."

"Yes, it does," Jacob said grimly. He was now staring steadily at Graham. Graham was grinning. He looked like a monkey baring his teeth.

"Is this your work?" Jacob asked.

Graham laughed and slapped his knee theatrically. "You think I created a dust storm? Who am I, God?"

Jacob shook his head and fixed his eyes back on the road.

"Definitely not," he muttered under his breath.

"How far away from Phoenix are we?" asked Sage.

"We just crossed into Arizona," Bob yelled over his shoulder.

"At least another four hours."

"Can we just go around it?" Robbie asked.

"Only if we want to skip the show and drive to California instead," Mickey commented. "Look at the size of that fucker."

"Dude," agreed Fiddles.

I looked at Jacob. "What do we do?"

He didn't look too happy. He shrugged. "Bob? Have you dealt with this kind of crazy shit before?"

"Yup. Nothing this big though. We should be fine. The green machine should keep out most of the dust. We'll just pull over, far off the road. We won't be able to see anything soon."

"America," Jacob muttered to no one in particular. "You always have to make everything so big."

Sage adjusted in his seat and grabbed my hand, giving it a squeeze. I gave him a small smile of thanks.

The storm moved fast. Bob pulled the bus a bit off the road and other cars on the highway began to do the same. Considering how busy Interstate 10 was, this was actually an impressive feat and an incredibly eerie sight.

We waited, holding our breaths, sitting absolutely still, as if the cloud was a voluminous monster hunting and stalking us. The bus began to shake from the winds, windows rattling. Grains of sand hit the glass with a peppery sound. Then the cloud was upon us and daylight was eaten from above, plunging us all into a gritty darkness. The sound was deafening, a mixture of howling winds and scratching sand, like someone was running their nails down the side of the bus. I gripped Sage's hand, all too certain that demons were outside, circling the bus, figuring out a way to get in.

All of us sat there in wonder and fear for what seemed like forever.

"Is this ever going to end?" Robbie asked. He sounded scared. I could barely see him in the murky dimness, but I could tell he was chewing on his nails.

"It will at some point," Bob said from the front. He reached down to the console and flicked a switch. The light in the kitchen came on, giving us all enough room to see each other. Understandably we looked scared to death, and ghoulish too, our faces swamped by shadows. Bob turned on the radio, I guess to lighten the mood, and The Allman Brother's "Midnight Rider" came on. A gorgeous tune reminiscent of sunny skies, not being trapped on a bus in a sandstorm.

"How long has it been?" asked Mickey after a few minutes.

Jacob was in the middle of pulling out his pocket watch when there was a slow knock at the bus door.

We all jumped, my heart trying to beat its way up my throat.

"Who the fuck is out there?" Robbie asked.

We all stood up, trying to get a look.

There was a knock again. You could barely see a white fist as it met with the door.

Bob was worried. "They're crazy for being out there. Maybe they need help."

He went to pull on the lever that would open the bus door.

"Don't!" Sage shouted, his voice booming above the wind and sand. "Don't open the door, Bob."

Bob paused and shot us a funny look. "Why not? They could be hurt."

The knock came again.

"Sage is right, don't open the door," Jacob reiterated, trying to convince him.

Bob looked at me. I gave him a look that I hope told him "remember what we talked about."

It seemed to work. He nodded at me, biting his lip and slowly sitting back down.

"Why can't he open the door?" Fiddles asked.

"Probably too much dust," Mickey told him. "It'll come right in."

"But what if they're hurt like Bob said?" Graham got to his feet.

Jacob put his hand out, holding him back. "No one is opening that door, especially you."

"Why especially him?" Robbie asked.

"Yeah, Jacob," Graham repeated, a taunting look in his dark, demonic eyes. "Why especially me?"

The knock happened again. Mickey stood up and started looking around him. "This is nuts. Anyone at least know where the flashlight is so we can light up this fucker?"

Meanwhile, Fiddles drummed on his knee and sang along to the song, "But I'm not going to let them catch me, no, not going to let them catch the midnight rider."

"I'm going for it," Graham said, trying to push past Jacob. Jacob responded by winding up and clocking Graham right in the face, sending him backward onto the couch.

"Holy fuck!" Robbie shouted, jumping to his feet.

Graham stirred, holding his bleeding face, while Jacob turned around and sneered at the band like a cornered animal. "No one," he bellowed, "but no one is allowed to open that door. No matter what happens! Is that understood?"

Silence and Greg Allman's voice filled the room. I looked at everyone. We were all scared as shit. Mickey, Fiddles, and Robbie seemed glued to their spot.

Sage put his arm around me and whispered into the top of my head, "It's going to be okay."

Mickey looked at us and at Jacob. "Can someone please explain what the hell is going on?" His eyes were glistening as if he were on the verge of tears.

Jacob shook his head. "You wouldn't believe us if we tried."

Robbie opened his mouth to speak when he was cut off by a cacophony of dozens of fists pounding on the bus. We were surrounded, long white limbs pounding on every available window and down the sides of the bus, long pale fingers splayed against the glass like ghosts through the sand. It was deafening. Terrifying. And there was no way we'd be getting out of this alive.

"Drive, Bob," Sage said, softly at first. Then, when no one moved, everyone's eyes still drawn to the hands and fists that were pounding on the bus, he yelled, "Drive! Drive! Move it! Drive,

Bob, fucking drive!"

Bob snapped out of it and dropped back in the driver's seat. He turned the key in the ignition. The bus sputtered but wouldn't turn over.

"Oh, no, no, no," I cried, panic spreading in my bones like cancer.

"What's going on?" Robbie yelled. "Sage, why…"

The pounding continued. I tried not to look at the skinny arms as they slid down the glass, fingers itching to come in and grab us and take us to Hell.

"Fuck, it's the battery," Bob yelled, trying again and again to start the bus. "It's dead!"

Mickey reached over and switched off the radio. Without the music, the pounding was more real, more horrific.

"Did you have to listen to the fucking Allman Brothers!" Jacob yelled.

Graham started laughing hysterically from the couch, blood spraying out of his mouth. A tooth flew out and landed in the aisle at Jacob's feet.

And just as quickly as the thrashing started, it ended.

Our eyes flew to the windows. The people were all gone.

The only sound was the blasting wind and sand.

We were alone.

"Okay." Robbie breathed out slowly. "Someone explain who those people were and what the fuck they were trying to do."

We were all still, afraid to move, afraid it would attract them if we did.

Bob was the first to break the spell and he tried the engine again. It started with a loud roar.

I clapped loudly, almost hysterical, and Bob laughed with a sick sense of relief.

"Thank the lord!" he proclaimed.

"You guys?" Robbie asked again, needing answers.

I was about to exchange a look with Sage to see if either one of us was going to say something when Graham's laughter stopped.

"They're coming," he whispered, his eyes closed, blood pouring out of his nose and mouth.

Bob turned in his seat to shoot him a look when there was a horrific crash, the sound of a dying metal beast, of a bus being broken as some speeding object smashed into its side. I was thrown out of Sage's grasp and chucked across the bus, my head slamming into the cupboards above the couch. Blood filled my eyes. There was the sound of breaking glass, people screaming horrifically like they were being tortured. The bus rolled and tumbled over and over: blackness, sand, wind. I felt hands and legs touch me briefly, and by the time I knew to reach for them they were gone.

When it all came to a stop, the metal groaning from all around, I didn't know if I was alive or dead. Everything was dark. I groped around for a feeling of something familiar. I found a small, short box and a handle. A cupboard. I moved my hands up, amazed that they weren't broken, and they met with something stuffed. A mattress. I tried to think where I was. Maybe in the rear bedroom? All I knew was I had been tossed far when the bus tumbled, spinning me around like a rag in the washing machine.

A cry broke my concentration. I turned in the direction of the sound, and when my eyes adjusted to the darkness, I could see shadows. There was a light coming from the end, very faint, and with it came sand and wind. I figured that I was at the rear, the bus was lying on its right side, and all the windows at the front were broken.

"Hello!" I called out, choking on the incoming dust. I wiped the blood off my forehead and pulled my shirt up to cover my nose and mouth.

"Dawn?" I heard a weak voice. My heart spasmed at the quiet fear and desperation that gripped it. It sounded like Mickey.

"Mickey? Where are you? Are you hurt?"

Where was everyone else? Why was no one else talking?

He coughed in response. It sounded wet and ragged.

I got to my feet, grabbing onto the side of the bed that was jutting out. I stumbled over a pillow and fell against the wall. Only it wasn't the wall. It was the side of the bathroom and a huge obstacle I had to climb over in order to get to Mickey and the front. I was dizzy, woozy, and my head was leaking blood from where I had bashed it. It took all the strength I had to try and pull myself up. I collapsed in a heap on top, almost falling through the open door into the bathroom. With shaking arms I reached over and pulled myself across the gap.

"Help," Mickey cried, closer now.

"I'm coming," I told him, coughing again, my legs dangling in the bathroom. I slithered across the rest of the wall and immediately met the two bunks. Mickey's labored breathing was coming from the top one, my bunk.

I leaned over the edge, feeling for him. I touched a leg and he cried out in pain.

"Sorry!" I waited a few seconds, wanting my eyes to adjust but I could only make out blurry shadows. "Are you hurt?"

"Y-yes."

"Where?"

"My…shoulder," he broke into a leaky cough. "M-my chest."

"Do you know what happened?

"I don't know. Something hit us. Robbie was beside me, I heard him beside me just after it all stopped. Now I don't hear him anymore."

I listened. All I could hear was the wind whistling, the grit flying into the bus. I couldn't hear Robbie. I couldn't hear anyone else.

Oh God, let Sage be okay, I prayed. It was the only moment of fear I would give myself.

"Mickey, you're going to be alright. I'm going to find the light, okay? I know there's one somewhere to the side of your head, where the ceiling would be."

"I can't move."

"That's okay, stay still. I'll find it."

I tried to lean over as far as I could without falling over on him, balancing my torso on the edge of the bunk. I reached and fumbled with my hands and eventually found the light switch.

"Close your eyes," I warned him. I squinted mine in preparation and flicked it on.

Mickey was lying below me, on the wall beside my bunk. His eyes were squeezed shut. His chest and shoulder were covered in blood, his shoulder twisted, his chest sunken in as if something heavy had slammed into him. His face was ashen, paler than death against his dark beard. I almost cried out but bit my tongue hard, not wanting to scare him.

"Okay, Mickey," I said.

He opened his eyes slowly, blinking hard at me. "Your head."

"I hit it," I said. "I'm fine."

"Where's Robbie?" he started coughing. Blood bubbled out of his lips.

I grimaced at the sight and looked over the edge of the bunk. I could barely see him in the space beside the other bunk but Robbie was there, lying on his stomach. For what it was worth, I couldn't see any blood in the darkness and after a few seconds, I saw his back rise and fall.

"He's there," I said turning back to Mickey. "He's alive."

Mickey smiled then wheezed and groaned. Sweat appeared on his pale forehead.

"Hey, you'll be fine," I lied. "Hang in there, boyo. I'm going to go see where everyone else is and get help."

"I'm sorry, Dawn," he said.

His voice cracked. It broke my heart.

"For what?"

"I should have been nicer to you. I wasn't. I'm sorry. Please, please go visit Noelle when this is all over."

"Mickey…"

"Promise me. She needs a friend. She never had any. She only had me. Promise me, please."

I tried to smile. The sadness felt too heavy on my lips. "I promise."

"Thank you," he said softly. Then his eyes closed and his final breath escaped his bloodied lips.

My chest was heavy, feeling like I was being choked from the inside. My throat was thick and I was unable to swallow. I couldn't do this right now. I couldn't grieve. I'd lose it. Mickey was dead, there was no way I could do anything for him anymore. He was dead.

I looked away and made a point to never look back. I shuffled myself along the side of the bunk and carefully dropped myself onto the back of the couch. The wind was lessening, calming down to a dull roar. I could see the shattered windows, edges of glass splattered with blood. The sand seemed to hover in the air, floating around like I was in a ghostly snowglobe.

I reached down to my feet, balancing on the cushions, and felt around for the light switch on the wall. It came on, flickering. Fiddles was lying in front of me, eyes rolled back in his head, still as death. His head was twisted at a gruesome angle, almost hanging down to his shoulder.

Keep it together, keep it together, I chanted to myself, closing my eyes at the sight. Get out now.

I stepped around Fiddles, a few tears leaking from my eyes, and tried to keep the feeling down that was bubbling up inside.

The windshield was completely shattered and sand had piled in, half burying the only way out. I got on my knees and began to crawl through, clawing through the sand like I was climbing a dune at the beach, keeping my back low so the sharp blades of glass didn't pierce my back and sides.

I was halfway out when I felt something thick and unstable beneath me. It was soft. It was a person.

I felt around and touched a side, a chest, an arm. I didn't know if they were alive or dead. I pushed on the arm, trying to flip the person over, praying over and over again that it wasn't Sage.

The person finally gave, sand sifting to make room, and with one thump I was looking straight into Bob's white face. A huge piece of glass was sticking out of one bloody hole that used to be an eye, the rest of the glass lodged deep in his brain.

That did it. Bob was gone. My dear Bob was dead. Bob who had the mortgage and the wife and loved Elvis. Bob whose twinkly eyes and many stories would be going to the grave with him.

I couldn't hold it together any longer. I screamed, taking in half the desert in my lungs. I flipped him over so the glass wouldn't cut me and I scampered out of the bus. I dragged myself along, my breath hitched, nerves crying out, until I felt solid ground and stony earth beneath me. I got to my feet and looked around. I could just the see shape of the bus, lying on its side. One half of it was crushed in where something had hit it. Only something the size of a semi or another bus could do that.

I was too distraught to think properly. Where was I again? Arizona. The highway. I needed to get help. I needed to find Sage. Where was he? Where was Jacob?

I looked around, not knowing what direction to go. I was blind in the dim storm. I walked haphazardly, tripping over rocks, ignoring the cuts and bruises I could see on my legs.

"Sage!" I called out. "Jacob?!"

My voice echoed eerily. I heard nothing but the wind brushing past. My eyes watered from the sand.

I was about to call again when I heard coughing to my left. I ran awkwardly in that direction, my leg starting to hurt, until I saw a fallen shape on the ground.

I fell to my knees beside it, scraping my skin.

It was Jacob.

"Are you okay?" I cried out. I put my hand to his weathered forehead. It was hot. His eyes were closed painfully.

"Rusty?" he asked, choking a bit on the words. "I'm fine. Are you hurt?"

"Just my head. What about you?"

"Bloody leg."

I looked down. His leg was bloody indeed. It was crooked and a piece of white bone was jutting out of his torn brown pant leg. I nearly vomited on him.

"I think it's broken," I said feebly.

He coughed. "No shit. Where is everyone else?"

"Mickey, Bob, and Fiddles are all dead. Robbie is still on the bus. He's alive but unconscious, I think anyway. I haven't seen Sage or Graham."

"I think we can assume they're gone together," he said between coughs. "His birthday isn't until tomorrow at midnight. There's still time. We can get him back. I think I know where he might be."

"You're going to help me?"

"Of course, you natty bird." He closed his eyes and let out a moan, his legs stiffening out straight. "But first, I need help. Go run to the road. It should be right ahead of you. Get someone to drive to a payphone. The storm is lessening."

I patted his shoulder and got up. "Don't die on me, Jacob."

"It would be my first occupational hazard," he answered. "I don't plan on it."

I nodded, and finding the last reserve of my strength, I started running. It wasn't long before I began to see the shapes of waiting cars and was almost to the road when a dark figure stepped in front of me.

"I've been looking for you," said a coolly sardonic voice. "Sage's lovebird."

It was Graham.

I cried out and turned around to run away from him, only to find Sonja, Terri, and Sparky standing right behind me, eyes black, mouths open in a pointy, demonic grin.

There was a blunt thud at the back of my head and a starburst of pain. I was out before the ground met my face.

CHAPTER TWENTY-THREE

I dreamed I was a little girl again. I was playing at the edge of the swimming holes that perforated the Columbia River, dipping my toe into the cool water but afraid to go in.

"Come on, baby Dawn," my mother encouraged. I looked up. She was standing in the water, wet hair cascading down the sides of her face. She looked young, strong, and beautiful. "Come in the water."

I shook my head. I wasn't a strong swimmer back then.

"I promise to hold onto you," she cooed. "I won't let you go."

She opened her arms and motioned with her hands. Her smiling face was glowing.

"Come on," she said again.

I hesitated. Then I walked in until I was up to my knobby knees, then I plugged my nose and jumped in the rest of the way.

It was dark and cold underneath the water but I surfaced, my lungs gasping for breath.

"You can do it, baby Dawn."

I doggy paddled toward her and when I was close, she reached out and grabbed me. I clung to her shoulder like she was a life preserver, instantly calmed by the feeling of her skin against mine.

"See, I told you I wouldn't let you go."

I relaxed, resting my head on her shoulder.

Suddenly my ear was being tickled by water. Rising water. I looked up. My mom was staring forward with a blank look on her face.

"I won't let you go, baby girl," she whispered absently. Her words were ghosts that floated up in the air.

Now the water was up to my chin. We were sinking.

"I won't let you go," she said again.

I gasped for air as we were pulled down.

"I won't let you go."

The cold water covered my head. I opened my mouth to scream but water rushed in and filled my tiny lungs.

My mother mouthed the words, "I won't let you go."

* * *

When I came to, I was lying on my back and my world was rocking back and forth, a shifting, splashing sound filling my ears. I opened my eyes to see a black, star-lit sky, open and expansive, stretching from one dark-hilled horizon to the other. The moon was full and radiating against the darkness. I felt terror wrap around me like a cold blanket, holding me still.

I tried to raise my head. Pain erupted from several points and stars spun in my dizzying vision. I let out a cry, unable to feel anything except the terror, except the pain.

A splash came from my left. At first it was just a sound. It continued, and soon I was being flicked with cold water, making me flinch involuntarily. Each movement caused the pain in my head to explode.

A vicious, melodic laugh erupted.

"Wakey wakey," came a girlish voice. "Your savior is here."

"Dawn!" It was Sage.

I tried to sit up but my world was immediately rocked. I tensed, trying to steady my arms, realizing it wasn't just the blows to the head that had made me dizzy, but that I was lying on something extremely unstable. The lower half of my body, my legs particularly, was sloping downwards and thick vinyl was rubbing against my skin.

"Take it easy," the girl said. "You don't want to drown yet."

I forced my eyes open and waited for the spinning to stop. When it did, I saw a lake lit by moonlight. I was lying down on an inflatable raft that was bending awkwardly in the middle. I looked down at my legs. There was a thick, very heavy chain wrapped around them from my ankles all the way up to my knees. I couldn't move my legs to save my life and I realized that was the point. It was a miracle the raft had just enough air in it to stay buoyant with all the weight.

To one side of me, floating in the water up to her chest was one of the most beautiful and terrifying people I had ever seen. Long alabaster hair, sculpted cheekbones, and iridescent eyes that looked like they were made of gold silk. For all her beauty, there was something so immensely dreadful about her that my skin crawled, like at any moment her face could change into something so horrific that I'd die from fright.

I managed to tear my eyes away from her hypnotizing gaze and looked to the shore. Sage was only a few yards away. My brilliant Sage. Somehow, he was here too. He was shirtless, his chest cut up and bleeding, on his knees in thick red soil. He was watching me with total agony on his face. I couldn't tell if it was for me, for himself, or for everyone else. Half his band, half his friends, were dead.

Graham was standing behind him, his arms crossed like a smug bastard, his lower half human, his head was one that belonged on a demonic worm, with a round toothy hole for a mouth. I shivered at the image, the inhuman blending of drummer and demon, the way his mouth dripped black and red splotches of clumpy blood onto the ground.

Naturally, the GTFOs were all there. Beside him were Terri, Sparky, and Sonja, all looking like the life-sucking groupies that they were.

They weren't alone. As I looked closely around the tree-lined lake, I saw many bobbing heads in the water—demonic faces in all shapes and sizes. Red glowing eyes. Protruding tongues and razor teeth. Weeping skin covered with maggots.

Something big splashed in the distance—a dark, undefinable shape under a bright moon. I caught the gleam of moving scales and an incredible sense of size. I saw the dark creature moving underneath the water toward me like a stealthy submarine.

This was Lake Shasta. And though I was close to shore, I knew I was in the deep end.

"I'm Alva," the woman said. She took her hand out of the water and offered it to me. I stared at her like she was a fucking idiot.

Her uncanny eyes narrowed for a second, and in that second her hand transformed into a long tentacle. She swiped it at me and it raked across my chest, pulling away skin with a hundred tiny, blood-sucking mouths.

I screamed at the pain and she laughed in retort, her golden eyes flashing into black, empty holes with no way out. I felt like I was being sucked into them, into a cold, hellish eternity.

"Let her go!" Sage yelled, his voice carrying clearly from the muddy shore. "She has nothing to do with this."

Alva looked at him dryly, her face transformed back to normal in an instant. "You asked for her, Sage. You asked for this."

"I never asked for you to kill her. I never asked for anyone to be killed and you know it!"

"Well, you should have been more specific when you made the deal," she said, sounding bored. She caught me staring at her and smiled very, very slowly. Her incisors were as sharp as shark's teeth and they cut into the side of her mouth where the wounds flayed open like torn paper. "Sorry this has to be so dramatic, Dawn. We like to have fun when no one's watching. And part of the fun is killing you in a most terrifying way. Now we know your mother died some years ago. Slit her wrists and drowned in the bathtub. We thought that was too cliché for you though."

"But you can't do this," I yelled, trying to keep the raft level. Water was splashing over the sides, swamping me. "The bargain's not even being fulfilled. There's supposed to be a published article. I haven't even finished writing it!"

Alva laughed. "Oh, that doesn't matter. We found it on the bus and finished the rest for you. We mailed it to Barry Kramer today. The fact-checker can't check facts when the whole band is dead."

"You're not supposed to kill him," I sneered. I didn't know where I was finding the courage. "It's not in the code."

"Screw the code," Alva sneered back. A small, revolting worm slid out of her ear and traveled down to her chest, leaving a black, slimy trail. "The only reason we follow the code is because we're made to. But you don't see one of the Jacobs around right now, do you?"

"You answer to someone."

"Yes. His name is Lucifer and I can tell you that he's not a fan of the code either. It's just something we have to do for that other guy."

I assumed she meant God. How diplomatic of him to have a deal with the devil himself.

"Besides," she continued. "You're what Sage asked for. He wanted someone to love. We gave that to him, and now we're taking it away, just like we took away every other person. He got off easy with his wife just leaving, but later we decided it lacked impact, you know?"

She giggled and splashed around in the water, treading it playfully, her appearance slowly becoming more monstrous. "To tell you the truth, Sage has been a fun contract to fulfill and an even funner one to collect on."

"Funner is not a word," I seethed. Always a journalist, even to the end.

She shrugged. "You should really choose your last words more carefully. Perhaps you should tell Sage you love him. Give him a bit of happiness before we take it away again."

I looked over at Sage on the shore. His eyes were conflicted, probably over a million different things. Graham had a firm grip on both his shoulders with talon-like claws, and the others were standing close by. He didn't have a chance in hell of saving me. They were going to drown me, here and now, and he'd be powerless to stop it. He'd have to watch it all. I wondered what happened on the bus, if he had to see the others dead.

"Well, you love him don't you?" Alva prodded, annoyed.

It wasn't until that moment that I realized I really did love him. I loved him before as one loves their idols. And I loved him now as a similarly damaged soul. A kindred spirit. It was a budding love, new and growing, built on attraction, on trust. I trusted him. I knew he'd try and save me if he could. But things weren't looking in his favor.

I would have told him. But it didn't feel right. It was a private thing from me to him. The demons didn't deserve to hear it.

"Okay, well at least you love her," Alva said to Sage. Her voice was deeper now as she slowly changed forms, more and more wriggling black worms coming out of her skin, bursting free of her face and neck like out of a rotten apple.

Sage shook his head.

Alva lowered her eyes. They were no longer gold. There was no longer anything beautiful about her. "You can't hide the truth from us. I can sniff it out of you."

"I'm not hiding anything," Sage said. His voice was cold and steady. He looked at me, a full apology brimming in his eyes. "I'm sorry, Dawn."

The confusion was a pleasant distraction. "What?"

"Yes, what?" Alva repeated, her voice growling.

Sage shrugged. "I...I don't love her. I barely know her."

Alva laughed. It was short and bursting with uncertainty.

"What do you mean you don't love her? Of course you do."

"I don't," Sage said in such a way that I believed him. "I don't love you, Dawn, I'm sorry. I like you a lot. An awful lot. But I don't love you."

I heard Alva make a sputtering sound. I heard the sound of my heart breaking.

Alva's depthless eyes were on me, reading the shock on my face. Then they turned into tiny black points and speared Graham with terrifying intensity. "Graham. You told me he was in love with her."

Graham looked flustered and changed back into human form, his gaping worm mouth shrinking into a hole. Everyone was looking at him, even Sage.

"What? He is in love with her. I know it."

"I'm not," Sage pleaded.

"Okay, can you guys stop rubbing it in!" I yelled, even though part of me wanted Sage to continue. The fact that he didn't love me was the only thing that was keeping me alive.

"Graham," Alva growled. She swam around the raft until she was between me and the shore and I caught long black tentacles and flickering tails drifting behind her. "Explain."

"I..I...," he looked at everyone, his face flickering from demon to human like someone flipping channels on a TV. "Chip. The sound tech. He said he caught them having sex on the floor. He says he talked to Dawn's friend and she said she was in love with him."

"I don't give a fuck if Dawn's in love with him!" Alva yelled, a ferocious sound that boomed across the lake, causing the water to ripple. I could hear something large and terrible surfacing behind me but I didn't dare look. "She's not part of the deal. The deal was we take what Sage loves. Does he love Dawn or not? Tell me you know this for a fact."

Graham's monstrous mouth flapped soundlessly for a beat or two. "They had sex! They've been spending all their time together! I've seen the way he looks at her."

He was losing the argument and fast. You could hear it in his tone. For the first time ever, Graham sounded scared. And whatever scared Graham was bound to terrify me.

Alva's stare flamed. Her voice rose. "You know, for a demon, you're a hell of a romantic, Graham. And a fucking moron. Love is more than just sex and longing looks. Fuck…look at all the fucking time we just wasted. Now this isn't even part of the contract."

I had to wonder what a head demon like Alva knew about love, but I pushed it out of my head and tried to think of what to do next. With chains that would surely sink me and a monster somewhere out in the deep, there wasn't much I could do except watch and wait.

"Maybe he's lying," Graham supposed, grasping for straws. My heart did a sick little dance at the idea. But his love would mean death and I wasn't a fool.

"He's not. I can tell," she said through grinding teeth. The water in the lake began to shake and ripple like it was being bustled by an underwater earthquake. A thick coat of black liquid began to bleed out of holes in her body and spread out across the water's surface like an oil spill. If I looked close I could see faces in the oily matter, screaming soundlessly at me, souls trapped in a never ending hell.

I looked away from the sight. Alava turned around in the water and aimed her gaze at me. Her eyes looked dead. "Kill him."

Everyone on the shore looked at each other.

She whipped around and screamed, "Kill him! Not Sage! Graham! Kill Graham! Kill him now! Kill him now!"

Any wonder whether demons could be killed was gone. Graham shoved Sage to the ground and started to run into the woods, but Sparky transformed into a black worm with multiple human-like legs and leaped onto Graham's back, taking him down. He thrashed as Sonja and Terri reached for him with their long, growing fingers. There was a scream and ripping sounds, wet cracks that rattled across the lake. Sage was on the ground nearby, face down, covering his ears from the sound. Terri and Sonja stood up, a bloody limb in each arm. They took the arms and tossed them into the lake where a dozen tentacles reached out of the dark water, dragging the limbs under the surface in a feeding frenzy.

The final rip was the loudest. I closed my eyes just as I saw Sonja holding up Graham's half human, half demon head. She brought his face up to hers as if she was going to kiss it and began to eat it instead. Talk about every rock star's worst nightmare.

Alva turned to me, and if she wasn't a disgusting, oozing demon, she might have looked sheepish. "Drummers are the worst."

"So what do we do with Sage?" Terri yelled. She kicked Sage in the side and he cried out in pain. "Can we have our way with him before we kill him?"

I was about to tell her that I would rip her tiny tits off if she dared lay a hand on him when Alva calmly said, "We aren't killing him."

I started. "What?"

She swam back toward me, looking beautiful again. "It's true it's not in the contract. We don't *have* to kill him."

"You're letting him live?" I asked hopefully, not daring to believe it.

She shrugged, drops of oily water rolling off her shoulders. I could almost hear screaming. "I think he's got a lot of talent. He could do better than that silly band."

I looked over at Sage, not trusting a word she was saying. Judging from the expression on his face as he pushed himself off the mud, he felt the same way.

"You," Alva said sweetly, placing razor sharp claws along the edges of the raft and gazing wickedly at me, "aren't an exception."

"What?"

"I might get in shit for totally breaking this contract before it even gets off the ground, but you bother me. It must be the groupie thing."

"I'm not a groupie." I couldn't help but protest. My pettiness no longer surprised me.

"Dawn Emerson's famous last words," she said with a smile of black shark teeth. "It's better than 'funner's not a word.'"

And then she poked her fingers into the raft.

Sage screamed my name from the shore.

The GTFOs laughed.

The raft popped and hissed and the water began shaking again, waves growing and rising. The raft was deflating fast and I was sinking into a black pool of tortured faces.

Alva smiled and started swimming back to shore just as Sage was launching himself into the lake. He started doing an incredibly fast breaststroke toward me, the thick water barely slowing him down. Alva walked out of the water, stark ass naked, and sat in the red clay with the demon groupies on either side of her like they were whale-watching.

Sage got to me fast but not fast enough. The raft was almost entirely under and I was no longer floating. I could feel hundreds of slimy hands grabbing me everywhere, trying to pull me down, the Damned wanting to claim another companion.

Sage grabbed me by my shoulders and held on tight.

"I'm not letting you go," he cried frantically. His face was close to mine and I could see the anguish in his clear eyes, the green turned silver by the moon.

"It's okay," I said, feeling the raft totally disappear beneath me. My legs began to feel heavy and I was pulled downward. Whether it was by the chains or the screaming souls, I didn't know. It didn't matter.

"No!" he screamed at me, trying to stay above water. "Try, Dawn, try swimming so we can make it to shore."

"And then what?" I asked, meaning the demons who were watching gleefully. "Then what happens?"

"At least you've tried," he said, straining, trying to keep both of us above water. I could tell he was losing strength fast. "This doesn't have to be your destiny. Neither me nor they have the power to decide that."

I nodded and tried to kick a bit. I could only move my legs like a mermaid and it was clear it wasn't getting me anywhere.

"Come on, please, angel."

"I'm trying," I cried, but got a mouthful of water. I was

growing so tired.

"Try for me. Please, for me. I can't lose you. I can't, Dawn, I can't. You're my hope."

He yanked at me, giving all he had, and tried to swim for shore. I gave as much as I could but I was losing the battle. My head went under the water. A child's voice whispered into my ear, "Play with us."

Sage pulled me up and I gasped for breath. His face was wet, but I couldn't tell if it was tears or lake water that streamed down his cheeks. I would have loved to see those dimples again. I would have loved to hear him laugh again. I would have loved for him to be inside me again.

"I love you," I whispered.

He pulled me close and kissed my forehead.

"You're my hope. I'm not letting go of that."

He wrapped his arms around me and we both began to sink under the water.

I opened my eyes and saw only him, his eyes open too, his face glowing from the filtered moon like the statue of an angel lit beneath a ghostly heaven.

I moved in to kiss him, my lips touching his with my last breath. The bubbles around us stilled, the hands stopped, and Lake Shasta welcomed us with open arms, leading us to her silky red floor.

This was it.

My dad, Eric, Mel, my mother, Sage, the band, Jacob, even my horse, they all flashed through my brain, and with the last strength I had, I managed to shed a tear for everything I was going to lose.

All was still. All was black.

A sputtering, low drone filled my head.

A stabbing feeling in my side.

I was rising fast.

My ears popped.

Hands grabbed my shirt and struggled. I was yanked up hard

by hands that were under my arms.

I was thrown into something hard and metal. A tinny sound on impact.

There was a pause. A groan.

Something else landed hard next to me. Something heavy smacked me in the face.

My eyes opened and a rush of water came out of my lungs.

I heaved and heaved, getting it all out, trying to get air back in.

"Easy now," came a familiar voice.

I took in one clear breath and was fully conscious of my surroundings. I was on the floor of a metal boat. Sage was beside me, coughing violently. Jacob was at the helm of the boat, one leg in a cast. He grinned down at us.

"Hope you know you've turned me into a criminal," he said, gunning the boat harder. We bounced hard along the water. "I had to steal some nice old chap's livelihood. Think how much trout this boat takes in each year."

I touched Sage on the shoulder to let him know I was okay and sat up, poking my head over the side of the boat. We were just about to ram into the shore where Alva, Sonja, Terri, and Sparky were scrambling to their feet.

Jacob killed the throttle to neutral and we coasted along gently.

"Good evening, ladies," he called out. "How are you?"

"You asshole," Alva screamed, blood flying from her mouth.

He shrugged. "You kidnapped my client, you cunt. As if I'd let that pass."

"You're supposed to be in hell!"

He gave her a dry look. "Did you really think a mere semi-truck smashing into a tour bus would kill me? Ladies, I toured four cities with Led Zeppelin and I survived that."

Alva glared at him. "You're getting off on a technicality here."

"And you're losing on a technicality. You want to try and test the code again, I'm going to be in your face. And if it's not me, it's another Jacob, or another Jacob. There are just as many of us managers as there are demons."

"Enjoy it while it lasts then," Alva sniped. Her silky eyes rested on me and I felt a vague burning in the back of my head. I hoped it was a concussion.

"Thanks, ladies. Remember to buy Sage Knightly's solo album when it comes out, it's sure to be a real hit."

Jacob gunned the engine to a roar and we sped away from the muddy banks. But it wasn't loud enough to drown out Alva's final cry.

"Be careful what you wished for, Dawn!"

I looked at the guys for confirmation but Jacob was grinning like a madman, piloting the small fishing boat at breakneck speed and Sage was coughing into his arm, his muscles tense.

I sat back and closed my eyes, not daring to fall asleep. Soon though, the lull of the waves and drone of the engine made the world fade to a gentle velvet black.

CHAPTER TWENTY-FOUR

I don't remember much about what happened next. I remember being carried out of the boat and into a car. The next thing I knew I was being lowered into a hard bed with scratchy sheets. My eyes opened briefly and I saw Sage peering down at me, his lips curled into a hint of a smile.

Then I woke up. I sat up in a strange bed and looked around a strange room. It was wood-paneled, but real wood, like the room was made out of logs. There was a chair and a table and the bed I was lying in, completely naked. My chest and forehead were bandaged up, as were a few places on my legs.

Beside me, lit by the sun that was streaming in through the single window, was Sage. He was sleeping on his back, his head tilted to the side. He was naked too, at least from the waist up, and his firm, thick chest and rigid abs were bandaged. His face looked peaceful, his lips almost smiling in his sleep.

I thought back to the night before. Jacob. He came and got us out. Where was he? I looked around the room for a sign then spotted a letter on the table.

I got up and tried to walk over but ended up limping. I'd done something to my ankle during the bus accident, or maybe it happened when Graham and the GTFOs bashed me on the head and I woke up on the raft. It didn't matter. It hurt.

I made a mental note to try and find painkillers somewhere and snatched the letter up.

The cover said Dawn and Sage and had a heart drawn around it. It felt thick in my hands.

I ripped it open and wasn't surprised to pull out a letter from Jacob. I peered into the remainder of the envelope. There was a small wad of folded bills.

Like the enigmatic manager himself, it was short and to the point.

Dawn and Sage,

I hope this finds you well. I did the best I could with your injuries, but my skills only go as far as bandaging up Robbie after he's passed out on the bathroom floor. Speaking of Robbie, he's fine. He's in a hospital in Tucson with some minor injuries. Noelle is doing better too..

Hybrid is over, as you both know. That was one of the things that had to be taken away from you. But that's now in the past and you're probably better off for it. Sage you're twenty-eight. You're free now. Your life starts today. I suggest, if you know what's good for you, to start working again right away. And on music. I'll take care of you financially. I've included a bunch of money I took from the band over the years. Don't worry, I knew I'd be giving it back to you one day, I just hoped I'd still have a job. No matter though, I'll find work and so will you. If you struggle, look me up. I love having assistants.

As for you, Dawn, you're a trooper through and through. Sorry you got dragged into this whole deal with the devil bit, but the truth is, even though you are Sage's hope and his biggest fan, you're just a better writer than that arsekisser at Rolling Stone. My wish for you is to enjoy your young life while you can and to love the ones you're with. Don't be like the rest of the youth who piss away their time with false promises of tomorrow. You know better now. Use your time wisely.

Take care, both of you.

I'll be seeing you soon.

Jacob.

I fished out the wad of bills from the envelope. Instead of a bunch of ones and tens like I'd assume his cockney ass would leave, it was a wad of hundreds. Sage was well-taken care of.

"What's that?" Sage asked wearily. "And who are you, a naked angel?"

I shot him a smile, overjoyed to see him alive and well.

"It's from Jacob," I said, climbing into bed with him. I handed him the letter.

He looked over it, smiling from time to time and frowning sadly the rest. He peered in the envelope and whistled.

"I don't think the man has much faith in me," he remarked, leaning over to put it on the bedside table.

"Don't be ridiculous," I admonished him. "You think they took everything from you?"

He gazed at me with dull eyes. "Almost everything."

I placed my hands on both sides of his gorgeous face, feeling the stubble beneath my fingers. "You're still the most handsome man I've ever seen with a body that any man would kill for. That's still here."

He looked down sheepishly. I held his face firmer.

"And you're still a talented musician."

He attempted to laugh but I tightened my grip. "I'm serious. Remember that song you wrote when you were young? You played it for me in the hotel room in Atlanta? When did you write that? Was it before or after you made the deal?"

"Before."

I exhaled loudly, a rush of relief flooding through me. "See, it was in you all this time."

"You're sounding corny now."

"No, Sage Knightly, you're the borderline corny one."

"I thought you would have forgotten all that."

I gently tapped the side of my head, carefully avoiding my injuries. "Journalists forget nothing."

He smiled, bright and beautiful, before it quickly faded. He shifted uncomfortably and looked down at his hands, dark bronze against the white sheets.

"I'm sorry about earlier."

"You'll have to be more specific," I said. "A lot has happened."

"I'm so sorry about everything," he whispered. "I'm sorry for everyone."

His eyes began to well up and I pulled his head into my chest, holding him there for comfort. I let him cry quietly for a few minutes. I didn't say anything, I didn't try and make him feel better. I just held him. I needed it just as much as he did.

When it was over, he wiped away his tears with an embarrassed look on his face. He shot me a quick glance then looked out the window at the blue, blue sky.

"I'm sorry if I made you feel stupid," he muttered.

"What?"

"Last night. When…when I told you I didn't love you."

"Oh hush now," I said, dismissing his sincerity with a wave. "That should be the least of your concerns."

"I know it hurt you and hurting you was the last thing I wanted to do."

I fixed my gaze on him. "Sage. Listen. There were two ways last night could have gone. You could have told me you loved me and I would have died. Or you could have told the truth, which you did, and the truth would have saved me. In theory anyway. Look, I'm a romantic like any other girl. But when it comes to life or love, I choose life. I'm here right now, ready to live and love another day. I could never regret that. I'm glad you didn't love me. You gave me my life by doing so."

"But," he began.

I put my fingers to his lips. "But nothing. You and I respect each other, we trust each other, and I dare say we find each other immensely attractive. I think that's a pretty good situation we're in, don't you agree?"

His gaze intensified, a subtle warning of what was to come next. His lips opened and took in my fingers, sucking on them slowly. I couldn't help but smile.

"Careful," I told him. "We're not exactly in tip-top shape."

He licked the length of my finger then gingerly placed his hands on either side of my face.

"I'll be gentle," he murmured.

We slowly fell back into the bed and played out a dance that could have been choreographed, grazing over our injured areas, gently stroking and teasing the more eager areas. He licked and sucked at my nipples in a slow, melodic fashion as I teased the sensitive places on his hard chest, going round the bandages like a rat in a maze. When he finally entered me, filling me with need and heat, it was like we were born again, free and unbandaged. He held my hands above my head, much like that teasing time in the hotel room, and gave everything he had to me, letting me lie back and enjoy it all—from the view of his perfect body, a body I knew had the strength of many men, to his expressive face that betrayed a wealth of complex emotions. We both came at the same time again, but this time, instead of being fast and furious, it was achingly slow, and when I let go, I let go of a few tears I hadn't yet found the time to shed.

Afterward, we held each other tightly, his naked cock pressed against my ass, his arms wrapped around me. I studied the snakes and Mexican skulls on his arms, wondering about the story behind each one. I could only hope I'd be given the time to learn them.

Outside, the Northern California sun streamed in the window. The sky was a brilliant blue and the leaves of a nearby oak had turned a golden red.

Summer was over.

A new season had begun.

EPILOGUE

I was lying on my bed listening to Alice Cooper's "School's Out" when the phone rang downstairs.

I leapt to the floor, yelling, "I'll get it," and quickly ran down the stairs, taking them two at a time.

My dad was sitting on the couch watching his favorite Saturday morning Warner Brothers cartoon like he always did, sipping a glass of apple juice. He gave me a knowing smile as I moseyed into the room.

"It's always for you," he said. "I don't even know why I bother."

"Ha ha," I answered. I tried not to peer at the glass of juice in his hand, tried to hide the ever present wonder if it was something alcoholic. But of course it wasn't. Not that it would stop me from worrying, but my dad hadn't had a drink for almost nine months.

A lot had happened during that time. After what happened at Lake Shasta, I went with Sage to live at his father's for a few days while I organized my flight home. His father was back in dire straits and the property was about to be seized. But thanks to the money that Jacob had left Sage, he was able to get his dad out of the red for the time being.

Sage decided he would take Jacob up on his offer and work as a manager's assistant. We said our goodbyes at the Sacramento airport. He wanted me to join him but I had unfinished business at home that I couldn't ignore any longer, not even for a rock star. I had my family. I had a relationship with Mel that I needed to repair. I had school and a career that was only just starting. I still had a calling I needed to find but I knew I wouldn't find it in a rock star's shadow.

And yeah, I say rock star because that's what Sage is and what he will always be. The talent he has was God-given, not brought on by any contract. After a few months of working for Jacob and working on his craft, Sage released a solo album, creatively titled "Sage Wisdom" (groan). I bet Jacob came up with the name considering how redundant it is. Anyway, the song he played for me in the hotel room ended up being called "A World of Want" and it was quickly climbing up the charts. The last time I heard from him he was about to go tour in Europe, where the audience was more accepting of experimental music.

I didn't hear much from Jacob except in a postcard that told me he was proud of me for landing a part-time writing position with Creem Magazine. After I learned the article was sent in to be published, I called up Barry and got him to read me the end of it, the part I didn't write. I was certain that the demons would have made some crazy libelous shit up but they didn't. They actually went into my notes and composed the end from interviews I did with Noelle, Robbie, and Mickey. There was no Sage, but Barry didn't even care—he said it kept together the idea of the man as a mystery. It really was the article of the century and was printed around the world. I, Dawn Emerson, recorded the fall of Hybrid.

The funny thing was, I didn't mince words either. I talked about demons and Graham and deals and the GTFOs but everyone thought it was some clever, poetic metaphor for the demise of the band. And I couldn't argue with anyone. Who would believe me?

Well, Mel did. Eventually I won back her trust. It took a few months of harassing her house until her mother had enough and forced us to make up. Once I told her the reason behind things, she came around, slowly but surely.

As for school, well, I just finished a few weeks ago. Todd is working for the paper in Spokane, but I'm working for Creem and Creem always rises to the top.

"Are you going to answer it or not?" My dad yelled good-naturedly. "I want to see the coyote get the road runner for once."

I snatched up the phone before it could annoy my dad anymore.

"Hello?"

There was a crackle and a pause. Then, "Dawn?"

"Sage?" I asked. He sounded so far away.

"Hey, angel, how are you? I hope I'm not waking you up."

I looked at my watch. "It's ten thirty in the morning, I'm no longer a lazy college student."

"I figured that. Congratulations. Welcome to the real world. How does it feel?"

"Eh, it's okay. I think I might look sexier in this so-called real world, though."

I didn't have to look at the couch to know my dad was looking mighty disturbed.

"I don't think that's possible," Sage growled seductively. "Listen, what are you doing next month? Is May busy for a retired rodeo queen?"

I laughed. "No. Not yet. There's supposed to be a bunch of good albums released that I'll have to review right away but that's about it."

"How do you feel about flying to Paris and meeting me there? I'm about to go on tour and I'd love a sexy, talented journalist to cover it."

My heart felt like it was being massaged. "Are you kidding me?"

"Do I ever kid? I'm serious. Tell me when you're free and I'll fly you over here. I'll take care of you, angel." He lowered his voice. "I really miss you."

I shot a look at my dad. He was pretending not to listen to every single word.

"'I really miss you too," I told him. My insides ached just thinking about him. When you've been with someone for weeks straight during a traumatic experience, someone you've fallen in love with...your idol. And then you're pulled apart and the only thing you get from him for months is to hear his raspy, whiskey-soaked voice on the radio, in a song he sang privately to you, it hurts. It damn hurts.

"So you'll come? Tell me the dates and I'll make the arrangements."

My heart soared in relief.

"Can you call back later tonight? I need to talk it over with the family."

"Of course. Talk to you soon."

He hung up and I was left staring dumbly at the receiver like I had done so many months ago. I could still hear Alice Cooper blaring from my bedroom.

My dad was staring at me expectantly. "Well?"

"Sage wants me to cover his tour in Europe next month."

My father shook his head and turned his attention back to the cartoon. "I swear, 1975 is going to eat us alive."

I took that as a sign of approval. I walked over to him and was halfway across the room when the front door slammed open.

"Dawn, Dad!" Eric cried out. My ever jumpy heart leapt to my throat.

I turned around, expecting to see Eric covered in bruises again.

Instead I saw his increasingly handsome, smiling face.

"What?" I asked. I exchanged a look with my dad and he shrugged.

"It's gone!" He exclaimed. "It's gone, it's gone, it's gone!"

I didn't dare let my mind jump to the conclusion it wanted to, that he was speaking normally and his face and body was completely still and relaxed.

"What's gone, son?" my dad asked.

"Look at me!" He grinned and held himself completely motionless. "I didn't have an episode all day, even when Pete Weatherby got in my face. It's gone. The Tourette's is gone. It's a miracle!"

He began dancing around the room and swept me up into an enthusiastic embrace. I hugged him back and fought back the urge to cry. Not because I was happy.

Because I was afraid.

They had found me.

I held Eric tightly while the words echoed in my head.

Be careful what you wished for.

ABOUT THE AUTHOR

The daughter of a Norwegian Viking and a Finnish Moomin, Karina Halle grew up in Vancouver, Canada with trolls and eternal darkness on the brain. This soon turned into a love of all things that go bump in the night and a rather sadistic appreciation for freaking people out. Like many of the flawed characters she writes, Karina never knew where to find herself and has dabbled in acting, make-up artistry, film production, screenwriting, photography, travel writing and music journalism. She eventually found herself in the pages of the very novels she wrote (if only she had looked there to begin with).

Karina holds a screenwriting degree from Vancouver Film School and a Bachelor of Journalism from TRU. Her travel writing, music reviews/interviews and photography have appeared in publications such as Consequence of Sound, Mxdwn and GoNomad Travel Guides. She currently lives on an island off the coast of British Columbia where she's preparing for the zombie apocalypse.

CPSIA information can be obtained at www.ICGtesting.com
Printed in the USA
LVOW12s2231300314

379602LV00004B/302/P